The Mandala of Sherlock Holmes

The Mandala of Sherlock Holmes

The Adventures of the Great Detective in India and Tibet

A Novel

Jamyang Norbu

Based on the reminiscences of
Hurree Chunder Mookerjee
C.I.E., F.R.G.S., Rai Bahadur

Fellow of the Royal Society, London

Fellow of the Royal Geographical Society, London
and recipient of Founder's Medal

Corresponding Member of the Imperial Archaeological Society of St. Petersburg

Associate Member of the Royal Asiatic Society of Bengal, Calcutta

Life Member of Brahmo Somaj, Calcutta

BLOOMSBURY

Published by Bloomsbury, New York and London
Distributed to the trade by Holtzbrinck Publishers

Cataloging-in-Publication Data is available from the
Library of Congress

ISBN 1-58234-328-4

First published in India by
HarperCollins Publishers India, New Delhi, in 1999
First published in the United States by Bloomsbury as
Sherlock Holmes: The Missing Years in 2001
This paperback edition published in 2003

2 4 6 8 10 9 7 5 3 1

Printed in the United States of America by
R.R. Donnelley & Sons, Harrisonburg

I travelled for two years in Tibet, therefore, and amused myself by visiting Lhassa and spending some days with the head Lama. You may have read of the remarkable explorations of a Norwegian named Sigerson, but I am sure that it never occurred to you that you were receiving news of your friend.

Sherlock Holmes
The Empty House

Is not all life pathetic and futile? ... We reach. We grasp. And what is left in our hands at the end? A shadow. Or worse than a shadow — misery.

Sherlock Holmes
The Retired Colourman

The Mandala (Tib.: *dkyil-'khor*) is a sacred circle surrounded by light rays or the place purified of all transitory or dualist ideas. It is experienced as the infinitely wide and pure sphere of consciousness in which deities spontaneously manifest themselves ...Mandalas have to be seen as inward pictures of a whole (integral) world; they are creative primal symbols of cosmic evolution and involution, emerging and passing in accordance with the same laws. From this perspective, it is but a short step to conceiving of the Mandala as a creative principle in relation to the external world, the macrocosmos — thus making it the centre of all existence.

Detlef Ingo Lauf
Tibetan Sacred Art

From time to time, God causes men to be born — and thou art one of them — who have a lust to go abroad at the risk of their lives and discover news — today of far-off things, tomorrow of some hidden mountain, and the next day of some near-by men who have done a foolishness against the State. These souls are very few; and of these few, no more than ten are of the best. Among these ten I count the Babu.

Rudyard Kipling
Kim

When everyone is dead the Great Game is finished. Not before. Listen to me till the end.

Rudyard Kipling
Kim

Contents

Preface

Too many of Dr John Watson's unpublished manuscripts (usually discovered in 'a travel-worn and battered tin dispatch box' somewhere in the vaults of the bank of Cox & Company, at Charing Cross) have come to light in recent years, for a long-suffering reading public not to greet the discovery of yet another Sherlock Holmes story with suspicion, if not outright incredulity. I must, therefore, beg the reader's indulgence and request him to defer judgement till he has gone through this brief explanation of how, mainly due to the peculiar circumstance of my birth, I came into the possession of this strange but true account of the two most important but unrecorded years of Sherlock Holmes's life.

I was born in the city of Lhasa, the capital of Tibet, in 1944, the year of the Wood-Monkey, into a well-to-do merchant family. My father was an astute man, and having travelled far and wide — to Mongolia, Turkestan, Nepal and China — on business matters, was more aware than most other Tibetans of the fragility of our happy yet backward country. Realising the advantages of a modern education, he had me admitted to a Jesuit school at the hill station of Darjeeling in British India.

My life at St Joseph's College was, at first, a lonely one, but on learning the English language I soon made many friends, and best of all, discovered books. Like generations of other schoolboys I read the works of G. A. Henty, John Buchan, Rider-Haggard and W. E. Johns, and thoroughly enjoyed them. Yet nothing could quite equal the tremendous thrill of reading Kipling or Conan Doyle — especially the latter's Sherlock Holmes adventures. For a boy from Tibet there were details in those stories that did at first cause some bewilderment. I went around for some time thinking that a 'gasogene' was a kind of primus stove and that a 'Penang lawyer' was, well, a lawyer from Penang — but these were trifling obstacles and never really got in the way of my fundamental appreciation of the stories.

Of all the Sherlock Holmes stories the one that fascinated me most was the adventure of *The Empty House.* In this remarkable tale Sherlock Holmes reveals to Dr Watson that for two years, while the world thought that the great detective had perished in the Reichenbach Falls, he had actually been travelling in my country, Tibet! Holmes is vexingly terse, and two sentences are all we have had till now of his historic journey:

> I travelled for two years in Tibet, therefore, and amused myself by visiting Lhassa, and spending some days with the head Lama. You may have read of the remarkable exploration of a Norwegian named Sigerson, but I am sure that it never occurred to you that you were receiving news of your friend.

When I returned to Lhasa on my three-month winter vacation, I did try and enquire about the Norwegian explorer who had entered our country fifty years ago. A maternal granduncle thought he remembered seeing such a foreigner at Shigatse, but was confusing him with Sven Hedin, the famous Swedish geographer and explorer. Anyway the grown-ups had far more serious problems to consider than a schoolboy's enquiries about a European traveller from yesteryear.

At the time, our country was occupied by Communist troops. They had invaded Tibet in 1950, and after defeating the small Tibetan army, had marched into Lhasa. Initially the Chinese had not been openly repressive and had only gradually implemented their brutal and extreme programmes to eradicate traditional society. The warlike Khampa and Amdowa tribesmen of Eastern Tibet staged violent uprisings that quickly spread throughout the country. The Chinese occupation army retaliated with savage reprisals in which tens of thousands of people were massacred, and many more thousands imprisoned or forced to flee their homes.

In March 1959, the people of Lhasa, fearing for the life of their ruler, the young Dalai Lama, rose up against the Chinese. Fierce fighting broke out in the city but superior Chinese forces overwhelmed the Tibetans, inflicting heavy casualties and damaging many buildings. I was in my final year at school in Darjeeling when the great revolt broke out in Lhasa. The news made me sick with worry about the fate of my parents and relatives. There was little information from Lhasa, and what little there was was vague and none too reassuring. But an anxious month later, All India Radio broadcast the happy news that the Dalai Lama and his entourage, along with many other refugees, had managed to escape from war-torn Tibet and arrived safely at the Indian border. Two days later I received a letter with a Gangtok postmark. It was from my father. He and the other members of my family were safe at the capital of the small Himalayan kingdom of Sikkim.

From the beginning my father had not been taken in by Chinese assurances and display of goodwill, and had quietly gone about making preparations to escape. He managed to secretly transfer most of his assets to Darjeeling and Sikkim, so that we were now in a very fortunate situation compared to most other Tibetan refugees, who were virtually paupers.

After graduating I decided to offer my services to help my unfortunate countrymen. I travelled to the small hill station of Dharamsala where the Dalai Lama had set up his government-in-exile, and was soon working at the task of educating refugee children. The director of our office was an old scholar who had previously been the head of the Tibetan Government Archives in Lhasa, and a historian of note. He had a wide knowledge of everything concerning Tibet and loved nothing better than to share it. He would hold forth late into the night in a ramshackle little teashop before a rapt audience of young Tibetans like myself, and imbue in us the knowledge and wonder of our beautiful country.

One day I asked him if he had ever heard of a Norwegian traveller named Sigerson having entered Lhasa. At first he also thought that I was asking about Sven Hedin, quite an understandable error, as Tibetan geographical accounts, rather inaccurate and fabulous when dealing with far away land, were inclined to treat the Scandinavian and Baltic nations as homogeneous feudal dependencies of the Czar of Russia. But on explaining that the Norwegian had travelled to Tibet in 1892 and not 1903 as the Swede had done, I managed to ring a bell somewhere in the old man's labyrinthine memory.

He did remember coming across a reference to a European in government records for the Water-Dragon Year (1892). He remarked that it had happened when he was collating state documents in the central archives in Lhasa for the preparation of the Thirteenth Dalai Lama's official biography. He had noticed a brief memo regarding the issuing of road pass for two foreigners. He was sure that one of the foreigners referred to was a European though he could not recollect his name. The other person mentioned was an Indian. He remembered that very well, for in later years the Indian had come under strong suspicion of being a British spy. His name was 'Hari Chanda'.

I was staggered by the significance of this revelation for I too had heard, or rather read, of Hurree Chunder Mookerjee (to give the full name and its more anglicised spelling) in Rudyard Kipling's novel *Kim*. Few people outside India are aware that Kipling actually based his fictional Bengali spy, the fat, ingratiating, loquacious, but ever resourceful Hurree Babu, on a real person — a great Bengali scholar, who had on occasion spied for the British, but who is now more remembered for his contributions to the field of Tibetology. He lived most of his adult life in Darjeeling and was somewhat of a celebrity in that small hill town, what with his C.I.E., F.R.S. and the great respect that the leading British notables at that time had for him. He died in 1928 at his home, Lhassa Villa.

The next time I went to Darjeeling to visit my family who were settled there, I took a walk on the Hill Cart Road to Lhassa Villa. It was occupied by a retired tea planter, Siddarth Mukherjee (or 'Sid' as he insisted I call him), a great-grandson of our famous scholar-spy. He listened patiently to the rather long and involved story I had to tell him. Hurree Chunder Mookerjee had published a book on his trip to Tibet, *Journey to Lhassa through Western Tibet*, but had made no mention in it of any European accompanying him. He had probably done so on the insistence of Sherlock Holmes who was, at that time, trying to keep the knowledge of his existence a secret from the world. I hoped that if I could gain access to Hurree's notes, letters, diaries, and other private papers I might find some reference to Sherlock Holmes, or at least to a Norwegian explorer.[1] Sid was thrilled to learn that

1. I thought I had finally managed to run our elusive Norwegian to earth when I came across this title at the Oxford Book Store, Darjeeling: *A Norwegian Traveller in Tibet*, Per Kvaerne, (Bibliotheca Himalayica series 1 Vol 13), Manjusri, New Delhi, 1973. Unfortunately this was the account of an actual Norwegian, and a missionary at that.

his great-grandfather could possibly have known the world's greatest detective, and was more than willing to help me in my quest. Most of Hurree's papers had been stored in some large tin trunks up in the attic of Lhassa Villa after his death. It took me about a week to go through all the musty old documents, but aside from a bad cold, had nothing to show for it — not a single reference to anyone who could remotely have been Sherlock Holmes. My disappointment could not but have shown. Sid was very kind and tried to cheer me up by promising to get in touch with me if he would come across anything that could contribute to my research.

So the years went by. My work took up all my time and energy and I had almost forgotten my abortive search when, just five months ago, I received a telegram from Darjeeling. It was short, but exultant:

Eureka. Sid

I packed my toothbrush.

Sid had greyed a bit, and Lhassa Villa hadn't weathered too well either. I noticed that a part of the back wall of the bungalow had collapsed. Sid was tremendously excited. He sat me down hurriedly, stuck a large whisky pani in my hand and let me have it.

Just a week before, Darjeeling had experienced a fairly severe earthquake — geologically speaking, the Himalayas being a rather new range, and still growing. By itself the quake was not strong enough to do any serious damage, but an unusually long monsoon had softened the mountain sides and undermined a number of houses. Lhassa Villa had not been severely damaged, only a part of the back wall had collapsed. When checking the damage Sid had discovered a rusty tin dispatch box embedded in a section of the broken wall.

Extricating it from the debris, he found that it contained a flat package carefully wrapped in wax paper and neatly tied with stout twine. He had opened the package to find a manuscript of about two hundred-odd pages in his great-grandfather's unmistakably ornate running script, and had excitedly commenced to read it, not pausing till he had finished the story, sometime in the early hours of the morning. And it was all there. Hurree *had* met Sherlock Holmes. He *had* travelled with him to Tibet — besides getting himself into some unbelievably strange and dangerous situations.

So the Babu had not been able to resist the urge to commit a true account of his experiences to paper, but had taken the precaution of sealing it within the back wall of his house; maybe with the hope that it would come to light in a distant future when 'The Great Game' would be over, and when people would read of his adventure in company of the world's greatest detective, with only wonder and admiration.

Sid took out the manuscript from a chest of drawers and put it in my trembling hands.

Knowing that I was a writer of sorts, Sid insisted that I handle the editing and the publication of the manuscript. But aside from providing some explanatory footnotes, I have had to do very little. The Babu was an experienced and competent writer, with a vigorous and original style that would have suffered under too heavy an editorial hand.

Sid and I are going halves on the proceeds of the book, though both of us have agreed that the original manuscript and the copy of the Tibetan road pass that was with it, should, because of its historical importance, be entrusted to some kind of institution of learning where scholars and others could have free access to it.

Tibet may lie crushed beneath the dead weight of Chinese tyranny, but the truth about Tibet cannot be so easily buried; and even such a strange fragment of history as this, may contribute to nailing at least a few lies of the tyrants.

October 1988

Jamyang Norbu
Nalanda Cottage
Dharamshala

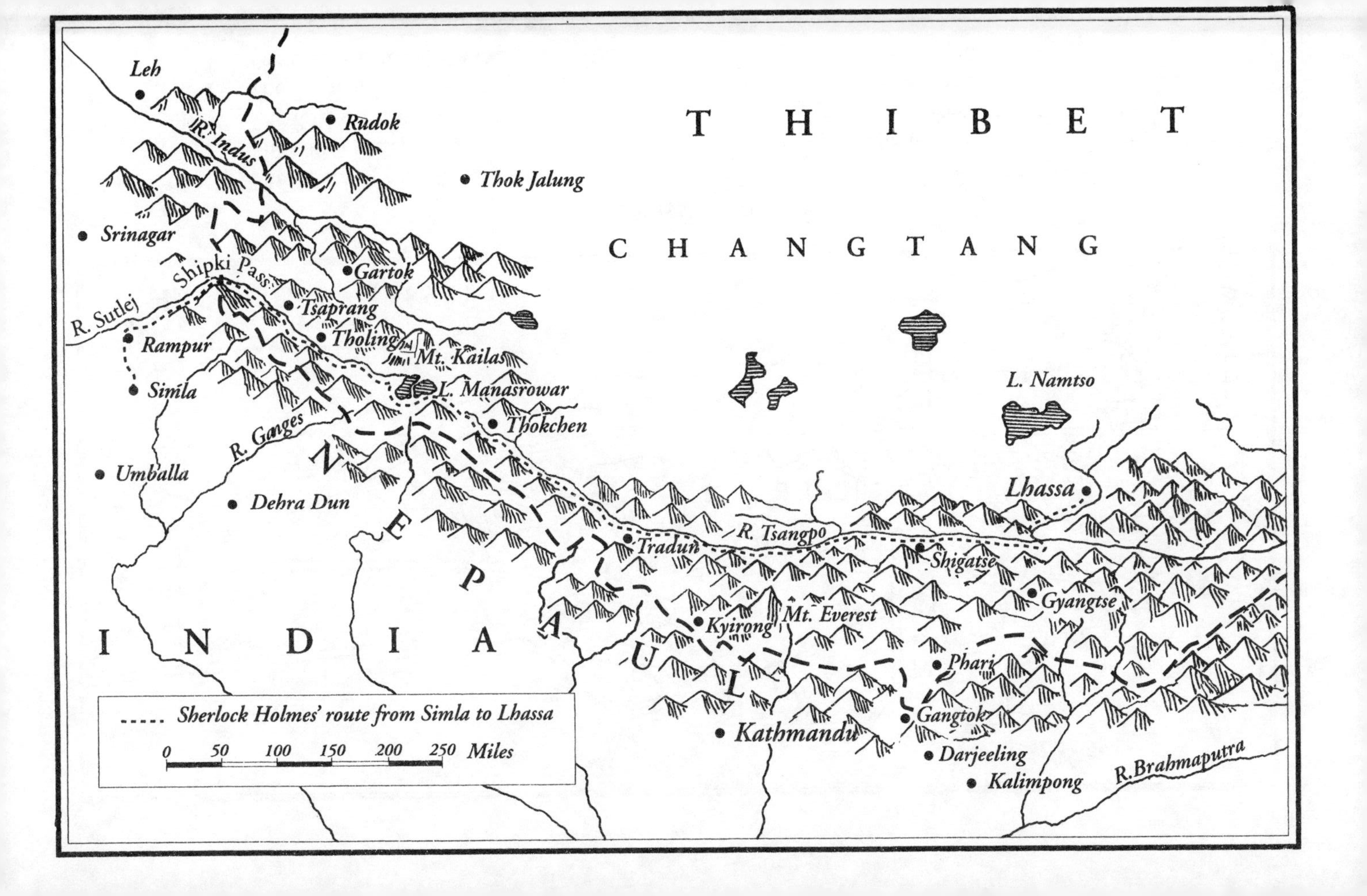
THIBET
CHANGTANG
INDIA
NEPAUL
Leh
Rudok
R. Indus
Thok Jalung
Srinagar
Shipki Pass
Gartok
Tsaprang
R. Sutlej
Rampur
Tholing
Mt. Kailas
Simla
L. Manasrowar
Thokchen
R. Ganges
Umballa
Dehra Dun
L. Namtso
Lhassa
R. Tsangpo
Tradun
Shigatse
Gyangtse
Mt. Everest
Kyirong
Phari
Gangtok
Kathmandu
Darjeeling
Kalimpong
R. Brahmaputra
Sherlock Holmes' route from Simla to Lhassa
0 50 100 150 200 250 Miles

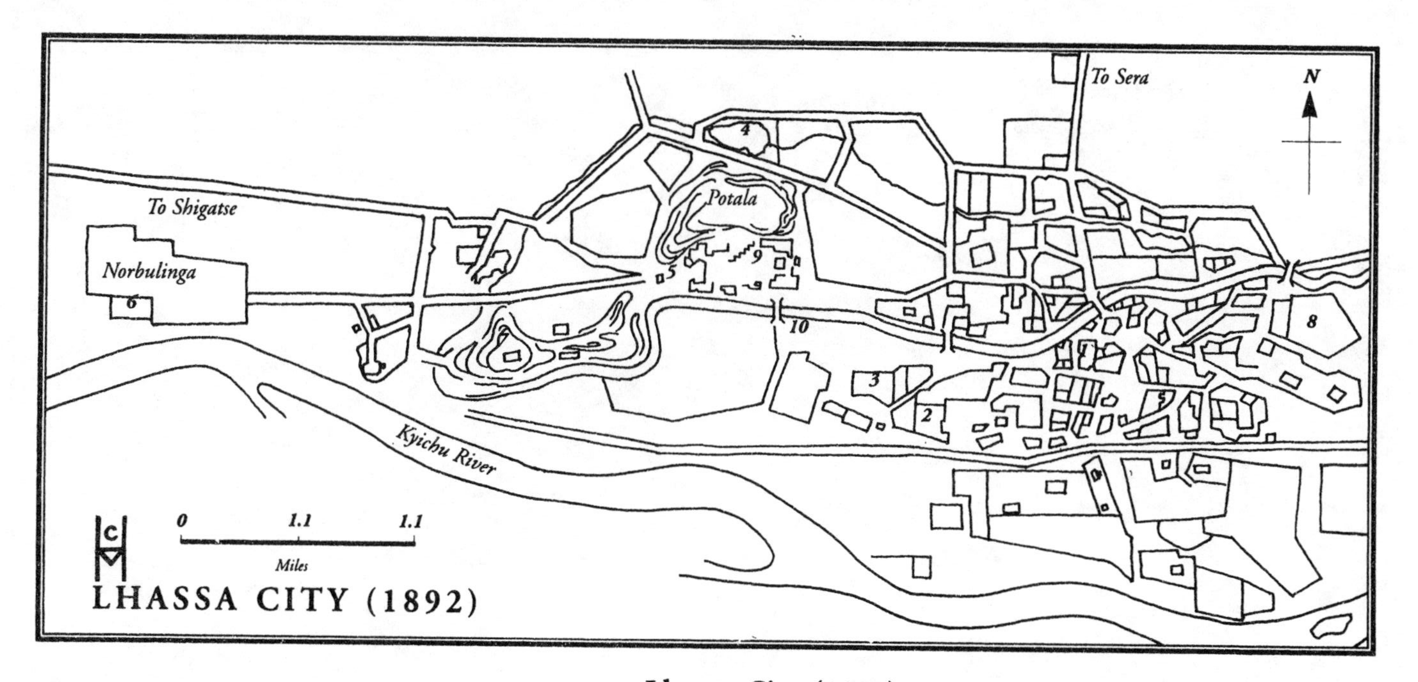

Lhassa City (1892)

1. The Central Cathedral
2. The Chinese Legation
3. The Kashgar Caravanserai
4. The Serpent Lake and Temple
5. The Gateway to Lhassa (Stupa)
6. The Guards' Barracks
7. The Iron Hill Medical College
8. The College of Occult Sciences
9. The Shol Village
10. The Turquoise Bridge

Introduction

'The Great Game...' Good Heavens! Could anyone think of a more infelicitous and beastly awful expression to describe the vital diplomatic activities of the Ethnological Survey — that important but little-known department of the Government of India, which in my very humble capacity, I have had the honour to serve for the past thirty-five years. This excretious appellation was the creation of one Mr Rudyard Kipling, late of the Allahabad *Pioneer*, who with deplorable journalistic flippancy, managed, in one fell stroke, to debase the very important activities of our Department to the level of one of those cricket matches so eloquently described in the poems of Sir Henry Newbolt.

I am not fully cognisant of how it all came about, but very unfortunately Mr Kipling managed to acquire details of the affair concerning 'The Pedigree of the White Stallion,'[1] which he coolly published in the Sunday edition of the *Pioneer*, 15th June 1891, entitled, 'The Great Game: The Lion's Reply to the Bear's

1. Kipling expanded and incorporated this account in his novel *Kim*, published in 1901.

Intrigues.' Essentially it concerned five confederated kings on the North-West frontier of India (who had no business to confederate) commencing earnest but secret negotiations with a firm of gun-makers in Belgium, a Hindu banker in Peshawar, an important semi-independent Mohammedan ruler to the south, and — the greatest cheek of all — a Northern power whose interest could, in no way, be said to coincide with that of the Empire's.

The Department had not been wholly unexpectant of such a development, and I had been assigned north for more than a year to keep a sharp eye on the doings of our five rajah sahibs. It is not necessary for me to elucidate the *modus operandi* of the following; suffice it to say that by establishing amicable relations with an underpaid secretary and transferring a large amount of rupees, I managed to arrange the betrayal of some vital *mursala*, 'King's letters,' or state correspondence which let all the cats out of the bag, so to speak. I had forwarded the revelations via E.23, C.25, and eventually K.21 to Colonel Creighton, the head of our Department.

The government acted with unusual promptitude and despatch. An army of eight thousand men besides guns were sent north, and it fell upon the five kings ere they were ready. But the war was not pushed. The troops were recalled because the government believed the five kings were cowed; and it is not cheap to feed men on the high passes. It was not the best of solutions; in fact, I thought it the most reprehensible laxity on the part of the government to allow the five kings — who were as treacherous as scorpion-suckled cobras — to even live. But officially I am debarred from criticising any action of my superiors, and I am only stating this unofficially merely to elucidate the political situation.

When that issue of the *Pioneer* came out with Mr Kipling's indiscreet (to say the least) story, it caused a tremendous hullabaloo in the Department. The Colonel Sahib realised that the inspiration for Mr Kipling's tale had come from within, *ab intra*, so to speak, and was beside himself with rage at this most base act of treason. Normally an unemotional and reserved man, he stormed through the corridor of the departmental bungalow at Umballa with the 'righteous fury of a Juvenal.' Grim interviews were conducted in his office with all and sundry connected to the case, even I having to spend an uncomfortable hour under the Colonel's piercing eyes. Of course, I managed to acquit myself well enough, though to be scrupulously correct I must admit to shedding a little perspiration before the interview was finally terminated, *sine die*, and I was allowed to leave the room.

The resultant conclusion of the investigation revealed a less critical flaw in the integrity of our Department than we had initially feared. Two babus from the archives were sacked, posthaste, and a young English captain with literary ambitions (he had contributed poetry, among other things, to the *Pioneer*) was transferred to an army transport division in Mewar, to breed camels and bullocks for the rest of his career. Mr Kipling was informed, through the editor of the *Pioneer*, that his conduct in this affair had not been entirely gentlemanly, but that the government would take no action if Mr Kipling would refrain from the furtherance of his journalistic career in India, and return home to England — which he did.

To our relief all of us fieldmen were cleared, though C.25 felt that his izzat had been impugned by the Colonel's suspicions. But a Pathan is always touchy about matters of honour and horseflesh.

Then one day, the thin black body of E.23 was found in a dark gully behind the gilt umbrellas of the Chatter Munzil in Lucknow. A dozen knife wounds, besides other fearful mutilations, had precipitated the untimely demise of the poor chap.

I am a good enough Herbert Spencerian,[2] I trust, to meet a little thing like death, which is all in my fate, you know. But the long arms of the five kings beyond the passes, and also the nabob of that certain Mohammedan principality to the south, beyond the Queen's laws, (who had all been embarrassingly compromised in the aforementioned affair of 'The Pedigree of the White Stallion') did not only stop at death. Barbaric tortures, painful even to contemplate, generally preceded the vile act of murder.

Propelled by such uncomfortable ruminations, I hastened to petition the Colonel to grant indefinite leave, on full pay, to those of us who had been compromised by Mr Kipling's indiscretions, so that we could become fully incognito till matters had quietened down somewhat. The Colonel agreed to my proposal except on one point where he made a frugal amendment. Accordingly, K.21 was sent with his Lama to retire temporarily to a monastery on the Thibetan frontier, and C.25 to Peshawar to be under the protection of his blood-kin. And I, on halfpay, departed jolly quick from my normal stamping grounds in the hills, to the great port city of Bombay, to bury myself inconspicuously in that teeming multitude of Gujuratis, Mahharatis, Sikhs, Bengalis, Goanese, British, Chinese, Jews, Persians, Armenians, Gulf Arabs and many others that composed the multifarious population of the 'Gateway of India'.

Yet, in spite of everything, I must be grateful to Mr Kipling; for it was my secret exile to Bombay that directly resulted in my providential meeting with a certain English gentleman, in whose

---

2. Herbert Spencer, 1820–1903. Once immensely influential and internationally popular Victorian thinker, formulator of the 'Synthetic Philosophy' that sought to apply scientific, especially evolutionary theory not only to biology but to psychology, sociology, anthropology, education and politics.

company I embarked on the greatest adventure of my life, resulting (due to the subsequent publication of select ethnological aspects of the journey) in the fulfilment of my life-long dream to become a Fellow of the Royal Society.

But, far more than this great honour, I shall always cherish the true friendship and affection bestowed upon me by this gentleman, a man whom I shall always regard as the best and wisest I have ever known.[3]

---

3. By a happy coincidence Watson ends his account of Holmes's death at Reichenbach (*The Final Problem*), with a similar sentence. Probably Watson and Mookerjee were both unconsciously recalling the lines of another, more ancient, biographer on the death of his celebrated friend and mentor. Plato in the *Phaedo* wrote: 'Such was the end, Echecrates, of my friend, concerning whom I can truly say that of all the men whom I have ever known, he was the wisest and justest and the best.'

INDIA

1

The Mysterious Norwegian

The post-monsoon sky over the Arabian sea is hazeless and clear blue as a piece of Persian turquoise. The air, washed by the recent rains, is so fresh and clear that astride Malabar Point at Bombay one fancies that one can make out the coast line of Arabia, and even faintly smell in the breeze some of those '... Sabean odours from the spicy shore of Araby the blest.'[1]

Of course it is all pure romantic fancy on my part; the whole bally thing is too far away to smell or see, but from my vantage point I managed to spot what I had come all this way to look for.

Through a scattering of dhows with their graceful lantine sails arching in the wind, the *S.S. Kohinoor* of the Peninsular and Oriental Steam Navigation Company cleaved the blue waters, the twin black funnels of the liner trailing a wispy ribbon of smoke. The ship was late, it should have arrived this morning. Through

---

1. Milton, *Paradise Lost.*

a pair of sub-efficient binoculars I had purchased at Bhindi Bazaar, I could just make out the name on the port bow. I quickly walked over the road to a waiting ticca-ghari. Hauling myself up onto the seat, I signalled to the coachman to proceed.

'Chalo!'

'Where, Babuji?'

'The harbour, jaldi!'

He lashed the thin pony with a length of springy bamboo and the carriage trundled down Ridge Road. I popped a piece of betel-nut into my mouth and chewed it contemplatively while I once again reviewed my plan of action.

Four months had passed since I had arrived at Bombay. I had peacefully passed the time making ethnological notes on the cult of the local goddess Mumba from whom the city had taken its name. But the Colonel must have felt that whatever potential dangers there had been had receded by now (and that I had received enough salubrious divertissement on departmental half-pay), for just a week ago our neighbourhood postman, a bony old Tamil from Tuticorin, delivered a taar (which is the native term for a telegram) to my temporary quarters behind the Zakariya mosque.

The missive, addressed to 'Hakim Mohendro Lall Dutt' — one of my more usual aliases — was couched in the characteristic innocent circumlocutions prescribed by the Department for ensuring the safety of our correspondence, *sub rosa*. The gist of the message was that a Norwegian traveller named Sigerson, probably an agent of an unfriendly Northern Power, was arriving at Bombay on the *S.S. Kohinoor*; that I was to ingratiate myself to him, possibly as a guide or some such, and learn the reason for his coming to India.

In preparation for this, I affiliated myself, in purely supernumerary capacity, to a shipping agency belonging to an old Parsee acquaintance of mine.

'Hai, rukho,' shouted the driver to his nag, pulling up the ticca-ghari before the gates of Ballard Pier. I got off, and despite the rascally Automedon's demand for two anna, paid him the correct fare of one anna, and hurried over to the pier. The harbour was crowded with merchant vessels and British warships, but I spotted the *Kohinoor* being slowly towed in by some smoky little tug boats.

The dark and dusty office of the harbour master was nearly empty except for a Gujurati clerk, sitting back in idle reverie at his desk, picking paan-stained teeth. A bounteous baksheesh of a rupee procured for me a quick peek at the passenger manifest of the *Kohinoor*. The Norwegian had Cabin 33, in first class.

When I got out of the office, docking procedures were already commencing and coolies and dockhands were rushing about the vast grey stretch of the pier hauling away on great thick ropes. The white liner towered above everyone and everything like a giant iceberg. Once the gangplanks had gone up, I in my capacity as shipping agent, got aboard the ship, and elbowing my way through the surge of harbour officials, coolies, lascars and what-not wended my way through crowded corridors, dining rooms, a card room, a billiard room and a stately ball-room, to the upper port-side deck and Cabin 33.

The Norwegian was in front of his cabin door, leaning over the railing and sucking on a pipe meditatively as he gazed down at the human maelstrom on the pier below. His person and appearance were such as to strike the attention of the most casual observer. In height he was well over six feet and excessively lean. When I addressed him, he straightened up from the railing and seemed to grow taller still.

'Mr Sigerson, Sir?'

'Yes?'

He turned to me. His thin hawk-like nose gave his expression an air of alertness and decision, and his chin, too, had the prominence which marks the man of determination. He definitely did not seem like someone to trifle with. I prepared myself to be humble and ingratiating.

'I am Satyanarayan Satai, Failed Entrance, Allahabad University,' I said, making a low formal bow and salaam. 'It is my immense privilege and esteemed honour, as representative of Messrs Allibhoy Vallijee and Sons, shipping agency, to welcome Your Honour to the shores of Indian Empire, and perform supervision of all conveniences and comforts during visitations and executions in the great metropolis of Bombay.' (It is always an advantage for a babu to try and live up to a sahib's preconception of the semi-educated native.)

'Thank you.' He turned and looked at me with a pair of remarkable eyes that were uncomfortably sharp and piercing. 'You have been in Afghanistan, I perceive.'

Of course I was not expecting this, but I trust I managed to recover my somewhat shaken wits fast enough to make an adequate, if not totally convincing, answer.

'Wha...! Oh no, no sahib. I am most humble Hindu from Oudh, presently in remunerative and gainful employment in demi-official position of agent, *pro tem,* to respectable shipping firm. Afghanistan? Ha! Ha! Why sahib, land is wretched cold, devoid of essential facilities and civilised amenities, and natives all murdering savages — Mussalmans of worst sort — beyond redemption and majesty of British law. Why for I go to Afghanistan?'

'Why indeed?' said he, with a low chuckle that sounded rather sinister. 'But to return to the matter at hand, I am afraid that it is quite possible for me to do without your services, useful and necessary though I am sure they may be. I have little in the way of luggage and can manage on my own. Thank you.'

In front of his cabin door was a Gladstone bag and a narrow oval case, much the worse for wear. It looked like a case for a violin, like the kind that Da Silva, the young Goanese musician who lived next door to me, used to carry his instrument in when he went off in the evenings to play dinner music at Government House.

This was, of course, suspicious in itself. No self-respecting sahib who travelled to India was without at least three steamer trunks, not to mention other sundry items of baggage like hat boxes, gun cases, bedding-rolls and a despatch box. Also, no English sahib, at least if he was pukka, played a violin. Music was the preserve of Frenchmen, Eurasians, and missionaries (though in the latter-most case the harmonium was a more favoured instrument).

And no sahib carried his own luggage. But that was just what he proceeded to do. With the Gladstone in his left hand, his violin case in his right, and his pipe in his mouth, he walked across the deck and down the gangplank, unperturbed by the bustling pierside crowd and the demands of the milling coolies to carry his luggage.

Of course this temporary setback to my plans was purely a matter of bad luck, or kismet as we would say in the vernacular. But I could not help but feel a slight unease at the perspicacity of the Norwegian. How in the name of all the gods of Hindustan had he known that I had been to Afghanistan? I will not deny that I was up in that benighted country not so very long ago. The first time, in my guise as hakim, or native doctor, I was discreetly pursuing some enquiries into possible nefarious connections between the five confederated kings and the Amir of Afghanistan, which unfortunately did not meet with any success. Much later, after the chastisement of the aforementioned kings, I was once again up in the snow-swept passes beyond the Khyber, this time posing as a payroll clerk to the coolies constructing a new British road; and one night, during an exploratory excursion in a horrible snowstorm, I was deliberately deserted by my Afridi guide and left to die. Whereof my feet froze and a toe dropped off ... but that is neither here nor there.

There was, *sine dubio*, something more to our Norwegian friend than met the eye. My curiosity was aroused. We Bengalis are — I say this in all humility — unlike most other apathetic natives, a race with burning thirst for knowledge. In short, we are inquisitive.

I followed the Norwegian off the ship through the bustling crowd at the pier side. His height made him quite conspicuous and I could easily spot his angular head towering well above the bobbing sea of humanity. I was careful not to reveal myself to him and took full advantage of the cover provided by the random piles of luggage and freight that covered the pier.

Peering over a pile of crate-boxes, I saw him enter the customs shed, which was a long kacha, or temporary, structure covered with a PWD type corrugated tin roof. I quickly walked to the shed and, sidling up to the open door, looked inside. The Norwegian had put his Gladstone and violin case on one of the long zinc-covered counters, and was drumming his thin elongated fingers impatiently on the top as he waited. Evening shadows were already long, and in the gloom of the dark building I did not immediately notice the young police officer in khaki drill who approached the Norwegian. He was a tallish, sallowish, DSP, or District Superintendent of Police — Sam Browne, helmet, polished spurs and all — strutting, and twirling his dark moustache.

I gave a little start. It was Strickland! By Jove. Events were definitely taking unexpected turns this evening. A word of explanation to the reader: Captain E. Strickland Esq., though nominally a solid and respected officer of the Indian Police was, in another sphere of his life, one of those shadowy players of the 'Game' (to use Mr Kipling's foul epithet) — and one of the best.[2]

---

2. Kipling's indiscretions regarding the Indian Secret Service do not seem to have been confined to just the affair concerning 'The Pedigree of the White Stallion'. Kipling readers will know that Strickland and his undercover activities are mentioned not only in *Kim* but in a number of short stories as well. Strickland is depicted as a proficient investigator, though certainly less cerebral than Holmes. He is a master of disguise and possesses a wide knowledge of native Indian customs and folklore, especially the more arcane and shady kind.

They told me that he was at Bikaner, that mysterious city in the Great Indian Desert (where the wells are four hundred feet deep and lined throughout with camel-bone) but I might have known. He was like the crocodile — always at the other ford.

He shook hands with the Norwegian and started to talk. It was impossible for me to overhear what they were saying because of the overpowering clamour of the pier. After a moment, Strickland spoke a few words to the half-caste customs officer and, picking up the Gladstone bag, proceeded with the Norwegian to leave the shed. I followed, a safe distance behind. Outside the gates Strickland hailed a ticca-ghari. Both of them got on the carriage, which then rattled out of the port area down Frere Road.

A fortunate instinct made me continue to keep behind the large Corinthian pillars of the main harbour buildings, for just then a small ferret-like man in dirty white tropical 'ducks' and an oversized topee emerged surreptitiously out of the darkness of the adjacent godowns and into the glare of the sizzling gas lamps that lit up the cab stand and the entrance of the Great harbour. His furtive manner betrayed the fact that he was secretly following either Strickland or the Norwegian, and as if in confirmation of my speculation he quickly made for one of the carriages in the line. Giving some inaudible instructions to the driver, he pointed distinctly in the direction of the fast disappearing carriage that his quarries had just taken. The driver whipped his beast and they rattled off in pursuit.

This was getting to be quite a lively evening, full of 'alarums and excursions' as the Bard would put it. I, in my turn, hailed a carriage and followed in consecutive pursuit, posthaste.

The evening life of the city had begun and the municipal lamp-lighters were nearly finishing their rounds. Dark sweating coolies hauling overloaded barrows mingled with white-robed clerks and subordinates from the government offices returning to their homes. Sweetmeat vendors and low-caste kunjris (vegetable and fruit sellers) plied their noisy trade on the pavements, their stalls lit by smoky flares, the acrid fumes of which mingled with the pot-pourri of other odours: spices, jasmine, marigold, sandalwood and the ever present dust. Yelling, near-naked urchins, darted about the street, clinging to the passing carriages and sometimes jumping on and off the clanging trams to the fury of the harried conductors.

At Horniman Circle a large wedding procession brought traffic to near standstill. Coolies carrying lanterns and flares lit up this colourful chaotic scene while a discordant native band, playing kettle-drums and shawms, provided a deafening but lively musical accompaniment to a group of wild dancers that preceded the groom. This splendid personage, dressed in the martial attire of a Rajput prince sat nervously astride an ancient charger. A veil of marigolds concealed his visage as he rode to his bride's home, clinging precariously to the pommel of his saddle.

I spotted the two stationary carriages about twenty feet ahead of me. The ferret-like man affected great interest in the procession though he often darted surreptitious glances at the other carriage to check on its progress in the congested traffic. He had a thin pinched face with an equally pinched sharp nose, and sported, quite unsuitable for his starved physiognomy, a set of rather flamboyant whiskers which I think are called 'mutton chops', and which were *en vogue* about a decade ago. He was a white man, of sorts, though definitely not a gentleman.

Finally, thanks to the firm supervision and energetic whistle blowing of a 'Bombay Buttercup' — the name by which traffic policemen in this city are known because of their distinctive circular yellow caps — the marriage procession turned towards Churchgate Station and traffic was permitted to proceed. A few minutes later the first carriage carrying Strickland and the Norwegian turned left towards Apollo Bunder and then into a side-street and up the driveway of the Taj Mahal Hotel. This magnificent structure, with its five arcaded and ornate balconied stories topped by a large central dome (with lesser ones at the corners), gives an appearance more of a maharajah's palace than a mere hostelry.

Ferret-face's ticca-ghari was nowhere to be seen. I looked carefully all around but it had disappeared. I paid off my driver outside the gates and walked up the driveway.

Despite the suspicious glare of the giant Sikh commissionaire, I entered the portals of this latter-day Arabian nights palace just in time to catch sight of Strickland having a few words with a European in full evening dress, whom I correctly surmised to be the manager of the establishment. The manager then politely ushered Strickland and the Norwegian down a corridor away from the lounge and then returned a short moment later, alone. I quickly crossed the lounge, trying my best to be inconspicuous. A severe looking burra mem, most probably a Collector's lady, attired in a flawless white evening dress, glared at me through her lorgnette. A flicker of her eyelids, half closed in perpetual hauteur, gave me to understand that she thought my presence irregular. I smiled ingratiatingly at her, but with a disdainful sniff she went back to her reading. Nobody else paid any attention to me.

Along the corridor were the rest rooms, and at the end, the manager's office. I tiptoed over to the door and managed to hear, somewhat indistinctly, the voice of the Norwegian. There was a large keyhole in the door. I surmised that from where I was I could not be seen from the lounge, and that if anyone did come down the corridor I could discreetly retire into one of the rest rooms. So, offering up a quick prayer to all the variegated gods of my acquaintance, I bent over and deftly applied my right ear to the keyhole. I admit that it was a caddish thing to do, but natives in my profession are not expected to be gentlemen.

'I do apologise for any inconvenience you may have had to undergo,' Strickland's voice sounded as clear as if he was speaking right beside me. 'But Colonel Creighton only received the telegram from London two days ago, and he rushed me off here as quickly as possible to receive you.'

'I hope that information of my arrival here has been kept absolutely confidential.'

'Certainly. Only the Colonel and I are in the know.' Strickland paused slightly. 'Well, to be scrupulously honest, someone else has also been informed, but right now that doesn't really matter.'

'Nevertheless, I would appreciate your telling me about it.'

'You see, about three weeks ago we received a message from one of our agents, an Egyptian chap at Port Said. He reported that a man claiming to be a Norwegian traveller, but with no gear or kit of any sort, had landed at Port Said off a bum boat, and had booked a passage to India on the P&O liner, *Kohinoor*. We have issued standing instructions to all our chaps at those stations to report on all Europeans, who could in any way, be travelling to India for purposes other than the usual. You see, for the past few years we have been having a deuced lot of trouble with the agents of... let us say, an unfriendly Northern Power — stirring up trouble with discontented native rulers and that sort of thing. So before the telegram from London got to us, the Colonel sent one of our fellows here to check up on you. But it's all right. Seems I got to you before he did.'

'Well, I wouldn't know....'

There was a brief moment of silence and, suddenly the solid door I had been leaning against was whisked away and a very strong hand dragged me into the room by the scruff of my neck. It was a very ignominious entrance on my part, and I was truly mortified.

'What the Devil....!' exclaimed Strickland, but then he saw my face and held his peace. The Norwegian released his forceful hold on me and turned back to close the door. He then walked over to the old baize-covered mahogany desk and, seating himself behind it, proceeded to light his pipe.

'I have been listening to him for the last five minutes but did not wish to interrupt your most interesting narrative.' He turned and once again subjected me to his penetrating gaze. 'Just a little wheezy, Sir, are you not? You breathe too heavily for that kind of work.'

'I am afraid it's all a....' Strickland tried to intervene.

'No need for any explanations, my dear Strickland,' said the Norwegian with a dismissive wave of his hand. 'Of course, everything is perfectly clear. This large but rather contrite native gentleman is without doubt the agent that Colonel Creighton sent to keep an eye on the sinister Norwegian. At least his appearance and abilities do credit to the Colonel's judgement. A man of intelligence, undoubtedly, and a scholar — or at least with interest in certain abstruse scholarly matters. Also a surveyor of long standing and an explorer who has spent a great deal of time tramping about the Himalayas. And, as I had occasion to inform him at an earlier meeting, someone who has been to Afghanistan. Furthermore, I am afraid he is connected with you, Strickland, in a manner not directly involving your Department; would it be correct of me to say, through a secret society?'

'By Jove!' exclaimed Strickland. 'How on earth did you guess all that?'

'I never guess,' said the Norwegian with some asperity. 'It is an appalling habit, destructive to the logical faculty.'

'This is most wonderful,' I blurted out unwitting, somewhat confused by the shock of such unexpected revelations.

'Commonplace,' was his reply. 'Merely a matter of training oneself to see what others overlook.' He leaned back on his chair, his long legs stretched out and his fingertips pressed together.

'You see, my dear Strickland,' he began, in a tone reminiscent of a professor lecturing his class, 'despite the deceptively sedentary appearance of the gentleman's upper body, his calves, so prominently displayed under his native draperies, show a marked vascular and muscular development that can only be explained in terms of prolonged and strenuous walking, most probably in mountainous areas. His right foot, in those open-work sandals, has the middle toe missing. It could not have been cut off in an accident or a violent encounter as the close adjoining digits do not seem to be affected in any way; and we must bear in mind that the toes of the foot cannot be splayed like the fingers of the hand for any convenient amputation. Since the generally healthy appearance of the gentleman would point against any diseases, like leprosy, I could safely conclude that his loss must have occurred through frostbite — and the only mountains in this country which receive heavy snowfalls are the Himalayas.

'I also noticed that he had a nervous tic in his right eye, oftentimes an occupational disorder afflicting astronomers, laboratory technicians and surveyors, who constantly favour a certain eye when peering through their telescopes, microscopes or theodolites. Taken along with the fact of his strenuous jaunts in the Himalayas, surveying would be the most acceptable profession in this instance. Of course, surveying is an innocent occupation, not normally associated with people pretending to be what they are not. So in this case I concluded that he had practised his skills in areas where the true nature of his work and his identity had to be concealed, that is in hostile and hitherto unexplored areas. Hence our Himalayan explorer. *Voilà tout.*'

'And my intelligence and scholasticism?' I asked amazed.

'That was simple,' he laughed. 'The degree of intelligence could easily be deduced by the larger than normal size of your head. It is a question of cubic capacity. So large a brain must have something in it. The scholarly drift of your interests was easily discernible from the top of the blue journal I noticed peeping coyly from your coat pocket. The colour and binding of the *Asiatic Quarterly Review* is a distinctive one.'

'But Afghanistan?' I managed to squeak.

'Is it not obvious? I will not insult the intelligence that I just lauded by describing how easily I came about it.'

There was a distinct twinkle in his eyes as he turned to Strickland. 'And when the shirt of an English police officer reveals the distinct outline of a peculiar native amulet, which is strangely also worn, this time more openly, around the neck of our native gentleman here, surely some kind of connection can be postulated. On the balance of probabilities the chance of both of you belonging to some kind of society, possibly a secret one, is therefore high. Moreover, in my readings on the subject, I have been informed that next to China, this country is the most infested with such organisations. Ryder, in his *History of Secret Cults,* is very informative on the subject.'

'By Thunder!' exclaimed Strickland, shaking his head in wonder. 'It's a good thing we aren't living in the Middle Ages, Mr Holmes, you'd have surely been burnt at the stake.' He leaned back on his chair and sighed, 'The Saat Bhai or Seven Brothers was an old Tantric organisation that had long been extinct, but which Mr Hurree Chunder Mookerjee here, revived for the benefit of some of us in the Department. This amulet, the hawa-dilli (heart lifter), was given to me by the blind witch Huneefa, after the initiation dawat or ceremony. She makes them only for us. The old hag actually believes she's making them for a real secret society and she inserts a scrap of paper in each bearing the names of saints, gods and what not. The amulet helps us to recognise one another if we've never met before or are in disguise. Of course the whole thing is unofficial.'

Strickland's tone gave me to understand that the so-called 'Norwegian' was not an outsider but someone definitely connected to the Department, probably in an important and influential way.

'You see, Sir,' I explained helpfully, 'it is also a kind of insurance. There is an established belief among natives that the Saat Bhai is not only extant but that it is a powerful society with many members.

And most natives, if they are not too excited, always stop to think before they kill a man who says he belongs to any specific organisation. So in a tight spot — if someone is attempting to cut your throat or something — you could say, "I am Son of the Charm," which means that you may be a member of the Saat Bhai — and you get — perhaps — ah, your second wind.'

'I used to belong to a lot of cults and things,' sighed Strickland wistfully. 'But the powers that be felt that I was letting down the side by traipsing about the country in various native guises, and I was told to drop it.[3] All I've got now is the Saat Bhai, so I hope you won't peach on me.'

'My dear fellow,' said the Norwegian, laughing in a peculiar noiseless fashion, 'so long as your Society's soirees are not enlivened by human sacrifices and ritual murder, I will carry your secret to my grave.'

'Well then, that's that,' said Strickland brightly. 'I'd better get along and send a telegram to the Colonel of your safe arrival. The manager ought to have your suite ready for you by now.'

'Well, there is one little matter that needs to be taken care of.' The Norwegian looked at me. 'Mr Mookerjee has, through his own exertions, discovered quite a bit about my affairs, and I feel that it is pointless, maybe even unwise, not to take him fully into our confidences.'

'Of course,' Strickland replied. 'Huree here is the soul of discretion, and you can trust him to keep a secret.' He turned to me with a superior smile. 'Well Huree, this gentleman on whom you unwisely inflicted your irrepressible curiosity is none other than the world's greatest detective, Mr Sherlock Holmes.'

'By blushes, Strickland,' he said in a deprecatory voice.

At that moment a blood-curdling scream burst through the corridors of the Taj Mahal Hotel.

---

3. For a fuller account of Strickland's problem, see Kipling's short story 'Miss Yougal's Sais' in *Plain Tales from the Hills.*

2

The Red Horror

The unlikely concurrence of Strickland's amazing revelation and the spine-chilling scream somewhat ruffled my normal orderly thought processes. But Strickland was quickly on his feet. 'What the Devil!'

Another scream rent the air.

'But quick, man ...' Sherlock Holmes shouted. 'It came from the lounge.'

We tumbled out of the manager's office and rushed down the corridor. As we ran, one shocking thought sprang suddenly into my mind. Sherlock Holmes had died two months ago. Every newspaper in the Empire, indeed throughout the world, had reported the tragic story of his fatal encounter with the arch-criminal Professor Moriarty at the Reichenbach Falls in Switzerland. How the deuce an' all had he sprung back to life? But before I could even begin to address this question, I came upon a scene so bizarre and terrifying that I shall probably carry its dreadful memory to my grave.

The lounge, lit by three brilliant Venetian chandeliers, was half-full of formally dressed ladies and gentlemen, every single one of them staring with a look of utmost horror at the top of the staircase that bisected the rear of the lounge. The screamer was the old burra mem who had earlier disapproved of my presence in the hotel lounge. She was now standing in the front of the company at the bottom of the staircase, and preparing to release yet another of her piercing distress signals.

On the upper landing — the focus of everyone's petrified gaze — was a figure of pure horror, straight out of Jehannum. It was a man — or at least had the shape of one — covered so entirely in blood that not a single detail of apparel or anatomy could be distinguished behind that ghastly shimmering surface of red. The scarlet figure stumbled forward blindly. The red surface of its face opened to reveal a black hole from which an anguished animal howl burst out, ending in a dreadful gurgle as if it were drowning in its own life-blood. Then slowly it keeled over, and rolling down the stairs came to a stop at the bottom, right at the feet of the burra mem, spattering her pristine white gown with blood.

The lady gave another piercing scream and fainted dead away.

Strickland rushed over, followed by myself, and we lifted the old lady and carried her over to a *chaise longue* where the terrified looking manager and ladies ministered to her.

'Please keep away from there,' shouted Strickland over the ensuing hubbub. 'I am a police officer, and there is no cause for any alarm.' He motioned to the manager who quickly came over to him. 'Send a messenger to Inspector MacLeod at the Horniman Circle Police Station,' he ordered, jotting down something on a chit which he handed over to the manager.

The manager was plainly shaken. 'It's most terrible business, Sir, such a thing has never ...'

'Snap out of it man!' Strickland cut him off impatiently. 'Send someone to the thana at once.'

Sherlock Holmes was kneeling beside the bloody figure, peering intently at the pupil of the man's eye that he had opened by pinching back the eyelid. As Strickland hurried over, Holmes shook his head grimly.

'He's dead as Nebuchadnezzar.' Sherlock Holmes wiped his fingers on his handkerchief. 'Extraordinary amount of bleeding here ... humm ... from just about every part of his body.'

Though a man of culture, and thus naturally averse to blood and violence, I have, due to the exigencies of my profession, seen death in many forms and circumstances. But this prostate figure — its shape and features masked entirely by this horrible covering of blood, looking not human but like a shapeless crimson monster — raised an amorphous terror in my heart. Of course, I did not reveal it.

Mr Holmes seemed more stimulated than shocked by the situation. There was no trace there of the horror which I had felt at this distressing sight, but rather the quiet and interested composure of a holy sadhu, seated cross-legged on his buckskin mat, meditating on the mysteries of life and death.

He wiped the dead man's face quickly with his handkerchief. I noticed no sign of any wound on the skin, but seconds later its features were once again covered with blood.

'Most singular,' was his only comment as he tossed away the blood-soaked handkerchief. He turned to Strickland, 'Could I trouble you to remain here and make sure everybody keeps well away from the body while I take a look around upstairs?'

'Certainly. I'll join you as soon as MacLeod and the boys get here.'

Sherlock Holmes turned to me, 'Would you care to accompany me, Mr Mookerjee? There may be questions to be asked and my ignorance of Hindustani will certainly create difficulties in that event.'

'It would be an honour, Sir, if any of my trifling abilities could prove to be of service to you.'

I had imagined that Sherlock Holmes would at once plunge into a study of the mystery, but nothing appeared to be further from his intention. With an air of nonchalance which, under the circumstances, seemed to border upon affectation, he ambled slowly up the staircase. On getting to the landing he gazed vacantly around him at the ceiling, the bloodstained floor and walls (which were like those of a slaughter house). Having concluded his rather perfunctory scrutiny, he loped noiselessly over to the left corridor, following an unmistakable trail of clear red footprints and large splotches of blood.

About five rooms down the corridor the footprints ceased, and only a few drops of blood spotted the carpet. Holmes tested the two doors on either side of this point in the passage, but only the door on the right, the one for Room 289, was open. The key still in the keyhole. Holmes pushed open the door of the room and peered in.

'Humm, it seems empty enough.'

'Are you expecting to find anybody, Sir?'

'Why do you ask?'

'Well, Sir, if the individual of enquiry is contemplating any untoward act of violence, I would not like it to occur as an unexpected incident. My nature is averse to any such shocks.'

'So you think our victim was murdered.'

'What other explanation is there?'

'Dozens. Still it is a cardinal error to theorise without sufficient data. Hulloa! Who's that?'

At the end of the corridor an old bhangi appeared, carrying his short-handled broom.

'He is only a sweeper, Sir, most probably an employ of the hotel.'

'Get him here for a minute, will you?'

'Most certainly, Sir. Bhangi! Idhar aao, jaldi!'

The old man padded softly forward on his bare feet, and, approaching us, saluted Mr Holmes.

'Namaste, sahib.'

'Ask him if he saw anything unusual a short while ago.'

'Listen thou, old man,' I asked in the vernacular. 'Hast thou seen anything not of the usual a little time before?'

'I saw nothing, Babuji but yes,' his ancient visage lighted up, 'I heard a loud scream, like that of churail.'

'All whom God has given ears heard that,' I interrupted impatiently. 'Now listen well, servant of Lal Beg (the god of the sweepers). This tall sahib is a sakht burra afsar of the police. A man is dead. Yes, that was what the screaming was about, and the sahib is investigating. If thou desirest to retain thy nowkri at the hotel, tell me everything.'

'Hai mai!' he wailed. 'What zoolum. I saw nothing, Babuji. Nobody came this way. Only another Angrezi sahib was leaving by the rear staircase.'

'Is it normal for sahibs to use the rear staircase?'

'Nay, Babuji. That is for the servants of the hotel.'

'Gadha! Why did thou not say so in the first place?'

I paused to explain to Mr Holmes what had transpired between the sweeper and myself.

'Now then, old man,' said I, fixing him once again with my stern gaze, 'how did this sahib look, and when did he leave?'

'Babuji,' he wailed again, 'all Angrezi sahibs look alike.'

'You may find yourself in a nizamut,' I said sternly, 'if you don't start remembering, jaldi!'

'Babuji, all I saw was a thin sahib, not so young, with funny whiskers and a long nose. He looked very frightened when he ran past me.'

Sherlock Holmes's thin lips tightened when I told him this.

'Ask him when exactly the man left.'

'He says, just now, Sir, just before we called him.'

'By thunder! Where's that staircase?'

'The sweeper says it is at the end of the corridor, Sir, and that it leads down to the trade entrance.'

Holmes ran through the corridor and down the narrow staircase, leaving me no alternative but to follow him. We came out in a rush through the back door into a narrow alley. But obviously our prey had flown, for there, about a hundred yards ahead of us, an ecca ghari rattled furiously down the dark empty lane. As the ghari turned the corner into the main street, it came for a moment under a street lamp. The occupant happened to rise in his seat just then and turn around to look back. It was the ferret-face!

'I fear we are a trifle late,' observed Mr Sherlock Holmes, slipping a large revolver back into his coat pocket. 'You did not, by any chance, observe the licence number of the carriage?'

'No, Sir, but I did see something else.' I told him about ferret-face as we climbed back upstairs.

'Quite so, quite so. He was probably a confederate,' he remarked as we reached the corridor. 'I should have anticipated something like this. Why hullo, here's Strickland. The police force must have arrived.'

'Mr Holmes, have you discovered anything?' enquired Strickland eagerly.

'I could only make a cursory inspection of the scene of the crime, before my attention was diverted by another incident.' Sherlock Holmes proceeded to tell Strickland of the old bhangi's tale and our fleeting encounter with the mysterious ferret-face. 'So now with your permission, I will commence my examination.'

As he spoke, he whipped out a powerful lens and a tape measure from his pocket. With these two implements he moved noiselessly about the corridor, sometimes stopping, occasionally kneeling and once lying flat on his face. He stopped at one point and beckoned to Strickland and me. 'What do you make out of this?' he asked, pointing to something on the floor.

'It looks like a large clot of blood,' Strickland replied.

'Mmm ... a possibility; still, if you could lend me a handkerchief.'

I proffered mine. He took it and wiped the red lump of blood with it. Underneath it was grey.

'Why, it is a piece of India-rubber,' I exclaimed.

'You think so?' Holmes remarked. 'Well, I think that's all that can be got here. Let us now proceed further.'

Holmes entered the Room 289 and there devoted himself for fifteen minutes to one of those laborious investigations which form the solid basis of his brilliant successes. It was a memorable experience for me, to view, first hand, the actual *modus operandi* of a man whose incomparable achievements were famous throughout the world. The look of keen interest on Strickland's face showed that his feelings were much the same as mine. At the time I could not help but be slightly amused at the way Mr Holmes muttered away to himself under his breath the whole time, keeping up a running fire of exclamations and whistles suggestive of encouragement and hope, and the occasional groan or sigh which probably indicated otherwise.

Near the large bed he stopped and exclaimed, pointing at the floor. 'Well, well. What do we have here?'

'It looks like marks left by the legs of a chair,' suggested Strickland.

'Table, my dear Strickland, definitely a table. The impressions are too wide apart for a chair. The table is not normally placed here, for the impressions would be appreciably deeper and there would be a slight difference in colour from the surrounding carpet. Also the table was removed from this position only a short time ago. Observe the tufts of carpet-pile slowly springing back into place.' He straightened up and looked around the room. 'And there we have the very article.'

'But there's another one just like it on the other side of the room,' I interjected.

'Ah. But the probability of this one being the right table is higher. It is just a matter of convenience. One normally uses what is closer at hand.' He walked over to the table and inspected it. 'I perceive I am correct. Observe these heavy scratches on the varnish. Dear me, what a way to treat such a fine piece of furniture. Obviously someone has stood on the top of this table. Someone wearing heavy boots. Humm. Now let's see how we can fit it all together. Could you lend me a hand here?'

Mr Holmes and I lifted the table over to the bed and set it down carefully so that the base of the legs matched the indentations on the carpet.

'A perfect fit, Mr Holmes,' said I, in satisfaction. But Sherlock Holmes was already on the table and reaching out for a brass lamp of native manufacture that hung on a thin chain over the bed. The lamp, of Benaras metalwork, was wrought in the shape of a richly caparisoned elephant. Handling it gingerly with a handkerchief, he examined it closely with his lens. Finally, after about ten minutes, he let the lamp swing back over the bed, and hopped off the table.

'Ingenious. Sheer devilish ingenuity. I should not have expected less ...' He scrutinised the counterpane on the bed with his lens. 'Now logically there should be ... Ah! Just as I expected.' With the aid of a small penknife he scraped away some brown particles from the cloth and held it up to the gas light for examination.

'It is definitely sealing-wax. Do you not think so, gentlemen?'

'Holmes,' Strickland cried impatiently, 'is there a connection between all this and the dead man? Was the man murdered, and if so, how? And why the tremendous bleeding? I really think you might treat us with more frankness.'

'In all my experience I cannot recall a more singular and interesting study. My investigations are nearly complete, but I must verify a few more details before I can announce my results to you. I assure you, however, that I will only hold back the answers for the shortest possible period. In the meantime, I think you ought to know that our unfortunate dead man downstairs is a victim of both murder and accident.'

'You speak in paradoxes, Sir,' I interjected.

'You're making fools of us, Mr Holmes,' Strickland said angrily.

'Tut, tut, Mr Strickland. The first sign of choler I have detected in you. Still, it is my own fault. I should have made it clear.'

'Clear, Mr Holmes? We do not even know who the dead man is.'

'The dead man was a native servant of this hotel. He was without doubt murdered. But his death was an accident, in the sense that he unfortunately placed himself in a situation where the real victim should have been instead.'

'Then who was the murderer really after?'

'None other than myself, I should imagine.'

'You, Mr Holmes?'

'Oh, I must admit to a certain notoriety in criminal circles,' Holmes chuckled, 'but it's a long story and....'

A vague memory that had been bothering me for the last few minutes now suddenly sprang crystal-clear in my mind. 'The boat, Mr Holmes,' I cried.

'Well, what about it?' said Strickland irritably.

'The *Kohinoor* should have docked at least by midday, instead of which it could only do so late in the afternoon. If everything had gone according to schedule, Mr Holmes not only would have been in this hotel by the evening, but could have been in his room, maybe even this one, at the time of the incident.'

'And Mr Holmes would then have been the unfortunate victim instead of the other fellow?' asked Strickland.

'Possibly,' said Sherlock Holmes softly. 'Only possibly. I assure you gentlemen, that I am not boasting of undue prescience when

I say that I was anticipating an attack upon my person. I have had four such attempts made on me just this month, though I must admit that this particular one presents the most features of interest.'

'But the room,' Strickland exclaimed. 'How could the murderer have known that ...?'

At that moment a dour looking police officer in khaki drill walked into the room. He tugged at his ragged grey moustache worriedly as he spoke.

'The body's been taken down to the mortuary, Sir,' he said to Strickland in a strong Aberdonian accent. 'In all my years in the force I've never seen a bloodier mess than this. What could have caused such a horrible death?'

'It's anybody's guess, at the moment,' Strickland replied. 'But things should become a little clearer once the body's properly examined. Who's on duty at the laboratory now?'

'Probably old Patterson, Sir.'

'Tell him I want the autopsy performed right away. I'll be down as soon as I finish questioning Mr Sigerson and his native guide here. Mr Sigerson ministered to the dying man and may have seen or heard something that could have bearing on the case.'

'Estrekeen' sahib could lie like a thief when he had to.

'Then would it be all right if the hotel people were to clean up the mess? We've gone over everything with a fine tooth comb, but haven't turned up a thing.'

'All right. If you're sure you haven't overlooked anything.'

'Nae, Sir. I'm pretty sure I haven't,' replied the inspector, and then chuckled. 'They're having an old boy's reunion dinner downstairs — the United Services College, I think — and the manager is in a fair dither, what with the blood on the staircase and all.' He walked over to the door adjusting his topee. 'I'll leave Havildar Dilla Ram and two boys here on duty.'

'Thank you, MacLeod. Good night.'

After the inspector had left the room Holmes raised his eyes to to the ceiling and sighed. 'So the official detective force of the city of Bombay functions in much the same manner as old Scotland Yard.'

'Look here, Mr Holmes,' said Strickland in an injured tone of voice. 'I admit that all of us are absolutely baffled by this mystery, and I am sure you're not. You have thrown out hints here and hints there but I think we have a right to ask you straight how much you know about the business.'

'My dear fellow, I did not at all mean to hurt your feelings. Just a few more details to be confirmed, after which I assure you, all will be revealed. Now, I want you to be there at that autopsy and note every detail carefully. I have no hesitation in saying that the results may be crucial to the solution of the case.'

'Well, Mr Holmes,' said Strickland, somewhat mollified, 'you have a deuced round-the-corner way of doing things, but I've put up with your reticence for so long, that I ought to be able to bear it a bit longer, I suppose.'

'Good man,' laughed Sherlock Holmes, clapping him on the shoulder. 'And, now, for one last thing, and this may be more in Mr Mookerjee's field of interest; where could one obtain some books dealing with the flora and fauna of this country?'

'Well, Sir,' I replied, somewhat puzzled by his unexpected request, 'the best place would be the library of the Bombay Natural History Society. I happen to know the Secretary, Mr Symington, quite well (I had demi-officially provided him with rare specimens of Tibetan primroses) and their library facilities are excellent. But I fear they will be closed now.'

'Ah well, then tomorrow must serve,' said Sherlock Holmes compliantly. 'I expect you here, Mr Mookerjee, bright and early tomorrow, to take me there. Now let us proceed downstairs to arrange my accommodations and have a bite of supper.'

'You must be famished,' Strickland said ruefully. 'I really should have...'

'Not at all, my dear fellow,' Mr Holmes interrupted, leading the way out of the room. 'It has been a most instructive evening. I wouldn't have missed it for the world. Would you mind closing the door behind you? It would not do to let people know we have been snooping around here.'

The manager had lost no time in straightening things out, it seemed, for the hotel-sweepers were busy scrubbing the staircase. They had not yet got to the landing which was still awash with blood. Holmes stopped suddenly before descending the stairs and looked with a puzzled expression at the floor.

'Do you happen to notice anything peculiar about this blood?'

'Why, no,' said Strickland. 'There just seems to be a lot of it around. Why? Is there anything unusual?'

'Never mind,' Holmes replied, descending the staircase, but I overheard him muttering to himself, 'Remarkable, most remarkable.'

We were crossing the lounge to the reception desk, when the manager hurried over to us. 'A thousand apologies, Mr Sigerson. I have been most remiss in my duties as a host. But this terrible accident and...'

'It's quite all right. I've spent a useful half hour working out the details of my proposed excursions in this city with my guide, Mr Mookerjee, here. Now if I could trouble you...'

'Most certainly, Sir.' Mr Carvallo!' He beckoned to the clerk at the reception desk. 'A room for the gentleman.'

Mr Carvallo, a plump sleek young gentleman, probably of Portuguese descent, reached under his desk for a key and then rang the desk-bell with a thump of his palm. A native porter in hotel livery shuffled up. He was given the room key with some instruction. He retrieved Mr Holmes's meagre baggage from the manager's office and shuffled up the staircase. Sherlock Holmes started to follow the porter, but then turned around to us. "If you'll just wait for me in the dining room, I won't be a minute. I have to get a fresh handkerchief from my valise.'

Strickland and I walked over to the dining room where we were at a small table in a corner of the room. Obviously, the United Services College Old Boys' (with ladies) reunion dinner had not ended, for the centre of the hall was lined with large banquet tables and occupied by the formally dressed ladies and gentlemen who earlier in the evening, had received such a rude shock from our dead friend. Needless to say, the banquet did not appear to be a particularly cheerful one. As a turbaned waiter in white livery silently filled our water glasses, Mr Holmes stepped briskly into the dining room, laughing silently in his strange way as he seated himself and unfolded his napkin.

'It is most piquant. Can you guess which room I have been given?'

'Surely not...' I cried in amazement, but I was anticipated.

'Yes, 289.'

'By Thunder!' exclaimed Strickland' 'It must be that smirking manager. Let me take him down to the thana and I'll make him talk, as quick as Jack Ketch's gibbet.'

'Hold your peace, Strickland,' Sherlock Holmes held out his hand in an imperious fashion. 'I assure you that I anticipated this very move. Furthermore, we have no proof of the manager's complicity in this business. Anyhow, whoever it is, we mustn't scare him off at this initial stage of the game.'

'But your life, man! Surely you're not going to sleep there tonight?'

'My very intention. Nothing will happen in that room tonight, my dear fellow. I am staking more than my poor reputation on it. And now let us not vex ourselves any further with these conundrums. Ah, this Solferino soup and roast chicken à la Moghul is the very thing. Could I propose a bottle of Montrachet to celebrate my...umm, somewhat eventful arrival onto the shores of the Indian Empire?'

3

Sherlock Holmes Reminisces

Over coffee Mr Holmes told us the story of the great deception he had performed on the world.

'You have by now heard of Professor Moriarty,' said Sherlock Holmes, pushing his chair away from the table and stretching his long legs.

'*The Times of India* carried an article about his criminal empire simultaneously with your obituary,'[1] I ventured.

'We received information from London about the Professor and his gang,' Strickland said. 'I also read quite a lively story about the whole business in the *Strand Magazine*.'

'That would be my friend Dr Watson's account of what he thought had happened,' Holmes remarked thoughtfully as he filled his pipe. 'In this entire business my only regret is the unnecessary

---

1. Probably the Reuter's despatch that appeared in all English papers on 7 May 1881, mentioned by Dr Watson in *The Empty House*.

alarm and distress I have caused him. But that couldn't be helped, I suppose. The stakes were too high, and Moriarty's minions too desperate.'

'Ay, there was a genius,' said Mr Holmes, puffing on his pipe. 'The greatest criminal mind of the century, but no one had heard of him. There lay the wonder of it. No doubt you have read the more lurid details of his career. In fact he was a man of most respectable origins. From a very tender age he displayed a precocious mathematical faculty which an excellent education developed to phenomenal heights. At the age of twenty-one he wrote a thesis on the Binomial Theorem, which has had a European vogue. On the strength of it he won the Mathematical Chair at one of our smaller universities. He is also the celebrated author of *The Dynamics of an Asteroid* — a book which ascends to such rarefied heights of pure mathematics that it is said that there was no man in the scientific press capable of criticising it. Unfortunately a criminal strain ran in his blood which was exacerbated and rendered infinitely more dangerous by his extraordinary mental powers. Dark rumours gathered round him in the university town, and eventually he was compelled to resign his chair and to come down to London.[2]

'For some years I had continually been conscious of some sinister and ubiquitous organising power behind the criminal world of London. For years I worked to uncover this conspiracy, and at last the time came when my researches led, after a thousand cunning twists and turns, to the late Professor Moriarty of mathematical renown. He was the organiser of nearly all that was evil and undetected in England, and possibly beyond. He sat motionless like a spider in the centre of its web, but that web had a thousand radiations, and he knew well every quiver of each of them. He did little himself. He only planned. But his agents were

---

2. A near identical thumb-nail biography of Prof. Moriarty is provided by Holmes to Dr Watson in *The Final Problem* and *The Valley of Fear.*

numerous and splendidly organised. This was the dark domain that I discovered, gentlemen, and which I devoted my whole energy to expose and break up.

'But the Professor was fenced round with safeguards so cunningly devised that at the end of three months I was forced to confess that I had met an antagonist who was my intellectual equal, if not superior. But I persisted with my investigations until one day the Professor made a mistake. It was a small mistake, I will grant you, just the merest oversight; but it gave me my chance. Starting from that point I wove my net around him.'

It is not necessary to relate here the full story that Sherlock Holmes told us about the brilliant way he managed to expose and trap the Professor and his organisation; and how Scotland Yard through its bungling allowed the Professor and some of his top henchmen to slip out of Mr Holmes's net. The reader will undoubtedly have read that special issue of the *Strand Magazine* where the entire story, including the subsequent meeting of Professor Moriarty and Mr Sherlock Holmes was excitingly related; and also, where, to the grief of an Empire, the mistaken conclusion was drawn that the great detective had perished in the thundering waters of the Reichenbach Falls.

Strickland and I listened entranced as Sherlock Holmes told us of his final moments with the professor.

'I had little doubt, gentlemen,' continued Mr Holmes. sipping his brandy, 'when the somewhat sinister figure of the late Professor loomed ahead of me, at the end of the only narrow track that led to safety, that I had come to the end of my fruitful career. His grey eyes were set with bitterness and malicious purpose. But he greeted me civilly enough. We had an interesting but brief conversation, and he gave me a sketch of the methods by which he had confounded the police force. I reciprocated with a few details of how I had managed to unearth his organisation and activities. I then obtained his courteous permission to write a short note for Dr Watson which

I left with my cigarette case and my stick. I walked along the pathway, Moriarty still at my heels, until I reached the end. Before me the thundering waters of the fall plunged deep down into a dreadful cauldron of seething and swirling foam. I turned around. Moriarty drew no weapon, but the mask of his calm exterior visibly began to break down. The great bulge of his forehead throbbed like a live thing. His eyes flashed a dreadful hatred, the like of which I had never seen before, and his mouth moved incessantly, no doubt uttering some curse for the damnation of my soul, but which I fortunately could not hear for the noise of the waterfall.

'Then with a snarl he hurled himself on me. He was like a madman and had the strength of one. Physically I am equal to most, but the fury of the Professor's charge initially confounded me. His long cadaverous fingers seized me by the throat, and proceeded to throttle me in a most alarming manner. His mouth, distorted with revengeful hatred, trickled with foam like a rabid dog.

'"Die, Holmes. Damn you! Die!" he screamed, spraying my face with his vile spittle. We teetered together on the brink of the fall. I have some knowledge, however, of *bujitsu*,[3] which includes the Japanese system of wrestling, and which has more than once

---

3. One of Dr Watson's less celebrated gaffes as a reporter is cleared up here. In *The Empty House* Watson records Holmes as crediting his defeat of Moriarty to his knowledge of ... '*baritsu* or the Japanese system of wrestling ...' In point of fact the word baritsu does not exist in the Japanese language. The actual term used by Holmes and correctly reported by Hurree is *bujitsu*, the generic Japanese word for the martial arts, which includes the Japanese system of wrestling (*jujitsu*) in addition to fencing, archery, etc. The Japanese statesman-scholar, Count Makino, also offered a similar explanation to account for Watson's error, in a paper read at the founding meeting of the Baritsu chapter of the Baker Street Irregulars in Tokyo, on 12 October 1948. (See *Foreign Devil: Thirty Years of Reporting in the Far East*, Richard Hughes, Andre Deutsch, Great Britain, 1972.)

been very useful to me. Gripping him firmly by the collar and applying a judicious foot against his stomach, I rolled over on my back throwing him clean over me.[4] With a scream he fell over the precipice. But the desire to live is a strong and desperate one in all beings. When I got up, rather shaken, I perceived that the Professor had managed to grip the edge of the precipice and somehow arrest his fall. He lay dangling over the dark furious chasm, his fingers scrabbling desperately to maintain a hold on the edge of the cliff. His eyes, wide with fear, met mine.

'"Help me, please," he croaked.

'At that instant I lost my sense of animosity towards the wretched man. I moved a step forward, not suspecting the base treachery that lurked in his heart. His right hand snaked towards my leg, nearly getting a grip on it. That was his undoing. His other hand, unable to bear his full weight, lost its grip. After a momentary effort to restore his hold, he plunged down the chasm. I saw him fall for a long way. Then he struck a rock, bounded off, and splashed into the water.

'For a while I was unable to move. Many men have hated me, but the implacable malevolence that Moriarty had directed at me left even my usually strong nerves somewhat shaken.

'I was just about to start back on the track when it struck me what a really extraordinarily lucky chance Fate had placed in my way. Moriarty was not my only enemy. There were at least three of his lieutenants who had escaped from the police net and would not hesitate to seek vengeance. They were formidable and dangerous men, and it would have been a willful act of self-deception if I thought I could avoid them perpetually. Foremost among them was Moriarty's own chief of staff. A man of the vilest antecedents but with a brain of the first order; as secretive and

---

4. Very similar to a sacrifice throw in Judo called *Tomoe-nage.*

unknown to most as his late master. The others were more openly notorious. You may recollect the case of L'Oiseau, the circus acrobat, of Niagara Falls fame, who murdered the Greek prime minister in his bed but escaped from police custody without a trace; and Luff, the so called 'Mad Bomber', whose explosive exploits filled the pages of our dailies just a couple of years ago. You see, Moriarty believed in the American business principle of paying for the best talents in their fields. And these fellows were the very best. One or the other would certainly get me. On the other hand, if all the world was convinced that I was dead they would take liberties; they would lay themselves open, and sooner or later I could entrap them.

'I managed to hide myself on a high ledge when the search party, organised by Dr Watson, arrived at the scene. At last, when they had all formed their inevitable and totally erroneous conclusions, they departed, and I was left alone.

'Suddenly a huge rock thundered past me and crashed into the chasm. For an instant I thought it was an accident, but a moment later, looking up, I saw a man's head against the darkening sky. Another stone struck the very ledge upon which I was stretched, within a foot of my head. Of course, the meaning of this was obvious. Moriarty had not been alone. A confederate — and even that one glance had told me how dangerous a man that confederate was — had kept guard while the Professor had attacked me. From a distance unseen by me, he had been witness to his master's death and my escape. He had waited and then, making his way round to the top of the cliff, had endeavoured to succeed where his master had failed.

'It did not take me very long to form my conclusions, gentlemen. I scrambled down onto the path, once nearly falling off into the chasm, when another stone sang past me. Halfway down I slipped, but by the blessing of God I landed, torn and bleeding upon the path. I took to my heels from the spot and managed to do ten miles over the mountains in the darkness.

Finally I came upon one of those shepherd huts that you find in the upper reaches of the Alps. It was empty and only a short beam of wood served to bar the stout door. I stumbled in, and fumbling in the darkness managed to find a battered tin lantern. By its cheerful light I proceeded to make myself at home. The household effects were somewhat primitive, but more than ample for my few needs, and indeed luxurious, considering the state of my present predicament. I washed and bound my wounds, which were, thankfully, of a superficial nature.

'It was with a light heart that I strode through the Alpine meadows the next morning. Though I took due precautions, I relegated most thoughts of Moriarty and his gang to the back of my mind. After all, the sun was shining, the snow on the mountain tops was virgin white, and my old cherry wood, which had survived my precipitous descent, was drawing very nicely. That evening I came to the town of Hospenthal. With the help of a guide I proceeded over the St Gotthard pass, which was deep in snow, and continued southward to the border town of Como. After ten days I reached Florence, the city of Dante — who when he remarked "*Nel mezzo del camin di nostra vita,*" could have been describing the position of my own life at that moment.

'I had wired to an old acquaintance in London for money.[5]

---

5. This was his brother Mycroft, as Sherlock Holmes was to later inform Dr Watson when he returned to London (see *The Empty House*). Holmes had also previously confided to Watson, though in a somewhat roundabout way, that Mycroft was actually the chief of British Intelligence. In *The Greek Interpreter* Holmes remarks that Mycroft occupied 'some small office under the British Government' though he was in truth 'the most indispensable man in the country.' In *The Bruce Partington Plans* Sherlock Holmes further confides to Watson that Mycroft's unique governmental position was that of a 'central exchange for incoming data' and that 'Again and again his word has decided the national policy.'

He was my only confidant, and it was he who wired to Colonel Creighton to assist me here in India. For you see, by then it was quite clear that I would require some active assistance especially when in unfamiliar surroundings, if Moriarty's avengers were not to succeed altogether. Four separate attempts were made on my life: the one that came closest to taking it was in front of the Gezirah Palace Hotel in Cairo, where I was set upon by two black-cloaked figures wielding over-size scimitars. I had fortunately taken the precaution of purchasing a hair-trigger and a hundred Boxer cartridges, so the conflict was rather one-sided.

'And now we have this bizarre murder, which if my theories are correct, is the latest, and so far the most interesting attempt on my life. But the temptation to form premature theories upon insufficient data is the bane of our profession. Nothing can be concluded till the results of the autopsy are released. I expect you, Strickland, to fit in this final piece of the puzzle tomorrow. Until then, good night.'

As my ghari moved along the dark streets of the city carrying me back to my lodgings, I tried to sort out in my head the events of the day. How had that poor man been murdered? Why all that blood? How did it all tie in to the manager and Moriarty and the ferret-face? But it was beyond me. I knew I had to wait till the morrow for an answer.

That night I had frightening dreams.

4

Flora and Fauna

Despite a somewhat restless night, I made my way early next morning to the hotel. Once again I was subjected to the hostile glare of the Sikh commissionaire, but I managed to avoid the manager and the desk clerk in the hall and quickly made my way up to Sherlock Holmes's room.

'Come in, come in,' a sharp voice cried out, as I knocked on the door of Room 289.

The room was full of dense tobacco smoke, but a single open curtain permitted a little of the early morning sun to shine into the room. He sat with legs crossed like a native rajah, on a kind of Eastern divan that he had constructed on the floor with all the pillows from his bed and cushions from the sofa and armchair. The effect of oriental splendour was heightened by the resplendent rococo purple dressing gown he wore and the opulent hookah that was laid out in front of him — the long satin-covered tube ending with a delicate amber stem that he held pensively between his thin long fingers. His eyes were fixed vacantly up at the corner of the ceiling. The blue smoke rose languidly from the hookah-bowl, while he remained silent, motionless, a shaft of sunlight shining on his strong aquiline features.

'Good morning, Mr Holmes. I perceive that you favour the native pipe today.'

'It has its virtues,' he replied languidly, 'especially during such sedentary moments. It is a recent discovery of mine that the balsamic odour of the native tobacco is peculiarly conducive to the maintenance of prolonged periods of meditation.'

He puffed thoughtfully. The smoke bubbled merrily through the rosewater.

'You have not slept, Sir?' I enquired solicitously.

'No. No. I have been turning over our little problem in my mind — besides a few other things. Tell me ...' he said suddenly, '...what is the meaning of life, of this perennial circle of misery, fear, and violence?'[1]

'Well, Sir...' I began, somewhat at a loss for words. 'I am, if you will pardon the expression, a scientific man, and therefore at quite a disadvantage when expressing opinions on such... ah... spiritual matters. But a Thibetan lama whom I once had the privilege of interviewing, for strictly ethnological purposes on matters of Lamaist ritual and beliefs, was of the opinion that life was suffering. Indeed, it was the primary article of his credo.'

'Wise man,' Holmes murmured, 'wise man.' He was silent for a while. His eyes gazed into space with a strange burning vacancy. For just a moment it seemed to me that beneath his calm, rational, superior self there struggled another more intense and restless soul — not at all European — but what would be recognised in

---

1. Holmes expresses a similar thought at the conclusion of *The Adventure of the Cardboard Box.*

the East as a 'Seeker'. Then with a conscious effort he broke off his singular reverie.

'Have you breakfasted?' he asked. I noticed an empty breakfast tray pushed away to the side.

'A cup of coffee? No? Well then, if it is not too early, could I trouble you to accompany me to the Bombay Natural History Society that you mentioned last night.'

'Mr Symington, the secretary is at the premises quite early, Sir. He works on his own researches there as it is much cooler in the mornings.'

'Excellent. Then let us not waste any time.'

He carefully coiled up the tube of his hookah, and taking off his dressing gown, put on the grey linen jacket he had worn the day before. Unlike most Europeans in India he did not wear a pith helmet or a topee, but made do with a light cap, of the kind which I think is called a deerstalker.

We quickly made our way downstairs. Before leaving the hotel Mr Holmes went over to the reception desk where he scribbled a chit and sealing it in an envelope handed it to one of the hotel clerks there. I suspected that the note was for Strickland. Then Mr Holmes and I left the hotel in a ghari.

There was the tang of saltwater in the air as we rattled down the beach road, where near-naked boys were selling coconut water, fresh in its own shell, and two ash-covered sadhus were performing their sun worship in the sea. Things were less peaceful at the Borah Bazaar where shopkeepers, vendors, tongawallahs, coolies, and pedestrians of all kinds were noisily beginning their day. Finally we arrived at the brick bungalow of the Bombay Natural History Society.

We waited in a large hall while the chaprasi went to find Mr Symington. The whole place was filled with an extraordinary variety of rather moth-eaten exhibits of stuffed birds and animals behind labelled glass cases. After a few minutes the chaprasi returned.

'The sahib awaits you. Please come this way.'

Stumbling over stuffed crocodiles and the hoofs of sambhar floor rugs, we followed him through a corridor and into a long chamber lined and littered with bottles of various chemicals. Broad, low tables bristled with retorts, test-tubes, and little Bunsen lamps, with their blue flickering flames. An overpowering smell of formaldehyde permeated the air. It did not seem to bother Symington, who sat behind a long marble-topped table sorting out what looked to me like dirty duckweed with the aid of a pair of tweezers. He was a small, untidy man with a bald shining head that was covered scantily on the sides and back with tufts of grey hair. Raising his head slightly he peered through his thick spectacles with weak watery eyes.

'Hello, is that you Mookerjee?'

'Yes, Mr Symington. How are you?'

'As well as can be expected. By the way, I never got the chance to thank you for that specimen of *Primula glacialis.*[2] It's a real feather in my cap, you know. Even Hooker[3] never got one.'

---

2. The only other reference I have uncovered on this unique plant is by Peter Goullart in *Princes of the Black Bone,* John Murray, 1959. Goullart mentions: 'I was told by an eminent botanist that high up on the slope of Minya Konkka, shooting through the snow, grew a remarkable primrose, called *Primula Glacialis,* one of the rarest flowers in the world discovered by a Catholic priest. It rivalled the sky in the purity of its blue colour and delicacy of its contours.... Why did the most beautiful, most enchanting and delicate blossoms on the planet grow so high and under such impossibly hard conditions, braving frost, hail, landslides and cruel winds, out of reach of humanity?'

3. Sir Joseph Dalton Hooker travelled throughout India (1848–50) particularly the Sikkim Himalayas, to study the distribution and evolution of plants. He was one of the most eminent of nineteenth century scientists and a close confidant of Darwin.

'Well, Sir, the true specimens only grow around twenty thousand feet. It is difficult for human life to manage at those heights.'

'But somehow you did, didn't you, you old devil,' he chuckled, pushing up a pair of spectacles that always had a tendency to slip down his nose. 'Now, who is your friend here?'

'Mr Sigerson is from Norway, Sir. He is a ... an ... ah ... explorer.'

'An explorer? How interesting. Very glad to meet you, Sir. How can I be of service to you?'

'If it is not too much trouble,' said Sherlock Holmes, 'I would like to consult whatever literature you may have on *Hirudenia*.'

'*Hirudenia?* Ah. You have come to the right place. We have every standard work on the subject, including a few very special and important reports that I may presume to say are not to be found anywhere in Europe at present. Please follow me.'

He led us into a long narrow chamber lined on either side with tall mahogany bookcases. He opened the glass-framed doors of one and peered short-sightedly at the collection of books inside.

'Could I trouble you for that?' He turned around, pointing at a low step-ladder nearby. I carried it over to him.

'Thank you.' He climbed up the first three steps and, peering closely at the spines of the books on the top shelf, commenced a litany of the names of the authors, who were, I suppose, all experts on '*Hirudenia*', whatever that was.

'Fowler ... Merridew ... Konrad ... Hackett, humm ... Hackett. Don't think he'd be any good to you; fellow deals with *invertebrate phyla* in general. Konrad and Merridew are best especially on the *hirudenia* of this country.' He pulled out two slim volumes and, blowing the dust off the top, handed them to Holmes. 'Hope you find what you need in here. Not too fond of them myself. Strictly a flora man. Blood thirsty brutes killed half my pack animals on an expedition once. Well, I will leave you to your research.'

Holmes sat on the step-ladder and began reading. He flipped over the pages of the first book impatiently, and when he got to the end put it aside with a snort of disgust. He must have found what he was after in the second book for he suddenly stopped flipping the pages and gave a little cry of triumph.

'Ha! Ha! Capital!' he chuckled, twitching with excitement, poring carefully over the page, underlining each sentence with a nervous finger. He occasionally paused to scribble brief notes on his cuff. After a long time he turned to me, shaking his head with feigned sorrow. 'Ah, me! It's a wicked world; and when a clever man turns his brain to revenge, it is the worst of all. I think I have enough information now...'

'Mr Holmes! You have solved...'

'Exactly, Mr Mookerjee. Only that I arrived at my conclusions last night, aided in part by the invigorating fumes of a few ounces of native tobacco. This ...' he said, closing the book with a thump, '... is merely confirmation.'

'But I don't understand how...'

'Patience,' he replied. 'All will be revealed in good time, I assure you. I have my own peculiar way of working, which you must forgive me. And now for a little recreation. I would like to avail myself of the services you offered to me on our first meeting aboard the ship, and be introduced to the sights of this city.'

We left the library and, going down to the laboratory, said goodbye to Symington. The old botanist shook Holmes by the hand and made a not very subtle bid to elicit information about Holmes's purported explorations.

'Well, Mr Sigerson, I wish you the best of luck in your venture. Mookerjee here knows the ropes and ought to be able to safely guide you to ... ahh ... where did you say you were going to pursue your explorations?'

'I did not,' said Mr Holmes, the merest hint of amusement colouring his voice. 'But your cooperation has been invaluable, and it would be ungrateful of me to be reticent. In all confidence, I am telling you that it is my intention to enter Thibet and visit the fabled city of Lhassa.'

As I had feared, Symington at once began to greedily enumerate a long list of plant specimens we were to obtain for him in the highlands of Thibet.

'... remember, I want the Blue Poppy and the *Stelleria decumbens*, root and all ... and don't get discouraged by the spines ... the *Gentiana depressa* must be of the dwarf variety otherwise ...'

Offering tactful but non-committal replies, I managed to finally extricate Mr Holmes and myself from the company of Symington, who would have even walked with us down the street with his endless catalogue of botanical needs, if we hadn't luckily chanced upon a ticca-ghari at the gate of the bungalow. We hurriedly boarded the carriage and fled.

Sherlock Holmes leaned back on the cracked leather seat of the ghari and chuckled. 'The etymology of the word "enthusiasm" can be traced back to the Greek *enthousia,* meaning to be possessed by a god or demon. But it never occurred to me till today how true the word has remained to its origin.'

'I'm afraid I put you in a false position, Mr Holmes,' I apologised, 'by claiming that you were an explorer.'

'Nonsense, Huree. Your explanation, though spontaneous, was prescient. On the conclusion of this case I intend to undertake an exploration and make my small contribution to the furtherance of human frontiers.'

'But why Thibet, Mr Holmes?'

'Is it not obvious? It is one of the last of the secret places of the earth, defying the most adventurous of travellers to force open its closed doors.'

'You will never get there,' I thought to myself. 'You, Mr Holmes, may be the world's greatest detective, but the priestly rulers of Thibet do not love foreigners, especially Europeans. No man ever gets even close to the Holy City without an official passport, and none are ever issued to white men. Even I only succeeded in reaching about halfway to Lhassa before the authorities discovered my true identity and nearly had my bally head cut off.'

'Of late...' continued Sherlock Holmes, '... I have been tempted to look into the problems furnished by nature rather than the more superficial ones for which our artificial state of being is responsible. Of these the ultimate problem is the meaning of our existence. It is in the hope of some explanation that I must go to Thibet which, rightly or wrongly, has been reported to be the last living link that connects us with the civilisations of our distant past, and where is preserved the knowledge of the hidden forces of the human soul.' He lit his pipe and puffed meditatively. 'There is nothing in which deduction is so necessary as in religion. It can be built up as an exact science by the reasoner.'[4]

The carriage trundled down Hornby Road towards the Mumba Devi Temple, and I performed my duty as a guide explaining to Mr Holmes the cult of the goddess Mumba (a form of Parvati, consort of Shiva) from whom the city had taken its name. Mr Holmes, like Strickland (thus unlike most other Englishmen) was a good listener, and his interest genuine and scientific. It was therefore a great pleasure for me to explain to him the sights of the city, frequently illuminating my discourse with jolly interesting and pertinent anecdotes. It is not generally known, for instance, not even to the citizens of this fair metropolis, that there was human occupation in the area even during the Stone Age. Very

---

4. Sherlock Holmes makes very similar statements in *The Final Problem* and the case preceding it, *The Naval Treaty.* It is interesting that the metaphysical strain in him should surface so conspicuously on these two occasions just before his final encounter with Professor Moriarty — surely the most deadly, yet significant, moment in his life.

recently, Paleolithic stone implements have been found at Kandivli in Greater Bombay by a scientific acquaintance of mine, a Mr Cunningham of the Royal Asiatic Society.

North of Greater Bombay are the Kanheri caves (which is a very jolly holiday spot) and the site of an ancient Buddhist University. More than a hundred caves have been discovered filled with gigantic Buddhist sculptures. The Portuguese who obtained the islands in 1534 presented them to Britain in 1661 as part of the dowry of Catherine of Braganza, sister of the king of Portugal, when she married Charles II. Ever since then, under the aegis of the Viceroy of India, Steward of our Most Gracious Majesty, the Queen Empress, this city has seen such tremendous progress, *pro bono publico,* in industry, building, education, and what not, that it is, without doubt, the foremost megapolis in the Empire — after London, of course, which I have not yet had the privilege of visiting.

Mr Holmes and I spent a most pleasant day touring the city and only during the late afternoon, after examining the delightfully didactic exhibits at the Victoria and Albert Museum, did Mr Holmes make reference to the murder case again.

'Well, I think we have refreshed our minds enough for the day,' he said, climbing into a carriage parked outside the Museum gates. 'Strickland will have set the stage by now for the final resolution of our problem. Kindly instruct the coachman to take us back to our hotel.'

Mr Holmes tossed a coin to an urchin begging for alms and leaning back on the carriage seat, smoked a cigarette. He then gave me certain instructions. 'Now, Huree, it is vital that you follow my directions to the letter. When we arrive at the hotel you will accompany me to the lobby where you will bid me goodnight and make a conspicuous departure. You will then make your way to the alley behind the hotel and, using the trade entrance, make your way to my room unnoticed. Knock softly, three times, at the door, and Strickland will let you in. From then on you are to follow his every instruction. As for myself, I will inform the manager or the desk clerk that I am somewhat exhausted by my excursions today, and that I wish to retire early, after having a quick supper in the dining room. That ought to give our friend, whoever he may be, enough time to make his own preparations.'

I was, of course, thrilled to the bone to know that the dénouement of this affair was in the offing, and it consoled me somewhat for Mr Holmes's frightful uncommunicativeness about the case. We arrived at the hotel. Once within the lobby I bade Mr Holmes goodnight and left through the front entrance, inevitably under the contemptuous gaze of the commissionaire. As my carriage moved across the driveway I had a fleeting glimpse of Mr Holmes addressing the Portuguese desk clerk, who was obsequiously poised in his usual half-bowing state.

5

The Brass Elephant

Outside the gates of the hotel I paid off the carriage, but the blighter of a ghariwallah demanded double the usual fare as he had carried an English sahib besides myself. I gave him a flea in the ear for his impudence, and quickly made my way to the rear of the Taj Mahal Hotel. By now it was dark. I moved carefully, keeping close to the shadowy side of the alley. I waited for a moment behind a pile of empty boxes, while a couple of sweating coolies carried large slabs of ice through the rear entrance of the hotel. When they left, I crossed the alley and entered the building. I climbed up the dark stairs and hurried down the brightly-lit corridor. There was no one about. I knocked sharply, three times, on the door of Room 289. An irate Strickland opened the door and practically dragged me in.

'Do you have to make such an infernal racket? Come in quick, man. He ought to be here any minute now.'

We concealed ourselves behind a grilled marble screen between the room and the balcony window. I was curious to know why Mr Holmes had posted Strickland to guard his room, and the identity of the mysterious intruder who was expected; but if my years with the Department have taught me anything, they have taught me to hold my water when ill-temper rules the roost; if I may be permitted the expression.

We remained standing silently behind the screen. Through the grille of the screen I could now discern the shadowy outlines of the objects in the room. Strickland sniffed suspiciously.

'What a horrible smell,' he whispered irritably. 'You wouldn't by any chance be using some kind of perfume, would you, Huree?'

'Certainly not, Mr Strickland,' I whispered back crushingly. 'The aroma happens to emanate from a brand of hair-lotion of which I make daily applications on the scalp. It is a very superior and expensive medicant, retailed at one rupee and four annas a bottle and manufactured by Armitage and Anstruthers at their *modern* plant in Liverpool. I highly recommend it, Mr Strickland, it would do wonders for your *coiffure*.'

He sighed. We resumed our vigil in dignified silence. Suddenly Strickland gripped me strongly by the arm. There was a slight rattle of a key opening a lock. The door opened noiselessly and for a moment a man's outline was clearly silhouetted by the gas lights in the corridor. The door closed quickly. The figure, furtively, made its way across the room to the bed. A match was struck. The glow revealed the fat nervous features of the Portuguese desk clerk. He lit a small candle and placed it on the dresser near the head of the bed, then quickly moved a table from the corner of the room (the very same table Mr Holmes had commented upon yesterday) to the side of the bed. Picking up the candle he climbed on the bed and then onto the table. He reached out for the brass elephant hanging over the bed and pulling it close to him he proceeded to perform a series of furtive operations whose exact nature we could not clearly discern from our coign of vantage.

The awkwardness of having to hold a candle in one hand, and arrest the swing of the elephant with the other, made his face shine with sweat and twitch with anxiety. He extracted an object from his jacket pocket that looked like a small container, and transferred something from it to the lamp. Finally he lit the lamp on the howdah of the brass elephant and let it swing gently back over the bed.

Then he got off the table and, placing it back in its corner, proceeded to wipe his face with a large handkerchief. He then left the room furtively, locking it behind him. Strickland and I stayed behind the screen for another ten minutes till three sharp raps came from the door. Strickland opened it with a key that he drew from his pocket. Mr Holmes walked in and looked up at the lighted elephant lamp that now swayed only imperceptibly.

'Ha! I see we have had our visitor. Capital, capital,' he remarked, rubbing his hands together. 'Oblige me by turning up the gas. We may have to entertain again this evening, and this time it would not do for our friend to view the consequences of his deed only by the light of this remarkable lamp.'

Mr Holmes's cheeriness did not dispel my fears. The lamp was definitely not your usual *objet d'art*, and being in the same room as it made me a trifle nervous.

'I hope it is not malignant in its operation,' said I, voicing my concern.

'Not at the moment, but we shall know very soon.' He turned away from the lamp and looked at Strickland. 'Now, Strickland, pray enlighten me as to the details.'

He stretched himself out on the sofa as Strickland informed him of all that had transpired in the room.

'I followed your instructions to the letter, Mr Holmes. At five o'clock, just before sunset, I entered the hotel unobserved, from the trade entrance, and picked up your key from under the cocoanut matting in front of the room. Since then I have been waiting — and a good long wait it has been.'

'Ah, but one propitious of a very satisfactory conclusion,' laughed Sherlock Holmes, 'as the incident you observed a little while ago will have augured. But we anticipate. Let us examine all our data before we proceed. What was the coroner's report?'

'Well, Mr Holmes, the coroner, Dr Patterson, was completely stumped. He says he's never had to deal with a case like this before. There are no indications of any kind of poison having been administered, nor are there any significant wounds to justify the tremendous bleeding — aside from a few superficial bruises that the deceased probably sustained falling down the staircase. In fact when the coroner had washed the body to examine it, there was practically no blood at all in his veins. I have never seen a paler native body in all my years in the force.'

'You are certain there were no wounds?' said Holmes insistently. 'No marks at all? Not even some insignificant puncture in the skin, around the back of the head or neck?'

'Mr Holmes, if you are thinking that the man died from a snake bite, I can assure you that it wasn't so. No reptile, however poisonous, could have . . .'

'Were there any puncture marks?' Holmes interrupted impatiently.

'Well, there were some slight scratches on the back of his neck, but nothing you could call punctures. I've seen all kinds of snake bites in this country and know the pattern they leave on the skin. These were lighter, mere nicks and . . .'

'This is the pattern of the scratches, isn't it?' said Holmes, holding out a slip of paper on which he had made some marks.

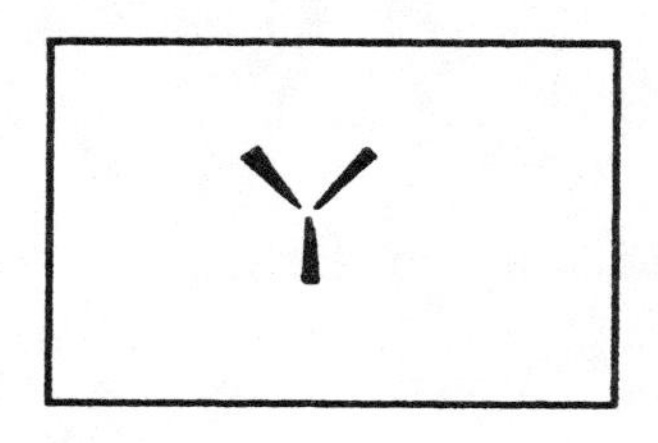

'How the Devil ...?' Strickland exclaimed, astonished.

'I thought as much,' cried Holmes, snapping his long fingers. 'My case is complete, gentlemen. It is now time to bring matters to a close. Strickland, could I trouble you to escort Mr Carvallo, the desk-clerk, up to this room. I fear that only the majesty of your official presence will succeed in persuading him to come up here again. You will bring him straight up to the bed and make him sit by the side.' Holmes began to arrange a few chairs to face the bed. 'Then you will seat yourself on this chair, if you please; Huree, you here. I'll take the armchair in the middle. I think we will then be sufficiently imposing to strike terror into a guilty breast.'

Strickland left the room and returned shortly with the Portuguese clerk. The fellow shrank back in evident surprise and fear at our judicial appearance, but Strickland firmly propelled him over to the side of the bed.

'Sit down, Mr Carvallo, sit down,' said Sherlock Holmes pleasantly. 'We are sorry to interrupt you in the performance of your duties, but as you will appreciate, the investigation of last night's tragedy must take priority over all other matters. No, no, please, sit in the middle of the bed, the edges are so uncomfortable, you know. You need not stand on ceremony with us.'

The desk clerk was attempting to sidle to the edge of the bed, occasionally casting furtive glances at the brass lamp above him. His nervous face was covered with perspiration, even more than when I last saw him.

'Very good,' said Holmes, leaning back in his armchair. 'Now, Mr Carvallo, will you please tell us the truth about yesterday's incident.'

The man turned white to the root of his hair.

'I do not know what you mean, Sir,' he managed to stammer.

'Come, come. You must not think us so simple-minded.'

'Sir, I am absolutely ignorant of what happened.'

'This is most unfortunate,' said Holmes, shaking his head. 'But I will make some suggestions that may serve to dispel the grievous lapse in your memory. We have every cause to believe that you were the instrument of yesterday's tragedy. We are prepared to make the concession that the dead man was not your intended victim, though I doubt that the point will sufficiently impress a judge to deter him from sending you to the gallows. Your real victim was myself, was it not, Sir? It was also some mistake on your part — the result of nervousness, maybe — that caused the premature operation of the device. Did you use too little wax? Maybe you accidentally jolted the thing when setting it up? You will not tell. Dear me, how very unkind of you.'

The blighter licked his thick, dry lips, but said nothing.

'Ah, well. It is a minor point and we can come back to it later when you feel more cooperative.'

'Oh! no, you don't,' said Strickland fiercely, pushing the now terrified clerk firmly back on the bed that he had again surreptitiously tried to vacate.

'No, Mr Carvallo,' said Mr Holmes, shaking an admonitory forefinger. 'You will sit there quietly till I have finished what I have to say. Now, where was I? Ah, yes. How did the unfortunate hotel servant die? I think in all probability he was passing by this room, and, looking through the open door — that you had in your nervous haste forgotten to close — saw the counterpane on the bed somewhat disarranged. Another act of gross negligence on your part, I am afraid. Being a conscientious employee of this hotel, the man stepped into the room and, bending over the bed, proceeded to straighten the counterpane. That was when it happened, did it not? Well. We can never be sure now. But I think my reasoning is sufficiently correct, at least to convince a jury. Do you not agree, Strickland?'

'Absolutely,' said Strickland grimly.

'Please! Please!' whispered the clerk hoarsely. The wretched man was now positively shaking with terror, and his large frenzied eyes gazed as if mesmerised at the brass elephant lamp burning above him.

'The elephant interests you?' said Mr Holmes, affecting to examine the lamp with a collector's curiosity. 'It is definitely of a very superior workmanship, Benaras brass, I should say; though this is the first time I have come across one with a lamp under the canopy. Very clever, if you think about it. Very clever indeed.' He managed to inject a hint of menace into his concluding words.

Galvanised by terror, the clerk leaped from the bed and collapsed before Mr Holmes. He clung to Holmes's legs and sobbed: 'I confess. I confess. The thing is in the lamp. It is a trap. Let me out of the room before ...'

Just then there was a sharp click from the lamp, and as we looked up a little hatch swung open from the bottom of the elephant and a small, bright object fell on the bed. The clerk screamed with horror. The thing was red and shiny, no longer than six inches and about the thickness and shape of a piece of garden hose. It rose up, one end poised in the air, wiggling from side to side.

'What the deuce is it?' said Strickland.

'Devilry,' answered Holmes, reaching into his pocket.

Just then the thing stopped swaying, stiffened for a moment, then with remarkable speed, began to move towards us. Though the desk-clerk's terror was certainly most contagious, my scientific curiosity compelled me to observe the curious method by which the creature effected locomotion. The moment it dropped its upper end on the ground its rear end rose up and wiggled forward. The upper end rose again and looped forwards with the rear end following immediately. The creature performed this operation with surprising speed and came rapidly towards us.

The clerk backed away in horror and tumbled backwards over

my chair. Strickland and I, though certainly not as frightened as he was, recoiled slightly from the advancing creature, vaguely aware of the menace that lurked in it despite its insignificant size. Only Sherlock Holmes was absolutely unperturbed. He remained calmly seated in his chair, and, as the thing got near his legs, reached into his pocket, pulled out a silver salt-cellar, and bending over poured the contents over the creature. As soon as the salt touched its body it began to squirm and flick about violently, as if in tremendous agony.

'Why, it is a leech!' I exclaimed in surprise.

'But not your common or garden variety,' said Holmes gravely. 'This one is a Giant Red Leech[1] of the Lower Himalayas, *Hirudinea Himalayaca Giganticus*, of the genus *Haemadipsa*. We must thank a kindly providence for restricting its existence to the small district of Kaladhungi in the Western Himalayas. Only its extreme rarity has cloaked its well-deserved reputation as a deadly killer. You may know that the saliva of the common leech contains chemical substances that not only anaesthetises the wound area, but also contain the anti-coagulant *hirudin*, which is used medically, and which prevents the blood from clotting. My reading this morning at the Natural History Museum informed me that the Giant Red Leech is not only much larger than the common leech, of which about three hundred species are known, but that its saliva contains these chemicals in concentrations *many thousands of times stronger*.'

'No wonder the poor chap bled as extensively as he did,' I said, in dread awe.

'That is not all,' said Holmes grimly, checking the notes on his cuff. 'Two other complex chemical substances are present in the Giant Leech's saliva. One activates the allergy reaction system

---

1. Could this have any connection with 'the repulsive story of the red leech' that Dr Watson mentions in his introduction to the adventure of *The Golden Pince-nez*?

in the body tissues to produce *histamine*, an *amine* concentrate formed from *histidine*, which dilates blood vessels and the pores of the skin. The third substance causes massive *Paroxysmal tachycardia*, a condition in which the heart suddenly commences to beat at an extraordinarily rapid rate — from two hundred and fifty to three hundred beats a minute — for a considerable period of time. So, once the saliva was absorbed into the blood-stream you would have a cumulative situation where a tremendously agitated heart would violently pump all the enervated blood from the body out of every dilated pore in the skin.'

'My God,' said Strickland with a shudder. 'But how did the creature get to him in the first place?'

'It dropped on the back of his neck when he bent over to straighten out the bedclothes.'

'That explains the marks on his neck,' exclaimed Strickland.

'Yes. The leech has three jaws, set with sharp teeth, that make the typical Y-shaped incision that I sketched for you a little while ago. The jaws and suckers on the mouth grip the flesh tenaciously. It is possible that the victim managed to tear the leech off his neck only after he rushed out into the corridor in panic. That is where the blood stains start. He then probably flung the horrible thing on the ground and stamped it to death. Huree, you may remember it as the "piece of India rubber" that I discovered yesterday in the corridor. But of course the leech had already injected its deadly saliva into the man, and from then on there was nothing any one could have done to prevent his heart from pumping his life blood out of his body. There was so much anti-coagulant in the blood that even after spilling on the floor and being exposed to the air for more than an hour, it showed no sign of drying.'

'You chanced to remark on it yesterday when we were coming down to the lobby after your investigations, Mr Holmes,' I exclaimed, remembering.

But Sherlock Holmes was already occupied in climbing onto the table he had pushed by the bed. He reached for the lamp, and, holding it delicately with a handkerchief, unfastened it from the chains that suspended it from the ceiling. He then jumped lightly off the table and placed the elephant on it.

'Humm. Ingenious. A unique and terrible weapon,' said he, examining the elephant closely. 'And yet such an exquisite work of art. Notice how the heat of the lamp inside the canopied box ...'

'The howdah, Sir,' I corrected him.

'Thank you,' he replied brusquely, '... how the heat of the lamp inside the howdah is transferred to the belly of the elephant by these copper wires. The heat gradually melts the wax that holds this small hatch in the elephant's belly and then, after a period of time regulated by the thickness of the wax used, allows the hatch to fall open and lets the creature out. I experimented on the hatch last night and discovered that it would not be possible for it to remain closed — once the lamp had been lit — for longer than two hours. So I was reasonably sure that no one would prepare the devilish thing again before the evening. Just to be on the safe side though, I asked you, Strickland, to be in my room before sunset. When I met Mr Carvallo in the lobby I informed him that I would be retiring after an early supper. So our friend was able to time his move nicely, while I had a light repast and thereafter borrowed a full salt-cellar.'

'But what went wrong yesterday, Mr Holmes?' I asked.

'Our nervous friend here ...' Holmes turned to the clerk, who was cowering in the corner of the room, '... used too much heat to stick the wax on the hatch yesterday, thereby causing a portion of it to drip on the counterpane. This thinned the seal and caused the premature opening of the hatch. But I apportion too much blame to you, Mr Carvallo. It was, after all, a most desperate commission, and remarkable that such a faint-hearted person as yourself should have attempted to undertake it. It would tax the limits of any man's courage to handle such a creature once — but twice! That was above and beyond the call of duty. Or was it because your master does not tolerate failure? A hard man, is he not? It would be difficult to imagine someone more unforgiving than the villain whom you have the misfortune to serve. What kind of hold does he have on you?'

'I cannot tell.' The wretch sank his face in his hands. 'It is too late,' he sobbed. After a while he raised his head and with great effort attempted to get a hold of himself. Taking a deep breath he spoke, a note of hopeless defiance heightening the pathos in his voice. 'No, gentlemen, I cannot tell. Whatever fate the law may impose on me, it will be a kinder one than what I will surely suffer if I betray my master.'

'Oh, you think so, do you?' said Strickland harshly, snapping a pair of handcuffs on him. 'Let me tell you, my man, that if I have anything to say about it you'll hang from the highest gallows in the Bombay Presidency.' He turned to me. 'Kindly ring the bell, Huree.'

A little while later Inspector MacLeod and two constables came in. Strickland gave them a number of instructions, after which they left with the wretched prisoner.

'The power of fear,' said Holmes gravely, settling himself in an armchair. 'I should not have underestimated it. Observe how even such a piteous wretch as our Portuguese clerk could steel himself to defy us, when the fear of Moriarty's retribution cast its dark shadow over his heart.'

'But he is dead,' I argued. 'You said ...'

'The man is dead,' corrected Holmes, 'his work lives. The Professor may lie at the bottom of the Reichenbach Falls but his charming society still has the power to reward, and, what is more relevant to our case, to punish those who betray it. Here in India, over a vast criminal empire, rules a bosom friend of Moriarty. That is the man who has inherited his dark mantle. That is the man who is after me now.'

'Give me his name, Mr Holmes,' said Strickland, 'and I'll soon have him sweating behind steel bars.'

'I commend your energy, Strickland. But I fear that such a direct course of action would prove futile. Colonel Sebastian Moran is a most cunning and dangerous adversary. At the moment the only net we have is too frail to hold such a formidable prey.'

'But, dash it all!' cried Strickland. 'The man is an honourable soldier.'

Holmes threw up his hands in resignation. 'Our net is indeed weak when a representative of the law fails to recognise his foremost adversary.'

'You astonish me, Mr Holmes,' Strickland remonstrated. 'You expect me to believe that an English gentleman, a former member of Her Majesty's Indian Army, the best heavy-game shot in India, a man with a still unrivalled bag of tigers, is a dangerous criminal. Why, I was with him just two nights ago at the Old Shikari Club. We played a rubber of whist together.'

'Well,' shrugged Sherlock Holmes, 'I suppose you cannot really be expected to have seen through the fellow's masquerade. After all, a couple of months ago Scotland Yard didn't even know of the existence of Professor James Moriarty. But believe me when I tell you that after the Professor, our Colonel Moran is probably the most dangerous criminal alive.'

He reached into the inside pocket of his coat and pulled out a slim morocco-bound notebook. 'Humm. Let's see what we have here on him. Just a few items I've copied out from my index of biographies. Ah! Here it is.'

He handed over a card to Strickland. I rose, and, standing behind Strickland, studied it over his shoulder:

Moran, Sebastian, Colonel. Unemployed. Formerly 1st Bangalore Pioneers. Born London, 1840. Son of Sir Augustus Moran, C.B., once British Minister to Persia. Educated Eton and Oxford. Served in Jowaki Campaign, Afghan Campaign, Charasiab (despatches), Sherpur, Cabul. Author of *Heavy Games of the Western Himalayas* (1881); *Three Months in the Jungle* (1884). London Address: Conduit Street. Clubs: The Anglo-Indian, The Tankerville, The Bagatelle Card Club. Address in India: Auckland Villa, Lahore Cantonment, Clubs: The Punjab (Lahore), The Old Shikari (Bombay), The Black Hearts (Simla).

'But Mr Holmes,' I objected, 'the gentleman's career is that of an honourable soldier.'

'It is true,' Holmes answered. 'Up to a certain point he did well. He was always a man of iron nerve, and no doubt you, Strickland, have heard the story of how he crawled down a drain after a wounded man-eating tiger. There are some trees, Huree, which grow to a certain height, and then suddenly develop flaws. You will see it often in humans. I have a theory that the individual represents in his development the whole procession of his ancestors, and that such a sudden turn to good or evil stands for some strong influence which came into the line of his pedigree. The person becomes, as it were, the epitome of the history of his own family.'

'That is surely rather fanciful,' Strickland reproached.

'Well, I don't insist upon it. Whatever the cause, Colonel Moran began to go wrong. Surely, Strickland, that if the Hyderabad card scandal did nothing to sully the good Colonel's reputation, then the mysterious death of his native butler must have at least given the police force some doubt as to his continence.'

'Mr Holmes, we are aware of certain blemishes on Colonel Moran's record, but it takes more than some suspicious occurrences to charge a man with being the leader of a dangerous criminal gang.'

'No doubt you are right,' said Holmes testily. He took a cigar from a box on the table and lit it. He then leaned back on his armchair, and, gazing at the ceiling, began to blow great clouds of smoke into the air. 'Well, it is a very long shot, but I must play it if my poor little reputation, such as it is, is not to suffer shipwreck.

Now Strickland, since you happen to play cards with Moran, you will surely have noticed a peculiarity in his right thumb.'

'He has a long, heavy scar running diagonally across his thumb. The result of some accident with a hunting knife.'

'Actually he received the injury in a struggle with a knife-wielding woman whom he had foully betrayed and ruined. But that does not concern us at present. Now, Huree, if you could kindly spare me a lead pencil from that fine array of writing paraphernalia you have displayed in your breast pocket, I will attempt to provide a demonstration of my claim that Colonel Sebastian Moran was the real perpetrator of this dreadful crime.'

Mr Holmes took a penknife out of his pocket and began to sharpen my pencil. He shaved off the wood and exposed more than a couple of inches of the soft lead, which he then delicately scraped with the knife over a clean sheet of paper. After about ten minutes he had a small pile of very fine black powder. Then going over to the elephant, he began to examine it minutely with the aid of his lens. The elephant glittered as Mr Holmes turned it this way and that, inspecting it under the gas; but I noticed that he was careful not to handle it except with a handkerchief.

'Mr Carvallo. Mr Carvallo,' he muttered to himself, 'you should not have fondled this thing so much with your sweaty hands.'

After a good twenty minutes, during which his brow seemed to furrow deeply with mounting frustration and annoyance, he sprang up from his chair with a cry of satisfaction. 'Ha! Ha! Capital. Now if I could trouble you gentlemen to come closer, I may be able to amuse you with this parlour-trick.'

As we gathered around him Sherlock Holmes picked up the sheet of paper and gently blew some of the fine graphite powder onto the surface of the elephant, on its left flank. He then tapped the elephant lightly with the penknife, till all the excess graphite powder fell off on the table. As if by magic a number of finger and thumb prints appeared on the part of the elephant which had received the powder. The black lines and whorls of the impression stood out clearly against the light yellow of the brass lamp.

'Now,' said Holmes, 'most of these belong to the sweaty fingers of our Portuguese friend, but if you will observe here closely ...'

Using the tip of the penknife as a pointer he indicated a large clear impression — a rough ridged thumb print with a diagonal line running across it.

'It is not conclusive evidence,' said Sherlock Holmes, folding the penknife and putting it back in his pocket, 'but it may serve to demonstrate that Colonel Sebastian Moran did, at sometime, handle this object.'

'This is most wonderful verification, Sir; *quod erat demonstrandum*, if I may be pardoned the expression,' I exclaimed in admiration.

'I owe you an apology, Mr Holmes,' said Strickland ruefully. 'I should have had more faith in your marvellous faculty.'

'You give me too much credit, Strickland. I must admit to some luck in this instance. On the balance of probability, I could not have hoped for such a perfect sample of the Colonel's thumb print, especially as the clerk had managed to obliterate nearly all previous fingerprints left on it by his injudicious handling of the object. But I took my chance for "*à vaincre sans péril, on triomphe sans gloire*". Corneille has such a very neat way of putting these things. But for incontrovertible proof you would need a sample of Colonel Moran's thumb print to compare with this one on the elephant. As you may know, no two human fingerprints are ever alike.'

'Yes, Mr Holmes,' answered Strickland, 'I have heard something of the kind; though till this day I was not aware that it could be used to practical advantage, especially in the solution of a crime.'

'A wide range of exact knowledge is essential to the higher development of the art of detection,' Sherlock Holmes explained in a didactic manner. 'The Babylonians pressed fingerprints into clay to identify the author of cuneiform writings, and to protect against forgeries. Fingerprints were also used by the Chinese at an early date for purposes of identification. You may not be aware that I am the author of a trifling monograph upon the subject. In my work entitled *Upon the Distinction and Classification of Human Finger and Thumb Prints* I enumerate five main groups of characteristic details and other sub-classification by which fingerprints may be systematically classified and recorded. I devote two whole chapters to the methods by which fingerprints may be detected upon objects such as glass, metal, wood, and even paper. I myself have developed a method, which you have seen crudely demonstrated, by which near invisible fingerprints can be enhanced or developed by the delicate application of fine powders whose colours contrast favourably with the background surface. The powders adhere to the lines of the prints because of the body oils and sweat always present on the surface of the human hand and which is invariably left on any surface we touch. Such developed fingerprints could be photographed to provide, let us say, evidence in court.

'In the monograph I also provide incontestable evidence of the superiority of the fingerprinting system over Monsieur Bertillon's[2] system of "anthropometry" for the identification of criminals. But I weary you with my obsession for minutiae.'

'Not at all,' Strickland said earnestly. 'It is of the greatest interest to me. Surely such a system as you have described would revolutionise police work.'

---

2. Alphonse Bertillon (1853–1914), the great French detective, was the father of the revolutionary system of classifying and trapping criminals by measuring and recording certain unchangeable parts of the human body. He called his invention 'anthropometry' or body measurement.

'Undoubtedly, but it is not in the province of a lone consulting detective to apply such a system to its fullest productivity. It would require the resources of a large official organisation, like that of Scotland Yard, to record the prints of every criminal or suspect they may come across, and register them in such a way that any one of them is always ready to be had for comparison with fingerprints found at the scene of the crime. But the Scotland Yarders are not men who would entertain any sympathy for revolutionary systems.'

'Well, Mr Holmes, I would consider it a signal of honour if you were to permit me to apply your system of fingerprinting in this country.[3] The Imperial Indian Police, in spite of many shortcomings, is still young enough to be occasionally pioneering.'

'The honour would be mine, Strickland. There are no patents on my methods. I only ask you to keep my name out of it, especially if the results of your endeavour should be fruitful enough to warrant the attention of the press. At present it suits my purpose to let the world think I am dead. I am sorry I do not have a copy of my monograph here with me, but you can get it from Huber in London, if you wish. They also have some other small works of mine that may interest you. The one entitled *Upon the Distinction Between the Ashes of Various Tobaccos* may prove useful to you. If you can recognise the black ash of a Trichinopoly at the scene of a murder, why, you could then count Colonel Sebastian Moran as one of your suspects — for I know he smokes them.'

'Well, Mr Holmes,' said Strickland with a little laugh, 'Trichinopoly or Lunkah, you can rely on us to have the Colonel

---

3. In 1896, in the district of Hooghly in Bengal, the Inspector General of Police introduced, for the first time anywhere in the world, the system of fingerprinting for identifying criminals. Only in 1901 did Scotland Yard adopt the Henry system of classifying prints by patterns and shapes.

behind bars before long. Once that desk-clerk has had time to reflect in the solitude of his cell, he will consider a full confession and transportation to the Andaman Islands preferable to stretching on the gallows.'

Just then there was an urgent knock on the door. Strickland went over and opened it. Outside in the corridor was a nervous-looking native policeman.

'Havildar, kya hai?' demanded Strickland.

The policeman mumbled something inaudible. Strickland turned a very worried face to us.

'The clerk's just been shot in front of the police station.'

6

A Shot in the Dark

Without a word Sherlock Holmes rushed out of the room. Strickland and I followed him out of the hotel to the rank of carriages that stood outside the hotel gates. As our carriage rattled down Frere Street towards Horniman Circle, Mr Holmes lit a cigarette and puffed at it in an abrupt and vexed manner.

'It was criminally careless of me not to have anticipated Moran's move,' said he. 'Now I fear that the one frail thread we had to tie up this case has just snapped.'

'But we still have the evidence of the thumbprint, Mr Holmes,' I suggested. 'Would it not suffice, in the *ad interim*, to secure the detention of Colonel Moran, till a more formidable case has been formulated?'

'My dear Huree, the evidence of the thumbprint would be too *outré* for any magistrate to think of issuing a warrant against a person of Moran's standing. We must not also forget that our old shikari is a man of diverse resources; he would flick away any such obstacles as we could, at the moment, put in his way.'

'I fear you are right, Mr Holmes,' said Strickland dejectedly. 'We needed that blasted desk-clerk's confession, and now he's dead. I should have warned MacLeod....'

'The fault is entirely mine, Strickland,' said Sherlock Holmes gravely. 'You could not have foreseen such an eventuality. But hulloa! I see we have arrived at our destination. Nothing less than a murder would draw such a mob — if the morbid curiosity of the London crowd is anything to judge the rest of humanity by.'

Indeed, the crowd before the Horniman Circle police station was so large that the progress of our carriage was severely impeded. In spite of my remonstrances, barefooted little street urchins clambered like monkeys all over our carriage to secure a loftier view point. Finally Strickland and the police sergeant had to dismount and force their way through the press of bodies. After paying off the ghariwallah, Mr Holmes and I followed.

'Chale jao, you chaps,' Strickland shouted above the hubbub, 'move along there.' Swinging his swagger-stick vigorously before him, he managed to clear a path through the throng. Some constables spotted us and, brandishing their lathis, came to our assistance. Once we got through the crowd I saw a large pool of blood on the ground. The body had been removed to the police station. Inside, a visibly distraught Inspector MacLeod met us, his grey scraggly moustache looking more dishevelled than ever.

'I'm very sorry about this, Sir,' he stammered. 'For the life of me I just can't imagine ...'

'My dear MacLeod,' Strickland interrupted, 'just tell us exactly what happened ...'

'Well Sir,' the inspector began, 'I escorted the prisoner from the hotel in the police victoria. I had two constables with me. When the victoria got to the thana and I was alighting, something struck the prisoner on the chest, mutilating it horribly. The effect was that of a gun-shot wound, but it could nae have been one, since neither I nor the constables heard the sound of a fire-arm being discharged. We managed to get the wounded man inside and Dr Patterson immediately attended to him, but it was nae use. He died a few minutes later.'

A stout middle-aged Englishman in a white surgical gown came out from another room. I presumed this was Dr Patterson.

'Good evening, Mr Strickland ... gentlemen,' he greeted us quickly and turned to Inspector MacLeod. 'Your man was definitely shot, MacLeod, and here's the bullet that did it. I just got it out of his chest.'

He held out a white enamel dish in which a single bloodstained bullet rolled to and fro. Sherlock Holmes bent over to examine it.

'A soft revolver bullet,' he declared. 'As you will perceive, it expanded considerably after discharge, thus inflicting the horrible mutilation on the body that Inspector MacLeod described.'

'But it could nae have been a revolver,' cried the bewildered inspector, tugging his scraggly whiskers in irritation. 'As I said before there was no sound of a gun being fired. And at this time of the night there is nae so much ado in the streets, that a pistol shot could nae have been heard.'

'See for yourself then,' Sherlock Holmes replied, pointing to the small bullet in the dish.

'I am nae denying it is a bullet, Sir,' protested the nettled inspector, 'but Captain Strickland, Sir, you know that the whole courtyard in front of the station is well lit with gas lamps. I am willing to stake my pension that there was nobody around the prisoner and me, at least within pistol range.'

'But further away,' suggested Strickland, 'on the other side of the street maybe.'

'That's a good eighty feet or more away,' replied the inspector, 'and I can nae be sure.'

'Was there any traffic on the street then, any carriage passed you by at that moment?'

'Nae, I am sure of it. Well there was this van — one of those covered delivery things — parked in front of one of the shops on the other side of the street. But nae even a crack shot could have hit a man at that range with just a pistol — especially at night.'

'Wouldn't it be rather late to make deliveries?' remarked Holmes, walking to the open window and peering out into the night. 'It is not there now, at any rate.' He turned away from the window to face us. 'Dear me. Dear me. What a singular problem.'

Something in his tone caught my ear. It seemed to me that the tone of his voice, far from sounding puzzled, hinted at privileged information. Strickland may have detected it too, for he immediately attempted to end the discussion and get Sherlock Holmes out of the police station.

'Well, there's nothing more we can do tonight,' said Strickland briskly, moving to the door. 'MacLeod, first thing tomorrow I want you to question all the shopkeepers and residents around here for any unusual activity or suspicious persons they may have seen at the time of the shooting.'

The crowd outside the police station had by now dispersed. The glow of the gas lamps fell on the prone figures of a few beggars sleeping on the hard pavement. The twanging of a sitar drifted faintly through the still night air. For a moment I thought of the plump Portuguese clerk now lying lifeless on a concrete slab in the police mortuary, while his soul was beginning its journey to 'that undiscovered country from whose bourn no traveller returns.' A constable flagged down a carriage for us and we rode back to the hotel, savouring the coolness of the late night air.

Sherlock Holmes seemed visibly distraught, his sharp face under his deerstalker cap was bent morosely low. He was so wrapped up in his own musings that he did not seem to hear Strickland's query. 'How was it done, Mr Holmes?'

'What?'

'The shooting, Mr Holmes. How was the Portuguese fellow done in?'

'Oh, that,' replied Holmes rather indifferently, raising his head slowly, 'just an air-gun.'

'What do you mean?'

'An air-gun, my dear Strickland. Or rather an air-rifle. Believe me such a thing does exist.[1] A unique weapon, noiseless and of tremendous power. I knew Von Herder, the blind German mechanic who constructed it to the order of the late Professor Moriarty. It fires a soft revolver bullet. There's genius in that, for who would expect such a thing from an air-rifle? Moran has, on more than one occasion, attempted to bag me with that thing, but fate has been kinder to me than to the Colonel's tigers.'

'But he will surely try again,' I expostulated, 'if we do not manage to arrest or incapacitate him. It is a most dangerous situation for your life and limb, Mr Holmes.'

'I am by no means a nervous man, Huree, but I see your point of view. What course of action would you recommend?'

'Discretion being the better part of valour, I would advise a speedy retreat from this most insalubrious metropolis,' I suggested.

'Huree is right, Mr Holmes,' said Strickland, 'Colonel Moran has tremendous advantages here. Apart from the size and turmoil of the city, which hinders effective police work, there are numerous criminal organisations in Bombay that Moran could easily recruit for his foul purpose.'

'I would recommend a sojourn to Simla, Mr Holmes,' said I. 'The climate there is delightful at this time of the year and is

---

1. In spite of its seeming novelty, the air-rifle had been in use earlier in history. Louis XIV hunted deer with one. It even saw military service when the French used it quite successfully against the Austrians in the Napoleonic Wars. An air-rifle was also used by Lewis and Clark on their celebrated expedition.

admirably adapted to the European constitution. Ah ... "the verdant hills, the crystal streams, the cool mountain winds perfumed by the breath of eternal pine trees..." or so we are informed in Towell's *Handbook to Simla*.'

'You mustn't let Hurree's poetry discourage you, Mr Holmes,' said Strickland. 'Yes, Simla *is* the best place for you to retire at the moment. Though it's the summer capital of the government, it is small enough for us to keep an eye on all unusual visitors, and the natives are simple, honest hill-folk. Moreover, Hurree here is in his element up in the hills, and could watch your back effectively.'

I was glad to learn that I would be accompanying Sherlock Holmes to Simla. Just the two days I had known him assured me that furthering the acquaintance of this remarkable person would not only prove instructive, but exciting as well.

'The Frontier Mail to Peshawar leaves tonight at one o'clock, Mr Strickland,' said I, consulting my Indian Bradshaw and the large silver turnip watch I had inherited from my father. 'If it would not be rushing things for Mr Holmes, we have about two hours in which to catch it.'

'Well, I am an old campaigner,' replied Sherlock Holmes, 'and two hours would be more than sufficient for me to collect my gladstone from the hotel.'

'Then it's settled,' said Strickland, as the carriage stopped in front of the hotel door. 'The sooner you leave Bombay the less chance of Moran being able to have another go at you. Hurree ...' he turned to me, '... collect your kit from your lodgings and meet us at the Victoria Terminus — at the book stall by the first class waiting room.'

7

The Frontier Mail

Surely the Victoria Terminus is the most magnificent railway station in the world. It was opened five years ago on the happy occasion of our August Sovereign the Queen Empress's Golden Jubilee, and its splendour and opulence was acclaimed throughout the land — only Lady Dufferin, the Vicereine, not approving, considering it '... much too magnificent for a bustling crowd of railway passengers.' This vast edifice is architecturally a harmonious blend of Venetian, Gothic, Neo-classical, Hindu and Islamic styles. The columns supporting the roofs are made from dark granite especially imported from Aberdeen, providing the whole majestic composition with a touch of Imperial sternness.

With my back to one of these stern granite columns and my suitcase and bedding-roll at my feet, I observed the milling multitudes arriving and departing, picking their way through supine, sheeted figures — third class passengers, who had taken their tickets overnight and were sleeping on the platforms.

Sweetmeat sellers, water carriers, tea vendors and paan-bidi wallahs pitched their sales-cries above the everpresent roar of this teeming humanity.

I purchased a copy of the *Times of India* from the A.H. Wheeler book stall, which also had on display Mr Kipling's works in their distinctive green covers (Indian Railway Library, Rs 1) for the amusement of passengers with long journeys ahead. As I paid the stall-keeper and tucked the newspaper under my arm, I got a glimpse of a small thin man in dirty white tropical 'ducks' and an oversize topee. He darted out of an inter[1] waiting room door and suddenly vanished in a crowd of Sikh cavalrymen. Ferret-Face! Was it really him? A lot of people in this country wore oversize topees and dirty 'ducks', but again…

Before I could sort my thoughts out properly someone tapped me on the back of my shoulder, startling me.

'Oh! It's you, Mr Strickland,' I exclaimed, much relieved.

'Now listen to me, Hurree. I've managed to get a first class *coupé* for two from the government quota, so you can travel with Mr Holmes without any problems from other European passengers.'

'Oh, there will be no problems, Sir.'

'I don't know, Huree. I'm not easy in my mind about letting you and Mr Holmes make this journey.'

'But why, Mr Strickland? We agreed that …'

'I know Mr Holmes is safer out of Bombay, but a moving train does seem like an ideal place for another attempt …'

'Not to worry, Sir. I will maintain a constant vigil.'

The Frontier Mail roared into the station, only a few minutes behind its scheduled arrival time of 1.45 a.m. The sleeping figures on the platform sprang to life. The normal hubbub of the station

---

1. Intermediate. One of the many classes on Indian trains in the past. Between third and second class.

now rose to a terrific crescendo as yelling passengers gathered up their boxes, bedding-rolls, children and relatives, and made a mad dash for the carriage doors and windows. A collective insanity seemed to overtake the vendors, coolies and beggars as they shrieked and howled to attract custom or charity.

We collected Sherlock Holmes from the first-class waiting room. Assisted by a porter wearing the red regulation shirt and brass arm band, who carried our few items of luggage on his head, we jostled our way through the teeming crowd and finally got to our carriage. As a precaution against dacoits Indian trains do not have corridors, and each carriage is entered independently from the platform. A rowdy group of tough-looking British soldiers — 'tommies' from the Royal Warwickshire Regiment — occupied the carriage immediately behind ours.

'Are you armed Mr Holmes?' enquired Strickland.

'I have a hair-trigger. I thought it as well to carry it.'

'It would be a considerable relief to me if you would keep it near you night and day, and never relax your precautions. Huree is an old hand at this kind of thing and you can rely on him implicitly.'

'Most certainly. Well, *Au revoir* then, Strickland. I cannot thank you enough for your help.'

'Goodbye Mr Holmes,' said Strickland as the train began to move down the platform and the child beggars made last frantic efforts to elicit alms from the passengers on the train. 'Goodbye Hurree. Mind you don't get careless.'

Shooing away the little beggars hanging onto the carriage windows, I leaned back in my seat and fanned myself with the newspaper as the train pulled out of the station on its long journey to Peshawar, at the foot of the Khyber Pass. The train would be proceeding via Deolali, Burhanpur, Khandwa, Bhopal, Jhansi, Gwalior, Agra, Delhi, Umballa, Amritsar and Lahore, but we would have to get off at Umballa and take a pony trap to Simla.

Mr Holmes had his head out of the window and was looking down at something outside. After a little while he pulled his head in and, settling back in his seat, lit his pipe. I put my luggage away neatly on the overhead rack, and popped a paan into my mouth. Chewing it slowly I cast my mind over the events of the day. All of a sudden I remembered Ferret-Face.

'Something the matter, Hurree?' Holmes's calm voice broke into my reverie. 'You look like you've just swallowed a thrupenny bit.'

I told him about seeing Ferret-Face at the station.

'But I really could not be sure, Sir,' I said. 'It all happened so dashed quickly.'

'Hmm. Still, it would be imprudent not to regard it as a fortuitous warning. Moran now probably knows of our flight from Bombay.'

It was not a very comforting thought. To be subjected once again to murderous fauna and expanding bullets, especially within the narrow confines of a moving railway carriage, was a trifle rich for my blood. But Sherlock Holmes thankfully diverted my mind from such distressing cogitations by diverting the conversation to more comforting and scholastic directions.

'Ethnology being your metier, Huree,' said Holmes, 'could you kindly tell me whether the representation of an open hand has any symbolic meaning in this country?'

'An open hand? Well, it is a commonly known symbol of the goddess Kali.'

'Pray, enlighten me as to the details.'

'Well, Mr Holmes, Kali is certainly not your usual benign divinity. No indeed. She is the very fierce and terrifying aspect of Devi, the Supreme Goddess; probably the most virulent deity in the Hindu pantheon. She is depicted as a hideous hag smeared in blood, with bared teeth and a protruding tongue. Her four hands hold, variously, a sword, a shield, the severed hand of a giant, and a strangling noose. Her rites involve sacrificial killings — at one time, of humans. Kali is supposed to have … aah … developed her taste for human blood when she was called upon to kill the demon Raklavija.

'But it is all gross superstition and savagery, Mr Holmes, quite unsuitable for the scientific mentality. I, myself, am a Brahmo Somajist,[2] eschewing such barbarity and esteeming instead the noble principles of reason and humanism, as expressed in the *Upanishads*, which represents the true philosophic teachings of uncorrupted Hinduism.'

Taking his pipe out of his mouth, Sherlock Holmes leaned forward.

'Interesting,' said he, 'but does this fiend or the open hand symbol have any connection with something other than mythology — with crime, maybe?'

'Why, yes, Sir. She was worshipped by the Thugs.'

'Ahh … I remember reading about them a few years ago. Some kind of professional murderers — were they not?'

'Yes, Mr Holmes. They were members of a well-organised confederacy of assassins who travelled in gangs throughout India for more than three hundred years.'

'Pray, continue,' said Holmes, as he leaned back on his seat, placed his fingertips together and closed his eyes.

'The *modus operandi* of these dastardly murderers was to

---

2. The Brahmo Somaj or Divine Society was founded in 1828 by Raja Ram Mohan Roy, the great Indian reformer and doyen of the Bengal Renaissance. He took his stand on the principles of reason and the rights of the individual as expressed in the *Upanishads*. These he said were basic to both Hindu and Western thought and formed a basis upon which they could mutually borrow. He attacked the institution of sati and abuses of caste, advocating the raising of the status of women and the abolition of idolatry.

worm their way into the confidences of wayfarers and, when all was hail-fellow-well-met, strangle them from behind with a handkerchief that had knotted into one of its corners (to give it a better grip) a silver coin consecrated to Kali. All this was done according to certain ancient and rigidly prescribed forms and after the performance of special religious rites, in which the consecration of the pickaxe and the sacrifice of sugar formed a prominent part. Although their essential religious creed was worshipping Kali, there were traces of Islamic practices present in their rituals. The fraternity possessed a jargon of its own called Ramasi. They also had signs by which its members could recognise each other.'

'When did the authorities learn of the existence of this organisation?'

'Definite evidence of Thuggery was only secured when Lord William Bentinck was the Governor-General of India; that would be around the 1830s, at the time of the Company Bahadur — The Honourable East India Company. His Lordship appointed Captain Sleeman to do the needful regarding this outrageous defiance of British Law. In five years no fewer than three thousand Thugs were caught and convicted; one of them admitting to no less than seven hundred and nineteen murders, with many others not too far behind this shocking tally. Over four hundred Thugs were eventually hanged and the rest transported, probably to the Andaman Islands.'

'So the whole brood was wiped out?'

'Well ... that would be the position of things ... ah ... *ex officio*, but it is not exactly *e concensu gentium*.'

'Some of them survived?'

'Not many, but enough to maintain the organisation. When young Captain Sleeman went after them, the Thugs were operating in Central India, mostly in rural areas and the jungles. Those who stuck to the outbacks were caught, sooner or later. Only the few who changed their habits and departed to the big cities like Calcutta or Bombay survived. That is why I wanted you to leave Bombay, Mr Holmes. They are there still, murderous as ever, ready to sell their services to the likes of Colonel Moran.'

Outside Bombay the train slowed down and stopped at a small station. Probably the tracks were not clear ahead and the points had to be changed. A harassed looking Eurasian ticket-collector entered our carriage, his sour face, under an uncomfortably large pith helmet, glistening with perspiration. He eyed me in a very unpleasant way. 'Hey you, Babu! What are you doing here? Nikal jao Jaldi!'

'This gentleman is travelling with me,' said Holmes quietly but firmly. 'We have taken the whole *coupé*. Here are our tickets.'

Wiping his face with a none too clean handkerchief, the ticket-collector pored over the damp sheaves of passenger lists on his clipboard, and at last grudgingly punched our tickets. Just as he was leaving Sherlock Holmes spoke. 'Excuse me, would you by any chance have a piece of chalk with you?'

The ticket-collector seemed rather surprised by Mr Holmes's request, but extracted a small stick of white chalk from the pocket of his faded blue uniform and proffered it to Holmes. Ticket-collectors and guards generally carried pieces of chalk with them to put temporary markings on the side of carriages for the purpose of identification.

'Thank you very much,' said Holmes as the ticket-collector tucked his clip-board under his arm and left. I also got out of the carriage to search for the dining-car. It was, thankfully, not too far away, and I was able to purchase some cold Murree beer for Mr Holmes and tonic water for myself. Clutching these I hurried back and I was just in time, for as soon as I reached our carriage the train started.

Mr Holmes was also outside the train, and he climbed in after me. As he reached for the door I noticed that his hands were covered with chalk dust. He then went into the toilet attached to our carriage. When he came out I noticed that he had washed his hands thoroughly.

As the train picked up speed and roared through the hot Indian night, Mr Holmes and I settled down to our journey. Drinking the cold beer and tonic water, and eating Cabuli grapes and pistachio nuts I had earlier purchased at the Bhindi Bazaar, we discoursed amicably on matters of life, art and philosophy before finally turning in for the night.

Around three o'clock in the morning I was rudely woken from my slumbers by a tremendous commotion from the neighbouring carriage — even a fire-arm being discharged. Probably the tommies had had too much to drink and were, as usual, being obstreperous and a disgrace to their uniforms. Someone also seemed to be yelling something, in Hindustani, but I could not be sure. After a while the uproar subsided and gentle Morpheus once more enfolded me into his embrace. But just before falling asleep I thought I heard Sherlock Holmes chuckling to himself in the darkness of the carriage.

I awoke to find Mr Holmes up in his purple dressing gown, smoking his pipe and reading *The Times of India*, while a railway bearer in white livery was serving breakfast on the raised drop-leaf table.

'Good morning, Huree,' said Holmes, turning a page of the newspaper. 'I trust you are well rested.'

'Oh yes, Mr Holmes. I slept like a baby. Only the bally hullabaloo in the next carriage disturbed my slumber somewhat. Surely it woke you up too, Sir?'

'Babuji!' said the bearer, who had, rather impertinently, been listening in on our conversation. 'Last night two dacoits broke into the next carriage.'

'How did you know that?' I asked in the vernacular.

'Babuji, I entered this rail-ghari with chota-hazris at Jalgaon junction early this morning. There policewallahs took one dacoit from the next carriage. The ticket-babu told me that two dacoits had tried to rob a carriage full of Angrezi soldiers. Hai! Bewakoof! On learning their mistake, one fool jumped out of the window. The other was shot in the leg by a soldier sahib's bundook. I must go now to serve other hazris.'

'It is dashed unusual of dacoits to enter a carriage full of armed soldiers,' I mused, after translating the waiter's story to Mr Holmes. 'Generally, criminals of this sort are more careful and prepared in their enterprises.'

But Mr Holmes did not seem to share my doubts. There was a knowing twinkle in his eyes.

'By Jove, Mr Holmes,' I exclaimed, 'I perceive you have a fair idea about the matter. I beg of you not to perpetuate my ignorance.'

'Well,' said he, putting away his newspaper, 'it all begins with the drawing of an open hand. Remember I asked you last night what it might mean.'

'Yes, Sir. I told you it was the symbol of Kali.'

'I noticed such a sketch done in chalk, on the side of our carriage, just before the train left the station at Bombay.'

'But I saw nothing.'

'You saw, but you did not observe. The distinction is clear. For example, you must have made hundreds of train journeys, and frequently seen the wheels on the carriages.'

'Yes, Sir.'

'Then how many are there on each carriage?'

'How many? Four, I suppose. I cannot be sure.'

'Quite so! You have not observed. Yet you have seen. That is my point. Now I know that there are eight wheels on every carriage because I have both seen and observed. But getting back to the subject at hand: when I first saw the drawing I knew that it could only be either one of two things: a child's innocent scrawl, or a mark left for some definite purpose. When you informed me that the handprint was a symbol of the goddess Kali, and consequently of the Thugee cult, I knew that the game was up and our flight had been discovered.'

'But who could have done it? Mr Strickland only made reservations for our compartment just before the train came into the station, and we have been inside the carriage ever since then.'

'It could have been any one of those beggars clinging to our carriage windows. Probably Moran had taken the precaution of having watchers at the station, just in case I made a bolt for it.'

'Probably Ferret-Face was one of the watchers, Sir.'

'It is more probable that he was the organiser, and had a number of watchers covering various places at the station and reporting back to him when they spotted anything.'

'Yes, of course. I stand corrected, Mr Holmes.'

'Now, I could not call for police assistance merely because of the drawing, even supposing that we could find such help on a moving train. We must bear in mind that the police would have wanted to know my position in the scheme of things, which would have been rather awkward to explain. There was also the possibility that Moran could have disguised some of his men as policemen to take us unawares. So with not many options left, I rubbed out the sketch on the side of our carriage and chalked a similar one on the side of the next carriage, the one full of armed soldiers.'

'Acha! Of course. So they were Thugs who entered the carriage last night, not dacoits. Goodness gracious! If it were not for your vigilance, Mr Holmes, there would have been handkerchiefs twisted around our throats this morning. Baapre-baap!'

'It need not have come to that. There was always my revolver. But that would have been cutting it rather fine. Now what do we have here?' Holmes raised the cover of a dish and sniffed appreciatively. 'Ah, bacon and eggs. Could I serve you some, Hurree. If I am not mistaken, the consumption of a few rashers of bacon does not constitute any fundamental violation of observances in your particular faith.'

We arrived at Delhi that night around eleven o'clock. I got up from my berth and peered out of the carriage window at the unlovely, fortress-like station built of dull red sandstone. It was hot, much hotter than Bombay — and very dusty. A lone bhisti spraying the platform from his buffalo-skin mussak, did not help to settle the dust or cool the air. The beggars were noisier here. I purchased a paan from a one-eyed vendor and chewed it till the train thankfully pulled out of the station. A little breeze wafted though the coach and I fell back to sleep.

Next morning at five o'clock the train rolled into Umballa city station where Mr Holmes and I disembarked. A light drizzle had settled the dust and freshened the morning air. As we breakfasted at the small but clean station restaurant, the Frontier Mail pulled out of the station on its long journey to the railhead at Peshawar.

There being no railway line to Simla at the time, we took the tonga service of the Mountain Car Company, which was available right at the railway station, and rattled off to Kalka, which is the first stop *en route* to Simla.

8

Under the Deodars

The tonga is a sturdy two-wheeled cart drawn by a single or two horses in curricle style, having back-to-back seating accommodation for four to six persons, apart from the driver. Since Mr Holmes and I had taken the whole tonga exclusively for ourselves, there was more than ample room for us and our few articles of luggage. Our tongawallah, or driver, was a shrivelled old greybeard with a dirty red turban wrapped around his bony head; but he kept the brace of the Kathiawar ponies moving at a brisk pace on the Kalka road, in the freshness of the rain-swept dawn.

For hours the tonga rattled along the hard, kankar-surfaced road, only stopping occasionally at a roadside parao, a travellers' resting place, to allow the ponies a breathing spell. We used the opportunity to stretch our legs and drink the jaggery-sweetened mahogany brown tea, which is the only kind of beverage available in these simple places.

About thirty-five miles out from Umballa city I espied the

distant mountains floating above the far northern horizon. The slight shower early that morning had cleared the air so that the peaks were pellucid and brilliant against the sunny blue sky.

'Look Mr Holmes, the Himalayas! The abode of the gods — or so we are informed in the *Skanda Puranas*.'

Sherlock Holmes lifted his head. An extraordinary change came over his face and his eyes sparkled like stars. All men are affected by their first view of the Himalayas, but in Mr Holmes's case it was as if his cares and worries had, at least momentarily, been lifted from his shoulders; as if he had been away on a long voyage and had now finally come home. For some time he gazed silently at the distant peaks.

'How does that thing by Beethoven go?' he murmured to himself. '"On the heights is peace — peace to serve." Tra la la ... la ... la ... la ... la la ... lirra ... lay ...'[1]

Mr Holmes reached for the violin case by his side and, working the catches open, pulled out a rather battered-looking instrument. Tucking the violin under his long chin he set about tuning it. Finally he commenced to play. His eyes took on a dreamy look as the haunting notes flowed from his instrument. He was probably playing the piece by Beethoven. I really did not know. I must confess to a slight ignorance in matters musical.

Be that as it may, Mr Holmes's musical accomplishments were of a nature to move the feelings of the most hardened Philistine. I was bewitched. The old tongawallah gave a happy cackle, and even the tired ponies seemed to become more sprightly.

Indeed with the inter-mingling of other sounds: the steady rattle of the cart, the rhythmic clip-clop of the ponies' hooves, the murmur of the distant Gugger river, and the songs of the doves and barbets in the shady jamun trees lining the road, a strange,

---

1. Probably 

fascinating symphony of nature was, in my fancy, performed before the approaching presence of the Himalayan foothills.

The piece ended and the last memorable notes faded away. I sat silent for a moment, and then broke out in spontaneous applause. 'Wah! Mr Holmes, Bravo! You have more talents than the god Shiva has arms.'

Sherlock Holmes smiled and bowed his head slightly. The great detective, in spite of his cold, scientific mind and masterful ways, could be moved by a genuine appreciation of his powers.

We stayed at Kalka that night. Early next morning we were on the road to Simla. Past the nearby Pinjore Gardens the road climbed and dipped about the growing spurs, the sound of gurgling mountain streams was everywhere and the chatter of monkeys filled the Deodar forests covering the hills. Traffic increased on the road. British officers on Badakshani chargers, Pathan horse-dealers astride spirited Cabuli ponies, native families packed on slow bullock carts, passengers like us on noisy tongas, and even a turbanned mahout on a solitary government elephant — wended their various ways, at various speeds, on this winding mountain road.

Gradually the air became colder, the vegetation more lush, and the road steeper as we neared Simla. Mr Holmes puffed contentedly on one of the many pipes he always seemed to have about him and hummed snatches of a tune to himself, gently waving his long, thin fingers in time to his humming. The horrors of Bombay seemed far away: the sinister Colonel Moran, Ferret-Face, the blood-covered corpse, the dead Portuguese clerk, and the nocturnal Thugs, seemed to take on the distant, unreal quality of a half-forgotten nightmare.

But I reminded myself that I had been charged with Sherlock Holmes's safety, and, though I had till now done little to merit this great trust, I must not, for the honour of the Department, be caught off my guard again. So I was jolly careful when we finally got to Simla and kept my eyes peeled for any further possible mischief initiated by Colonel Moran.

Simla, the summer capital of the Government of India since 1864, is a most delightful and sophisticated town. The European section of the town — with the church, the Mall, the Gaiety Theatre, the Viceroy's residence, and all the better buildings, houses and shops — is situated on the heights of the hills and inter-connecting ridges. Lower down is located the native bazaar — a veritable jumble of rusty tin and wood houses packed so closely together on the steep mountainside that they give the disconcerting impression of being stacked, willy-nilly, on top of each other.

After tiffining at Peleti's and installing Mr Holmes at Dovedell Hotel, I made my way to the lower bazaar where I maintained a modest apartment. Nikku, my faithful servant, poured me tea and gave me a report on events in Simla. Afterwards I set out to meet certain people: rickshaw-pullers, saises, shopkeepers, government clerks, hotel employees, beggars and a pretty little Mohammedan lady of easy virtue, all of whom were not averse to providing me information or performing small commissions — on the provision of pecuniary remuneration, *ad valorem*. Thus I made pretty dam' sure that neither Colonel Moran, his confederate Ferret-Face, nor any of their hired cut-throats could commence nefarious activities, or even arrive at Simla without the fact becoming first known to me — me, Hurree Chunder Mookerjee M.A.

After two days I managed to rent a small but fully-furnished cottage for Mr Holmes — Runnymeade, near Chota Simla. The previous occupant had been a notorious poodle-faker, a doyen of the Simla smart-set who, due to a number of causes, including inebriation, fell off his horse nine hundred feet down a ravine, spoiling a patch of Indian corn.

I was afraid that in spite of my efforts Mr Holmes was not very *comme il faut*, socially speaking. One would have thought that after all the difficulties and dangers he had undergone he would at least relax a bit and enjoy himself with the other holidaying Europeans at the hill-station. But he did nothing of the kind. He did not call on the Viceroy or sign the guest list at Government House, or even drop cards at the residences of important officers and personalities — in fact he did not even have cards printed. As a result he was not invited to the great balls and banquets, or even asked out to dinner; a situation which he maintained just suited him 'down to the ground'. The tournaments of the Simla Toxophilite Society, and even the polo matches and horse races at Annandale left him cold.

I was really at my wits end trying to make him enjoy himself. But at the same time one had to be quite wary about attempting to persuade Mr Holmes to do anything he did not so desire. There was that in his cold, nonchalant air which made him the last man with whom one would care to take anything approaching a liberty. Knowing his liking for music, I thought it would not be improper to suggest a visit to the Gaiety Theatre, where at the time a comic operetta by Messrs Gilbert and Sullivan was being performed. It was only much later I learned that his musical interests leaned towards violin concerts, symphonies, and the grand opera.

'An operetta. A comic operetta?' exclaimed Sherlock Holmes, a tinge of horror colouring his voice.

'Yes, Mr Holmes,' said I, a trifle defensively, 'and a jolly entertaining performance it is too — from what I've heard. The whole of Simla is talking about it. Why, His Excellency the Viceroy has seen it twice already.'

'Which is, no doubt, why it should recommend itself to me also. No, no. Let His Excellency do what he will. As for me, *odi profanum vulgus et arceo*. Horace's sentiments may not be exactly democratic, but at least they reflect mine at the moment.' He handed me a long list. 'Now, Huree, if you *really* want to make yourself useful, you could go down to the chemists, and get these reagents for me.'

This was another thing that I found rather difficult about Mr Holmes. As the reader will have realised by now, I am a scientific man, but I do draw the line at performing malodorous experiments in the living room. But not Mr Holmes. On the very first day that he set up house at Runnymeade Cottage, he made me get him a whole collection of beakers, retorts, test-tubes, pipettes, bunsen-lamps, and chemicals, (some of which were not immediately available in Simla) which he happily set up on a few shelves in the corner of the living room, spilling acids and what not on a beautiful Georgian table which he used as a work bench.

I shuddered to think of the day when I would have to return the cottage and its furnishings to that hard-faced Oswal Jain, who was the housing agent, for it was not only the table which would have to be accounted for but also the deep gash on the teak mantlepiece where Mr Holmes had transfixed all his unanswered correspondence with a Thibetan ghost dagger he had purchased from a curio dealer at the bazaar. The mantlepiece itself was always a mess, with a litter of pipes, tobacco-pouches, syringes, penknives, revolver cartridges, and other debris scattered over it.

But all this was nothing. One day the simple pahari man-servant I had got for Mr Holmes came running into my apartment, yelling that there had been shooting and murder up at the cottage. With my heart beating furiously, I rushed up to the cottage, only to discover Mr Holmes hale and hearty, lounging in an armchair in a room filled with cordite-smoke. By his side was his hair-trigger and a box of cartridges, and the wall opposite him, to my horror, was adorned with a mystical OM, done in bullet holes.

But one thing I could not really object to was Mr Holmes's compulsive bibliophilism since I was thus inclined myself, although I never did have the means to indulge in it to the happy extent as he did. He bought books not by the niggardly volume, but in large piles and generous bundles, which were scattered higgledy-piggledy all over the cottage, much to the distress of the pahari servant. Indeed Mr Holmes and I never went for a walk around the Mall without finally ending up browsing at Wheeler's, or Higginbotham's Book Depot.

But Sherlock Holmes's favourite was the Antiquarian Bookshop belonging to Mr Lurgan. Stacks of strange and rare books, documents, maps and prints, covered with layers of grey dust, rested between all manner of strange merchandise. Turquoise necklaces, jade ornaments, trumpets of human thigh-bone and silver prayer wheels from Thibet, gilt figures of Buddhas and Boddhisattvas, devil masks and suits of Japanese armour, scores of lances, khanda and kuttar swords, Persian water jugs and dull copper incense burners, tarnished silver belts that knotted like raw-hide, hairpins of ivory and plasma, and a thousand other oddment were cased, piled or merely lying about the room, leaving a clear space only round the rickety deal table, where Lurgan worked.

He was an employee of our Department, of course, and extremely efficient at training chain-men and preparing them for great excursions into the unknown. He was very knowledgeable and an able linguist, speaking English, Hindustani, Persian, Arabic, Chinese, French and Russian fluently. We shared similar interests in strange religions, and native customs, though I must admit to not being altogether comfortable in his company. He had the disconcerting ability of being able to dilate the pupils of his eyes and closing them to a pin-prick, as if at will. He had strange mesmeric powers too, that I had on more than one occasion seen him use on people; and he was reputed to have dabbled in jadoo, magic! Lurgan was surely the most mysterious character ever employed by the Survey of India. He was very vague about his antecedents, claiming to be partly Hungarian, partly French and partly Persian, changing one or the other every now and then to suit his queer humours. Only Colonel Creighton knew Lurgan's real story; and the Colonel being the insufferably close-mouthed gentleman that he was, would probably carry that information with him to his grave.

Lurgan enjoyed Mr Holmes's company — though I had not told him who the Norwegian explorer really was — and between long bouts of speculation on nature, metaphysics, and the vagaries of the book-trade in Simla, served us small nutty biscuits and green china tea in exquisite egg-shell cups.

One evening when returning to Runnymeade Cottage from Lurgan's shop, Sherlock Holmes turned to me. 'Lurgan says you speak Thibetan.'

'I have some modest abilities in that direction.'

'Modest?' said Mr Holmes dryly. 'You are the author of a definitive work on Thibetan grammar, and the compiler of the first Thibetan–English dictionary.'

'Not really the first, Mr Holmes. Oh no. My late guru, the great Hungarian orientalist, Alexander Csoma de Körös, not only produced the first Thibetan–English dictionary, but pioneered the whole modern study of the Thibetan language and civilisation.'

'How were your interests first directed towards this field?'

'Well, Sir. It is a long story, but I will be brief. I finished my M.A. from Calcutta University in 1862, when I was a young man of twenty-four. Being favourably known to Sir Alfred Croft, the director of Public Instruction of Bengal, who has always been my good friend and mentor, I was appointed to the post of headmaster of the Bhutia Boarding School in Darjeeling. At that pleasant hill station on the border of Sikkhim. I met Csoma de Körös.

'He was an extraordinary man and a great scholar, truly one of the greatest. He had left Hungary as a young man and come to this Himalayan town to learn everything he could about Thibet. He believed that the Hungarian people, the Magyars, had, many centuries ago migrated to Hungary from Thibet; and everything about that strange country fascinated him. He was a very old man when I met him, and it is my great regret that I was not able to fully imbibe from this fount of wisdom, for he passed away a year later. But none the less, he fired in me a great inspiration to learn about Thibet.

'You see, Sir, after deep study of the Thibetan language and scriptures, de Körös was convinced that Thibet was the last living link that connects us with the civilisations of a distant past. That although the mystery-cults of Egypt, Mesopotamia, and Greece, of the Incas and the Mayas, had perished with the destruction of their civilisations, and are forever lost to our knowledge, Thibet, due to its natural isolation and its inaccessibility, had succeeded not only in preserving but in keeping alive the traditions of the most distant past — the knowledge of the hidden forces of the human soul and the highest achievements and esoteric teachings of Indian saints and sages.

'I applied myself with energy to the study of the Thibetan language and established friendly relations with the Rajah of Sikkhim (who is of pure Thibetan stock) and many of the leading lamas in that country, so that I was eventually not only conversant in the language but was able to read and understand many of their ancient books. The authorities eventually came to learn of my abilities in this arcane subject and decided that the interests of the Government of India would be better served if I were to quit the field of public education and join another department where my skills could be put to more … aah … vigorous use. And this is how I now happen to be here, Mr Holmes, at your service.'

'And a valuable one you would be performing for me, Huree, if you were to teach me the Thibetan language.'

'You do too much honour to my trifling skills, Mr Holmes, nevertheless the little I know is at your disposal. But I must warn you, Sir, that mere knowledge of the language would not help you to enter Thibet.'

'What do you mean, Huree?'

'Well, Mr Holmes, you may have heard of Thibet referred to as "The Forbidden Land" — and that is exactly what it is to all foreigners, especially Europeans. The priestly rulers of that country are jealous of their power, their wealth and their secrets, and they fear that the white man may take them away. Therefore Europeans or their agents are forbidden, on pain of death, to enter Thibet. The situation has taken a turn for the worse recently, since the Dalai Lama, the Supreme Pontiff of the Thibetan church and the ruler of the country, is now in his minority, and the power of the Imperial Manchu representative in Lhassa has gained ascendancy.'

'What do the Manchus have to do with Thibet?'

'Since the army of the Emperor Yung-Cheng entered Thibet at the beginning of the last century, the Manchu throne has claimed certain suzerain rights in Thibet, and has established two Manchu representatives called Ambans in Lhassa, the capital city. The exercising of imperial prerogatives in Thibet has had an uneven history, which has also affected the position of those wishing to travel to Thibet. At the moment, unfortunately, not only has the senior Manchu Amban in Lhassa, Count O-erh-t'ai, gained an ascendancy over the Dalai Lama and the Thibetan Government, but he also has an intense and virulent hatred for all Europeans, especially the English.'

'Hmm … I see. But have you yourself managed to get into Thibet?'

'Yes, Mr Holmes. The native has a few advantages in this respect. That is why the Department employs natives for conducting explorations and investigations in places like Thibet; especially from among those races living near the Thibetan frontier.

'I myself travelled to Thibet in the guise of a holy man, a pundit, but unfortunately aroused the suspicions of the authorities half-way to Lhassa, at the town of Shigatse, where the great monastery of the Teshoo Lama[1] is located. The Manchu officer of the small Chinese garrison there was one of the most unpleasant representatives of the Celestial Empire I have ever had occasion to encounter. The blighter would have beheaded me on mere suspicion — dam' his eyes!

'By Jove, Mr Holmes, you will appreciate the irrevocability of my position, but at the eleventh hour I was saved from the executioner's sword by the mother of the Teshoo Lama, whom I had earlier cured of a mild dyspepsia with an effervescent draught of my own preparation. The pious lady sent a large bribe to the officer in question, which fortuitously relieved him of most suspicions concerning my status and activities. But I was forced to curtail my explorations and retire posthaste, to Darjeeling. So you see, Sir, a visit to Thibet is not all beer and skittles, as they say. Besides, what with the altitude, snow-storms, wild animals, bandits and what not — it can all be very trying.'

'Well, Hurree, you have certainly made the perils of a Thibetan journey clear enough. But one must cross one's bridges when one gets to them. For the present I will, with your invaluable guidance, confine my explorations to the complexities of the Thibetan language.'

So I commenced giving daily lessons to Mr Holmes. He was an admirable pupil, and had an unusually sensitive ear for the subtle tonal inflections in the language, which generally drove most Europeans to despair. For instance, the Thibetan 'la' could mean a mountain pass, an honorific suffix tagged to a person's name, a god, a musk deer, wages, to lose something, or even one's

---

1. The monastery of Tashi-lhunpo, the seat of the Panchen Lamas. Early European travellers to Tibet and writers mistakenly referred to the Panchen Lama as the 'Teshoo' lama or the 'Tashi' lama, after the monastery.

soul, all depending on the exact tonal inflection used when pronouncing it.

Sherlock Holmes also found no difficulty in the usage of honorifics, for the Thibetan language is not one language but three: ordinary, honorific, and high-honorific. The first is used towards the common people; the second towards gentlemen; and the third towards the Dalai Lama. One may think that these distinctions are merely a question of prefixes and suffixes. But that is not the case at all: even the roots of the corresponding words in each often have no relation to one another.

But I will not burden my readers with any further digression into the subtleties of the Thibetan language, for such a subject can only be of interest to a specialist. Nevertheless, for those readers who would like to know more about the Thibetan language I can recommend my *Thibetan for the Beginner* (Re 1), published by the Bengal Secretariat Book Depot, and the *Grammar of Colloquial Thibetan*, (Rs 2.4 annas) by the same publisher.

9

A Pukka Villain

Runnymeade Cottage was just outside Chota Simla. Behind the cottage was a mule track which, seven miles beyond Chota Simla, led to the Hindustan–Thibet (or H–T) road. Sometimes our lessons would be disturbed by the sound of bells, as Thibetan traders plodded along the track with their panniered mules. Occasionally lamas in weathered wine-red robes would go past, twirling their prayer wheels, and half naked sanyasis with begging bowls of polished coco-de-mer and blackbuck skins would make their way to some distant cave-shrine, where they would spend the summer fed by the nearest village. Pahari herdsmen in warm putoo (home-spun wool) coats would pass through with their flocks of goats and sheep, sometimes playing strange tunes on bamboo flutes.

I would explain to Mr Holmes the background of these various people — their origins, religious customs and so on and so forth. He took a great deal of interest in them. Sometimes he would stop a Thibetan muleteer or a Ladakhi trader and try out his Thibetan on them. They would smoke his tobacco and laugh with amazement when the strange sahib spoke to them, haltingly maybe, but unmistakably in their own language. Months passed in this manner: in study, long walks and conversation, without even a hint of Colonel Moran or his society's activities ever disturbing the peace at Runnymeade Cottage.

It was this tranquillity that permitted me the leisure to examine Mr Holmes's personality and uncover traits in it that were not at all tranquil. He was not a happy man. It seemed that the great powers he possessed were sometimes more of a curse than a blessing to him. His cruel clarity of vision seemed often to deny him the comfort of those illusions that permit most of humankind to go through their short lives absorbed in their small problems and humble pleasures, oblivious of the misery surrounding them and their own inevitably wretched ends. When his powers thus overwhelmed him, Sherlock Holmes would, unfortunately, take certain injurious drugs such as morphine and cocaine in daily injections for many weeks.

Aside from this unhappy habit, there was much in Mr Holmes that was lofty and spiritual. He was celibate, and did not seem to have any desire for such human foibles as wealth, power, fame or comeliness. He could have been an ascetic in a mountain cave, for the simplicity of his life.

Strickland came up for Christmas. Simla was deep in snow, but up at the cottage, sitting before a roaring log fire, we warmed ourselves with potent beverages, and listened to Strickland's report. The case had made no progress. In spite of the strenuous efforts by the Bombay police, no link could be established between the dead Portuguese clerk and Colonel Moran. Also, no witnesses had been found who had seen anything remotely suspicious at the time the clerk had been shot in front of the police station. Strickland had attempted to rattle the Colonel's self-assurance by sending in 'beaters' to flush him out of his lair. He had posted policemen in civilian attire around the Colonel's house and club, and had even had half-a-dozen following him wherever he went. But Colonel Moran was not a man easily shaken by such tactics, and stuck to his daily routine as if the 'beaters' did not exist at all. Once, on leaving his club, he had even made one of the policeman hold his horse, and subsequently tipped him a rupee. A cool rogue, the Colonel sahib.

Strickland also had instructions for me from another Colonel, our department head, Colonel Creighton. I was to remain with Mr Sherlock Holmes for the time being and make myself useful to him in whatever way he wanted. I was also to take every precaution against any further attempt on Mr Holmes's life — and I was to look sharp about it! The last comment — quite uncalled for — was probably Colonel Creighton's way of expressing his disapproval of the way I had been caught with my dhoti down, when Colonel Moran's thugs had made their abortive attempt to murder Sherlock Holmes on the Frontier Mall. Being a scrupulously honest sort of chap I had not hesitated to include the incident in my report to the Colonel, even though it had not really shown me up in the best of lights. Even if I hadn't, the Colonel would have learnt about it one way or the other — he was that sort of person.

Well, we babus have our pride. I was determined never to have such an embarrassing situation repeated again. So I doubled my precautions, instructed my informers and agents to increase their vigilance, and even employed, full-time, a couple of little chokras, to keep an eye around the vicinity of Runnymeade Cottage for anyone who might take undue interest in the cottage or its occupant. In my line of work it is axiomatic that time and energy spent on precaution are never wasted. Sure enough, within a week the truth of this was demonstrated, Q.E.D.

One day one of the ragged little urchins, the one with the particularly runny nose, came running to my house at the lower bazaar. 'Babuji. A strange man appeared at the back of the sahib's house a short while ago,' the boy said, sniffing in a disgusting manner.

'And what of it?' I asked impatiently. 'All manner of men pass by the track behind the house.'

'Nay, Babuji. This man did more. He entered the house.'

'Kya? What manner of man was he?'

'He looked like a real budmaash, Babuji. He had long matted hair and was dressed belike as a Bhotia, in brown woollen bukoo and sheepskin cap. He also had a burra talwar, stuck in his belt.'

'And what of the sahib?' I enquired anxiously.

'We know not, Babuji. We saw him not.'

I imagined Mr Holmes peacefully sitting at his desk going over his Thibetan declensions, or happily performing one of his malodorous experiments, while an assassin silently approached him from behind, a glittering sword raised in his hands. I felt slightly sick.

Reaching under my bed, I quickly dragged out my tin trunk. Rummaging in it I finally found the small nickel-plated revolver that I had, some years ago, purchased at the Multani bazaar in Cabul. However, I must confess that I am a hopeless shot. In fact I could never quite get over the inconvenient but purely involuntary habit of closing my eyes dam' tight when pulling the trigger. But being ever averse to the crudities of violence I had always considered the bally thing as an object to be used more *in terrorem* than *in mortiferus* — so the standards of my marksmanship did not really matter too much.

I puffed up to the cottage behind the boy. The other chokra was waiting by the bend in the road, just before Runnymeade Cottage.

'Ohe, Sunnoo,' the boy with me called to his friend, 'what has happened?'

'Kuch nahin,' the other replied, 'the man is still in the house.'

'And the sahib?' I enquired anxiously, fingering the pistol under my coat.

'I have not seen him at all, Babuji.'

'What of the servant?'

'He went to the bazaar an hour ago — before the Bhotia man entered the house.'

'Both of you stay here quietly. I'm going to take a look,' said I, as confidently as I could. I was not very happy about it, but it had to be done. I approached the cottage from the east side where there were the least number of windows, walking as lightly as my hundred and twenty seers of corporeal flesh permitted. I managed to scramble over the picket fence without any difficulty — just a few scratches and a slightly torn dhoti — and sidled up to the stone wall of the cottage. Then I crept up to the front door and prepared for action. Girding up my loins — in this case quite literally as I had to tie the loose ends of my dhoti around my loins for the sake of comfort and convenience — and closing my hand on the butt of my revolver, I slowly pushed the door open.

The small parlour was empty, but I noticed that the door of the study-cum-living room was ajar. With nerves tingling I tip-toed over and peeked in.

A pukka villain of a hill-man stood by the side table near the fire-place, rifling through Mr Holmes's papers. He looked decidedly sinister. His small slanting eyes peered furtively at the papers that he clutched with thin dirty fingers. A scraggly moustache dropped around the sides of his greasy lips. His long hair matted with dirt complemented the filthy sheep-skin cap that partly covered it. He wore a bukoo, or woollen gown of Thibetan cut, and felt boots of Tartar design. His Thibetan broadsword, I was relieved to note, was firmly in its scabbard, stuck into the belt of his robe. He looked quite the budmaash, or desperado, and was probably one of those bad characters from the upper reaches of Gharwal who specialised in robbing pilgrims proceeding to Mount Kailash.

But what was he doing? If he was a robber, he should be packing away whatever articles of value he could lay his hands on, and not poring through other people's correspondence — which he certainly could not read in any case. There was a mystery here, and I would not solve it by dithering in the parlour.

Cocking the hammer of the revolver, I entered the room. 'Khabardar!' I said in a brave voice. He turned towards me slowly. The blighter looked even more villainous than I had previously supposed. His greasy lips curled into a sneer and he placed his hands akimbo on his hips. 'Take heed, budmaash,' I expostulated firmly. 'Thou hast only to touch the hilt of thy sword and I will most surely blow thee to Jehannum on a lead ball.'

He must have been impressed by my stern demeanour for he suddenly fell on his knees and babbled apologies and excuses in a queer mixture of bad Hindustani and Thibetan. 'Forgive thy slave, Lord and Master. I only came to take back what is rightfully mine. What was stolen from me by the tall English sahib. My sacred ghau, my charm-box. Even now it hangs there on the wall of this unbeliever's house.'

Mr Holmes stealing his charm-box? What tommy-rot did this smooth-tongued villain expect me to believe. I moved my head to look at the wall where he was pointing but there was no charm-box there. When I turned back to the rascal to give him a piece of my mind, Sherlock Holmes stood smiling at me by the fireplace.

'I do wish you wouldn't grip the revolver so tightly, Huree,' said he in his dry, unemotional way. 'After all, the thing may have a hair trigger, you know.'

'Good Heavens, Mr Holmes!' I cried in amazement. 'This takes the bally biscuit. How the deuce an' all ...'

'Confess that you were absolutely taken in,' said he, chuckling to himself and throwing his cap, wig, and false moustache on the armchair.

'Why, certainly, Sir. It was a most extraordinary thespian

performance. But you should not pull my leg like that, Mr Holmes. I was very worried about your safety.'

'I owe you an apology for that. I certainly did not intend this disguise to be some kind of practical joke on you. This is my passport to Thibet.'

'But surely it is too dan...'

'You were fooled by it, were you not? You thought I was a Bhotia trader.'

'A Bhotia bandit, Sir. Not a trader.'

'But a Bhotia, nonetheless.'

'Well, I cannot deny that, Mr Holmes ... By Jove, you were, if I may say so, a Bhotia to the boot heels; a Bhotia *ad vivium*, if you will pardon the expression. But I must still beg you not to be rash, Sir. After all I am responsible for your welfare — and a trip to Thibet demands much more than an adequate disguise. You will require pack animals, provisions, medicines, tents, tin-openers, etcetera, etcetera — and at least the services of an experienced and faithful guide.'

'Someone like yourself, perhaps?'

'Me, Sir? Ah ... ahem. Well. I was really not implying that at all. But for the sake of argument — why not?'

'Why not, indeed. So why don't you come with me?'

'Mr Holmes, it is a deuced attractive proposition. After all I am a scientific man, and what is a little danger and discomfort to the insignificant self, when weighed against the opportunities to extend the frontiers of human knowledge — which we will, no doubt, be doing on this proposed venture.'

'No doubt.'

'But alas, Sir. I unfortunately happen to be in official harness, and can only proceed on such voyages on receipt of authorised instructions, *ex cathedra*.'

'Which would be Colonel Creighton's?'

'Most unfortunately, yes, Mr Holmes.'

'Well, I shall have to speak to the Colonel about it, won't I?'

'But the Colonel will surely object. He may even blame me ...'

'Spare me your anxieties, I beg you,' he said, raising his hand in an imperious manner. 'Leave it to me.' He took off his Thibetan robe. 'Now I would be much obliged if, on your way home you would kindly return this costume to Lurgan, and that horrible wig and moustache to the manager of the Gaiety Theatre.'

Carrying these articles of disguise, I left the cottage. Mr Holmes was so masterly in his ways, and his requests so definite that it was difficult to question his actions — but I was still considerably worried. Colonel Creighton was a very suspicious man. He knew how keen I was on another opportunity to go to Thibet, and that I strongly resented the Departmental ruling that I was not to enter Thibet because of my last mishap there. Old Creighton would certainly conclude that I had deliberately influenced Mr Holmes to make this dangerous journey, so that I could accompany him.

I sighed unhappily. The Colonel could be very hard on those whom he felt were flouting Departmental discipline. I expected a very unpleasant interview with him soon. I was not disappointed.

Three weeks later Colonel Creighton came up to Simla. He met Mr Holmes, in fact they dined together a couple of times and seemed to enjoy each other's company. I was not invited, so I did not know what exactly passed between them. My own meeting with the Colonel took place in the storeroom behind Lurgan's shop. For at least an hour I was subjected to one of the most embarrassing and uncomfortable interviews in my career. The Colonel surpassed himself in his suspicions and nasty insinuations. Finally, with what seemed to be a great deal of reluctance and bad grace, he accepted my explanation.

'So, all right. Let's say for the sake of argument, that you didn't put him up to it. Then who did? Why the blazes does he want to go to Thibet, of all places? He's a detective, isn't he, not an explorer.'

'Well, Sir. In spite of my efforts to dissuade him, he is determined to go. That is all I can say.'

'Well he can't. And that's that.'

'Begging your pardon, Sir, but it would be very difficult to stop him, apart from restraining him physically. He has impressed me as an extremely resourceful and determined gentleman. He could pass himself off as a native any day.'

'Is he that good? In his disguise, I mean?'

'I am not exaggerating, Sir, when I say that, till now, I have never seen such a master of the art.'

'Hmmm ...' the Colonel looked thoughtful, 'and how is he managing with his study of the language?'

'Well, he is not absolutely fluent yet, but competent enough to pass himself off as, let us say, a ... a Ladakhi or some such person. Ah yes, a Ladakhi disguise would be the most suitable thing for Mr Holmes. It would conveniently explain the few undisguisable elements of his features — like his prominent nose, for one thing.'

'Yes, and the spring caravan to Lhassa from Leh leaves in a few months. Why is it, Huree, that I still cannot get over this very nasty suspicion that you have very conveniently arranged matters to suit your needs.'

'Oh Sir! I assure you that ...'

He dismissed my protestations with a wave of his hand.

'Anyway, as you said, we can't stop him. There are a number of reasons why we can't, not least of all, London — but that doesn't concern you.' He looked out of the window down at the red tin roofs of the houses in the bazaar below. Finally he turned around and shrugged his shoulders. 'Ah well, the violence and dangers he might face in Thibet will probably be no more than what he has already encountered in this country. And what about you, Huree? Mr Holmes asked me if it were possible for you to accompany him to Thibet.'

My heart leapt with joy; but I was careful not to let anything show on my face. 'Me, Sir?'

'Yes, you, Huree. What do you think about it?'

'Well, Sir, I am naturally pleased that Mr Holmes should regard my services so highly. But my accompanying him to Thibet is, of course, quite out of the question — without Departmental approval,' I added, conscientiously.

'Yes, of course, quite,' said the Colonel dryly. 'Now Hurree, as you well know, and have made sure, you are going with Mr Holmes to Thibet. But don't think you can spend your time there peacefully collecting data on quaint native customs and religions. I want work!' He opened his despatch box and delved into a mass of letters and documents.

'Why, of course, Sir,' I replied with dignity.

'Hmm ... Now listen carefully.' He held out a letter written on rough Thibetan paper; the kind manufactured from the bark of one of those species of *Daphne* plants (*Edgeworthia gardneri*) which comes mostly from Bhootan. 'This is a secret report I received from K.21 just a week ago. His monastery is, as you know, close to the main caravan route from Kashgar to Lhassa, and is therefore a good place to pick up news from the Thibetan capital. Evidently things are not as they should be in Lhassa. There are rumours that two senior ministers have been removed in disgrace from the cabinet, and a much respected abbot of the Drepung monastery gaoled like a common criminal. K.21 feels that the Manchu Amban is behind these events, and it is probably an attempt to undermine the position of the Grand Lama and strengthen Chinese influence in Thibet. It seems that these particular ministers and the abbot wanted the young Grand Lama to be enthroned before his constitutional age. They were opposed to the Regency, which has acquired the reputation of being influenced by the Chinese representative, the Amban.'

'Would that be Count O-erh-t'ai, the man who hates the English?'

'Yes, and we've found out why he's so rabidly xenophobic. It seems that his father, the Marquis T'o-shih, was burned to death when British troops set fire to the Imperial Summer Palace in Pekin.'[1]

'And he now wants to ensure that no one but China has any influence in Thibet.'

'Exactly. The Thibetans haven't taken too kindly to his meddling though. We have reports of angry mobs demonstrating before the Chinese legation in Lhassa, and the possibility of the Emperor despatching more Chinese troops to reinforce the garrison in Lhassa.'

'By Gad, Sir. That is a pretty kettle of fish that is boiling there. I myself have been the recipient of such snippets of rumours from certain Bhotia merchants of my acquaintance.'

'I need to have more than rumours. It is vitally important that you get to Lhassa and learn the truth of the situation there.'

'Not to worry. Sir. This time I will most assuredly not fail to get to Lhassa; and once there ascertain the veridicality of the situation.'

---

1. In 1860 an Anglo-French expedition led by Lord Elgin occupied Peking after defeating Imperial Chinese forces and forcing the Emperor to flee to Jehol. Every palace, temple and mansion in the capital was thoroughly plundered, and the Imperial Summer Palace burned to the ground. The occasion that provoked this war was the 'Arrow' incident of 1856, when a Chinese-owned but Hong Kong-registered ship, the *Arrow*, was forcefully boarded by Chinese police at Canton for the alleged purpose of searching out a notorious pirate. Incidentally, Elgin is buried in an old church yard at Dharamsala, the present headquarters of the Dalai Lama in northern India.

THIBET

10

More Bundobust

Sherlock Holmes was eager to be off, but the Colonel and I counselled patience. The passes would be snow-bound till late spring, and the Leh–Lhassa caravan[1] wouldn't start till then. It was also felt to be wiser not to join the caravan at Leh itself, as there was a Thibetan trade agency there whose officials might take an undue interest in our *bona fides*. Instead we would travel by the Hindustan–Thibet road and cross Thibet over the Shipki *la*, or Shipki pass, and as if by a happy chance, encounter the caravan somewhere around the vicinity of Kailash, the holy mountain.

---

1. This annual trade caravan was also a tribute envoy to the Grand Lama from the king of Ladakh. Known as the Lopchag (annual prostration) mission it was established in the seventeenth century at the end of the Ladakh–Tibet–Mongol War. See 'The Lapchak Mission from Ladakh to Lhasa in British Indian Foreign Policy,' John Bray, *The Tibet Journal*, Vol. XV No. 4.

In the meantime there were preparations to be made. I have, for very sound reasons, always taken pride in my faculty of organisation, or bundobast, as we call it in this country, and the reader must forgive me for the rather detailed description I have provided of the extensive arrangements I made to ensure the success of our expedition.

In order of importance, the first thing I had to do was hire our expedition sirdar. We were very lucky to acquire the services of Kintup, a sturdy mountaineer of Sikkhimese extraction, who had on previous occasions performed a few commissions for the Department,[2] and had also been my guide on my last abortive trip to Thibet. He was living in Darjeeling at the time, eking out a living as a tailor. But I telegraphed him a message and some TA (travelling allowance) money, and he arrived in Simla a week later, eager to be off on another adventure.

'This time we *will* get to the Holy City, Babuji,' he reassured me, his rough callused hands clasping mine in greeting. 'We will not make the mistake of staying overlong in Shigatse, as we did the last time.'

He was a thickset, active man, with a look of dogged determination about his rugged, weather-beaten features. He had

---

2. In 1881, Kintup (or K.P. as he is listed in Departmental records) was sent secretly to Southern Tibet to throw marked logs into the Tsangpo river to prove its continuity with the Bhramaputra. This intrepid spy pushed his way through unexplored jungles infested with wild animals, cannibals and head-hunters, and after four years of thrilling adventures and narrow escapes finally managed to throw the marked logs into the river. But there was no one watching for them below in Assam as the officer in charge of the experiment had died. For a full account of Kintup's feats see 'Exploration on the Tsangpo in 1880–4', *Geographical Journal* XXXVIII (1911). *Survey of India Records IX*, L.A. Waddel.

all the alertness of a mountaineer, and with the strength of a lion he was a host in himself. He and Mr Holmes took to each other at once.

We also hired two other men. To look after our pack animals we got Shukkur Ali Gaffuru, whose father was a man of Yarkand and mother a Lamaist of Spiti, the mixed race being called Argon, generally distinguished by physical hardihood and loyalty. For our cook we got Jamspel, a cheerful young Ladakhi who, in spite of certain limitations in his culinary ability was not averse to bathing occasionally, and was skilled in lighting and maintaining yak-dung fires under all circumstances and climatic conditions.

Kintup and I travelled to nearby Narkhanda for the animal mela, or fair, where we purchased twelve sturdy mules to carry our baggage and provisions. For riding we purchased five shaggy little tats, or hill ponies, which in spite of their ludicrous size and hirsuteness, were stronger and better equipped to survive in the desolate highlands of Thibet than most horses.

I also had to arrange for the purchase or preparation of various other items: tents, saddles, pack-saddles and panniers, *yakdans,* which are small leather-covered wooden boxes such as are used in Turkestan, kitchen utensils and dekchis frieze blankets, gutta-percha undersheets, a tent-bed for Mr Holmes, bashliks, rifles, knives, note-books, writing material, talkan, or roasted barley meal, which the Thibetans call *tsampa*, preserved meat, tobacco, etcetera, etcetera. I instructed Jamspel to bake a large quantity of *khura*, or hard Ladakhi biscuits, which keep practically forever. I was rather partial to them and they were very good to nibble on to relieve the tedium of a long journey.

I managed to order a complete medicine chest from Burroughs and Wellcome of London, with drugs prepared specially for a high and cold climate. All the remedies were in convenient tabloids, and stowed in a robust and beautifully crafted wooden chest.

At this point I think that I ought to inform the reader of

certain other preparations I made demi-officially in the larger interests of science and Imperial advancement. We fieldmen were not only in the business of collecting political information, as my previous conversation with Colonel Creighton may have led the reader into believing. In fact the bulk of our duties, the rice and daal of departmental activities, was concerned with geographical and ethnological information. Therefore, we fieldmen, or to use the proper Departmental term, chainmen, were trained and equipped essentially to perform such tasks.

Initially we were trained in route survey and reconnaissance work. We were taught the use of sextant and compass, and how to calculate altitudes by observing the boiling point of water. But since this bally business cannot be conveniently conducted because of the deplorably suspicious and hostile nature of the ignorant inhabitants of unexplored lands — and since it is occasionally inexpedient to carry measuring chains and other conspicuous tools of the trade — the Department has devised some very ingenious methods and contrivances to circumvent suspicion and hostility.

First of all we were trained to take, by much practice, a pace which, whether we walked up mountains, down valleys, or on level ground, always remained the same — thirty inches in my case. We also learned how to keep an exact count of the number of such paces we took in a day, or between any two landmarks. This was done with the aid of a Buddhist rosary, which you may know comprises one hundred and eight beads. Eight of these were removed, leaving a mathematically convenient one hundred, but not a sufficient reduction to be noticeable. At every hundredth pace a bead was slipped. Each complete circuit of the rosary therefore represented ten thousand paces — five miles in my case, as I covered a mile in two thousand paces. Because the Buddhist rosary has attached to it two short secondary strings each of ten smaller beads, these were used for recording every completed circuit of the rosary.

Not only was the Buddhist rosary ingeniously adapted to the purpose of exploration, so were prayer-wheels (*mani lag-'khor*). These were fitted with a secret catch which enabled one to open the copper cylinder and insert or remove the scrolls of paper bearing one's route notes and other intelligence. Compasses were also concealed inside the wheels. Larger instruments like alt-azimuths and chronometers were concealed in specially-built false bottoms in *yakdans* while secret pockets were added to our clothing. Thermometers, for measuring altitude, were concealed in hollowed-out staves, and mercury — necessary for setting an artificial horizon when taking sextant readings — was hidden in a secret cowrie shell and poured into a pilgrim's bowl whenever needed.

Lurgan, who had a great facility for deception, had devised most of these contrivances, and had taught us fieldmen how to use them.

11

On the Hindustan–Thibet Road

'Ho there, Gaffuru.' The deep booming voice of Kintup was strangely muffled by the dense fog of the early morning. 'Tighten the girth of the bay mule lest he throws his load.'

He finished checking the loads on the mules and the trappings on the ponies, and then walked over to me, his thick felt boots softly crunching the gravel on the garden path of Runnymeade Cottage.

'Babuji, thou may'st tell the sahib that all is ready for the journey.'

I stepped into the cottage where Mr Holmes was bidding farewell to old Lurgan. A month earlier, Colonel Creighton had revealed to him the true identity of Sigerson, the Norwegian traveller, and had recruited Lurgan to help in the preparations for the journey. He turned to me as I entered the room.

'Ah, I think old Huree Babu here wants to tell you that everything is ready for your departure, Mr Holmes.' He reached into his coat pocket and pulled out an old tartar pipe, beautifully chased with silver and with a jade stem. 'It is an Eastern custom to offer a gift to the departing traveller. Anyway, I don't see how you could go on smoking that very English cherrywood in your Ladakhi disguise. Please, I insist.'

Mr Holmes accepted the gift and thanked Lurgan warmly. Lurgan turned to me and handed me a cylindrical iron pen case of Thibetan design.

'Seeing that your modern binoculars made the Chinese authorities suspect you on your last trip, I thought it as well that we were more circumspect this time. You just take off the cap and peer through it from the small hole at the bottom and — hey presto! It's a telescope. Is it not clever? I think it is the best thing I've done since the hollow prayer wheel. Well, old chap, best of luck. Do try not to create a diplomatic incident again. It just upsets the Colonel, and you know how difficult he is to work with then.'

We rode silently out of the garden. I turned round in my saddle to see Lurgan's dark outline against the comfortable glow of the open cottage door. He raised his right hand in farewell. I shivered a little, as much because of the penetrating chill of the foggy morning as at the realisation that once more I was leaving comfort and security to face the hardships and perils of the unknown. As I have confessed before, I am an awfully fearful sort of man — which is a serious detriment in my profession — but somehow or the other, the more fearful I become, the more dam' tight places I get into.

Yet fear at least performs the useful function of making one careful. I had taken a number of precautions to ensure that anyone taking undue interest in our activities would not learn very much. Even our silent, stealthy departure on this dark morning was one of my attempts to 'muddy the well of inquiry with the stick of precaution,' as they would say in Afghanistan.

Our small khafila wended its way out of Chota Simla on to the Hindustan–Thibet Road, planned and commenced in 1850 by Major Kennedy, secretary to Sir Charles Napier who completed the conquest of the Punjab and Sind. This redoubtable feat of Imperial road building majestically traverses the lofty barriers of the high Himalayas for two hundred and three miles to end at Shipki *la* on the Thibetan frontier.

Gradually the darkness was dispelled, though the clammy mist clung cheerlessly to the cold mountainside. The indistinct shapes of our animals and riders merged like wet inkstains with the dark outlines of trees and bushes, while the muffled clip-clop of shod hooves, the creak of strained leather, the steady breathing and occasional snorts of our patient beasts filtered so faintly through the mist that they seemed like sounds from some half-forgotten dream.

'*Lha Gyalo*! Victory to the gods!'

The deep voice of Kintup, riding in the lead, rolled back to us. This Lamaist invocation, generally shouted by Thibetans at the start of a journey, or at the top of a pass or mountain, was taken up softly by his co-religionist, Jamspel, our Ladakhi cook. I rode beside the lanky figure of Sherlock Holmes, muffled in a sheepskin-lined Ladakhi robe, and sitting awkwardly astride his small hill pony.

'Well, Sir,' I ventured, 'we begin our quest.'

'"*Caelum non animum mutant qui trans mare current*." Horace is not too reassuring about the benefits of travel, but let us pray that our passage over these mountains will provide us more inspiration than he got from his sea voyage.'

From Simla, the first day's journey towards the interior of the mountains is usually Fagu, a distance of fourteen miles. Here, and for several stages farther, as far as the road lies through British territory, there are dak bungalows provided by the government for the accommodation of travellers upon the payment of a small fixed sum per day. Though often in bad repair, and therefore very uncomfortable in rainy weather, these houses are a very great convenience, as they enable travellers to dispense with the carriage of tents.

The road from Simla to Fagu followed the course of the main range, not always on the very crest of the ridge, but seldom at any great distance from it. About four miles from Simla there was a sudden increase in the elevation of the range, and at the same time it turned very abruptly towards the southeast. The road ascended the steep face of the ridge in a series of zigzags. Near the top of the ascent it suddenly surfaced from under the thick fog to present us a dawnlit view of the remarkable peak of Shali, right across the valley in the northeast, its bold rocky mass seeming to overhang the Sutlej valley.

We arrived at the Fagu bungalow in the late afternoon, in the midst of pelting rain. However, drinking mugs of hot tea and warming ourselves before a bright fire, we soon forgot the discomforts of the wet ride. For two more days we rode along the crest of the main ridge past the hamlets of Matiana, Narkhanda, and Kotgarh; the last being the seat of an establishment of European missionaries performing noble works of charity and conversion among the artless people of these hills.

From Kotgarh we commenced our descent from the main ridge down into the valley of the Sutlej river. The road was very steep and the change in vegetation dramatic — one moment alpine, the next, tropical. The heat also rapidly increased till the road reached the bank of the Sutlej, at the village of Kepu. We continued our journey up the valley to Nirat, a distance of seven miles, and next day arrived at Rampur, the capital of Bushair.

The district of Bushair is an independent hill state governed by a Hindu rajah. His dominion also extends over Kunawar, the district further up the valley whose inhabitants are Tartar by race and Buddhists of the Lamaist persuasion.

The town of Rampur is on a small level tract of ground about a hundred feet above the river which it overhangs. The houses are substantially built, but mostly one-storied, with steeply sloping slated roofs. The town has a good deal of trade with Thibet, principally in shawl wool, and is the seat of a small manufacturing unit of soft white shawl cloth. The river here is crossed by a rope suspension bridge. It consists of nine stout ropes, which are stretched from one side of the river to the other. The width of the Sutlej at the bridge is about two hundred and eleven feet.

The Sutlej is one of the four major rivers whose source is the most sacred mountain of Kailash and the fabulous dual lakes by it. The Thibetans fancifully regard it as flowing from a peacock's mouth, and have thus named it. The Indus, the Bramhaputra and the Karnali rivers also have their sources in the same area and are called, 'Flowing from the Lion's mouth, Flowing from the Elephant's Mouth, and Flowing from the Horse's Mouth' respectively, by the Thibetans, who, like most other Asiatics, prefer the fabulous explanation to the scientific one.

We stayed at Rampur for two days as guests of the old whisky-loving rajah. He was well-disposed towards me as I had, in a previous passage through the town (in the role of a hakim) successfully treated him for gout, and members of his rag, tag and bobtail court for various other ailments.

From Rampur onwards, the valley of the Sutlej narrowed and the mountains became more lofty and precipitous. After four days, when we reached the town of Chini, the lush vegetation of the lower valley had given way to occasional wind-racked junipers and desiccated shrubs. The breeze now had a knife-edge to it which caused me to tie the hanging lappets of my moth-eaten rabbit-skin cap down firmly over my ears.

But nothing seemed to bother Mr Holmes. The windier, the colder, the bleaker, and the closer to Thibet we got, the more cheerful and animated he became. When he was not asking me incessant questions about the Thibetan language and customs, he was humming snatches of tunes to himself and smiling in an enigmatic way.

From Chini — nothing more than a large collection of rude stone huts inhabited by sallow, greasy, duffle-clad mountaineers and their equally greasy sheep — we wended our way up to Poo, the last but one village before Shipki *la*, and Thibet. It is normally a five-day ride from Chini to Poo, but it took us six. You see, we ran into something unexpected on the fourth day.

12

A Dam'-Tight Place

Around noon that day we stopped for a rest and a meal. While Kintup gave the animals their feed bags, Jamspel bustled about with his pots and pans, and Gaffuru started a small yak-dung fire. Sherlock Holmes reclined on a flat sunbaked rock and smoked his tartar pipe in tranquil contemplation. I walked over to the edge of the road. Far below, the surging waters of the Sutlej river roared by.

The track wound in and out of the mountainside following the meanderings of the river. A couple of furlongs further up the road a narrow bridge had been erected across the river which was not more than seventy feet in width at this point. The bridge was of the kind called *sanga* by the hill people, which means a wooden bridge or a bridge of planks, contrasted with *jhula,* a rope bridge. The pier of the bridge on the left bank was formed by an isolated rock that jutted out precariously from the cliff side.

Taking out the pen-case telescope from my pocket, I focused

it on the cliffs on the other side of the river. I tracked their whole length, as far as they were visible, but save for a solitary lammergeyer feeding on a dead lamb, detected nothing. But, 'one has checked nothing unless one has double-checked everything,' as we say at the Department. So once again I raised the telescope to my eye and commenced vigilant observations, mumbling to myself all the while. A deplorable habit — but one that I had unconsciously acquired over the years in an attempt to commit to memory all that I was observing.

'What's that? Rather a funny-looking rock there. Looks more like a bally topee than anything else. By Jove, it is a topee ... how the deuce an' all did it get there? ... Gosh! There's a head under it too ... let's have a better look. Oh, damn this beastly focus knob. It's too tight. Damn Lurgan ... aah ... that's better. Now ... What! Ferret-Face! O Shaitan!'

The head disappeared behind a rock just as I laid eyes on it, making me a bit unsure whether I had really seen it in the first place. I rushed back and told Sherlock Holmes what I thought I had just seen.

'Hmm,' he frowned, 'that fellow's getting to be a regular stormy petrel. We must leave this place at once. It is too exposed.'

'Yes, Sir! I will make preparations for departure at once. Arre, Kintup. Idhar aao.'

I explained the situation to Kintup and the others. Kintup (admirable fellow) was a veteran of many adventures and unperturbed by such unexpected contingencies. He immediately set about preparing for our speedy departure. The others followed his worthy example. Barely was the last mule loaded when Gaffuru, the Argon, cried out, pointing to the road below, the one we had passed just a short while ago.

'Dekho sahib! Riders.'

About a mile away, on the road below, a cloud of dust moved rapidly towards us. I whipped out my special telescope and focused it on the sight of a company of the most desperate looking bandits, armed to the teeth, whipping their shaggy ponies furiously.

'Look, Mr Holmes!' I cried, handing him the telescope. 'We are in mortal peril of life and limb.'

'So it would seem,' he replied, cool as a cucumber. He handed me back my telescope and, going over to one of the pack mules, pulled out a Martini-Henry rifle we had concealed, *pro re nata*, under its pannier. He began to load it rapidly. 'Get those mules moving up the track quickly. If we manage to cross the bridge before they get to us, we have a slight chance of holding them off from across the river.'

I at once perceived that Mr Holmes's plan was the only feasible course of action. Yet, it was a good three furlongs to the bridge, probably more, and the mules would slow us down a great deal — and in the meanwhile the riders would be catching up with us, fast. It would be touch and go, at best.

'Arre! Chalo! Choo, choo!'

Kintup, Jamspel and Gaffuru whipped the animals up the track while Sherlock Holmes, with his cocked rifle, and myself with my nickel-plated revolver, followed as rearguards. The road was, at this point, cut into the side of a near perpendicular cliff, winding in and out, following the twists and turns of the savage river a hundred feet below.

We had not covered more than a furlong when suddenly a crackle of rifle fire echoed from across the river and the rock face by our side spurted dust and stone chips. Our ponies reared and skittered with fright.

'By Thunder!' cried Holmes, 'they have some marksmen across the river. Take care, Huree.'

Hardly had Mr Holmes uttered these words when a bullet ploughed into the side of my wretched pony, which stumbled a few paces to the edge of the track and then collapsed with a piteous whinny. I myself tumbled ignominiously on the ground like a bally football, and would probably have rolled right off the road and plunged over the cliff and into the river, had not Mr Holmes quickly dismounted and providentially come to my aid. In the veritable nick of time, when I was just commencing my fatal descent over the cliffside, he grabbed me by the back of my collar and hauled me away from the precipice.

'Thank you for most timely assistance, Sir,' I managed to gasp.

'Not at all,' he said, as we hurriedly crawled behind a protective rock. 'I really cannot afford to lose my invaluable guide just at the beginning of this journey.'

More rifle fire bracketed us. Sherlock Holmes returned a few shots, but unfortunately his pony panicked in the noise and confusion and ran off. So both of us were now *sans cheval*. The main body of riders had by now come very close. Some of them had dismounted and were firing at us. It was an extremely alarming situation — let me assure you dear reader — to have all those deadly projectiles zooming around us like maddened bumble-bees. But by resourceful usage of boulders, rock faces and other cover available for concealment thereof; and also as Sherlock Holmes's standard of marksmanship was of a very high order — which somewhat dampened the initial ardour of the overboldened rascals — we managed not to sustain any injury for the time being.

There was a sharp bend in the track before us that prevented us from seeing the bridge. I hoped that our men had managed to get the animals across safely.

'The blighters are closing in, Sir,' I shouted above the crackle of another fusillade by the enemy.

'I see them,' he replied, reloading his weapon methodically. 'We have to move before they get close enough to be able to rush us. Now listen, Huree. As soon as I begin firing, I want you to get up and start running. Don't even pause before you get around that bend. Ready? Now off you go!'

Mr Holmes commenced an effective rapid fire that caused the opposition to keep their heads low. I sprang up from behind my boulder, banged off a few wild shots myself from my revolver, and bounded up the track — my bally legs exerting themselves eighteen annas to the rupee. Sherlock Holmes fired a few more shots and then came running after me.

Swarms of lethal missiles whizzed and crackled around us during our precipitous flight. It seemed to be an agonisingly slow and endless run, but I finally approached the bend, and with one last tremendous burst of energy, flung myself gratefully around that crucial corner.

I was just going to heave a massive sigh of relief when a shockingly unexpected sight caused me to renounce, forthwith, all further hopes of a continuing corporeal existence.

As implacable as death, Ferret-Face stood in the middle of the track. The first thing I noticed about him was the very large Mauser automatic pistol in his right hand, which seemed to be pointed straight at me.

'Angels and ministers of grace defend us.'

Behind him, in full battle array, were the wildest looking bunch of Thibetans I had ever seen. They were scattered about the road and hillside, behind boulders and tree-trunks, but their rifles, muskets and jingals[1] were charged and cocked, poised for firing. Sherlock Holmes came charging around the corner, nearly colliding into me, and was also confronted with this deadly *impasse.*

'What the Devil ...' he exclaimed, but realising the gravity of our predicament he composed himself admirably. With steady hands he lit his pipe and calmly proceeded to smoke as if he had not a care in the world. Ferret-Face raised his pistol. I saw his finger tightening around the trigger and I thought of the little

---

1. Jingals. Heavy match-lock muskets mounted on stands and worked by two men.

palm-lined village in lower Bengal where I was born. Tears welled up in my eyes.

There was a loud bang followed by a sharp volley of rifle-fire and the boom of discharged muskets. I felt like I fainted dead away, for everything seemed to become suddenly dark. But when I opened my eyes I realised I was still standing — and quite alive! And Sherlock Holmes was still standing besides me, smoking his pipe.

Ferret-Face and his men were still there before us, smoke curling from the barrels of their weapons. I turned around.

The road behind was strewn with the supine bodies of those villainous bandits who had attempted to assassinate us. They had been shot down by Ferret-Face and his men, when they had followed Mr Holmes and myself around the bend in hot pursuit — not expecting a hotter reception!

Some of the villains, specially those who had been at the rear of their column, had survived the fusillade, and were now in ignominious flight. Ferret-Face fired a few more shots after them to encourage them on their way and then restored his weapon to the wooden (stock-combination) holster strapped to his side. He came over to us and extended his hand to Mr Holmes. 'Mr Sigerson, I presume?'

'Yes.'

'My name is Jacob Asterman. I am an agent of His Holiness, the Grand Lama of Thibet, and I have been instructed to deliver to you this special passport, permitting you and your companion to visit the holy city of Lhassa.

13

Passport to Thibet

At a sign from Asterman a young Thibetan of refined appearance came forward and, bowing low, gave him a document wrapped around an arrow. This was what the Thibetans called a *da-yig*, or 'arrow-missive', which indicated that the document was an official one. Asterman made a formal bow and handed the 'arrow-missive' to Mr Holmes who broke the wax seal, untied the string, and rolled open the passport. It was written in the elegant *umay*, or flowing script, which Mr Holmes had not yet mastered; so he passed it over to me. I read it aloud. A copy of the document and a translation in English is provided below for the reader's amusement:

> All governors, district officials, village headmen and the public on the route from Tholing to Lhassa — hear and obey! The foreigner, Si-ga-sahab (Sigerson sahib) and his companion the Indian pundit bearing a godly name, Hari

Chanda, are making an honourable journey to the abode of the gods (Lhassa). On their journey, all district officials are required to provide them four riding ponies and whatever pack animals required, complete with all necessary saddles, harnesses and fittings. Customary payments will be made to the owners of the animals thus hired, and proper receipts obtained from them. At all halting places, fodder must be provided for the animals owned by the bearers of this passport. Furthermore, fuel must also be provided to them, and when required, passage on ferries, coracles, and ropeways. All must be provided without fail on this journey. There must be no delays or hindrances.

The first day of the second moon of the Water Dragon Year.
The seal of the Grand Lama of Thibet.

Addendum: This passport it accompanied by two 'robes of the gods,' of the ashe, or middling quality, to welcome the honourable visitors.

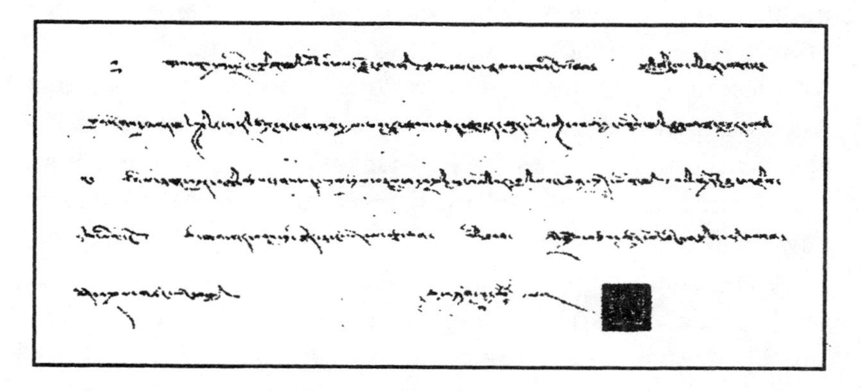

The Thibetan who had been carrying the 'arrow missive,' — and who seemed to be some official functionary — reached into the folds of his robe and extracted two white silken scarves, the 'robes of the gods' grandly referred to in the passport. These scarves, generally called *khatags*, are used by Thibetans and other Tartars to grace every ceremony or occasion in their lives. They are used to welcome guests, to bid goodbyes, to petition lords, to worship the Buddha, to propitiate the gods, to celebrate weddings, and to mourn at funerals. The white colour of the scarves serves to denote the purity of the giver's motives.

He unfurled the scarves and, bowing low, handed one each to Mr Holmes and myself.

''pon my word,' said Holmes, accepting the scarf graciously, and making a slight bow in return. 'This is rather a singular turn of events. What do you make of it, Hurree?'

'By Gad, Sir, this takes the bally bun, if you ask me. My brain is totally at sixes and sevens — though I must say that the passport does appear to be genuine.'

'Oh, but it is,' said Asterman quickly, a note of consternation in his voice. 'The Chief Secretary of the Grand Lama himself has issued it and personally ordered its delivery to you. This ...' he pointed to the square red seal on the document inscribed with minute Sanskrit letters, 'is the seal of the Grand Lama. There is no other like it in all of Thibet and Greater Tartary.'

Observing our quizzical expresions he added, 'Ah! I see that you require further explanation. Very well. We shall proceed to my encampment across the river, where you shall have rest, refreshments and answers. Your men and animals are there right now, all safe and sound.'

We crossed the bridge and, proceeding a few hundred yards up the track, came upon a level tract of land. A few cotton tents and a large shamiana were erected in a circle around a small fire. Kintup and the others were squatting on the ground by the fire, but when they saw us they came running to greet us. I noticed that Mr Holmes was touched by the evident happiness of the men to see us alive and unharmed. Kintup told us that they were sure we had been killed, especially after hearing the last thunderous discharge of weapons. They also thought that they themselves had been taken prisoner by one contingent of the bandits. Much to their relief, I was able to assure them that this was not so, and that Asterman and his men were our saviours rather than our captors.

Our 'saviour' ushered us to some low ottomans under the awning, and called for refreshments. It is strange how prejudices can alter the appearance of a person in one's eyes. Asterman now seemed to be a jolly decent sort of chap, nowhere approximating the role of the sinister 'Ferret Face' to which I had previously allocated him. He was somewhat garrulous though.

'Well, Sir, if you are to make any sense of it, I must tell you my story from the beginning.' Asterman took off his grimy topee to reveal a pink bony skull, sparsely covered with occasional strands of weathered grey hair. His thin, pinched face became very animated when he began to speak. 'I am, as you may have had occasion to observe, a Jew, Sir. An unhappy son of Shem, who because of history and circumstance has had to endure more than his share of the rigours of life.

'My family were originally from Alexandria, my father being the third son of David Asterman, one of the most prominent merchants of that city. But my father wanted to strike out on his own, and, taking his birthright, he and my mother set out for Calcutta, where he set himself up as a spice merchant. But he was improvident, Sir, and though he had only one failing — horses — it was enough to cause the ruination of our family and his own early demise of a broken heart. May his soul rest in peace. To support my old mother and my many brothers and sisters, I tried to operate a kabari, a second-hand shop at Bow Bazaar in Calcutta, but it was a disheartening venture. I lacked capital and skill, and try as I might I could never make enough money to raise my family above penury. But we were a pious family, Sir, and faithfully kept God's commandments. Though we were close to despair we did not lose faith in the Almighty. He had caused ravens to feed Elijah in the wilderness, surely he would not let us perish altogether. Then one day an unusual customer came to the shop.

'He was a young gentleman of medium stature and decidedly oriental features. He wore outlandish but rich silken robes, and was accompanied by a Kayeth, a bazaar letter-writer, who was obviously acting as his interpreter. The letter-writer explained to me that the gentleman was from Bhotiyal, or Thibet. The letter-writer had, a number of years ago, plied his trade up in the small township of Kalimpong, on the border of Thibet, and had picked up a bit of the language there. The Thibetan gentleman was desirous of obtaining a special item, and had approached a number of shops in the city for it, only to be turned away in disbelief and, occasionally, ridicule. Finally he had decided to give up. The letter-writer had urged him to make one last attempt, and had persuaded him to enter my humble shop. I attempted to set him at his ease, and politely enquired about the item he desired to purchase. He replied simply that he wanted a "thunderbolt"!

' "Now Jacob, my son," I told myself, "this is not the moment to display surprise or mirth. Fools do not wear such expensive silks (my grandfather had dealt extensively in silks and I knew a fine piece when I saw one), nor are they accompanied by interpreters to translate their follies. There may be some profit to be made in this, just at the cost of a little patience and courtesy."

'So I decided that there was a misunderstanding,' continued Asterman, taking a sip of tea, 'probably enlarged by the letter-writer's incompetence as an interpreter. I patiently questioned the Thibetan gentleman many times about the exact nature of the item he wanted, about its shape, colour and properties, but got nowhere. Then I remembered that in the collection of second-hand books in the shop, there was an old Thibetan–English dictionary that I had purchased from the effects of a deceased missionary. I rushed to the back of the shop and found it lying on a pile of musty *Blackwoods* magazines. The moment I showed the dictionary to the Thibetan gentleman I knew that our troubles were over. He was clearly an educated person — in his own way — for he flicked over the pages of the book eagerly till he found what he wanted. With a little cry of satisfaction he pointed to a spot on the page, and urged me, in his queer gibberish, to look there.

'To be fair to the letter-writer, the literal translation of the Thibetan word was "thunderbolt", but what it actually meant, and what the Thibetan gentleman was actually looking for, was meteorite iron.

'I managed to obtain a quantity of it for him from a dealer who supplied minerals and geological specimens to schools and colleges. He paid me a handsome commission, and since then has used me to locate many strange and fabulous things. He himself was an official of the Grand Lama, and was seeking these things for his master. I never knew why he wanted them, and I did not think it my business to ask. For making magic,[1] maybe? Anyway, I was well recompensed for my troubles, though I had my occasional failures. But it is surprising what you can find, no matter how fantastic it may be, especially when you are being liberally paid to find it, and have *carte blanche* as to expenses. I could tell you some strange stories of my ventures for these things. Why, the single occasion when I had to bargain for a Phoenix egg from the treasure trove of the Grand Mage of Kafiristan, would make a more exciting tale than all of Mr Haggard's novels.'

---

1. Asterman was not exactly wrong. Tibetan tantric ceremonies require many strange objects for their efficacy. The meteorite iron was probably used to cast ritual implements like 'ghost daggers' (*phurba*), bells (*drilbu*) and 'adamantine sceptres' (*dorjee*).

'It is all very interesting, no doubt,' said Sherlock Holmes dryly, 'but I would be much obliged if you would tell me how you came to know of our presence in these hills, and why we have been so singularly honoured with a passport to Thibet?'

'Certainly, Mr Sigerson, most certainly,' replied Asterman, a trifle abashed. 'I was just getting to that. But first some more tea.' He clapped his hands imperiously and one of his men padded over. 'More tea for our guests here. Their cups are empty. Have the sahib's servants had food and drink too? Very well, you may go.' He then turned to face us with a quizzical expression.

'Well, Sir, as I have told you, there is very little that surprises me now, but the whole business concerning you has been one big Chinese puzzle to me. Four months ago the Grand Lama's official — the same one who came to me for the 'thunderbolt,' and indeed the one who gave you and the babu your white scarves of welcome — provided me instructions to locate a certain *chilingpa*, or European, in whom they were greatly interested. This was the first time they had asked me to find a person, and I wasn't too sure what I was getting myself into. But they promised to pay me well if I found him. They could only give me a garbled version of your name, Mr Sigerson, but they provided me a full and accurate description of yourself, including the date and time your ship would dock at Bombay harbour.'

I felt an uncomfortably prickly sensation at the back of my neck.

'But how could they have known?' Sherlock Holmes muttered, his brow knitting into a puzzled frown.

'Oh, but they did, Sir,' protested Asterman. 'God strike me if I am not telling the truth. They even mentioned your pipe and violin-case.'

'And you followed Mr Sigerson from the harbour to the hotel,' I prompted, 'didn't you?'

'Yes, I did, Babuji,' he replied, grinning in amusement, revealing yellow, crooked teeth. 'Don't think that I didn't notice you on the carriage behind me. Though I will confess that I didn't think you had anything to do with Mr Sigerson, till much later. It was the murder at the hotel that told me I had let myself in for more than I had bargained for.' He shivered slightly. 'I still have nightmares about the ghastly blood-covered figure lurching towards me in the hotel corridor. I fled the place in terror. Fortunately I had taken the precaution of retaining my carriage at the rear of the hotel. So I managed to get away quickly, just in the nick of time, for two policemen came after me from the service entrance.'

So, Asterman had not recognised us in that dark alley.

'Well, Sir,' continued Asterman, 'that night I returned to my lodgings determined not to involve myself any further in this dreadful business. But on further reflection during the night, I realised that I had a commitment to my employers and had to at least let them know of your whereabouts and plans. So the next day I hung about the vicinity of the hotel and watched your comings and goings; and when you left the hotel with your baggage late in the evening, followed you to the railway station. I baksheeshed the reservation wallah, who told me that you had purchased tickets to Umballa. I guessed then that you were going to Simla, and I was right.

'I had to go to Darjeeling to make my report. The young official, whose name is Tsering, or "Long Life", seemed to think it of great consequence. He asked me a lot of questions about you, Mr Sigerson. He was, moreover, very upset to hear about the murder at the hotel. Finally I told him that I was very sorry, but that I could not go on any further with this dangerous commission. He told me that this business was extremely important and they would pay me whatever I wanted to see the thing through. I named a ridiculously high sum to discourage him, but, to my dismay, he readily agreed. Anyhow, if I survive this, my family and I are set up for life. Tsering then gave me my instructions. He said that you would make an attempt to enter Thibet in the spring, and that on the way your enemies would attempt to kill you. It would then be up to me to save you. He himself would cross the border from Tholing, which is just across the Shipki pass, with a contingent of armed troops and join me to assist you. He would also have an official passport for you to enter Thibet.

'I'm afraid we cut it rather fine, Mr Sigerson. The troops only managed to get here a day ago, and though we scouted the whole area, and managed to locate the main body of bandits, we missed the three riflemen they had placed across the river. It is rather unusual for armed bandits to prowl these areas, and even more unusual that they should just be waiting for your small caravan. Why, just this morning a long mule train carrying merchandise passed along this road — but they just ignored it. You do seem to attract danger Mr Sigerson: first the murder at the hotel, and now these bandits. Why, Sir ...' he continued, putting a conspiratorial finger to his lips, 'there must be something terribly important behind all this. No? Maybe I ask too much ... I must really learn to mind my own business.'

'Well, Mr Asterman,' Sherlock Holmes said with a smile, 'seeing that my companion and I owe our lives to you, it would be churlish of me not to relieve your curiosity. I regret that it is not possible, at the moment, to let you know everything about myself or my companion, but I can tell you that a dangerous criminal organisation has, of late, made a number of attempts on my life. The murder at the hotel was one of the particularly interesting ones. You see ...'

Without revealing his true identity or the exact nature of the criminal organisation behind the crime, Sherlock Holmes told the story of the brass elephant lamp and the giant killer leech. Even with the modifications, it was an exciting tale. Asterman was entranced. I noticed that Mr Holmes was careful to credit the police force with the solution of the case, and appoint himself in the role of the confused victim.

'What a story, Sir! What a story!' exclaimed Asterman. 'It terrifies me to think how close I was to death in that hotel corridor. Pity the police could not apprehend the mastermind behind the crime. Would have saved me a lot of trouble too, with these bandits — I suppose he must have employed them.'

'Most certainly,' replied Mr Holmes, filling his pipe from a grey leather pouch.

'It was most reprehensible laxity on my part, Sir,' I remarked apologetically, 'but for the bally life of me I cannot understand how they could have known of our journey. I made sure that our preparations aroused no one's interests or suspicions.'

'I'm sure you did, Huree. But we are not dealing here with ordinary criminals, as I have had occasion to point out before. This organisation is unique in the annals of crime.'

Asterman scratched his pink pate and remarked cheerfully, 'Well, Mr Sigerson, you need not worry about them once you enter Thibet. I doubt if these criminals, unique though they may be, can succeed in entering this country when hardened explorers have failed. But it still puzzles me as to why the Thibetan authorities gave you and the babu here a pass to enter Thibet. Ah, well, Tsering will explain it to your sooner or later. He will be escorting you to Lhassa.'

'Why do you think they gave us a road pass, Mr Holmes?' I enquired that night, in our small tent. I was warmly ensconced inside my sheep-skin sleeping sack, but the memories of the events and revelations of that exciting day prevented sleep. Sherlock Holmes was half inside his sleeping sack, and, leaning back against his rolled up *poshteen*, was smoking his pipe.

'It is a piquant question, is it not?' A blue spiral of smoke rose from his pipe. 'But it will have to remain a mystery, at least till we get to Lhassa, for I do not have any answers. Still, we could possibly venture to discount any malevolence in their intentions, for if they were laying any kind of trap for us, why go about it in such a deuced round-the-corner way? Why send Asterman to rescue us from Moran's hired ruffians, and then lure us into something else? No, it cannot be that. Anyhow, there is insufficient data for the problem to be capable of an immediate solution. We shall just have to trust in a merciful providence, Huree, when we cross our Rubicon — that pass — tomorrow.' He put away his pipe and leaned over to blow out the candle. 'Good night.'

'Good night, Mr Holmes.' I could see that we were going to get into a good many dam'-tight places before all this was over. I sighed and pulled the top of the sleeping sack over my head.

14

On the Roof of the World

The next day we set out for Shipki *la*. We were to be escorted to Tholing, the chief town of the first Thibetan district across the frontier, by the soldiers and the young official, Tsering. Tsering wore his hair long in a top-knot and disported the long turquoise earring that denoted his status as an official and a gentleman. He was a conscientious young man, ever alert to our needs, but rather nervous. No doubt the responsibility of looking after the guests of the Grand Lama himself was an onerous one. Mr Holmes was also the first European he had ever met, socially, apart from Asterman, who in any case was not really a sahib.

Asterman bade us farewell. He was thankful to have concluded his part in the affair and looked forward to setting up a prosperous business with the rich reward he had received. As far as Mr Holmes and I were concerned, he had earned every pie of it, and more. We wished him well in his proposed venture, and watched him trotting off on his goose-rumped mare, down the long winding road back to Simla.

The Shipki pass is not a very impressive one, as far as Himalayan passes go, being only 15,400 feet above mean sea level, but the tightening I felt in my lungs, and the slight fibrillation in my heart told me that once again I was in a land where I really had no business to be. The pass was excessively windy and beastly cold. The Thibetans, alongwith Kintup and Jamspel, piled up stones on a cairn as an offering to the mountain gods, and shouted their salutations.

'*Lha Gyalo!* Victory to the gods!'

The more pious ones strung coloured prayer flags of cheap cotton from wind-weathered poles stuck on the cairns. This custom of the Thibetans has been much misunderstood by European travellers to the Himalayan frontiers, some of whom have observed that the natives were wont to worship mountains and stones. In truth, the Thibetans consider such inanimate objects sacred only by virtue of their being a residence of a god or *lha* who is present as *animus assistentis* and not as *animus animantis*. Some of these *lha* have their counterpart in the Roman *numina*.

Mr Holmes also laid a *khatag* on the top of a cairn. He noticed me looking at him and chafed me in a light-hearted way. 'Come on, Huree, pay your respects to the gods, like a good babu. We are in their provenance now. From here on, science, logic and Mr Herbert Spencer simply cease to exist. *Lha Gyalo*!'

I had never seen him quite so cheerful and light-hearted before. It could have been the rarity of the air. Altitude affects people in strange ways. While it just gave me occasional headaches, it appeared to make Mr Holmes happy. He had also gradually stopped taking those injurious drugs.

That night we halted at a little village at the foot of the pass. We pitched our tents by the side of a small brook, under an enchanting grove of apricot trees. Unfortunately it was not the right season for the fruit, but the sweet scent of the blossoms was sufficient to make our repose pleasurable.

But from then on the land became increasingly waterless and desert-like, what geographers would describe as a *dorsum orbis*. After two days we reached the town of Tsaparang, once the capital of the ancient Thibetan kingdom of Guge, abandoned around 1650 because of incessant wars and a drop in the water table. The citadel of the kings, an impregnable fortress, stood on the top of the sheer cliffs that rose above the ruins of the city. I had learned from certain records in the archives of the Asiatic Society that the first Catholic mission station had been founded here in 1624. The Portuguese Jesuit, Antonio de Andrade, had formed a Catholic community and is reported to have built a church. I told Mr Holmes this strange story and both of us searched for traces of a Christian building in the ruins, but found nothing.

'Did the good father succeed in converting many of the natives?' asked Holmes, knocking the ash out of his pipe against the side of a broken wall.

'Not very many, I would think. Thibetans are notorious in missionary circles for their obstinacy in clinging to their idols and superstitions.'

'They revel in their original sin, do they?' chuckled Mr Holmes. 'Anyhow, there is a surfeit of religion in this country already. Why should the missionaries want to bring in another?'

Next day we rode into Thöling, the other capital of the kingdom of Guge. This town is more populated and relatively prosperous. It has a picturesque monastery with golden canopies and spires, and is considered to be the largest and the oldest monastery in western Thibet. Unfortunately we could not visit it as we had to meet the governor of the district.

His servants were waiting for us outside our allocated quarters, a small whitewashed structure made of sun-dried bricks. As we dismounted they all doffed their caps and bowing low stuck out their tongues. It seemed to me to be an excellent example of the 'self surrender of the person saluting to the individual he salutes,' which Mr Herbert Spencer has shown to lie at the bottom of many of our modern practices of salutation. They had presents for us from the governor: entire carcasses of sheep, bags of cheese and butter, trays of eggs, and sacks of *tsampa*, which is the staple food of all Thibetans. After resting for a while and refreshing ourselves, we went to pay our respects to the governor at his official residence, a gloomy stone mansion on the edge of the town.

His name was Phurbu Thondup or 'Thursday Wish-Fulfilled', and he was a man of Falstaffian proportions, larger even than myself. He was dressed in yellow silk robes and wore the long turquoise earring and top-knot, like Tsering. But to indicate his superior rank — he was a fourth ranker to Tsering's sixth — he had a small gold amulet in his piled-up hair. The nobles in Thibet are ranked in seven classes, to the first of which only the Grand Lama belongs. Yet in spite of his apparent seniority, the governor was very deferential to Tsering and addressed him with great politeness. There was something more to our young friend than met the eye. Phurbu Thondup cleared his throat noisily and ceremoniously before relating the latest instructions he had received from the Grand Lama's secretary.

We were to travel as swiftly as possible to Lhassa. Advance arrangements had been made at all the villages and nomadic encampments on the way, and also at the isolated *tasam* houses, the small caravanserais in which one can change a mule and find lodgings. But we were to try and be as inconspicuous as possible. We were to be especially careful, he continued, when we got to Shigatse, and on no account should we go anywhere near the Chinese consular office there.

Oh ho! So it is politics, I thought. Could our *entrée* into Thibet have some kind of connection with the troubles that the Thibetans are having with the Manchu Amban in Lhassa?

I confided this to Sherlock Holmes on our way back from the governor's mansion, but he did not seem too impressed with my conjecture.

'I am not saying you are wrong, Huree, but as I gave you to understand before, it is a cardinal error to theorise without sufficient data. Consider the contrary. Wouldn't inviting a foreigner to Thibet, if discovered, cause a more serious problem with the Manchu representative, whose xenophobia, I have been given to understand, is unusually virulent, even for the normally suspicious Chinese? So spare me such further speculations, I beg you.'

Early next morning, shivering and grunting in the morning chill, I slung my umbrella (tied on both ends with a piece of string like a rifle-sling) across my back, and climbed sleepy-eyed onto my pony.

For a week we rode by the banks of the Sutlej river, across a country that had an original beauty in spite of a certain barrenness. All kinds of small birds flitted about the gorse bushes and rocks, while lumbering saurus cranes picked for fish in the shallows. We also had our first encounter with the kiang (*equus hemionus*), the Thibetan wild ass. A large herd of this most graceful animal sauntered up to have a look at our caravan. Their curiosity satisfied, they turned all at once, as if at a single command, and trotted off in the most elegant manner.

Fortunately for these birds and beasts such opportunities afforded for shikar did not seem to delight Mr Holmes. It was an unusual attitude on his part as every other Englishman I knew revelled in the slaughter of tigers, deer, pigs, birds, fishes and what not. Mr Holmes's aversion to blood-sport raised him in the esteem of the Thibetans, and also Kintup and Jamspel who subscribed to the Buddhist and Jain doctrine of the sacredness of life in all its forms. We also came across a number of nomad encampments with their herds of sheep and the famous yaks of Tartary (*bos grunnions*).

Then, as we were approaching the *tasam* at Barga, a chain of glaciers, gleaming in the evening sun, came into view, and with it the towering Gurla Mandatha peak and the most holy mountain of Kailash. This mountain is sacred not only to Buddhists, who consider it to be the abode of the deity, Demchog (Skt. Chakrasamvara), but to Hindus as well, who regard it as the throne of Shiva. Because of this many Buddhist and Hindu ascetics and pilgrims have been drawn to the area for the past two thousand years or so, to worship the mountain, to practise austerities by it, and to go around it in holy perambulation. The Thibetans call Mount Kailash, Kang Tise, or Kang Rimpoche, the Precious Mountain, and it plays an important role even in the pre-Buddhist shamanist religion, Bon. Mount Meru, the central mountain axis of Hindu and Buddhist cosmology is probably founded on the unique physical and geographical properties of Kailash.

We were desirous of travelling around the mountain like pilgrims — I would dearly have loved to make observations and measurements of the mountain from various points — but Tsering had his instructions and was reluctant to waste even a single day. Finally we arrived at a compromise of sorts. We would forgo the trip around the mountain, but would make the journey past it and the sacred lake at a slower pace, so that we could, at least, have the leisure to appreciate the remarkable beauty of the place.

For a couple of days we rode across the great plains of Barga, by the mountains and the long stretch of glaciers, till we reached Manasarover. We set up our tents by the shores of this holy lake, which is probably the highest body of fresh water in the world. I made a number of scientific studies of the lake, the results of which have been published in my first account of this trip, entitled: *Journey to Lhassa through Western Thibet* (Elphenstone Publications. Calcutta. 1894. Rs 3.8 annas.) of which the *Statesman* was kind enough to remark: 'a monumental work of exploration and scientific survey.' This present account, for reasons of space and suitability, does not contain the scientific details of our travels and explorations. So readers desirous of such information are advised to purchase the above-mentioned book from any bookshop in the Empire.

The mountain is reflected in the waters of the Manasarover, which, along with the surrounding land, is of awesome beauty, probably unequalled in the world. I found additional joy in the knowledge that few explorers had ever laid eyes on it, much less studied it scientifically as I had the opportunity to do. I bathed in the lake like the other pilgrims, though my motives sprang more from considerations of hygiene than piety. It was freezing cold either way.

Our next stop after the lake was the settlement of Thokchen, or 'Great Thunder', which, belying its impressive name, consisted of a single house. The house was, furthermore, virulently lousy. We passed the night in our tents.

From then on we followed the Bramhaputra river or Tsangpo, as the Thibetans call it. Fed by numerous small streams, the river grew bigger and bigger as the days passed.

Except for a little rain and a couple of sharp hailstorms, we were fortunate to have generally fine weather. I usually rode with my blue and white umbrella open to shield myself from the sunlight, which, due to the altitude and the thinness of the air, was very strong. Unexpected gusts of wind would sometimes blow the umbrella inside-out, or away, to the vast amusement of Kintup and the other servants, who would ride wildly after it and hunt it down as if it were a rabbit or something. But the worst of the winter gales were over, and the summer dust storms yet to commence, so one could quite comfortably read a book sitting on one's pony, under the cool shade of an open umbrella — or as it so often happened to me, fall into a brown study.

'You are probably right, Huree,' Mr Holmes's voice broke into my reverie on one such occasion. 'Science alone cannot answer all the questions of life. Man's higher destiny can be discovered only through religion.'

'Precisely so, Sir.' I agreed, 'Though it troubles me ... Good Heavens, Mr Holmes!' I cried. 'How the deuce an' all could you know my innermost thoughts?'

Sherlock Holmes chuckled, and leaning back on his saddle pulled the reins to make his pony accommodate its speed to mine.

'How do you think? Through magic? Clairvoyance maybe? Or just through a simple sequence of plain, logical reasoning?'

'For the life of me, Sir, I cannot see how reasoning could have enabled you to follow the course of my mental processes. My thoughts were all tightly locked up in my bally head like meat in a coconut. No, Sir! The only explanation is jadoo. Probably you enlisted the aid of some mind-reading djinn like Buktanoos or Dulhan, or Musboot — maybe even Zulbazan, son of Eblis.'

Sherlock Holmes laughed out loud. 'I really hate to disillusion you about my familiarity with the denizens of darkness, but the whole thing is absurdly simple. Let me explain. I have been watching you for the last ten minutes or so. You had Herbert Spencer's *Principles of Biology* open in your hand and were reading it with great interest. You then put the book down on the front of your saddle — open, somewhere in the middle — and you became thoughtful. Your eyes narrowed. Obviously you were thinking over what you had just read. If I am not mistaken, Spencer discusses certain theories of Mr Darwin and others somewhere in the middle of the book — about the continuing development of species from simple to complex forms. I could not be absolutely certain of this, but you helped to confirm my hypothesis by altering the manner of your reverie and observing the wild animals and birds around us in a deliberate and inquiring manner. Your views seemed to agree with that of Spencer's for you nodded your head on a couple of occasions.'

Mr Holmes lit his tartar pipe and, blowing out a stream of white smoke, continued. 'But then your thoughts were rudely interrupted. Do you remember the pitiful remnants of a gazelle killed by wolves that we passed just a little while ago? It seemed to upset you. It is all very well to talk or write about "the survival of the fittest"[1] in a warm comfortable drawing room in London; but actually encountering this aspect of nature even in the insignificant death of a poor gazelle, is a humbling experience. The frown darkened on your face. What theories could explain the misery, the violence, and the brutality of life, you seemed to ask? You thought of your own brushes with violence and death. I noticed that you looked down at your right foot where you once lost a toe, and nearly your life, and shiver a little. Your expression deepened into one of sadness, the melancholy that comes with the awareness of the permanence of our human tragedy.

'Then you noticed the gleaming towers of the monastery in the distance, and your thoughts seemed to lift a little from their previous despondency. You gazed up at the open sky. Your expression was quizzical but not entirely melancholy. Probably you were asking yourself if religion had the answer to human suffering, where science did not. It was then that I ventured to agree with you.'

'Wah! Shabash! Mr Holmes. This is more astounding than any magic,' I exclaimed, amazed at this revelation of yet another facet of his genius. 'You followed my thought process with extraordinary precision. A most remarkable feat of reasoning, Sir.'

'Pooh. Elementary, my dear Hurree.'

'But how was it done, Mr Holmes?'

'The trick is to construct one's chain of reasoning from the initial premise of umm ... let us say, "dependent origination", to use this profound Buddhist concept. Then from a drop of water

---

1. A phrase coined by Spencer in 1852.

you could logically infer the possibility of a Pacific or a Niagara without having seen or heard of one or the other. So all life is a great chain, the nature of which is known whenever we are shown a single link of it.'[2]

The monastery was perched on a hill, below which was the settlement of Tradun. It was a regular bustling metropolis for those parts, consisting of over twenty houses, besides a number of nomad tents scattered over the bleak plains. We were somewhat close to the kingdom of Nepaul from here, and I noted three distant ice peaks rising from that direction.[3]

It took us another three weeks to get to Shigatse. We were fortunate to be able to visit the great monastery of Tashi Lhunpo and see its treasures; but we avoided going anywhere near the Chinese consulate, which was to the west of the town. Kintup and I had too many unhappy memories of the place from our last visit. We heard all kinds of rumours in the bazaar about the intrigues of the Manchu Amban in Lhassa and his assistant here in Shigatse, and the imminence of an invading Chinese army. But we could place no credence on any of these stories.

From Shigatse it was about a ten-day journey to Lhassa.

---

2. Holmes expresses something very similar in his article 'The Book of Life', which Watson mentions (rather disparagingly) in *A Study in Scarlet*, his first published account of his meeting with the great detective. It is remarkable that neither Watson nor the generations of Holmesian scholars should have noticed the clear spiritual bent in Holmes's character.
3. Annapurna, Dhaulagiri, and Manaslu.

15

The City of the Gods

We reached Lhassa in the late afternoon of the 17th of May, 1892. When we came around the last bend on the pilgrim road from Gyangtse, we had our first view of the great Potala palace floating high above the green barley fields of the Kyichu (Happy River) valley.

The Potala was initially constructed in the Water-Bird year (1645) by the fifth Grand Lama, or Dalai Lama, to give his actual title. There is evidence to suggest that the central structure, the 'Red Palace', had been in existence since the seventh century, the time of the ancient Thibetan kings. The building is named after Mount Potalaka in South India, one of the holy mountains of the Hindu god Shiva. Buddhists, however, believe that the mountain is sacred to Avalokitesvara, the Buddha of Compassion, whom they maintain is the Grand Lama, in his divine form. The Potala palace would be a formidable structure anywhere in the great metropolises of the world, but in the bleak wilderness of the

Thibetan landscape such a monumental creation of human genius and energy assumed awe-inspiring dimensions.

Only one white man, Thomas Manning, had ever set eyes on it before;[1] and in our Department only K.21 had seen it before me. I humbly thanked my Maker for granting me this privileged sight. I could see that the scene had a similar effect on my companions. Tsering, Kintup and the other Buddhists dismounted and prostrated themselves on the ground in reverence. Even Gaffuru, the staunch Mohameddan, was moved to offer a respectful salaam towards it. Mr Holmes's eyes seemed to fill with a calm bliss as they gazed at the distant Potala. His stern brows, ever knotted in intense cerebration, gradually relaxed, permitting a gentle smile to break out on his face.

All the trials and hardships of the journey seemed to magically lift off our shoulders. With light hearts and good cheer we proceeded to the holy city.

Following the pilgrim road we proceeded through an avenue of trees, passing gardens and orchards that supply the Lhassa markets with vegetables and fruits, across parks, past fields and shaggy stretches of woodland. The air was delightfully free from dust, that plague of Shigatse, and this was doubtless due to the marshes and far reaching network of streamlets which give Lhassa its refreshing green and luxuriant vegetation. Although the sparkling streams are teeming with fat trout, no fishing may be done here, nor any killing of birds, lest a transmigrated human-life may thus be sacrificed. The banks of these numerous brooklets are a mass of blossoms of wild flowers trying to outvie each other in gaudy tints: scented potentilla, magenta and blue daisies,

---

1. Huree is mistaken. John Grueber and Albert D'Orville visited Lhassa in 1661 and saw the Potala palace, although the construction was not fully completed till 1695.

buttercups, primulas and harebells. Up the valley one could see the fields of ripening barley stretching like a sea for miles. Harvesters had commenced work, singing in light-heartedness, the women wearing garlands of yellow clematis.

We passed a small funeral party. The dead body was carried doubled up in a sitting posture and wrapped in a blanket. Most probably it was being taken to a cemetery outside the city where it would be disposed of in the rather gruesome but traditional manner by being cut to pieces and fed to vultures and ravens. As Manning, in the account of his travels, quaintly puts it, 'They eat no birds, but, on the contrary, let the birds eat them.'

We entered the city by the famous western gate, which is actually a large stupa with a passage through it. With us was a group of noisy pilgrims from Tsang province, which helped not to draw too much attention to our small caravan. Our guide, Tsering, led us through streets crowded with pilgrims, monks, beggars, swaggering bravos and silk-clad gentlemen. Ladies wearing fantastic head-dresses rode by, accompanied by their servants, while their less fortunate sisters walked, some carrying small wooden barrels of water on their backs. Nomads, clad from head to foot in sheepskin, held each other's hands for safety. Women from Khams, or Eastern Thibet, with hair braided into a hundred and eight separate plaits, spun large prayer wheels in pious, if mechanical ritual. Merchants from Turkestan, Bhootan, Nepaul, China and Mongolia displayed in their stalls a rich array of goods: tea, silk, fur, brocades, turquoise, amber, coral, wines and dried fruits and even humble needles, thread, soap, calico, spices and trinkets from the distant bazaars of India. Lhassa is a surprisingly cosmopolitan town, with merchants and travellers from not only the countries I have just mentioned, *vide supra*, but also Armenians, Cashmiris and Muscovites.

Finally after what seemed like endless twists and turns through narrow streets and dark alleys, we came before a high wall

surrounding a mansion. Tsering banged his fist on the massive wooden gate and shouted for attention. A moment later the gate opened and we rode into a large courtyard. The gate shut quickly behind us. Mr Holmes and I were ushered into a well-appointed chamber, decorated in the Thibetan fashion with religious paintings (*thangka*) and ritual objects, and the floor covered with rich carpets and divans. We were served tea and Huntley & Palmer's chocolate-cream biscuits.

Tsering left to report our arrival to the Grand Lama's secretary. He requested us to remain in the house till he returned and not to go out in the streets. Anyhow, both Mr Holmes and I were tired, the exhaustion of the journey finally catching up with us. After a warm bath and a good dinner, served by silent, well-trained servitors, we went to bed. The beds were soft, the sheets clean, and the quilts warm. We slept like the proverbial logs.

I had just finished my morning ablutions, chanted a brief Brahmo Somajist hymn (of a theistical nature), and popped the first betel nut of the day into my mouth, when Sherlock Holmes appeared at the door.

'Ah! I see that you are up, Hurree,' he said cheerily. 'That is fortunate, for Tsering has news for us. He's waiting in the dining room.'

After breakfast we resumed our disguises and followed Tsering to the Norbu Lingka (Jewel Park), the summer residence of the Grand Lama. It was about two miles out of the city. The long, straight road leading to it was lined on either side with tall willows. During the spring and summer months the Grand Lama lives and conducts his business from this charming retreat which, with its gardens, lakes, menageries, pavilions and comfortable residential buildings, he finds more pleasant and habitable than the cold, gloomy chambers of the Potala.

The Jewel Park is surrounded by a high wall. We arrived at the front gate, which was guarded by a few armed soldiers. Clearly we were expected, for some grooms quickly appeared and relieving us of our ponies hustled us through the gates. We walked through a charming grove of conifers and willows till we got to the middle of the park, where the Grand Lama has his private garden and residence. It was surrounded by a high, yellow wall, with two gates guarded by giant warrior monks. We passed through the front gates into a magical garden, covered with fruit trees and gnarled, twisted junipers, reminiscent of a Japanese print. Throughout the ground there were fierce Thibetan mastiffs, straining at their chains, magnificent specimens of the breed. A sparkling brook wound its way through these trees to finally flow into a placid lotus-covered lake. Strange birds of exotic plumage fluttered about the branches. I even noticed a bright green Indian parrot sitting on the top of a peach tree solemnly chanting the mantra 'Om Mani Padme Hum'.

The actual palace was a modest-sized building which quite suited the bucolic nature of the surroundings. Monk attendants ushered us into a large reception room richly carpeted, whose walls were covered with finely executed murals of religious themes. The furnishing, though, was occidental, with comfortable arm chairs and low Regency tables. An ornate ormolu clock ticked softly on a Queen Anne sideboard, beside which stood a small man dressed in wine-red monastic robes, his bare head shorn in the prescribed manner. As he came forward to greet us, I noticed that his small dark eyes, with their typical epicanthic folds, were plainly short-sighted. He wore round spectacles of Chinese design, made of thick *bilaur* or crystal. His voice, though high, was strong and clear.

'Welcome to Thibet, Mr Sherlock Holmes, and you too, Babuji.'

16

Tea at the Jewel Park

So startled was I by this unexpected revelation of Mr Holmes's secret, that I hardly heard the Lama's words of welcome to myself.

'You have the advantage of me, Sir,' said Sherlock Holmes softly, ' ... in more ways than one.'

'You will forgive me. I am the Lama Yonten, Chief Secretary to His Holiness the Dalai Lama. Please, please be seated.' He waved us to the brocade-covered arm-chairs and summoned servants, who poured us tea out of a Crown Derby teaset. After the servants had left the room, the Lama resumed his conversation.

'You will, no doubt, be wondering how we came to know of your true identity,' he continued. 'The explanation is simple, though it may not convince one not of our faith. You will see much ignorance and superstition in this land, Mr Holmes, but there are

still some who have the power of the Third Eye. The Great Seer of Taklung, the "Tiger's Prophecy", is one such. His inner vision pierced the mists of time to find you.'

'I was aware that of late my reputation had been enhanced somewhat, thanks to my friend Watson's lively accounts of my work, but that it had transcended physical laws is somewhat surprising — though nonetheless flattering. Still, there is Tertullian's famous reason, *certum est quia impossibile est*,' said Mr Holmes shrugging his shoulders.

The Lama Yonten smiled, his face creasing like old leather. 'Mr Holmes, I assure you that no one in Thibet was even aware of your existence before the Great Seer discovered you in his vision. Indeed it came as a great surprise to me that he should have chosen a *chilingpa*, an outsider.'

'Chosen? For what?'

'To protect the life of my master, Mr Holmes,' said the Lama simply.

He walked over to the curtained window at the rear end of the room and, pulling apart the drapes slightly, beckoned to us. We joined him and looked out at an exquisite garden menagerie. Two beautiful gazelles grazed contentedly besides a spiral-horned argali *(Ovis orlentalis himalayaca)* and a few musk deer *(Moschus chrysogaster)*. A shaggy bactrian camel *(Camelus bactrianus)* gazed sadly up at the trees which were crowded with parrots, beautiful Cobalt Warblers of Severtzoff *(Leptopoecile sophice)*, colourful tits, and a red-headed species of some kind of wagtail that I could not identify. A few monkeys — the tailless variety from Bhootan — sat peacefully on the branches, grooming each other. At the back of the garden near the walls were a number of rather flimsy cages that contained the more ferocious members of this little zoo: two sleeping leopards, a red panda *(Ailurus fulgens)*, a badger (Tib. *dumba*), and a large Bengal tiger that paced up and down in its somewhat fragile looking cage, growling now and then as if fretting its captivity.[1]

A boy of about fourteen walked slowly up a path to the cages. His hair was cut short and he wore red monastic robes. He did not appear to be very healthy for his complexion was pale, in contrast to the ruddy skin of most Thibetans. But he had bright intelligent eyes that became animated with affection and joy when he talked to the animals. The creatures, too, appeared to be happy with their young visitor, and even the restless tiger stopped its pacing and settled down peacefully.

'He is the Dalai Lama ...' said the Lama Yonten, gently closing the curtains, '... manifestation of the Buddha of Compassion, the Ocean of Wisdom, the source of all happiness and prosperity in the Land of the Great Snows. Yet such is the darkness of this age that evil men would conspire to harm him.'

'Pray, if you could be more precise as to details,' said Sherlock Holmes.

'Of course, Mr Holmes. You will excuse me if I express myself clumsily, for the tale is as long and complicated as it is unhappy. Thibet is a small and peaceful country, and all that its inhabitants seek is to pass their lives in tranquillity and to practise the noble teachings of the Lord Buddha. But all around us are warlike nations, powerful and restless as titans. To the south there is the Empire of the English sahibs, who now rule the land of the Shakyamuni, and to the north is the Kezar of Oros, though fortunately he is far away.

---

1. Being Buddhists, the Dalai Lamas would, of course, never have had animals captured for their amusement. The animals in the menagerie were wounded or lost creatures rescued by pious travellers and presented to the Dalai Lama for safe-keeping. When there was an excess of animals at the zoo, the Dalai Lama would present them to government officials, who were obliged to give them a good home.

'But to the east is our greatest peril and curse, Black China — cunning, and hungry for land. Yet even in its greed it is patient and subtle. It knows that an outright military conquest of Thibet would only rouse the ire of the many Tartar tribes who are faithful to the Dalai Lama, and who are always a threat to China's own security. Moreover, the Emperor of China is himself a Buddhist, as are all the Manchus, and he must, at least for the sake of propriety, maintain an appearance of friendly amicability with the Dalai Lama.

'But what he cannot achieve directly, the Emperor attempts through intrigue. Over the years, through bribery, blackmail, and murder — conducted through his representative here in Lhassa, the Amban — the Emperor has slowly succeeded in getting very close to his goal. The present Amban in Lhassa, His Excellency, the Count O-erh-t'ai, is unfortunately, not only a most intelligent and dangerous man, but one with a smooth and persuasive tongue. He has succeeded in filling the head of the Regent of Thibet, the incarnate lama of the great Tengyeling monastery, with sacrilegious and treacherous ideas.'

'... that he, the Regent, should continue to remain in power even when the young Dalai Lama comes of the rightful age to assume power,' interjected Sherlock Holmes.

'Exactly, Mr Holmes, and since the Dalai Lama has now reached his majority ...'

'Excuse me for interrupting, Reverend Sir,' said I meekly, 'but is not His Holiness only fourteen years of age?'

'Yes, Babuji, and the previous Dalai Lamas were nearly all enthroned at the age of eighteen or nineteen. But years have really nothing to do with their coming of age. That great event is traditionally heralded by a sign — when the Ice Temple of Shambala, which is normally buried under a glacier in the north, opens itself from the great ice. In the past this has always happened when the Dalai Lamas were about eighteen years of age. But just a month ago, the "Watchers of the Ice Temple" reported that the temple had once again emerged from the great ice. The Regent, with the help of his ally the Amban, lost no time in countering this unexpected threat to their plans. They had two senior ministers of the *kashag*, the cabinet, arrested. Four members of the *Tsongdu*, the parliament, were expelled in disgrace, two of them being senior abbots of Drepung and Sera monastery. All these people were outspoken critics of the Regent's pretensions, and had declared that the Dalai Lama, in spite of his tender years, should be enthroned at once, as the heavenly sign had indicated.'

'Was there nothing that could be done to save them from incarceration?' I enquired politely.

'It was all we could do to prevent them from being executed,' replied the Lama with a shudder. 'The Amban had expended a great deal of energy and money to fabricate evidence and false witnesses to convict them. The Regent used all the weight of his authority to press these false charges and convict them of treason. They just stopped short of attempting to arrest the old prime minister and myself; and we never know when they may do it. But of much greater consequence is the life of our master, and we feel that yet again it is being threatened.'

'Again?'

'Mr Holmes, the last three incarnations of the Dalai Lama departed to the heavenly fields, or to put it in less respectful terms, died, before reaching their majority — all under very suspicious circumstances. One, at least, we know, was definitely instigated by the Chinese, though, as usual, there was no real evidence of their direct complicity. In any event, the political confusion and instability caused by these unhappy occurrences were very advantageous to the Chinese, who gradually increased their power and influence in Thibet. They are so strong now that we feel they may well be intending to make a final effort to gain full control of our country and end the glorious line of the Dalai Lamas for all time. Lies and false prophecies, undoubtedly originating from the Chinese legation, are being spread that the present Dalai Lama will not survive to his majority, and that he will be the last of his line. Unfortunately, these filthy lies have gained a certain credence as His Holiness is a sickly boy, and has only just recovered from a very serious fever. The Chinese have, also, not been slow to point out to the ignorant and superstitious that His Holiness is the thirteenth in the line of incarnations.'

'And you believe they will make an attempt on his life?'

'I am sure of it. The Amban himself has been heard boasting that the Dalai Lama's life was as secure as that of a louse squeezed between his fingernails. I have a man at the Chinese legation who provides me with information on what is going on there. So I have taken the precaution of having His Holiness's meals tasted twice: once in the kitchen and once again just before he eats. The guards have been doubled. I have even raised a contingent of warrior monks to guard the inner walls.'

'But you do not think it sufficient?'

'No, Sir,' replied the Lama tiredly, and the lines on his face seemed to deepen with his answer. He nervously fingered a string of jade worry beads. 'Most of my life has been devoted to study and meditation, and the prime minister is a very old man. Both of us are ill-suited to challenge the Amban's intrigues and the Regent's treacherous plots. But we had to do something. The life of our master was at stake. That is why we secretly sought the guidance of the Seer of Taklung. He is no mere bazaar soothsayer, Mr Holmes, but a *mahasiddha*, a great occult master, one whose transcendental wisdom arises not from dependence on mortal gods, but from his own subjugation of the illusion of duality, and the spontaneous realisation of the pure nature of primal emptiness. His is the highest vision.'

'And he recommended me?' said Holmes, slightly bemused.

'Yes, Mr Holmes, and I dread to think what the Regent will do when he discovers that I have permitted an Englishman into this country. But if my master is to be saved, the Seer's vision must be fulfilled — even if I have to pay for it with my head.'

In spite of his size and apparent nervousness, the Lama Yonten was obviously a brave and loyal man. I hoped that Mr Holmes would be able to do something to help him.

But Sherlock Holmes shook his head sadly. 'Sir, I represent justice, as far as my feeble powers go, but I really cannot see where I can be of help in this matter. You have taken all possible steps to protect your master. Everything he eats is double-checked for poison. The guards have been doubled, and you have also raised a contingent of … umm … warrior monks to protect him.'

'But the Amban knows all this,' protested the Lama Yonten. 'He will be sure to confront us with something unexpected. Not for nothing is he known as "the Father of Deception" among the people of this city, who hate him, and his strutting henchmen who never miss a chance to humiliate any Thibetan.'

'How many men … Chinese soldiers, does he have to protect him?'

'Not many. No more than two hundred. It would actually be no problem for us to storm the Chinese legation and wipe out everyone within. But that would give the Emperor the perfect excuse to send in an invading army and subjugate us once and for all. Something like that nearly happened when the loyal ministers were arrested and a large mob gathered outside the legation to protest Chinese interference in Thibetan affairs. I had to send palace guards to disperse the crowd, and make sure no harm came to the Amban or any Chinese there. It was a galling task for the men, and though I, as a Buddhist monk, have vowed never to harm any sentient being, it was not an easy decision for me to protect the evil men who were planning to harm my master.'

'But what can you expect me to do, Reverend Sir,' replied Sherlock Holmes, 'when even your own hands are so effectively tied? If there were only enough time for me to … '

'That is what we have the least of,' interrupted the Lama, 'if my man at the Chinese legation is right. Two weeks ago a closed palanquin arrived there in the dead of night. The occupant was received personally by the Amban, who conducted him to a suite of rooms at the back of the residency. My man did not see this mysterious guest, as the servants were warned to keep away from the gate at the time of his arrival. They were also warned, on pain of death, never to go near his rooms. The mysterious guest has brought his own retainers: silent, unsmiling fellows, I am told, in black livery. We don't know who the man is, but I expect the worst.'

'Do you think he could be some kind of hired assassin?' said I.

'It is probable. My man overheard a snatch of the Amban's conversation as he came out of this mysterious visitor's room. The Amban's face was flushed with excitement, and as he turned away from the door he smote his fist into the palm of his other hand and hissed: ' ... a few more days and it is ours.'

'Piquant,' observed Sherlock Holmes, ' ... but decidedly sinister. When was this?'

'Just two days ago.'

'Then you can expect it anytime now, whatever it is that the Amban and his nocturnal guest have concocted. You did not consult the ah ... Seer of Taklung, about this?'

'There was no time, Mr Holmes. It is a good five days' journey to the mountain of the Blue Crystal, where the Seer lives; and I cannot leave my master unattended, now that danger is imminent. Anyway, it is unnecessary. The Seer has spoken and you, Mr Holmes will surely triumph over our enemies. I have never known the Seer to make a wrong prediction.'

'There is always the first time,' Holmes sighed despondently and remained silent and deep in thought for a long time. Finally he leaned forward towards the Lama, and addressed him in a gentle tone. 'Excuse me, Reverend Sir. In no way do I wish to belittle your beliefs, but my entire career, indeed, my life has been based on logic and reason. Thus at the moment I really cannot see how I merit your assurances of my infallibility. The task that you wish me to undertake is too great, too complex, and too removed from the sphere of my experience, for me to accept with any hope of success. Indeed it appears that matters are now far beyond my control. You require the services of an army, Sir, not a consulting detective. I must regretfully decline the responsibility.'

The Lama Yonten looked dreadfully crestfallen with Sherlock Holmes's answer. I too, I must confess, was somewhat disappointed with my friend. I had become so accustomed to witnessing the fertility of his genius, and the awe-inspiring powers of observation and concentration that his great mind could bring to bear on any problem, that I had overlooked his inherent human limitations. Even the world's greatest detective could hardly be expected to challenge the ambitions of Imperial China, single-handedly.

The Lama rose, somewhat unsteadily, from his chair, and lifted his hands as if in a gesture of resignation. His eyes, through his thick spectacles, were sad and tired, though he tried not to betray in his voice the disappointment he must have felt.

'Well, Mr Holmes. I can see that your refusal is final. I know you are a brave and honourable man, and that you would not refuse to help us if you thought you could do so in any way. Therefore I will not attempt anything so vulgar as offering you wealth for your services, or persist in wasting your time with an old man's pleas. Goodbye to both of you. May the Three Jewels protect you on your journey home. Now if you will excuse me, I have certain duties to attend to.' He rang a small handbell. 'Tsering will see you to your residence.'

We bade him goodbye. As that small, disappointed figure shuffled off to an adjoining room, I could not but help feel slightly disappointed with my friend for giving up without even trying. He must have sensed my feelings, for as we descended the short flight of steps in front of the palace, Holmes turned to me and remarked: 'You disapprove of my want of enthusiasm in the matter, do you not?'

'Oh no, Mr Holmes,' I protested. 'I am sure that *ex facto,* your decision was one hundred percent correct. I just thought that with your great powers ... and that scoundrel of an Amban and how they nearly cut off my head ...'

At that moment Tsering came down the stairs to join us. He had just met the Lama Yonten, who had instructed him to let us know that preparations for our departure to India were being made, though they would take a few days to complete. In the meantime we were to remain in our quarters and refrain from going out into the streets.

Our ride back to the city was a melancholy one. Holmes rode slightly ahead, puffing at his pipe, deep in contemplation. I rode beside Tsering and attempted to be convivial, but he either sensed that something was amiss, or the Lama Yonten had told him of Holmes's refusal, so the conversation did not exactly proceed smoothly.

Dinner too, was not a very cheerful event. The filet of yak and Chinese cabbage in cheese sauce was delicious, but Sherlock Holmes ate very little, and conversed even less. After dinner I retired to my bed-chamber and spent an hour composing a report of the political situation in Lhassa for Colonel Creighton, which I would have to convey to a Newari merchant at the Barkhor market, in the centre of the city. He would take it to Darjeeling and deliver it to the Departmental agent there. I made no mention in the report of our meeting with the Lama Yonten.

I got into bed and tried to sleep. I heard Mr Holmes pacing up and down his room, which was next to mine. He walked exactly six steps, stopped, turned around (you heard a slight shuffle), then walked back six steps, turned around (you heard the shuffle again), and started again. Somewhere on the eleventh turn I drifted off to sleep.

AND BEYOND

17

The Flying Swords

A strong hand shook me by the shoulder, waking me from a deep sleep.

'Wha … who?'

I tried to blink away my drowsiness and noticed that it was still dark. The glow of a candle in his hand outlined the troubled face of Sherlock Holmes, and told me at a glance that something was amiss.

'Come, Hurree,' he cried, 'the game's afoot. Not a word! Into your clothes and come.'

'Why, Mr Holmes? What is the …' I began to ask, but he had already left the room. I did as I was ordered and was ready in a trice.

Tying the lappets of my old rabbit-skin cap under my chin, I ran out through the living room to the courtyard, where some of the servants were hurriedly saddling our ponies. In a very short time Mr Holmes, Tsering and I were on our steeds and out of the gates, Tsering leading the way through the dark, deserted streets.

For the bally life of me I could not comprehend what was going on. I attempted to ask Mr Holmes, but it was difficult to make enquiries when riding single file in narrow alleyways. I thought it indiscreet to shout. When we came to the outskirts of the city it was possible for the ponies to travel two abreast, and I thought that I would take this opportunity to ask Mr Holmes the reason for this nocturnal excursion. But no sooner had I begun to get my pony beside his, than we came to the Western Gate of the city, and were soon galloping furiously on the dirt road that led to the Jewel Park. No conversation was possible then.

A bright summer moon occasionally lit our way as it scudded through a cloud-patched sky.

A hard twenty-minute ride brought us before the main entrance of the Jewel Park.

Two soldiers, with rifles at the ready, ran out of a sentry box and challenged us. Tsering quickly dismounted and identified himself. He also made some enquiries, though I could not discern his exact words as he spoke softly.

'But it is very late,' one of the soldiers replied. 'He must have retired hours ago.'

'... and we cannot disturb him now,' said the other soldier.

Sherlock Holmes dismounted and walked over to them. 'Even as I speak ...' he said gravely, '... the life of the Grand Lama is threatened by a terrible danger. It is vital that we see the Lama Yonten.'

'But we have our orders,' one of the guards replied, slightly shaken by Mr Holmes's portentous declaration. 'We cannot desert our post.'

'A most commendable course of conduct,' replied Holmes rather sardonically, 'but surely one of you can guard the gate while the other goes to fetch the Lama Yonten.'

'Well, I don't know, Sir,' the soldier scratched his head bemusedly.

'If anything happens to the Grand Lama, I shall personally hold the two of you responsible,' said Sherlock Holmes in that stern, masterful way of his, which rather rattled the two simple fellows. 'Get a move on, man,' he urged.

Bewildered and not quite sure of themselves, they reluctantly opened a small door set into the main gate. One of the soldiers went through it and disappeared into the darkness.

We waited. Sherlock Holmes extracted a dark lantern from his saddle-bag and proceeded to light it. He then closed the shield and handed it to me. No gleam of light escaped but the smell of hot metal and oil told me it was ready for instant use.

'Keep it handy. We may have urgent need of it.'

Sherlock Holmes paced restlessly about in a fever of suppressed frustration, occasionally throwing out his hands as if chafing against the inaction. Finally, after about fifteen minutes, the gate opened and the small, cloaked figure of the Chief Secretary appeared, accompanied by our soldier, and a giant warrior monk.

'Mr Holmes, what a surprise ...' said the Lama Yonten.

'Reverend Sir,' interrupted Holmes, 'we have no time to lose. I fear an imminent attack on the person of His Holiness.'

The Lama looked up at Sherlock Holmes in a queer sort of way. Not puzzled or bewildered, mind you, though a bit dazed; but on the whole reassured and pleased. 'Then we must do something about it,' he said firmly. 'What are your orders, Mr Holmes?'

'Quick, follow me,' cried Sherlock Holmes, leaping past them and running into the Jewel Park. Mr Holmes was decidedly a swift runner and it was all we could do to keep up with him. We were permitted a brief pause by the inner wall, as the Lama Yonten ordered the gates opened. Then once again we were racing through the dark gardens. I must admit to tripping and stumbling a few times, but recovered swiftly enough to just about keep up behind Mr Holmes. He must have had the eyes of a panther for he sprinted unerringly in the darkness towards the palace building. On arrival, he paused briefly near the door to wait for the rest of us. As soon as I arrived he grabbed the lantern from me and entered the building. Past the reception hall we ran, coming to a long corridor with a number of doors on either side.

'This is His Holiness's bed-chamber,' whispered the Lama Yonten, pointing to the second door on the right. But Holmes did not seem to have heard him, for he quickly strode up the corridor to the fifth door on the left, and there paused to open the metal shield on the lantern and draw a revolver from the pouch of his Ladakhi robe. He then signalled me to push open the door. Slightly apprehensive, I leaned against it.

The door swung back somewhat awkwardly on its clumsy wrought-iron hinges. A shaft of light from the lantern cut through the darkness of the room to reveal a terrifying red face with long white fangs sticking out of a grimacing mouth. I gave a little start. Actually, I nearly screamed, but recovered my wits sufficiently — and in the jolly nick of time — to realise that the fearful apparition was nothing but the idol of a *yidam*, a wrathful deity of the Lamaist pantheon. We were obviously in some kind of chapel. Mr Holmes did not betray any surprise but kept the lantern shining steadily on the idol. Then he slowly moved the beam of light across the room, revealing more images of fierce tantric deities, peaceful Buddhas and Bodhisattvas, all disconcertingly life-like in the silence and gloom of the chapel. The heavy scent of juniper incense contributed to the mystery of the place.

The clear, effulgent beam of the lantern rested on the image of a divinity (or demon?) attired in black and holding two short swords, one in each hand. Its head was entirely wrapped in a black scarf, revealing only a pair of dark sinister eyes that glittered like moonstones.

Then they blinked!

'My gosh!' I exclaimed

'Look out! He's armed,' shouted Holmes, raising his revolver as the figure sprang forward to attack us.

Just as swiftly another figure — our warrior monk — leapt forward to confront the assailant. Our monk had also unsheathed his weapon — a heavy piece of iron in the shape of a large key, suspended from the end of a leather thong — which he whirled and flicked about him with practised dexterity and deadliness. Uttering savage yells both the protagonists gave battle. For a few minutes there was a confused melee of hurtling limbs and flashing weapons. By the solitary light of the lantern it was difficult to follow clearly the full course of the fray.

Awakened by the pandemonium, more guards and servants came shouting down the corridor, carrying candles and lamps. In the relative glare of the collective illuminations, our masked intruder appeared to become somewhat discomposed.

Then suddenly he initiated a flurry of wicked thrusts with his swords that caused our warrior monk to fall back a pace. That was all the masked intruder needed. He spun around, and running to the side of the room, jumped out of an open window — probably the same one he had entered by.

'After him!' shouted Holmes.

Our warrior monk unhesitatingly jumped through the window, followed by Mr Holmes and, slightly later, by myself. I am not the most agile of persons, I must admit, and I tripped on the sill and tumbled into a bed of rather prickly roses. I sprang up briskly enough, though, and sped after Mr Holmes. It was extremely difficult to see anything clearly in the infernal darkness, but I did manage to get occasional glimpses of Mr Holmes's running form, so that I was just able to follow him in the confusion of trees and bushes. Then the dark shadow of the garden wall loomed ahead and I saw Mr Holmes run into it — and disappear!

On reaching the wall — at the point of Sherlock Holmes' disappearance — I discovered a small but solid wooden door built into the wall. The door was open, so I went through it quickly. The moment I got to the other side, the moon came out from behind a bank of clouds, and I saw that we were outside the palace compound, on an open stretch of land, probably at the back of the Jewel Park. The pale moonlight clearly revealed the warrior monk and Mr Holmes running close at the heels of the black-garbed intruder who was heading for a small stone bridge arching over a little winding stream. Before the bridge was a palanquin borne by some half-a-dozen uniformed figures.

The intruder was now running very fast. He had transferred both his swords to his left hand, while with his right he extracted a white tubular object from the recesses of his clothes and held it forward, as if to hand it over to someone in that company ahead.

'Stop him!' cried Holmes, raising his revolver to fire.

But once again he was anticipated by our valiant monk. The fellow twirled his weapon rapidly over his head and released it in the direction of the fleeing intruder. The missile hummed across the distance and struck the man squarely behind the head with an audible crunch. He dropped in his tracks like wet buffalo dung. His two swords fell on the ground with a clatter, and the white cylinder rolled away from his lifeless hand. It was a rolled up scroll, or something like it.

Sherlock Holmes rushed forward to recover the object. Just then the thick curtains covering the sides of the palanquin parted slightly, and a sickly white hand emerged. The thin, gnarled hand described some strange gestures, like the passes of a way-side jadoo wallah, and — may I be born as a louse in a Baluchi's beard if I am lying — the scroll rose from the ground, hovered in mid-air for a brief moment, and then flew over to the palanquin, straight into the waiting hand. The hand, with the scroll, then quickly drew back into the palanquin and the curtains closed. A thin wailing voice came from within the palanquin, issuing some kind of order, for the uniformed men quickly shouldered the closed litter and prepared to leave.

Our warrior monk was clearly a chap with a bounden sense of duty, for he charged unhesitatingly forward to intercept the departing company. The thin hand emerged from between the curtains of the litter again, and made some more of those strange passes. As if at a command the two swords on the ground flew up into the air, flicked and swung around like the needle of a monstrous compass searching for the North pole, and, on pointing in our direction, suddenly froze. A split second later they shot forward like twin arrows.

The first one flew in the direction of the monk. The second sped straight towards Mr Holmes. He raised his right hand to ward it off. At the last moment it seemed to deflect the tiniest bit and, striking his right shoulder plunged into a tree trunk behind. With a cry Mr Holmes dropped his revolver. I ran up to assist, to resuscitate, but then noticed that the first sword had struck our warrior monk in the middle of his chest, impaling him like a lepidopterist's specimen.

For a moment I was transfixed with fear and indecision, but then noticed that the palanquin and its bearers were fast disappearing over the bridge and into the darkness beyond. I quickly picked up Mr Holmes's revolver and fired a few rounds at our departing foes. It was, of course, a futile gesture, made more so by my previously mentioned incompetence in matters concerning the discharge of firearms. But at least the report of the weapon served to draw the attention of Tsering and the others — who had lost their way in the park — and who now came quickly to our aid.

'What has happened ...?' Tsering cried, looking around him. 'Mr Holmes, you are hurt.'

'A mere scratch, my dear fellow,' said Holmes clutching his

right arm in pain, and not looking as well as he claimed to be. 'But how is he — the monk guard?'

The warrior monk — brave fellow — was dead as a door-nail. The sword had gone right through his heart. But he died partially avenged, for the masked intruder too — we discovered on investigation — was dead. The back of his head had been crushed by the force of the monk's missile. Tsering removed the black scarf from around the dead assassin's head.

'See the small burn-marks on his shaven head, Mr Holmes,' said Tsering, holding a lantern over it. 'He was a Chinese monk.'

'Hmm ... yes. I have heard that certain monasteries in China have the reputation of training their members to become skilled assassins rather than holy men.' Sherlock Holmes remarked, rather abstractedly. Then he clutched his arm tighter in sudden pain, and spoke in a low hiss. 'But we lose precious time. The palanquin must be followed.'

Mr Holmes quickly explained to Tsering about the cylindrical object being taken by the mysterious person in the palanquin, and instructed Tsering to take some guards and follow it.

'... it left a few minutes ago so it won't be too difficult to catch up with it. Keep a safe distance. And don't, if you value your life, try to stop or apprehend it. I just want to know where it is going.'

Tsering quickly went off with two soldiers, while some other guards carried away the two bodies. Mr Holmes's wound was now bleeding quite severely and his face was drawn and deathly pale, so I helped him back to the palace.

18

The Missing Mandala

The Lama Yonten quickly summoned a monk physician who bathed Mr Holmes's wound and treated it with some aromatic herbal salve. Servants also brought in hot tea and other refreshments, which were very welcome to us after our trying experiences of the night. As he was being tended, Sherlock Holmes narrated to the Lama the strange occurrences by the bridge. The Lama seemed much troubled by Mr Holmes's tale.

'This is terrible, terrible,' the Lama said, shaking his head from side to side. 'But at least you have, for the present, prevented an unthinkable evil and a national catastrophe.'

'Is His Holiness all right?' Holmes inquired.

'Yes. I have just come from his bed-chamber. He is unharmed. Fortunately the assassin must have made a mistake and entered His Holiness's chapel instead of his bedchamber.'

'Humm … perhaps,' said Sherlock Holmes speculatively. 'Though that could have been his intention all along.'

'What do you mean?' the Lama asked, puzzled.

'Well, when I was chasing the intruder, I noticed that he had something in his hand, which he tried to hand over to whoever it was in that covered litter.'

'I saw it too, Sir,' I ventured. 'It looked like a rolled-up scroll or a roll of parchment.'

'Exactly. Now it would not be unreasonable to assume that the article had been taken from the chapel. And, since our intruder did not strike me as a chance thief, one could possibly conclude that the man had intended to enter the chapel and steal the scroll in the first place.'

'So you do not think that he had any murderous intentions?' the Lama Yonten queried.

'I cannot really say,' answered Holmes, shrugging his shoulders. 'Of course, I must confess that such an intruder, armed with two wicked swords, is someone to whom one cannot confidently attribute peaceful intentions. But considering the facts it would seem that his principal task was not murder, but the purloining of some object from the chapel.'

'Well, it will not be difficult to verify,' said the Lama Yonten. 'The Senior Chapel Attendant is at this moment cleaning up the mess there. He will certainly know if anything has been stolen. I will have him summoned.'

He reached over for his small handbell, but Sherlock Holmes raised his hand.

'It would perhaps be more profitable to go there and look for ourselves.'

'But your wound, Mr Holmes?'

'A mere scratch. It does not prevent me from walking.'

'Very well,' the Lama nodded.

Holmes rose from the couch, grimacing slightly from the pain he must have felt. I started to go over to help him but he waved me away.

The chapel, now brightly lit with oil lamps, was still in some disarray, though a few monks were attempting to tidy it up and put everything in order. One of them — a wrinkled, toothless old chap with narrow squint eyes and hollow cheeks sprouting a few grey hairs — was clearly upset.

'Oh dear me ... oh ... oh ...' he wailed, holding up the remains of what had once been an exquisite Ming cloisonné vase. 'How can I get everything ready for the morning service?'

'Do not worry *kusho*,' said the Lama Yonten. 'His Holiness is confident that in your good hands everything will be in order. Now, is there anything missing?'

'Missing?' the greybeard threw up his hands and commenced his lamentations again. 'Oh! Were I to have as many eyes as the Za demon, it would be impossible to tell in this chaos.'

'Has something been removed from there?' asked Sherlock Holmes, pointing to the far corner of the back wall.

'Where did you say?' the old man peered about confusedly. Holmes stepped across the room and indicated the place. 'I think we had a ... now what was it? Oh yes, there was a *thangka* hanging there.'

'About two feet high and a foot and a half wide?' asked Holmes.

'How did you know ...?' the Lama Yonten began to ask, amazed, then he laughed. 'Ah, Mr Holmes, you noticed the discoloration on the wall where the scroll was hanging.'

'Yes, clear observation is the basis of any investigation.'

'Which *thangka* was it?' the Lama Yonten asked the old chapel attendant.

'Let me think. Yes, it was the one of the *mandala* of the Great Tantra of the Wheel of Time. The very old one.'

'Was it of any significant value?' asked Holmes.

'In terms of material wealth, not really so,' replied the Lama. 'There are others just like it. In fact one could commission an artist to paint one exactly like it for a small sum of money. But this one originally belonged to the first Grand Lama, or so I have been told, and therefore has greater spiritual value. Even then, I really do not see why anyone should risk his life to steal it.'

As we all began to leave the chapel, the Lama Yonten turned to the old attendant and offered him a few words of consolation and encouragement. 'Don't worry. You can take the vases and ritual implements from behind the Assembly Hall to replace the broken ones. Everything will be all right.'

As we once again settled down in the reception room, Sherlock Holmes lit his pipe and spoke to the Lama Yonten. 'Could you enlighten me as to the subject of the painted scroll? My knowledge of the symbolisms of your theology is very limited.'

'Well, Mr Holmes, let me first explain to you what *mandalas* are in general, before discussing that particular one.'

'Pray, if you would be so kind.'

The Lama took a pinch of snuff from a jade snuff bottle and delicately wiped his nose on a yellow silk handkerchief. After blinking once or twice he proceeded to give a detailed explanation on this unique cosmological and psychological aspect of Lamaist Buddhism. The Lama Yonten's explanation was very recondite, and certainly liable to be misunderstood by someone not familiar with the tenets of Lamaism. I have therefore taken the liberty of providing a simpler (and more scientific) version of his talk.

The *mandala* is a circular design of many colours and great geometrical complexity. Essentially it is a symbolic map of a world; the world of the human mind and consciousness. The various circles and squares composing it represent the various stages of psychic development on the long journey from ignorance to ultimate enlightenment. The final stage is arrived at in the centre of the circle, in which resides a Buddha or Bodhisattva who represents the final goal of the spiritual quest.

The particular *mandala* in question was of the Great Tantra of the Wheel of Time (Skt. *Sri Kala-chakra*). The most complex of such occult systems, this tantra was said to have been brought to Thibet from the mythical realm of 'Shambala of the North' in the eleventh century.

Shambala, in the Lamaist world system, is regarded as a wonderland similar to Thomas Moore's Utopia, the New Atlantis of Francis Bacon, or the City of the Sun of Campanella, where virtue and wisdom had created an ideal community. This fabled land is considered to be the source of all high occult sciences, far in advance of our world in scientific and technological knowledge. The sacred scriptures of Thibet prophesy that when mankind is finally enslaved by the forces of evil, the Lords of Shambala will, in the Water-Sheep Year of the Twenty-fourth cycle (2425), send forth their great army and destroy the evil forces. After that Buddhism will flourish anew and a Perfect Age will begin. The Lama Yonten of course believed implicitly in this charming myth, as did all other Thibetans and Mongols.

At the end of the Lama's story Sherlock Holmes stretched back on his couch and looked pensively at the ceiling. Then leaning forward again he asked, 'Did you not mention yesterday that the Grand Lama would be undertaking a retreat at a certain far-away temple?'

'Why, yes. At the Ice Temple of Shambala. He will be going there in a week's time.'

'Does this temple have any connection to "the Shambala of the North", that you were describing to us just now?'

'Most certainly, Mr Holmes. The temple, which is normally buried underneath the great ice, was the very spot where the messenger from Shambala originally expounded the secret science of the Wheel of Time to the first Grand Lama. Ever since then all Grand Lamas have been required by tradition to undertake a period of retreat there, prior to their enthronement. There, through prayer and meditation, they would establish cosmic communion with the occult forces of Shambala, which would then awaken their latent powers and wisdom, thus enabling them to rule this land wisely and protect it from the dark forces.'

'And the last three Grand Lamas — who died before their majority? They presumably did not get to go to this temple.'

'Alas, no. The schemings of evil councillors and Chinese pressure prevented them from doing so. It is now vital that nothing happens to prevent His Holiness from going to the Ice Temple and meditating there.'

'And after ...?'

'Our task will have been accomplished, Mr Holmes — yours and mine. It will then be out of our hands.'

The Lama Yonten peered rather short-sightedly towards the door, which was just behind my low couch.

'Is that you, Tsering?'

'Yes, Honourable Uncle.'

'Come in. Come in and sit down.'

I turned around to see Tsering standing by the door. So, he was the Lama Yonten's nephew. That explained the deference with which the governor of Tholing had treated him. It was prudent of the Lama to assign the care of his two potentially compromising foreign guests to someone close to him, in blood as well as trust. Tsering sat on a low divan next to the Lama and gratefully gulped down a bowl of hot butter tea served to him by a monk servitor.

'Well?' said Holmes, as Tsering put down his tea cup.

'It was no problem following them, Sir.' said Tsering, wiping his mouth with the back of his hand. 'And we were careful not to let ourselves be seen, as you instructed. We followed them out to the city, where they took the Lingkor road,[1] south of the Iron

---

1. The Tibetan *via sacra* circling the holy city. The street circling the main cathedral, the Jokang, is shorter though equally holy, and is known as the Barkor.

Hill. They carried on in an easterly direction, sticking all the while to the back streets till they came near the Kashgar caravanserai, which they skirted, and finally they entered the compound of the *yamen*, the Chinese legation.'

'Are you sure?' asked the Lama Yonten anxiously.

'I am certain. The main gate of the legation walls was open and the Amban himself with servants and guards was waiting. All of them bowed low as the palanquin went through the gates.'

'Then it is him!' the Lama Yonten went white as a sheet. His hands trembled.

'Who?' asked Holmes.

'The mysterious guest that arrived at the Chinese legation, the person within the palanquin who caused swords to fly, the power to whom even the Amban must bow. It is him. The Dark One!'

'The Dark One?' repeated Holmes rather incredulously, arching an eyebrow,

'Yes. He has returned from the outer darkness to destroy our master again as he swore to do eighteen years ago.'

'Reverend Sir,' said Holmes bemusedly, 'so far I have confined the limits of my investigation to affairs of this world. As I had occasion to remark before, the supernatural is definitely outside my sphere of competence.'

'Oh no, Mr Holmes. The Dark One is a living person, I assure you. He acquired the name because he turned away from the light of the Noble Doctrine and perverted sacred knowledge for the fulfilment of his greed and ambition. It is a black and sinister tale, but it is important that you hear it all — from the beginning.

'The College of Occult Sciences in Lhassa is the highest institution of occult knowledge and practice that exists in Thibet. Few but the best of scholars from the great monastic universities are admitted; and that too only after a rigorous and thorough investigation of each candidate. Every twelve years, when the calendar of the twelve beasts makes a full round, the college holds a great examination. In the year of the Water Monkey (1873), the College produced two of the greatest adepts of the occult sciences that the country had beheld for more than a century — ever since the Laughing Yogi of the Grey Vulture Peak covered the barley fields of Tsetang with his hand and saved them from a hailstorm.

'Great honours were bestowed upon them. The Grand Lama himself — the twelfth sacred body — attended their final examinations and afterwards invested upon them (with his own blessed hands) their white cloaks of occult mastery. Their fame spread beyond the frontiers of the Land of the Great Snows, even to the court of the Emperor of China; and they were invited to Pekin to hold services for the well-being of the Emperor and his subjects, and the protection of his hills and streams.

'It was there, Mr Holmes, that certain demonic ministers of the Emperor lured one of them into the ways of evil. With great cunning they filled his mind with every kind of filth and abomination — and even with the unthinkable ambition to take the Grand Lama's throne and rule Thibet. On returning to Lhassa both received suitable appointments at the Grand Lama's court. With the cunning of a serpent, the Dark One managed to conceal his foul intentions from nearly everybody, but inadvertently aroused some slight suspicions in the mind of his colleague, the Gangsar *trulku*, the former abbot of a small monastery in southern Thibet. This astute lama had noticed some slight but disquieting changes in the Dark One's behaviour in China.

'On the eve of the Great New Year's Festival, when everyone was busy preparing for the coming ceremonies, Gangsar *trulku* saw the Dark One enter the Grand Lama's chapel — the very one the assassin entered tonight — and strike His Holiness with a sword. The loyal *trulku* rushed in to save his master, but he was too late. In his brave struggle with the Dark One, he lost his life. Unfortunately for this incarnation of evil, the Grand Master of the College of Occult Sciences appeared upon the scene. Before the Dark One could strike again, the Grand Master projected a surge of mental energy which nearly destroyed him. His mind was partially shattered, and he lost his memory and most of his former powers. He was incarcerated in one of the deepest dungeons in the Potala. The Amban, however, on instructions from the Imperial court in Pekin, managed, through extensive bribery and coercion, to get him secretly released from his prison, and smuggled out of the country to China. Since then, we know not what became of him, for distance weakens telepathic waves. It is possible that he has recovered some of his old powers and put up some kind of mental screen.'

'How can you be sure that it is him?'

'I cannot, Mr Holmes — not absolutely, anyway. But I can feel his presence in my bones. Your description of the way in which the swords flew sounds very much like his handiwork.'

'In what way?'

'The Gangsar *trulku* was impaled from behind by a flying sword as he grappled with the Dark One.'

Although I had witnessed something of the sort tonight, my scientific training rebelled against accepting such superstitious magic without at least adducing some natural causes for the event. 'Cold steel should not levitate of its own volition, Sir,' I protested. 'There must be some scientific explanation for such unusual aviational phenomena.'

'The power of the human mind is limitless, Babuji,' the Lama Yonten attempted to explain. 'The only barriers that prevent its fulfilment are our own ignorance and sloth. Here in Thibet, through meditation and various yogic practices, adepts have trained the mind to concentrate, harnessing all its limitless potential to slay the demon of the ego, the source of all our miseries and sorrows.'

'... and to make swords fly through the air as well,' said Holmes dryly.

'The power of the mind is pure energy and thus essentially neutral — neither good nor bad. Therefore, before we permit any novice to undertake such occult training, we instil in him, through study and reflection, a true altruistic motive in his quest for such powers. Only rarely has this motivational training ever failed.'

'But it did in the case of the Dark One,' said Holmes.

'Unfortunately, yes.'

Sherlock Holmes drew on his pipe and gazed reflectively into the distance for a minute or two, before turning to us again. 'If we are to suppose that our mysterious friend in the palanquin tonight is the same "Dark One" who murdered the twelfth Grand Lama, then the theft of the painted scroll begins to take on a more sinister significance.' Holmes looked at the Lama Yonten gravely. 'You must be wrong, Reverend Sir. There must be something unusual about that particular scroll.'

'Maybe the painting was stolen in order to somehow disrupt the Grand Lama's proposed retreat at the temple,' said I venturing a new hypothesis. 'Does he, perchance, need the *mandala* painting for his meditations there?'

'Yes, he does, Babuji.' the Lama Yonten answered. 'But it is not necessary for it to be the same one. Any faithful copy of it will do. The *mandala* simply serves as a plan for the meditator to guide his psychic energies in the correct channels during his meditations. Why, at the Ice Temple itself there is a large stone *mandala* — a three dimensional one — of the tantra of the Wheel of Time. That would be more than sufficient for His Holiness's visualisation practices.'

'Then it only stands to reason that there must be something very special about the one that was stolen tonight.' said Sherlock Holmes testily.

'There is, Sir.'

The young lad whom we had observed the previous day playing with the animals in the menagerie now stood small and alone in the corridor. He was wrapped in a thick maroon cloak like the one Lama Yonten had on. The Lama Yonten and Tsering rose hastily to their feet. Mr Holmes and I followed suit.

'Your Holiness, you should be in bed,' said the Lama Yonten anxiously.

'But how can I sleep with so much going on? Anyway I wanted to see the foreigners.' He came over and stared at us with much curiosity, but also friendliness.

'You are from the Noble Land (Arya-varta or India)?' he enquired of me politely in a high boyish voice.

'Yes, Your Holiness. I come from the province of Vangala (Bengal) where the great sage Atisha[2] was born.'

'I hope one day to make a pilgrimage to all the holy places in the Noble Land — when all the present problems are settled.' He then turned to Sherlock Holmes and bowed his head once. 'I wish to thank you, Honourable Sir, for saving my life tonight. The Lama Yonten told me earlier that were it not for your vigilance and courage an assassin might possibly have ... harmed me.' He appeared a little troubled at this realisation, but then his boyish nature reasserted itself and he was all curiosity and questions again.

'But you do not look like a foreigner.'

'I am supposed to be in disguise as a Ladakhi,' said Holmes with a smile.

'You had better pretend to be half Kazakh then. That would explain the pale cast of your eyes.'

'Your Holiness is very observant,' said Holmes. 'Maybe that is why you saw something special about that stolen *thangka.*'

---

2. Atisha (Skt. Dipankarajnana., Tib. Jowo-je) 982–1055, was a great Buddhist teacher from Bengal who came to Tibet in the eleventh century to revive a Buddhism that had been weakened and corrupted after the break up of the Tibetan Empire.

'It has been hanging in the chapel ever since I can remember, and I never took any particular notice of it. But one day a monkey from the garden managed to enter the chapel and, besides breaking a few things, knocked the painting off the wall. After I had chased the animal out, I was picking up the scroll to restore it to its hook when I noticed some writing on the back.'

'Writing?' enquired Holmes, a hint of excitement in his voice. 'What exactly was on it?'

'Well, there were a few lines explaining that the *thangka* had been commissioned by my first body after his return from the realm of Shambala of the North. That's about all, I think. No. Wait a minute, there were also some strange verses, penned by the First Body himself.'

'Can you remember them?'

'No. I only glanced at them that once. They were very puzzling and I could not understand them. That is all I remember.' The lad must have realised how disappointed we were with his answer, for he looked up at Holmes anxiously. 'Is it very important? I do wish I could remember. I wish I could help.'

'Your Holiness must not worry,' said Holmes kindly. 'You have helped enough by letting us know of the existence of the verses.'

'Yes, and Mr Holmes will confound our enemies with his powers, my Lord.' the Lama Yonten tried to cheer up the crest-fallen boy. 'Now you must rest. The Venerable Physician Abbot has expressly instructed that you must have a great deal of rest if you are to fully recover from your illness.' The Lama Yonten looked up at the tall bearded monk who was standing at the doorway. 'Come, the Lord Chamberlain is waiting.'

We all bowed as the young Grand Lama bade us a polite fare-well and left the room with his chamberlain. I could not but help reflect on how, in spite of his illness, he was such a bright, intelligent boy, unspoiled by the loftiness of the unique position, gentle and courteous in spite of the treachery and violence surrounding him.

It saddened and frightened me to think what he might have to face very soon. Sherlock Holmes too seemed to share my sombre reflections, for he gazed silently ahead, grim-faced and pensive, his heavy drooping eyelids forming deep shadows under his eyes. The ticking of the ormolu clock filled the silent room.

'We must get it back!' cried Sherlock Holmes suddenly, smacking his fist into the palm of his hand.

'What?' I said, surprised.

'You mean the *thangka,* Mr Holmes?' asked the Lama Yonten.

'Yes. I am convinced that it is the loose thread that will unravel the mystery.'

'But, Sir, everything about this case is so bizarre and complicated.' said I.

'As a rule,' said Holmes 'the more bizarre a thing is the less mysterious it proves to be. It is your commonplace, featureless crimes which are really puzzling, just as a commonplace face is the most difficult to remember or identify.'

'But how can the scroll be the solution to this confusing business?'

'It is of the highest importance in the art of detection to be able to recognise, out of a number of facts, which are incidental and which are vital. Otherwise your energy and attention will be dissipated instead of concentrated. Now, if we overlook, for the moment, all the strange occurrences of the night, even the unfortunate death of our monk guard, what we have remaining is the theft of the painted scroll. That is the simple cause on which everything else, however bizarre, devolves.'

'But how can you get it back?'

'Simple. I mean to burgle the Chinese legation,' replied Holmes calmly. I was rather startled by the answer, though awed by the infinite resourcefulness and daring of my companion.

'But you can't do that.' the Lama Yonten wailed.

'I don't see why not. View the matter fairly. They burgled the

Grand Lama's chapel, so it seems only fitting and proper that we return the compliment.'

'Ah! A *quid pro quo*, Mr Holmes.' said I.

'Exactly.'

'There's bound to be an embarrassing diplomatic incident if you are caught,' the Lama said nervously.

'Well, we cannot discount that possibility entirely, can we now? But look at it this way. The only means we have of discovering our enemy's schemes is through that *thangka.* So either we avoid any incidents and wait for them to strike, or we take a risk and possibly confound their knavish tricks.'

'When you put it that way, I don't see what else we can do,' said the Lama Yonten glumly.

'Excellent!' cried Holmes, rubbing his hands together. 'Now let us work out the actual execution of our enterprise. Your mention of a diplomatic incident has given me a little inspiration. What if news of tonight's happenings were to somehow become known to the public?'

'There would be massive riots in front of the Chinese legation.' cried the Lama, throwing up his hands in horror.

'Exactly. Which would cause all the guards and other people there to rush to the front wall of the legation to defend it.'

'... we could then effect surreptitious entry through the rear.' said I excitedly. 'A most inspired *ruse de guerre,* Sir.'

''pon my word, Hurree,' said Holmes. 'You're getting to be as good a mind-reader as myself. But you have made one little error in your assessment. You are not going with me.'

'But Sir,' I protested, 'surely you will require assistance.'

'Two arrows in the quiver are better than one,' said Tsering gravely, 'and three better still.'

'No, Tsering.' said Sherlock Holmes firmly. 'Your task will be to ensure that a riot does take place before the legation gate, at the exact time I require it.'

'But the crowd may get out of hand,' the Lama Yonten worriedly fingered his beads.

'Quite so,' said Holmes suavely. 'That is why Tsering will be there. He will see to it that the mob, though suitably noisy and demonstrative, does not actually storm the legation or set fire to it.'

'That would be enough for the Emperor to send an army into Thibet,' muttered the Lama gloomily.

'Have a number of palace guards in mufti,' Holmes continued with his instructions to Tsering, ignoring the Lama Yonten's jeremiads, 'and post them in front of the crowd. Give them firm instructions to keep the mob from getting out of control.'

'Well, I think I could manage that, Sir,' said Tsering confidently. 'When do you want the riot to take place?'

'Tomorrow would be as good a day as any. I would need the cover of darkness, so it has to be in the evening. Now let me see ...' he turned to the Lama Yonten, '... by the way, did you not mention yesterday that you had a spy in the Chinese legation, posing as a servant?'

'Yes?'

'Would it be possible for you to summon him here tomorrow? I would require some information on the layout of the legation compound, and the exact whereabouts of the Dark One's suite.'

'I could have him here around noon tomorrow. Earlier? ... No. I don't think it would be possible.'

'Since daylight lasts till about six o'clock these days, I think it would be fine for the riot to take place after that. I will make my entry when the demonstration is well under way.'

'Right, Mr Holmes.' said Tsering, getting up from the divan. 'I'll move along to the city and spread the word at the *chang* taverns there. Will you be coming back to the city too?'

'I think it would be prudent if Mr Holmes and his companion remained within the walls of the Jewel Park,' said the Lama, 'now that they have been seen by the Dark One. Send someone to fetch their things from the city.'

A little while later Mr Holmes and I were shown into a well-appointed suite of rooms to the east of the main palace. It was three o'clock in the morning when we finally settled down but Mr Holmes did not make any preparations to go to bed. Instead he poured himself a measure of whisky from his silver travel flask, and filled his pipe from his grey leather pouch. He turned to look at me.

'You are not going to bed, Hurree?'

'No, Mr Holmes,' I replied in an injured tone. 'I hope I am not being tedious, but I would like to enquire if you have any cause to find my services unsatisfactory.'

'Of course not, Hurree. *Au contraire* ...'

'Then why the deuce an' all, Sir, do you not wish me to accompany you on your venture tomorrow?'

'My dear fellow. It will be extremely dangerous.'

'Dangerous, Mr Holmes?' said I indignantly. 'I have been in mortal peril since I first followed you off that ship: at the Taj Mahal Hotel with that beastly insect; on the train with those beastly Thugs; and on this entire journey with those beastly bandits and what not. What does some more danger matter to me now at this stage of the game?'

'You may have a point there.'

'And I really could be of invaluable assistance, Sir,' said I quickly, exploiting this first breach in Mr Holmes's resolution. 'I have some experiences of unlawful ingress into well-guarded buildings for the purloining of confidential papers.'

'Well, Hurree,' said Sherlock Holmes with a shrug, 'seeing that we've been together so far on this long journey, it would perhaps be amusing — if the worst came to the worst — having to continue it together in the hereafter.'

19

The Dark One

'It's nearly six o'clock,' I whispered, consulting my silver turnip watch. 'Why hasn't the bally crowd turned up yet?'

'One really cannot be expected to time a public riot as finely as a dinner appointment,' said Holmes, a trifle sardonically. He was leaning back comfortably on a pile of grain sacks in the corner of the room, smoking his pipe. 'Tsering is a reliable fellow. Give him a little time. He will come.'

I looked out of the small, rough window. Across the narrow street I could see the shadowy walls of the Imperial Chinese legation looming in the twilight. Mr Holmes and I were in a small store room at the back of an inn by the Kashgar serai, in the southern part of Lhassa, where the camel caravans from Turkestan — the beasts being of the shaggy, two humped species, *Camelus bactrianus* — ended their journey. Kintup had managed to secure this very convenient accommodation, just a stone's throw from the rear of the Chinese legation. The Tungan innkeeper had been informed that Mr Holmes and I were Ladakhi merchants waiting for a caravan to Yarkand.

Though the room was really not of a habitable standard — in fact it was filthy, verminous, and offensive to the olfactory organ — it was an ideal starting point for our venture.

But this stroke of luck had been offset by the bad news that the Lama Yonten's agent was unable to come and brief us on the layout of the legation grounds. The duties of the servants had increased two-fold with the arrival of the Dark One, and the agent had feared that his absence would be noticed. Still, he had agreed to meet us at the rear outer-wall of the legation as soon as the demonstration started, and lead us in through the trade entrance, which was usually securely barred and bolted.

And so we waited. I sat back, and watched the faint glow from Mr Holmes's pipe across the darkness of the room. As the darkness increased, this solitary light appeared to be like a faint star, alone in the vast emptiness of infinite space.

Suddenly, for no obvious reason, I felt very much alone and very afraid. And then that part of me, the rational, prudent part, that always pleaded for peace, stability and good sense (so far suppressed by the other part of me, the one that invariably got me into dam'-tight places) now rushed to the fore.

What in the name of Herbert Spencer was I, a respectable scientific man doing, embarking on this mad criminal venture — stepping into the veritable 'Jaws of Death' as it were, when I had only just managed to squeak out of them the last time I was here in Thibet? Of course, I sympathised tremendously with the plight of the Grand Lama, but when all's said and done, Imperial China is Imperial China; and one did not go around challenging a sinister and vindictive institution like that with impunity — especially when it was served by frightening blighters who impaled good men on levitating cutlery with mere flicks of the finger. And anyway, how could I, a lowly subordinate in a minor department of the GOI, be expected to help the bally Thibetans when even Sherlock Holmes, the world's greatest detective, the foremost upholder of justice, had just yesterday afternoon pleaded to be relieved of the task. Well he had, hadn't he? Hold on a minute though ... then why the deuce an' all did he change his mind about helping to protect the Grand Lama? And how the Dickens had he known that the Grand Lama would be needing help last night — at the very precise moment he needed it too. Ooooh, Shaitan!

For a few minutes I was rather overwhelmed by the ramifications of my questions. But then I realised that I was absolutely incapable of answering any of them. So I proceeded to ask him, *ex tacito,* of course. He did not reply immediately, but drew long on his pipe, which burned brightly. By its glow I saw a shadowy face that was much troubled.

'You would not call me an irrational man, would you, Hurree?'

'Of course, not, Sir. If I may say so you are the most rational, most scientific man I have ever had the privilege of meeting.'

'Yet reason or science had nothing to do with what I did last night.'

'Please?'

'I just *knew.* One moment I was smoking my last pipe for the night and thinking about our meeting with the Lama Yonten, and the next moment I knew for certain that a dangerous assassin was going to enter the Grand Lama's Summer Palace.'

'Like a premonition, Sir?'

'There was nothing vague about it. The singular thing was the absolute assurance I felt about this startling revelation. Yet there was no way to explain it in logical terms. It was a most peculiar experience.'

'Subsequent events proved you right, Mr Holmes.'

'Yes, and that makes it all the more disturbing.'

'But it did make you change your mind about helping the Grand Lama?'

'Well, it hurts my pride to leave unresolved bits of business lying around, Hurree. It is a petty feeling no doubt, but it hurts my pride. Hulloa! Hulloa! What's that?'

He got up from the sack of grain and quickly went over to the window. From the distance the rumbling sound of many people shouting was now audible.

'From what I can hear, Tsering seems to have a good-sized mob there. Is the dark lantern shielded?'

'Yes, Mr Holmes.'

'Good. Well, Hurree, before we start, I just want to say that I am very glad of your company tonight. Some situations in life are best faced with a true friend by your side.'

I was most touched by Mr Holmes's expression of affection and trust.

For a moment he gripped my right hand firmly in his. He then turned quickly and walked out of the room. I followed suit.

The main hall-cum-eating room of the inn was empty, and so was the kitchen. Everybody had gone out into the street to see what the commotion — which was getting louder and more threatening — was all about. From the black, grimy kitchen we stepped through a back door and into the alley at the back of the Chinese legation. A strong odour of camel dung and urine wafted through to us from the main serai grounds. At the east end of the alley which joined the Saddle-maker's Street, we could see a large boisterous procession of Thibetans carrying flaming torches and yelling threats and abuse. They poured past the alley to the front of the Chinese legation. Mr Holmes and I pressed ourselves against the back wall, taking advantage of the shadows, till the crowd had moved past. As the last of the Thibetans disappeared, Mr Holmes and I sidled by the wall to the other end of the alley and looked around. There was no sign of our contact. We waited.

By the sound of it the demonstration was hotting up. The crowd was lustily shouting fierce slogans denouncing the outrages perpetrated by the dog of an Amban. They sounded jolly obstreperous though, and what with their flaming torches and all, I hoped that Tsering would be able to keep control of the situation. Suddenly Mr Holmes stiffened. 'Don't make a sound,' he whispered. 'There's someone by the corner there. It could be our man.'

For the life of me I could not see anyone in that gloom, but as I had occasion to observe before, Mr Holmes had the most extraordinary powers of nocturnal vision. I tiptoed behind him as he moved swiftly and silently forward. An anxious whisper stopped us dead in our tracks. 'Here. Come this way,' a dark figure stepped forward out of the shadow of the wall and beckoned urgently to us.

As we got there I noticed a low door built into the legation wall. It was open. By it stood a small chap in dark-blue cotton suit of Chinese design and a black skull cap. He looked nervously around him like a scared rabbit, his prominent buck teeth emphasising the resemblance. 'Are you from the Lama Yonten?' he uttered in a croaking whisper.

'Yes.'

'Come in this way, quickly. I must close the door before someone notices.'

We entered a large courtyard filled with leather-covered chests, like the ones used to transport brick tea from China to Thibet. Probably the Amban supplemented his salary by trading in brick tea, which the Thibetans regarded as a delicacy. By the courtyard were some houses and behind them the main legation building, which was two stories high. Dark outlines of armed soldiers could be seen moving about on the roof of this building and on the outer wall in the front. Our diminutive guide crouched behind a pile of chests and signalled us to do the same.

'Now listen carefully. I have very little time. All the Amban's soldiers are at the front to prevent the mob from breaking down the gates. Everyone else has gone to the main legation building as it is the most defensible.'

'Where are the quarters occupied by the Amban's special guest? The one that arrived a few weeks ago.'

'Merciful Kuan-yin,' the man whispered very agitatedly. 'Keep away from him.'

'Where are they?' insisted Sherlock Holmes firmly, holding the man tightly by the shoulders.

'It's that large house … there on the left … the one nearest the wall. But I have to go now, the other servants might notice my absence.'

'You have been of great help,' said Holmes, releasing the timid fellow.

'Take care. And don't go anywhere near *him*,' he croaked, before scurrying off across the courtyard and vanishing into a patch of shadows between some houses.

I was rather shaken, I admit, by his dire warnings, and conspicuous display of fear. But Mr Holmes seemed totally unaffected by any such terrors. Silently but surely he made directly for the house that had been pointed out as the Dark One's quarters. I followed close at his heels. The house seemed to be unoccupied, for there were no lights shining from the windows, and no sounds of any kind either. As soon as we got to the house, Mr Holmes set about trying to open a window. With the aid of a springy dagger (which he had borrowed from Kintup) and a bit of stiff wire, he quickly managed to undo a catch and ease open a frame. He performed the task with a practised dexterity that in anyone else would be sufficient cause for grave suspicions. Once inside the room he pulled the heavy wool curtain over the window.

'Let's have some light then, Hurree.'

I slid open the shield of the lantern. We were in a small antechamber, empty save for a few small chairs around the sides. One door led through a short corridor to the front door. I pushed open the other to discover a large and opulent study. The room was lit by two oil lampions of Imperial Dragon design; one hung on brass chains from the ceiling, while the other rested on a small side-table. Thick damask curtains prevented the light from spilling through the windows. The study was furnished in a peculiar mixture of Oriental and European styles. The walls were covered with expensive brocade drapes on which hung heavy giltframed portraits of Manchu dignitaries in court dress. The cupboards, bookshelves, chairs and tables were made of black ebony of exquisite workmanship. The finest piece was a large desk with legs shaped like lion's paws, with a set of drawers fitted with jade knobs.

'I don't like it,' Holmes whispered, putting his lips near my ear. 'Something's not quite right here. Anyhow, we have no time to lose. Let's start with that.' He pointed to the desk.

We had just opened the third drawer when I felt a slight draft against my back, and turned around. Framed in the faint light at the doorway was the shadow of a crooked man, holding something in his hand.

'Perhaps this is what you are looking for,' he said in a low hiss that I felt I had heard somewhere before. Two Chinese soldiers in black uniforms and turbans emerged from behind him and stepped into the room, their rifles poised for action. The crooked man shuffled into the room dragging his right leg. The light revealed a cadaverous-looking blighter with a bent, broken body and a lame right leg, somewhat incongruously dressed in the rich silk robes of a high mandarin. His face was badly distorted, especially the mouth, from which a little trickle of saliva dripped. His complexion was a sickly white, and his eyes, deep within their hollow sockets, seemed to burn with a passionate light. But the most remarkable thing about him was the great bulge of his forehead, which moved and twitched on the occasions when he seemed to feel some great emotion.

'Moriarty!' cried Holmes.

My skin went cold at the name.

'Yes, it is I, Holmes.' His lips twisted in an ugly smirk. 'Come now, why do you not greet your old adversary more warmly. Are you so surprised to see him alive?'

Shocked as he must have been by the unexpected resurrection of his nemesis, Sherlock Holmes reacted with great composure.

'I must confess to just that,' admitted Holmes coolly. 'All the same, if you don't mind my saying so, you have not been wonderfully improved by your recent experiences.'

'Aaah … you mock me, Holmes. But you will pay … It was a wicked, cruel thing to throw me over the precipice … wicked! But did you know the great service you performed for me that day? You are puzzled? You think I am babbling … then listen. As I fell into space … and looked down on death, my memories suddenly came back to me. I remembered my true self … and I remembered my power … yes … my great powers. It was almost too late. I hit the side of a rock-face … and smashed my hip … my leg … my face … but then … aaaah … my power surged through me. So now I live … broken and in pain … but I live. You Holmes …'

'… will, no doubt, go the way of all flesh,' said my friend philosophically, moving a step forward. Immediately both the guards raised their weapons.

'No, no, Holmes. You will stay very still. You have so cleverly managed to give Colonel Moran the slip on every previous occasion. But this time, since you are dealing with me, his master, I must insist on a very different conclusion. So, both of you, take out your weapons … slowly. Put them on the ground … now move slowly to the other side of the room. Very good. Chen Yi, pick up the guns.'

While one guard trained his weapon on us the other stepped forward and picked up our pistols and stuck them in his belt. Moriarty hobbled painfully across the room to the ebony desk, and seated himself behind it. He then tossed the scroll he was carrying onto the desk.

'So you seek the Great *Mandala*. Much good will it do you, even if you have it. Fool. What can you know of its great secret, when you never even knew mine. You thought I was a genius when actually I was a man whose mind was shattered ... memories lost and mental powers reduced to only the intellectual functions. But just that paltry fraction of my power — and a little help from my Chinese friends, who helped to establish me in Europe to avenge themselves against the nations that had humiliated China — was sufficient to create the greatest criminal empire in the world. What can you do against me now? Now that my powers have been restored to me.'

He paused to see the effect of his speech on Sherlock Holmes, who, unperturbed as ever, looked straight back at him with calm dignity.

'You do not believe me? Maybe a demonstration would be in order. I owe you that, at least. You threw me into that chasm ... and, well, I am a man who believes in returning favours.'

He raised his hands, his fingers forming strange *mudras* or occult gestures. It may have been my overwrought imagination but I distinctively felt some energy move across the room. The lamps flickered, and I felt a strange sensation in the pit of my belly, as if a hand had grabbed me there. The two soldiers may have felt something too, for I clearly heard both of them suck in their breath in audible gasps.

The effect on Mr Holmes was alarming. His eyes grew wide with terror. His mouth opened to emit a sharp scream, which ended in a low, frantic gurgle. His body swayed forward, his hands stretched out, flailing wildly, as if he was balancing for dear life on the edge of something terrifying. I was certain that he was being subjected to some kind of powerful mesmeric force that actually made him see and experience falling over a precipice. I am not inexperienced with this strange force, having once been unhappily subjected to a séance by Lurgan[1], back in Simla — but I need not go into that now. But the suddenness and overwhelming force of this present phenomenon was beyond the bounds of anything imaginable. Slowly Mr Holmes seemed to lose his balance, and with a great cry fell forward onto the floor. In spite of the armed guards, who had their weapons trained on me, I rushed forward to assist my stricken friend.

Just at that moment the sharp report of rifle-fire broke into the room. What in heaven's name was going on out there? Had the Chinese soldiers commenced firing on the mob? Professor Moriarty dropped his hands and turned his head in the direction of the fusillade. He barked an order to a guard. 'You! Go to the front quickly and ask His Excellency the Amban what is going on. Report back immediately.'

I was tending to Mr Holmes and trying desperately to resuscitate him. I was very gratified to note that he was not deceased or even critically incapacitated. He was breathing heavily, gasping sometimes, but, feeling my hands on his shoulder, he opened his eyes. For just a brief moment he appeared somewhat bewildered — a state I had never seen him in before — but his indomitable strength of character quickly reasserted itself and his eyes resumed their normal alert and intelligent quality. I helped him to a chair.

'You have recovered, Holmes?' gloated Moriarty. 'Good. Very good. Pathetic as your mental powers are when compared to mine, they never fail to astonish me. Any other man would be a gibbering wreck by now. But I should not have expected anything less from the great Sherlock Holmes.'

---

1. Lurgan's power of mesmerism is described by Kipling in *Kim*. Lurgan hypnotises the eponymous hero into seeing a shattered water jug becoming whole again.

A few more bursts of gunfire echoed outside. Moriarty drew aside the curtain from the window beside him and peered out.

'Don't expect your dirty Thibetan friends to save you,' he said, turning around and facing us again. 'A few more volleys from the guard's rifles and they will all take to their heels. "A whiff of grapeshot" Eh! … "A whiff of grapeshot". Bonaparte knew how to deal with rabble.' The Professor bent forward over the desk and glared at Holmes with manic eyes. '… and he knew power; crude as his notions of it may have been, he knew how it had to be wielded — with force and ruthlessness!'

'Brag and Bounce,' I thought to myself. The blighter's conceit was really insufferable. I could not help but offer a refutation, though I regretted it the moment I did.

'Yet, if I may be permitted a historical retrospective,' said I, delicately, 'the Corsican brute ended his life as a wretched prisoner of His Sovereign Majesty, King George the Third.'

'Yes, fool,' he turned to me with a snarl. 'He failed because his powers were only those of the intellect, of military stratagems and political plots. Great as such an intelligence may seem to a dolt like you, they are as nought against the power of the primordial mind. But perhaps my demonstration on Holmes did not convince you. Perhaps you would like one yourself?'

Before I could offer a polite refusal he held up his right hand and pinched his index finger and thumb together. Although I was about ten feet away from that dreadful man, I distinctly felt something tweaking my nose — and hard! I nearly jumped out of my bally skin.

'Does this quite convince you now, my fat Hindu friend? Or perhaps a little more pressure would reinforce the salutary effect of this lesson.'

'Yeow! Ow! Ow!' I could not but help yell out. 'Eduff! I dink I am abdolutely codvinced. Yeow!'

He did not release my nose immediately, dam' his eyes, but

held on even more firmly for a few moments more, before finally letting go after a last savage tweak.

'Yeow!'

While I rubbed my poor nose, Moriarty leaned back on his chair and resumed his boasting speech.

'Awesome as the force I have just demonstrated may seem to you, it is nevertheless subject to the laws of nature and the cosmos, and thus inherently limited. Others, though only a few, possess such powers as mine. But there is a way to increase its strength — a hundred fold, a thousand fold — and I have, at long last, found the way.'

He raised a finger. As if at a command the scroll on the desk unrolled itself and lay flat on the surface.

'And this will lead me to it.' He pointed to the circular geometrical painting, its colours gleaming like living rainbows under his deathly white finger. 'And only I will be the master of it. This time none of those weak-minded lamas with their tiresome pieties will be permitted to come between me and my destiny.'

As Moriarty ended his mad diatribe, the yelling of the mob outside became distinctively louder; suddenly the window on his side, behind the guard, exploded, as a rock smashed through it and flew into the room. By Jove! The demonstrators were shying missiles in retaliation to the shooting. The guard turned around in surprise.

Mr Holmes did not hesitate to seize this opportune moment. He leaped forward and fisted the cad soundly on the side of his head. It was a well-executed and powerful blow — obviously Sherlock Holmes was fully versed in the manly art of pugilism — for the guard was effectively incapacitated by that single cuff.

The speed of my own reflexes were not very much behind those of Mr Holmes. My many experiences in various ticklish situations had honed my reactions to a fine edge; and anyhow, fear is always a powerful goad to speedy action. Such is the tremendous galvanic force of the trained human reflex, that before I had even conceived a thought of assailing my foes, my fingers were already curling around the base of the shining lampion on the small table by my side. And before Moriarty could have any idea of what I was up to, I had picked it up and hurled it straight at him.

Unfortunately, I missed. I was a good three feet off the mark. The lamp flew past the villain and struck the wall behind, and fell broken on the floor. He didn't even flinch, just looked directly at me with those terrifying eyes. I was, I will admit, a trifle abashed by this turn of events.

'I should opine that the damaged article was not particularly valuable …' I said, rather sheepishly.

'Silence, fool!' he snarled, the veins on his bulging forehead twisting and jerking in an appalling fashion. 'Did you think to save your miserable skin by such a pitiful trick?'

He raised his hands as if to deliver another one of his horrible spells, while I stood there helpless as a frog before a cobra. But then I noticed a flickering glow behind him, and suddenly the Professor was jumping about, screaming like a lunatic. The glow became brighter to reveal the flames devouring the edge of his robe and the carpeted floor, where the oil from the broken lamp had spilled and ignited.

'But quick man,' Holmes shouted. 'Run!'

I did not hesitate but made straight for the door, followed by Sherlock Holmes. I came to the ante-chamber and would have carried on running through the front door — and into goodness knows what other dangers — but was opportunely seized by the shoulders by Mr Holmes's strong hand and propelled to the window by which we had earlier effected ingress, and quickly bundled out through it. Without pausing for thought or circumspection, I sped on through the courtyard, once colliding with and overturning a pile of boxes, till I reached the back wall, where I frantically searched for the small door.

'Here, Hurree,' whispered Holmes, opening the small barred door. Oh, blessed relief.

We got to the other side with no further problems. We ran through the alleyway and up to the front of the inn where Kintup was waiting for us with our ponies. We rode swiftly away from that awful place, the drumming of our horses' hooves drowning the dying clamour of the mob.

20

To the Trans-Himalayas

A hot, satisfying repast of yak-tail soup and *momos* awaited us on our return to the Jewel Park. I gratefully tucked in. Food has always been a great solace to me in moments of difficulties and upset nerves, but Sherlock Holmes waved away the steaming dishes. It was one of his peculiarities that in his more intense moments he would permit himself no food — sometimes even starving himself for days during an investigation.[1]

'At present I cannot spare energy and nerve for digestion,' he said to the Lama Yonten, who seemed to understand and approve of Mr Holmes's abstinence, for he immediately ordered the waiters not to bother him further. Certain Buddhist and Hindu teachings consider the custom of fasting to be a great spur to the intellect. Mr Holmes though, was the first instance I had come across of a European practising this.

---

1. Watson also mentions this habit of Holmes. See *The Mazarin Stone.*

Instead he drew a cigarette from his case and, lighting it, related to the anxious Lama our adventures of the evening. The Lama Yonten was, predictably, horrified with the way everything had gone wrong, and how we had only managed to escape from the clutches of the Dark One by the skin of our teeth.

'Merciful Tara. This is terrible. It was unforgivable of me to allow you to put your lives at such risk.'

'You must not upset yourself over it, Reverend Sir,' said Holmes reassuringly. 'When all's said and done, we did manage to come out of it without too much damage.'

'Not quite, Mr Holmes. I just received word from Tsering that two men were wounded by the firing from the Chinese legation — though not mortally so — thanks be to the Buddha. But far more serious is the matter of your exposure to the Dark One, or Moriarty, as you know him. The Amban is bound to lodge a serious complaint to the Regent about unauthorised foreigners in the city.'

'With our *locus standi* in this country fast becoming a questionable one,' said Holmes, 'it is vital that we act swiftly.'

'The Regent will also lose no time in pressing charges of treason against me,' said the Lama Yonten mournfully. The Lama's melancholia was infectious and even dampened somewhat the tremendous *joie de vivre* I was experiencing from having survived that terrifying encounter with Moriarty. The Lama's low spirits also reminded me of the original purpose of our mission — and its failure.

'Oh! Dash it all!' I exclaimed, disgusted with myself. 'After all the trepidation and bother, and I did not even think to appropriate the bally scroll before fleeing the scene.'

'Don't be too hard on yourself, old fellow,' said Holmes, 'I nearly forgot too, in all that excitement.'

'You have it!' I cried with joy.

He pulled out the scroll from the pouch of his heavy robe. 'Yes. We have not yet met our Waterloo, Hurree — if I may resume

Moriarty's Napoleonic analogy — but this is our Marengo, for it began in defeat and ended in victory.'

He pushed the empty dishes on the table to one side, and, unrolling the scroll carefully, laid it flat on the surface of the table. He then methodically examined it with his magnifying lens.

The painting, on sized cotton, was about one and a half feet by two, but its rich brocade border brought it up to the measurements that Mr Holmes had mentioned earlier. The design of the *mandala* itself was exactly the same as others of the Kalachakra tantra that I had seen before, though the colours on this one were appreciably deeper, probably due to its great age.

'It has obviously been hung for a very long time,' commented Holmes, without looking up from his lens.

'Well, it has been there on the chapel wall,' said the Lama, 'ever since I can remember. And I entered the service of His Holiness's former sacred body as a boy.'

'... the design on the brocade,' observed Holmes' 'has become distorted by the stretching of the vertical weave in the material — the cumulative effect of time and gravity. Now let us see what we have on the other side.'

He turned the scroll over carefully. On the back of the painting were a number of lines of Thibetan writing in the uniform *uchen* print. It stated briefly, just as the young Grand Lama had told us, that the painting had been commissioned by the first Grand Lama after his meeting with the 'Messenger,' and his journey to Shambala; followed by the date and the seal of the Grand Lama. Below this were seventeen lines of verse. The first seven lines were a kind of benediction, while the remaining lines formed the actual poem, seemingly a description of the various parts of the *mandala* structure, but mixed with strange instructions. A queer rigmarole, with something of the flavour of a nursery rhyme. These seventeen lines were written in the cursive *umay* script, clearly penned with the angular nibbed bamboo pen that Thibetan calligraphers were wont to use. As I remarked at an earlier instance, Mr Holmes was unfamiliar with this script, and he now requested the Lama Yonten to read it to him. The Lama adjusted his spectacles and, bending over to peer at the scroll on the table, read the following lines in his high, sing-song voice:

Om Svasti!
Reverence to thee, Buddhas of the Three Ages and Protector of all Creatures.
O, assembled Gurus and Warriors of Shambala.
Out of your great compassion show us the true path.
When wandering through the delusion of samsara guide us on to the true path.

Facing the sacred direction
Turning always in the path of the Dharma Wheel
Circle thrice the Mountain of Fire
Twice the Adamantine Walls
Proceeding once around the Eight Cemeteries
And Once the Sacred Lotus Fence,
Stand before the Walls of the Celestial City.
Then from the Southern Gate turn to the East
Enter the inner-most palace from the Northern portals
And sit victorious on the Vajra throne. EE - TI!

'It is a lot of gobbledegook,' said I, when the Lama had finished.

'Nay, not necessarily so, Babuji,' objected the Lama Yonten. 'The occult sciences have always used inscrutable and symbolic language to safeguard secret knowledge and prevent its revelation to the profane.'

'So you think, Sir, that this has some hidden meaning?' I asked.

'Verily, though it be hidden from me.'

'And from anyone else, too, I should jolly well think,' said I, scratching my head absolutely mystified.

Sherlock Holmes absent-mindedly sipped a cup of Chinese tea — the only refreshment he had partaken of that day — and once again lit the unsavoury pipe which was the companion of his deepest meditations.

'I wonder ...' said he, leaning back and staring at the ceiling. 'Perhaps there are points that have escaped your Spencerian intellect. Let us consider the problem in the light of pure reason. The common denominator in the various pieces of our puzzle — the Grand Lama's proposed retreat, the Ice Temple, the *mandala* painting, and this cryptic verse — is some kind of connection to Shambala. That is our point of departure.'

'A somewhat broad one, Sir,' said I doubtfully.

'Well, let us see, then, if we can narrow it. As I focus my mind upon the verse, it seems rather less impenetrable. In spite of its cryptic nature, it is not too difficult to see that what we have here is a set of instructions.'

'It is a guide to Shambala!' I cried triumphantly.

'A guide?'

'I mean it is a description of the route to that place. We have the legend that the first Grand Lama may have travelled there. Probably he recorded the route of his journey.'

'Humm. Any other reasons for thinking so?'

'Well, there are also certain words in the message which provide indications of it being some kind of travel itinerary. We have the word ...umm "Proceed" in the twelfth line. Then ... let me see ... aah ... "direction" ... in the eighth and ninth lines. There are also the many references to "Mountains" and "Walls" and a "City." '

'Good Hurree, good! But not, if I may say so, quite good enough. There are difficulties with your theory. Consider just the tenth and eleventh lines ... "Circle thrice the mountain of Fire, Twice the Adamantine Walls" ... and others like it. Even if we were to assume that such places did exist, just going round and round them would not get us anywhere.'

'We'd be going around in circles,' I admitted, a trifle abashedly.

'Exactly. There are just too many references to circles in this message to make it possible that it is a physical description of a route to some actual destination.'

'You are right, Mr Holmes,' said the Lama Yonten. 'The message is probably symbolic. The circle, or the wheel, is the omniscient symbol of the essential principles of our faith; of cause and effect, of birth and death, indeed of the entire cycle of existence itself. Perhaps the message is nothing more than that — just a religious discourse couched in recondite metaphysical terms.'

'That really won't do, Your Reverence,' said Holmes, shaking his head. 'It hardly stands to reason that a man of Moriarty's unregenerate nature should take such trouble to steal a religious tract. No. The message definitely conceals something of great material advantage to the Professor. His own words seem to indicate that he is seeking some tremendous source of power.'

'But exactly what, Mr Holmes?' I demanded.

'There is an appalling directness about your questions, Hurree.' said Holmes, shaking his pipe at me. 'They come at me like bullets.'

'I am sorry, Sir, I did not mean ...'

Holmes waved away my apologies. 'The answer to your question lies in the Ice Temple. I really do not think we can form any further conclusions without paying a visit to the place.'

'Well, Mr Holmes,' said the Lama, 'we shall be there in a week, when His Holiness goes there on his retreat. That is if the Regent doesn't have me arrested first and the visit stopped.'

'Then the sooner we get to the temple the better,' said Holmes crisply. 'Is it possible for the Grand Lama's travel plans to be advanced?'

'That would go against tradition,' protested the Lama. 'The date for His Holiness's departure has been especially chosen by the State Astrologer.'

'Well, Sir,' replied Holmes, a trifle brutally, 'you will have to choose between flying in the face of tradition or seeing the end of everything you have worked for, not least, the life of your master.'

The Lama Yonten was silent for sometime, head bowed low, his hand turning the beads of his rosary with soft regular clicks. Finally he sat up and said resignedly at Sherlock Holmes. 'You are, of course, right, Mr Holmes. When shall we leave?'

'The sooner the better. We must not forget that Moriarty may be making a trip of his own to the temple, if he has not been too affected by tonight's mishap. Do you think it would be possible for His Holiness to start tomorrow?'

'Tomorrow,' the Lama Yonten wailed. 'That is impossible.'

But of course, it wasn't.

Next day at dusk a small cavalcade of riders departed inconspicuously from the rear gate of the outer walls of the Jewel Park, by the deserted shores of the Kyichu River. Only a few water fowls (Tib. *damcha*) watched the passing of the line of men and horses. I rode alongside Mr Holmes, just behind the Grand Lama and the Lama Yonten. Tsering, Kintup and ten Thibetan soldiers rode ahead. Our company had been kept small on Mr Holmes's insistence, he very correctly feeling that anything larger would adversely affect our speed, and, more critically, the secrecy of our expedition.

The young Grand Lama, far from objecting to Holmes's precipitous decision, had been tremendously enthusiastic about it and had refused to pay any attention to the Chief Secretary's many doubts. The Lama Yonten, to give him his due, soon recovered from his initial worries and quickly got down to making all the necessary preparations for our expedition — which were considerable. We could not just 'rough it' as the Grand Lama himself was travelling with us, and proper tents, provisions and bedding had to be arranged. But it was all very efficiently accomplished before the appointed hour of our departure.

The Ice Temple of Shambala was about a hundred miles north of Lhassa — three days' hard riding. It was located, quite uniquely, under a huge mass of trapped glacial ice, squeezed between a deep rift in the Trans-Himalayan range. The Thibetans called this mountain chain Nyenchen-thang-lha after the ancient (pre-Buddhist) mountain god who held court there. Normally this temple was buried under the glacier, even the entrance being entirely sealed off by a massive wall of ice. But for some hitherto undiscovered reason, this front cliff of ice melts and breaks away once in about half a century, permitting entry to the temple. The Thibetans believe that the ice wall opens at the time that the gods of Thibet consider it propitious for a Grand Lama to assume the throne of the country, and that it has unfailingly opened (though there is no scientific evidence for this) for every incarnation of the Grand Lama — though the last three were prevented from visiting it at the prescribed time. Hence their tragically short lives, and the evil times in the country.

There is a definite limit to the period that the Ice Temple is accessible. About three to four weeks after the initial opening, the glacier begins to move once again and gradually seals the entrance to the Temple, keeping it sacrosanct until the time that another incarnation of the Grand Lama should be ready to sit on the Lion Throne of Thibet.

No convincing scientific explanation has ever been offered for this *lusus naturae*, though its existence has been reported by certain Russian explorers. My own view on the subject is, I believe, so far unique — if I may be pardoned the term — though I do not insist that it is necessarily the only correct one. The reader may take it as a mere theory; but a theory formulated by an intelligent and empirical observer.

Two distinct facts may be noted: 1. That the glacier is forced to travel in a deep gorge. 2. That the rock-face in front of the gorge — lining the ice wall — is formed of a very hard granitic rock, while the walls of the gorge itself are made up of a softer limestone. Thus, in time, the inner gorge has worn away much more than the mouth, creating a point of tremendous concentration and compression in front of the glacier.

My theory is that the enormous pressure exerted by the entire glacier on this small opening causes a marked decrease in the temperature in the ice at this point, and a subsequent hardening of its consistency (a natural phenomena that can be observed when snow is compressed to form snowballs). Thus an unusually hard and cold ice wall is formed at the front, effectively preventing the gradual melting and movement of the whole glacier, as normally occurs in all other glacial activities.

But though nature can be impeded, it can, of course, never be entirely halted. Year after year, the pressure builds up behind the ice wall, until eventually a point of surfeit is arrived at in the front, when the temperature cannot drop any more, or the ice harden. This slow build up of pressure may take up to fifty years, hence accounting for its coincidence with the coming of age of the Grand Lamas. Once this crucial stage is reached, the entire front of the narrow ice wall breaks open to reveal the entrance to the hidden temple. The sudden drop of pressure and temperature in front causes the whole phenomenon to start all over again, and slowly, in the space of many weeks, the entrance to the temple is once again covered by a solid wall of ice.

It was nearly dark on the second day when we camped at the foot of the pass that led over the mountains. High above us, up into the dark cloudy skies, soared the white jagged peaks of the long mountain chain. Beneath the snows, the slopes were grey with bare rocks and boulders, only an occasional wind-racked dwarf pine and solitary patches of tough gorse providing some relief to this grim scene.

The Grand Lama did not seem to become in any way affected by our hard journey nor the desolation of the surroundings. In fact he seemed to be enjoying himself thoroughly. He was, after all, a boy, and what boy if unnaturally confined for a lifetime to the company of dull teachers, old retainers and guards, would not enjoy the freedom of such an outing — rough though it may be. He ran around the campsite throwing stones at the bushes and joining Mr Holmes asked him innumerable questions about his life, about England and the world. It surprised me to observe Mr Holmes listening and replying patiently to the boy's many queries. But as I had occasion to notice before, underneath that hard, rational exterior and the assured egotism that often annoyed many, he had a remarkable gentleness and courtesy in his dealings with women and children.

Next day we made our way up through the high and forbidding mountains. Our trail was covered with rocks and patches of ice, while higher up it was all snow. Our sturdy ponies plodded on the whole morning, wending their way through the bleak maze of icy peaks, while we huddled on our saddles trying to protect ourselves from the fury of the elements. I tried to shield myself from the occasional sleet with my trusty umbrella, but it was blown inside-out the very first time by a blast of freezing wind, and only after a monumental tussle did I eventually manage to close it, and put it away.

Tsering and the soldiers, who all had long hair, now rearranged their tresses loosely before their eyes to prevent snow blindness. The rest of us had to make do with strips of coloured gauze. At about two o'clock in the afternoon we rode through a particularly windy vale between two massive peaks and, crossing it, finally got the first glimpse of our goal.

The mountains opened up in front of us into a field of glistening snow about a mile long, that abruptly ended in a wide chasm that cut right across it in the dramatic manner of the Grand Canyon in North America. A natural bridge of ice spanned this chasm and was seemingly the only way across it. On the other side the snow field continued — littered with great chunks of icy debris — and was gradually hemmed in between sheer cliffs of rock that fanned out from the high narrow front of the glacial wall. This wall of ice stood at least five hundred feet high and about a hundred feet wide, smooth and vertical, like a gigantic pane of glass. At the base of the wall was a dark regular opening which I realised was the entrance to the Ice Temple of Shambala. The ground in front of the wall was covered with thousands of pieces of broken ice, giving the impression of a stormy, wave-tossed sea that had become suddenly frozen.

Shivering on the backs of our ponies, we surveyed this awesome scene. I also took the precaution of examining the various details of the surrounding topography with my small telescope.

'Well, Mr Holmes,' said I cheerfully, removing the instrument from my eye, 'it seems that your insistence on speed has paid dividends. We have certainly arrived here before Professor Moriarty and his Chinese chums. I can see no sign of any human presence around here.'

'But that is not as it should be,' said the Lama Yonten, worriedly.

'What do you mean, Sir?' asked Sherlock Holmes.

'Two monks, the "Watchers of the Ice Temple", live here, in a cave at the side of that ridge.' The Lama pointed to the mountain to our right. 'Besides their main task of reporting the opening of the temple entrance, it is one of their duties to prevent travellers from crossing that bridge and inadvertently profaning sacred ground. But where are they?'

'They may be in their cave. They may not have heard us coming.'

'That is not possible. The surrounding mountains funnel all sounds from the valley towards their cave. That is why it was chosen. They should have heard our arriving at least an hour ago, and come to receive us.'

'Humm. It would be well if we were cautious,' said Holmes

grimly, his brows knitting with concern, 'Let me have that spy-glass of yours for a minute, Hurree.'

'Certainly, Sir.'

He clapped the instrument to his eyes and made a systematic survey of the surroundings. The rest of us waited silently, A little chill of fear crept into me as I realised that I may have spoken too soon.

'The small wooden door to the "Watchers" cave is open and swinging about in the wind,' said Holmes anxiously. 'On the opposite ridge a flight of snow pigeons is circling nervously above its nests. Wherever *they* are, they are well-hidden.'

'We have to go between those two ridges to get to the ice bridge,' said Tsering gravely. 'I think they may be waiting behind them.'

'When do you think they will attack?'

'Probably when we get near the ice bridge and descend from our ponies to walk across. That would be the most dangerous moment. We would be trapped like bugs between the claws of a scorpion.'

'Well, we shall see,' said Holmes calmly. Turning towards us he addressed us in a firm, measured tone. 'We will ride single file, with His Holiness and the Lama Yonten in the centre. Tsering and I will ride in front with five soldiers. Kintup and the other five soldiers will follow the Lamas. You, Hurree, will bring up the rear. On the first sign of an attack we will race straight to the bridge and *ride across it.* It may seem a foolhardy thing to do, but it is the only chance we have against a large enemy force. Over here the valley is too flat and bare. Once we cross the ice bridge you, Tsering, will position the soldiers behind those large blocks of ice and hold off all pursuers. It will not be too difficult since they will only be able to cross the bridge single file. The Lama Yonten and I will take His Holiness inside the temple. Now remember, don't hesitate at the bridge. Ride straight across it. They will not be expecting us to do that, and it may provide us the necessary element of surprise for the success of our plan. Good Luck.'

It was the measure of the man's great personality, and the cool confidence and calm authority with which he outlined his plans, that not one of us raised a single objection or question, but prepared ourselves to carry out his orders. We rode single file across the vale. I rode in the rear, not feeling too happy with my position but prepared to take on the worst. I extracted the revolver, issued to me from the guard's armoury at the Jewel Park, from within the folds of my robe, and, throwing off the safety catch, stuck it in my belt in front of me. As we passed between the end of the two ridges, I noticed the flock of snow pigeons *(Columba leuconota)* fluttering above their nests, exactly as Mr Holmes had described; but I did not see any signs of the enemy. Maybe it was just a snow leopard *(Felis uncia)* that had disturbed the birds, I thought. Maybe there were no attackers after all. This happy inspiration greatly raised my spirits, for I had not looked forward to galloping across that ice bridge which was, at most, only a couple of yards wide, and probably slippery as the Devil as well. Just as I was feeling a bit relieved Mr Holmes raised a cry of alarm.

'They're coming! Ride on.'

I did not bother to look around but whipped my steed and got it moving at a rapid trot. I had just covered about a hundred feet when I saw a company of soldiers, all of them dressed in black, riding towards us from behind the ridge where the snow pigeons had been disturbed. I turned to look at the opposite ridge, hoping I would not see what I expected to see, but I did. Another company of riders came out from behind the mountainside and charged straight towards us.

For a moment both groups of attackers reined in their horses and looked around confusedly. They were obviously surprised at the way we were unhesitatingly racing towards the bridge. But they immediately recovered, and, shouting blood-curdling Chinese war cries, *'Sha! Sha!'* (Kill! Kill!) galloped towards us. By now our column of horsemen was proceeding at full speed, but the attackers began to gain on us. To make matters worse, they were closing in on our rear, where I was riding. I kicked my pony hard in the flanks to coax some more speed out of it.

As the animal accelerated forward I turned around in my saddle to observe my pursuers. There must have been at least sixty of the blighters *in toto.* They were wearing black uniforms and had black turbans wrapped around their heads. Belts of ammunition were slung across their chests, while on their backs were modern repeating rifles and large executioner's swords — or *da dao,* as the Chinese call them — just like the one that had featured so prominently in my near execution in Shigatse, on my previous visit to Thibet. By Jove. These were definitely Imperial Manchu troopers, not just the Amban's bodyguards.

Looking before me I saw that Tsering had reached the ice bridge. He did not hesitate — brave fellow — but spurred his mount on. The bridge curved up a bit towards the middle in an arch, so that a clear view was afforded me of his crossing. His pony's hooves scrabbled desperately to get a purchase on the icy surface, and somehow it managed to keep moving and soon got to the other side. Five of our soldiers followed without any problems, as did Mr Holmes, the Grand Lama and the Lama Yonten. The remainder were successfully making the crossing until the last Thibetan soldier in the column got to the bridge.

His pony scrambled up to the middle with no problem, but just when it was descending, its rear hooves slipped on the ice and it fell heavily on its side. Its legs desperately kicking and pawing the air in a vain attempt to right itself, the animal slid to the edge of the bridge. Then with a last pitiful whinny it fell into the chasm. The rider had tried to throw himself clear when the pony fell, but his feet had become entangled in the stirrups, and he was dragged over as well. He gave an awful cry as he plunged slowly into that bottomless gorge of ice, and the echoes of this human and animal terror reverberated through the mountains like a pronouncement of doom.

I urged my steed on desperately, but just as it got to the bridge I heard a crazed yell behind me and turned around. Close behind me were the Imperial troopers, waving their ugly swords in a very truculent manner. One soldier in particular, a pock-marked, yellow devil, was immediately behind me. He raised his huge sword. I flinched. There was a bang. A red splotch like a carnation in bloom suddenly appeared in the middle of his forehead; and with a look of infinite bewilderment fixed upon his face, he toppled backwards off his horse.

Our soldiers had already taken up defensive positions behind the blocks of ice and were firing at our attackers, who, in spite of their numbers, were in a very exposed situation. I quickly managed to cross the bridge as confusion struck my pursuers. Once across, I rode up to the ice wall and quickly dismounted, seeking cover behind the large chunks of ice strewn about the place. Tsering, Kintup and the soldiers had positioned themselves securely and obviously did not need my assistance, so I picked my way through the ice and followed Mr Holmes and the Lamas to the temple.

At the base of the gigantic ice wall was an entrance, rather like the mouth of a large cave, but cut more regularly, like an upright rectangle, and at least forty feet high. On either side of the entrance, upon huge pedestals of dark basaltic rock, were colossal statues of winged lions posing *en couchant,* and measuring about twenty-five feet from the crown of their heads to the base of the pedestals. They were unlike any representations of lions I had seen before. They were certainly not of Indian design. There was a hint of Babylonian influence in the wings, but everything else about them, the heads, the features, the lines and the postures were definitely not Mesopotamian, nor even of Asian or Chinese origin.

Could it be that these were the works of a lost civilisation that had existed thousands of years before the present-day Thibetans had inhabited the land? The fine condition of the statues, which were hardly damaged or eroded, could be explained by the fact that they were usually buried under the ice and only had to face periods of exposure twice a century. Maybe like Herr Schliemann, who had discovered the ruins of Troy just a few years ago, I had discovered an entire ancient civilisation unknown to anyone in the world. I decided to call it the Tethyian civilisation, after the prehistoric sea of Tethys from under which the plateau of Thibet and the Himalayan mountains had emerged many millions of years ago.

The noisy passage of a bullet past my head caused me to terminate my scientific musings, and clutching my umbrella, I quickly ran in through the vast temple door.

21

The Ice Temple of Shambala

Once my eyes had become used to the dimmer light inside, I realised, with some disappointment, that the interior of the cave was quite small — only about forty by forty feet. The walls were covered with strange carvings and inscriptions, reminiscent of Egyptian hieroglyphics but far more abstract and fantastic. The chamber was wretchedly cold and clusters of icicles hung from the corner of the ceiling and covered parts of the wall. A thick carpet of powdery snow covered the floor, and squeaked loudly under our boots.

The Lama Yonten was helping the Grand Lama to rest in a corner of the temple, and had laid his cloak on the ground for him to lie on. The young lad, it will be remembered, had only just recovered from a serious illness, and our desperate race across the bridge had overtaxed his frail constitution. I extracted a small hip-flask of brandy (which I carry only for medical emergencies, since I am a strict teetotaller) and, unscrewing the cap, poured some of the vital fluid down his throat. He coughed and gasped, but the colour began to come back to his bloodless cheeks.

Mr Holmes was unsuccessfully striking vestas against the wall in order to light our dark lantern. Somehow his matches had become wet, so I went over to him and proffered a box of dry ones that I fortunately had on me. He quickly lit the lantern. After he adjusted the shutters, it threw a brilliant beam of light onto the opposite wall. He directed the beam around the room, which was quite bare except for the wall inscriptions, until in the middle of the chamber, the light shone upon a strange multi-tiered structure which rested on a stone pedestal. A blanket of powdery snow covered the whole thing, making it look like a large wedding cake.

'That is the Great *Mandala*,' said the Lama Yonten. 'The very one used by the Messenger of Shambala when he gave the master initiation to the first Grand Lama.'

Sherlock Holmes went over to the structure and commenced to dust the snow from its surface with his muffler. I joined him in the task, until very soon we were done. The *mandala* was about six feet high, while the base, a one-foot-thick stone disc, was nearly seven feet in diameter. Progressively smaller stone discs, squares and triangles were meticulously stacked on top of it, one over the other, forming a structure halfway between a squat cone and a pyramid. On the very top was a tiny delicate model of a pagoda with a graceful canopied roof. Although the basic lines and circles of this *mandala* were nearly the same as that of the painted scroll, the stone *mandala* lacked the ornamentation and colours of the latter. It looked stark and utilitarian. More like the diagrammatic proof of a complex mathematical formula than a religious symbol.

While I held the lantern above him and directed its beam wherever required, Mr Holmes crouched to subject this strange structure to an examination with his magnifying lens. Five minutes sufficed to satisfy him, for he rose to his feet and put away his lens. Then, placing his hands firmly against the side of the thick stone disc, he proceeded to exert his full strength, in a somewhat oblique direction, against the weighty object. I did not notice anything, but some slight change must have occurred for Mr Holmes stopped and grunted in satisfaction.

'It moves,' he said, a note of triumph in his voice.

'What does it mean?' I asked.

'It means our little mystery, the riddle of the cryptic verse, is nearly solved.'

'I do not understand, Mr Holmes.'

'You will remember we agreed that the verse was a set of instructions, probably for the disinterment of something concealed — something precious. Since the symbolism of the *mandala* structure is used in the verse, what is more logical than to conclude that the instructions refer to an actual *mandala* — but one that is palpably whole and upright.'

'So that we can move around it in particular circles, like the instructions say?' said I puzzled. 'But ...'

'No no, my dear Hurree. Not to move around it but to *move* it. My cursory examination has revealed that this structure has not been hewn from the a single piece of stone but has rather been assembled — each layer of it — from separately sculpted pieces, each capable of being moved, or rather rotated, around a central axis.'

'Like the tumblers of a lock?'

'Exactly. Your choice of an analogy is a happy one, for this *mandala* is — if my reasoning is correct — a lock, albeit an unusual and considerable one.'

'But what about a key then, Mr Holmes. We do not have it.'

'Oh, tut, man. We need not be so literal. The verse is our key.'

'I have been very obtuse ...' said I, abashed, but Mr Holmes had no time for my self-reproaches, and was in a fever to begin testing his theory.

'Now, Hurree, if you could lend a hand here, and … excuse me, Reverend Sir,' he turned to the Lama Yonten, 'if you could kindly read the verse to us.'

The Grand Lama had now recovered and insisted on holding the lantern, while the Lama Yonten unrolled the *mandala* scroll and read the lines on the back. '*Om Svasti*. Reverence to thee …'

'We can skip the benedictory lines,' interrupted Holmes 'and proceed with the actual instructions.'

'As you wish, Mr Holmes,' replied the Lama, quickly perusing the verses, underlining the word with this bony forefinger. 'Let me see. Hmm … ah yes … the instructions start here. "Facing the sacred direction …" '

'What would that be?'

'North, Mr Holmes. Shambala is properly referred to as "Shambala of the North." '

'So that would necessitate us having our backs to the entrance and facing the *mandala* from that direction. Let us see now …'

'I have it, Mr Holmes,' I cried exultantly, scraping away the snow at the base of the *mandala* exactly across the entrance. 'There is a crossed *vajra*[1] inscribed on the floor here. This probably marks the direction from which we start.'

---

1. The *vajra* was originally the thunderbolt weapon of Indra, the Indian Zeus. The Buddhists changed it to the symbol of highest spiritual

'That is the very place where the Grand Lama must sit when meditating on the *mandala*,' said the Lama Yonten.

'So we can take it as our starting point,' said Holmes briskly. 'Now let us have the next line in the verse.'

' "... turning always in the path of the Dharma wheel ..." '

'Bear in mind, Hurree, that all our operations will have to be conducted clockwise. Pray continue, Sir.'

' "... Circle Thrice the Mountain of Fire." '

'That would be the base of the *mandala*. See the design of flames carved into the stone. Now, Hurree, let us attend to it with a will.'

It was not an easy task. Both Mr Holmes and I were grunting with the effort, but finally the giant disc moved slowly. As per the instructions we rotated that bally deadweight three times around its axis, finishing exactly where we started, by the crossed *vajra* mark on the floor. I collapsed with exhaustion.

' "... Twice the Adamantine Walls ..." ' the Lama droned on.

'Come on Hurree,' Mr Holmes exhorted me. 'This one will be easier. It's much smaller.'

Mr Holmes was right. The 'Adamantine wall' disc wasn't as heavy as the 'Mountain of Fire' disc, and we only had to rotate it twice. The 'Eight Cemeteries' disc was even easier, while the one after that, 'The Sacred Lotus Fence' disc, I managed by myself.

On the fifth tier the *mandala* changed shape; from the circular discs of the earlier mountains, walls and fences, to a square plinth

---

power 'the Adamantine Sceptre' which is irresistible and invincible. The double or crossed *vajra* (Skt. *visva-vajra*) symbolises immutability, and is hence used in designs of thrones and seats, inscribed on bases of statues, pillars, foundations of houses, anywhere where permanence is desired.

with protuberances on each side — the four walls of the Sacred City and its four gates.

'"... Then from the Southern Gate turn to the East ..."'

Following the instructions we turned the square plinth a three quarter turn. Now came the last item in the verse. 'The Innermost Palace', which was the pagoda with the canopied roof, on the very top of the *mandala*. It was a tremendously exciting moment. While Mr Holmes gave the little pagoda half a turn from the South to the North — as the instructions specified, we waited with bated breath for the result.

Nothing happened.

A cold chill of disappointment coursed through my body. It seemed to me that somehow Mr Holmes must have made a radical mistake in his chain of reasoning.

'We are undone, Hurree,' said he, a pained look on his face. He turned away, and biting hard on the stem of his pipe paced restlessly about the chamber, kicking up a small storm of powder snow in his wake. He kept up his choleric perambulations for about ten minutes, when all of a sudden a happy thought seemed to strike him. He brightened at once, and snapped his fingers.

'The *Vajra* throne,' he cried. 'We have omitted "... and sit victorious on the *Vajra* throne ..."'

'But that only seems to be a concluding symbolism of some kind, Mr Holmes,' said the Lama Yonten.

'We have moved everything movable in the *mandala*,' said I despondently. 'There is nothing more left to manipulate.'

'Let us see,' said Holmes, going over to the *mandala*. He carefully studied the pagoda on the top with his lens, and then with the thin blade of his pocketknife, gently prised open the miniature doors of the little temple. Within the pagoda was a tiny crystal throne carved in the shape of a crossed *vajra*. It was a beautiful thing. As the Grand Lama directed the beam of the lantern on it, Mr Holmes carefully studied this miniature *objet d'art* closely with his lens.

'But what shall we do now, Mr Holmes?' said I. 'We have no instructions about what to do with it.'

'Ah, but we do, Hurree,' said he cheerfully. He paused. 'We sit on it.'

With that he put the tip of his forefinger on the crystal throne and gently pressed it down. There was an audible click — as if some kind of lever had been activated. Then the crystal throne began to glow with an eerie green light. It slowly became brighter till its radiance suffused the North wall of the chamber with a light as brilliant as that of a full moon in mid-summer. The *mandala* itself began to vibrate spasmodically, the tremors increasing in intensity till the entire temple shook in an alarming manner.

To our consternation some of the icicles broke off the roof of the chamber and crashed onto the floor, throwing up sprays of snow. Mr Holmes quickly grabbed the Grand Lama and, doing his best to cover the lad's body with his own, retreated to a corner of the chamber. The Lama Yonten and I also hurriedly backed away from the *mandala*, which seemed to be the source of all this tremendous energy.

As I retreated to the rear wall, I tripped on a piece of fallen icicle and staggered backwards. I expected to fall against the wall and put my hands behind me to take my weight, but to my surprise I encountered nothing and fell clean backwards. Even more alarming was the fact that my descent backwards did not stop at the floor but continued in a precipitate and confusing manner for quite some time, till finally I landed with a painful bump, somewhere in utter darkness.

'Hulloa, Hurree! Can you hear me?' Mr Holmes's distant voice slowly filtered into my scrambled mind. I shook my head to clear it.

'I am here, Mr Holmes!' I yelled back.

'Are you all right?'

I took stock of my condition and situation. 'I think so, Sir. There are no bones broken, anyway.'

'Excellent. Where exactly are you?'

'I seem to be at the bottom of an awful abyss, Sir. I am of the opinion that the entrance should be somewhere in the middle of the wall opposite the temple door.'

'Good man. Hang on for a minute. I'll get a light down there soon.'

A few moments later a welcome glow of light appeared in the darkness above me. Gradually, as the light descended and became brighter, I was able to discern the comfortably familiar outline of Sherlock Holmes' tall figure, holding the dark lantern and walking down a long stone staircase — which must have been the one I had tumbled down. Behind him the two Lamas followed.

'You are to be congratulated, Hurree,' said Holmes cheerfully, coming up to me. 'The honour of discovering the secret of the *mandala* is yours.'

'Is this all, Mr Holmes?' said I, disappointed. 'All that mystery and noise and fuss, just to conceal a passage way?'

'Patience. We shall know when we get to the end of it.' He pointed the lantern in the direction opposite to the staircase. 'See, it does not stop here but continues much further.'

The Lama Yonten and the Grand Lama made solicitous enquiries as to my state of health subsequent to my sudden descent, and gave loud thanks to the 'Three Jewels', the Buddhist Trinity, for my deliverance.

We proceeded down the passage cautiously, with Mr Holmes in the lead holding the lantern, and the rest of us following closely behind him. Though the passage was very long it was surprisingly straight and true, without even the slightest bend, dip or rise during its entire length. The walls were constructed to an exactness that would certainly tax a modern engineer. As we proceeded, the light from the lantern shimmered off the surface of the walls. I reached out to touch it and was surprised to discover how smooth it was — smoother than marble, even glass. There were no seams or joints, no interruptions of any kind in the unnatural evenness of the surface. It had clearly been made by a people with very advanced technical knowledge. I mentally began to review all the bits of information I had now acquired about my Tethyian civilisation, and tried to classify them in some systematic order.

Suddenly Mr Holmes paused and signalled us to halt. He then directed the beam of the lantern straight to the floor, which like the temple, was covered with a thin carpet of powdery snow. We were probably arriving at a place where drifts of snow could somehow enter this subterranean corridor.

'What do you think of that?' he asked, indicating a number of footprints clearly impressed on the soft snow.

'Obviously someone has anticipated us,' said I, worried.

'More than one, I'm afraid. There are three distinct sets of impressions. I first observed them just a little way ago. One of them is obviously a cripple. Notice how the impression of the right foot is quite askew, and also blurred because he dragged that foot.'

'Moriarty!' I exclaimed in horror.

'Yes. As I expected, the Dark One has got here before us. One of his companions led the way, he came next, and the third followed as rearguard. There can be no question as to the superimposition of the footmarks.'

'Do you think the Amban is with him?' asked the Lama Yonten.

'Probably not. The two other impressions are from the same kind of footwear — cheap, cloth-soled Chinese boots, I would think; the kind that can be worn on either foot. I noticed the Chinese soldiers wearing them.'

I was not at all happy about our proceeding with this

particularly dangerous venture, especially when highly unscrupulous bounders, fully prepared to commit violences against our persons, awaited us at the end of it.

'Hadn't we better ...' I began to make a suggestion.

'We are doing so,' Holmes interrupted me rather brusquely. He extracted a revolver from within the folds of his robe and cocked it. 'It would be well if we were to proceed with all due caution. Hurree? You are armed?'

'Yes, Sir,' I said resignedly, pulling out the ludicrous weapon from my belt, and began to go through the motions of preparing it for the coming fray.

'You Hurree, will bring up the rear. If anything should happen to me, you will at once escort His Holiness and the Lama Yonten out of this place. Now close the shield of the lantern. We will have to manage in the dark.'

We moved very carefully along the passage, which now gradually, almost imperceptibly, became wider, and strangely less dark, or so I imagined. As we went forward the phenomena became more apparent. Unwilling to trust my own visual senses I tentatively imparted to Mr Holmes my assessment of the luminary intensification. He had noticed it too.

'You are right, Hurree, and it is getting progressively lighter further up the passageway. We must double our precautions. The light will make us more visible, and more vulnerable.'

For another half an hour we advanced stealthily. By this time the passage had so enlarged that it was now the dimensions of a large cathedral. It was also now quite simple to locate the source of our illumination. Hundreds of feet above us hung a massive roof of clear glacial ice, via which a remote daylight filtered through to provide a pale unearthly luminescence in the cavern below.

As we sidled by the left wall of the gigantic passage way, glancing nervously up at this tremendous anomaly of nature, the thought of those millions of tons of unstable ice poised menacingly above our heads did nothing to reassure me about the wisdom of our enterprise. A little way ahead there was a narrow opening in the wall — probably a cleft in the rock, but with the regular lines of an entrance of some kind. Maybe it was the beginning of a branch passage, or the door to a chamber.

Sherlock Holmes stopped a little way before the opening and, getting down on one knee, carefully inspected the white floor. 'I don't like it. The alignments of the footmarks change here. They do not all point forward as before, but instead point toward each other in a rough circle. Obviously they gathered around here to confer.'

Meanwhile I had proceeded to the side entrance to have a look inside. I was just stepping into the opening when Mr Holmes shouted a warning. 'Stop, Hurree It is a trap!'

Instinctively I drew back, which was most fortunate, for two shots rang out, the bullets whizzing perilously close past me. I pressed my back hard against the wall and tried to control my breathing and the rhythm of my heart, which were now totally at sixes and sevens. Pressing himself against the wall, Mr Holmes sidled up besides me. 'Moriarty and his men conferred here to prepare a trap for us,' he whispered. 'But in baiting a mouse-trap with cheese, it is well to remember to leave room for the mouse. The entrance was rather too obvious. The footmarks also provided a useful confirmation.'

'But what can we do now, Mr Holmes? I asked. We can only proceed at unequivocal peril to life and limb.'

'Let us not succumb to such morbid anticipations before having exhausted our own resources.' Holmes said sternly. 'First of all we must establish the exact circumstances of our adversaries. Hurree, if crouching very low, you could quickly peep around the corner and fire a few shots in their general direction, it may afford me the opportunity to make a quick reconnaissance. Are you ready? Now!'

I fired three rapid shots around the corner and whipped back to safety, just before a volley of rifle-fire crashed past me and echoed through the many miles of empty caverns. Mr Holmes had managed to duck back safely also, and he now stood with his back pressed to the wall and his eyes filled with frustration.

'The Devil take it!' he cried bitterly. 'They are unassailable.'

'How, exactly, Sir? I did not have time to see anything.'

'The two soldiers are entrenched behind large blocks of ice which provide them absolute protection against our bullets. There is no way they can be flanked, and they have a clear field of fire of the whole entrance. We are trapped here.'

'But we can always retreat, Sir.' I cried out at this folly, flinging my arms out in protest. It was very careless of me, I will grant you, to make impassioned gestures while under fire, for my left hand must have stuck out a bit beyond the corner. There was a sharp crack and I felt a sudden hot sear, as if a red hot poker had been pressed against the back of my hand. I had been shot. Good Heavens! I withdrew my injured limb with alacrity and tried to nurse it with my other hand, which held the revolver. Unfortunately, in the heat and confusion of things I must have dropped my fire-arm on the floor. More unfortunately still, the bally thing was cocked and ready to fire, and so it accidentally discharged a round.

'What the Devil ...?' Mr Holmes leapt back in alarm as the bullet zipped past his nose and flew up into the air.

Somewhat embarrassed by this unfortunate accident I lowered my head and affected to examine my wound with great interest. But to my dismay, Mr Holmes's reaction to this minor and absolutely unintended blunder of mine was rather violent and unexpected. He grabbed me by the collar and threw me brutally to one side. Recovering from this uncalled for assault on my person and dignity, I sought to remonstrate with him. 'Really Sir. Such behaviour is unbecoming of an English gentle...'

Just then a great mass of murderously jagged ice crashed down on the very spot where I had just stood. The accidental discharge had struck the ice on the roof and dislodged a large section of it. Mr Holmes must have seen this and taken effective steps to save my life. I censured myself for my want of faith. How could I have, for even a single moment, doubted the integrity of my noble and valiant friend.

'I … I …' I stammered an embarrassed apology.

But Mr Holmes was chuckling and rubbing his hands together. 'Ha ha! Capital! I never get your limits, Hurree.'

'But …' I began to ask. He held up his hand.

'Once again, Hurree, in your own inimitable fashion, you have demonstrated the solution, *le mot de l'énigme,*'

'But …'

'How is your wound, Babuji?' the Lama Yonten enquired solicitously, taking my injured hand in his. 'If I may …'

Fortunately the wound was only a superficial one. The skin at the back of my hand had been scored, but there was little bleeding. The Lama Yonten applied some herbal salve and bound it with my 'kerchief.

'Now Hurree,' said Holmes, methodically reloading my revolver, 'when I give the word, both of us will whip our weapons around the entrance and fire a few quick rounds — not at the soldiers, but at the roof above them — and then withdraw immediately.'

He handed me back my revolver. I knelt low near the floor just by the entrance. Mr Holmes crouched over me, his weapon raised by his head.

'Ready? Now!'

Both of us suddenly stuck our heads round the corner, rapidly fired half-a-dozen shots, and quickly ducked back to safety, just as the Chinese soldiers released a murderous volley in reply. With our backs pressed to the cold wall we held our breath and waited.

A couple of seconds later a thunderous roar burst through the entrance, followed by a veritable storm of powder snow which so filled the air that for a minute visibility was reduced to near zero.

Gradually the snow settled down and Mr Holmes and I, firearms at the ready, cautiously walked through the entrance. Our plan had succeeded beyond our expectations, for the two unfortunate Chinamen were completely buried under a mass of icy rubble. The effect had been much greater in this chamber, not only because of the greater amount of ammunition we had expended, but also as the roof was much lower at this point, with great jagged icicles dangling from it.

We circumvented the icy grave. The Lama Yonten muttered some prayers, probably for the souls of the two wretched men entombed there. On the other side, about forty feet away, was another opening. So, this chamber was some kind of vestibule. We crossed the room and walked through this new entrance.

We were now in an enormous, circular, hall-like enclosure, easily a few thousand yards in diameter, covered by a gigantic dome of ice that must have been at least half a mile high at its central point. All around this colossal rotunda were great statues — twenty in number — of grim warriors clad in strange armour. The figures were of gigantic proportions, on a par with the great Buddha statues I had beheld in the Bamiyan valley in Afghanistan. As we surveyed this awesome scene, which would have made Kubla Khan's 'stately pleasure dome' look like an inverted pudding bowl, the Lama Yonten chanced to see something.

'There is a light shining in the centre.'

I applied my telescope to my eye, but could not see very clearly. What with the cold and the damp, some condensation had formed on the inside of the eyepiece; and besides, the instrument was not a very powerful one.

'There is definitely an unusual coruscation in that vicinity,' I reported. 'But I cannot make out what is causing the phenomenon.'

'We will know soon enough,' said Holmes laconically. 'Let us move on.'

Twenty minutes walk brought us before a large column of ice — a truncated stalagmite — about six feet high resting on a square stone platform two feet above the ground. The column seemed to be made of an unusual kind of ice, metallic in appearance, and dark — but in a silvery kind of way like a moonlit sky. The strange sheen of the column's surface gave the illusion of not really being solid, but just an opening to deepest space. Little star-like specks of light reflected from the icy dome on its surface reinforced the illusion. But even more wonderful was what rested — or to be exact — what seemed to be suspended a few inches above the top of the column. A perfect crystal, about the size of a large coconut, blazed with an inner fire, its many, perfectly cut facets distributing the light in myriad magical patterns.

'It is the Norbu Rimpoche!' (Skt. *Chintamani*) whispered the Lama Yonten, obviously awe-struck. 'The great Power Stone of Shambala.'

'But that is a mere legend,' said I, sceptically, for I had often come across the story in my sojourns in the Himalayas and Central Asia.[2]

'Nay, Babuji.' The Lama Yonten interrupted me. 'I recognise the stone from the description in the *Sacred Tantra of the Wheel of Time.* It is written that the Messenger from Shambala planted two such Stones, one each at the psychic poles of our planet. The

---

2. Legends of the *Chintamani* stone are prevalent even beyond these places. It is believed that Tamerlane and Akbar possessed portions of such a stone, and that the stone set on Suleiman's (Solomon) magic ring was a piece of the *Chintamani.* Nicholas Roerich, the famous White Russian mystic, artist and traveller was convinced that the *Chintamani* was the *'Lapis Exilis',* the Wandering Stone of the old Meistersingers.

first was lost when the sacred continent of Ata-Ling was devoured by the great waves. The second was brought here to Thibet, but was believed to have been taken back to Shambala when the forces of evil gained ascendancy over our land.'

'Yet it has always been here,' said Holmes reflectively. 'Hidden in this vast cavern, the *real* Ice Temple of Shambala. Probably the location and secret of this temple were lost after the death of the ninth Grand Lama; and since then the entrance chamber has mistakenly been thought to be the actual temple.'

'Much was lost with the demise of the ninth Hallowed Body,' said the Lama Yonten, shaking his head sadly. 'But now the discovery of the True Temple and the Power Stone will ensure the rule of His Holiness and the future happiness of our nation. And it is thanks to you, Mr Holmes; you and your brave companion.'

'Are there no thanks for me?' A harsh sneering cackle broke the sanctity of the temple. 'For me, who first discovered the Great Stone of Power?'

22

The Opening of the Wisdom Eye

Both Mr Holmes and I raised our pistols as the broken, cadaverous body of Professor Moriarty, the Napoleon of Crime, The Dark One, shuffled and limped into view from behind the ice column where he had been hiding. 'Journeys end in lovers' meetings,' Moriarty said with false cheer. 'Excellent. Such a perfect reunion could scarce have been expected, even if I had mailed engraved invitations to everyone. We have, of course, Holmes, the busybody, his fat Hindu Sancho Panza — to whom I owe a little something — and, ... aah ... yes, the Lama Yonten, chief monkey to our brat here ... the last Grand Lama of Thibet.'

'Hurree, shoot him if he so much as twitches a finger,' said Sherlock Holmes grimly, raising his revolver and shielding the Grand Lama's body with his own.

'With pleasure, Sir,' said I resolutely, pointing my weapon straight at Moriarty.

Moriarty looked scornfully at us. His altogether unpleasant

appearance had definitely taken a turn for the worse since our last encounter at the legation, what with the acquisition of a number or recent weals and burn-marks. 'Do you think it is necessary for me to take those silly gestures and passes any more? You do not believe me. Look!'

A narrow ripple of movement seemed to pass in the air between his eyes and the Stone of Power; and then from the Stone a concentrated wave of some kind of energy shot out and struck our hands. Our weapons disappeared in a flash.

'I assure you, gentlemen,' said Moriarty, with mock civility, 'the very atoms that composed the metals of your primitive weapons have been shredded and scattered to the extremities of the universe. As a demonstration it was perhaps extravagant. You must forgive me this childish display. It is not every day that one discovers the most powerful well-spring of energy in the world.

'Though it was commonly believed that the Great Power Stone of Shambala had been lost or that it had returned to Shambala, I, through lengthy and arduous research, learnt of its continuing existence. In the course of my studies I also discovered that the key to its location lay in the painted scroll that hung in the Grand Lama's chapel in the Jewel Park. In my attempts to acquire the scroll, I was obliged to do away with the Grand Lama — this brat's predecessor — who was unfortunately in the chapel praying, no doubt for the benefit of all pathetic sentient beings. I also had to dispose of that ninny, Gangsar *trulku,* my erstwhile colleague, who blundered into the scene and made a typically posturing and ineffectual attempt to save the life of his wretched master.

'Unfortunately I was prevented from acquiring the scroll by the Grand Master of the College of Occult Sciences — curse him! — who, taking me unawares, destroyed much of my memory and power. It is fortunate for that puffed-up old dotard that he is dead, for I had much to repay him. But even with part of my mind shattered, a glimmer of my previous quest remained faintly in my memory. After my escape to China and my eventual settlement in England, I was unconsciously drawn to the scientific study of crystals and strange stones — even extraterrestrial ones[1] — which provided me some trivial recreation. Then you, Holmes, restored my powers to me, and I was once again able to embark on my true quest — and accomplish it.'

He hobbled towards the monolith and reaching up, lifted the crystal into his hands.

'Stop! It belongs to Shambala,' cried the Lama Yonten. 'You must not desecrate it with your profane hands.'

'Old Fool!' Moriarty cried harshly, his face distorted with anger and evil anticipation, the veneer of his false civility now beginning to crack. 'For too long have you and your pious kind sat on the greatest force in the universe and just wasted it. Compassion! Enlightenment! Bah! By my own efforts I have discovered the Stone of Power and only I will possess it. And it will be used as it was intended to be used — for power.'

Holding the Stone in both hands Moriarty raised it high above his head, till his entire body was bathed in its myriad flashes of light. It seemed that he was burning in a fierce pyre, but these flames did not consume — they healed, they restored! I could scarce believe my eyes, but there it was. Gradually Moriarty's crooked body straightened till he stood tall and erect. His near cadaverous body filled out with muscle and blood, his shoulders and arms broadened and his sunken chest expanded like a balloon. Wrinkles, scars and blemishes vanished from his face, which now became youthful and comely. But his eyes remained as ever dark and sinister, and his voice harsh and sneering.

---

1. In *The Valley of Fear,* Holmes tells Watson that Moriarty is the celebrated author of *The Dynamics of an Asteroid* — 'a book which ascends to such rarefied heights of pure mathematics that it is said that there was no man in the scientific press capable of criticising it.'

'Now, before I subject you to the Stone's awesome powers — though the effect will be somewhat different in your case — perhaps an explanation is in order. It may comfort you to know the precise workings of the force that will collect your final debt to nature. I will try not to be tedious, so bear with me ...'

He then embarked upon an extraordinary lecture which was chok-a-block full of very fanciful ideas and wild theories, that he, in a very superior way, considered to be more scientific than the scientific laws formulated by such great thinkers as Mr Dalton or even Mr Newton. Of course it was all bakwas, as we say in Hindustani. I am convinced that his tricks came from a knowledge of jadoo and the power of djinns and demons in his service. There was nothing scientific about it. I mean he even said that light waves were electric and magnetic vibrations, when everyone knows that light is just colours (VIBGYOR) as proved by Mr Newton in his famous prism experiment. Even more crazy was his idea that human thoughts were mere electrical discharges in the brain cells. I mean, how can a scientific man like me even begin to tolerate such ravings. If Moriarty was right then all we had to do for mental inspiration was to stick our finger into one of Signor Galvani's battery piles. Anyhow, I reproduce his entire lunatic lecture for the reader's amusement. That he conducted it in the most condescendingly superior and professorial manner will surprise no one.

'The Power Stone is essentially a crystal,' Moriarty commenced to address us, in a tone one would only be forgiven for adopting towards the village idiot. 'In structure a rhombic dodecahedron to be exact. Though certain elements in its composition are not of this world, its unique properties derive more from its nature as a crystal than anything else. Concerning the knowledge of crystals, our science is yet in its infancy, though the precise geometrical forms of crystals have excited the interests of many thinkers. Are not the five platonic solids, of which Plato had so much to say, just various crystalline forms? And we must not forget the diamond. A mere crystal of carbon, yet the most precious stone on earth.

'The crystal derives its unique quality from the symmetrical lattice structure of its molecules. The tighter the atoms of the lattice are packed together, the more pronounced the qualities of the crystal become and the more enhanced its ... aah ... special powers. For example, when the formation of carbon molecules is loose, it lacks a lattice structure altogether, and the result is charcoal or soot. With greater pressure, the lattice form is assumed in the formation of the carbon molecules and the result it graphite. When carbon molecules are subjected to tremendous pressure and the lattice structure is packed tight, diamond is formed. But if the molecules and atoms in the lattice form are compacted beyond a certain stage, some crystals develop extraordinary properties. For instance, the crystal of Iceland Spar only permits a certain plane of light to go through it. It may interest you to know, in spite of all the stupid opinions to the contrary, that light waves consist of electrical and magnetic vibrations taking place in all possible planes containing the ray. Thus the crystal of Spar puts the random electric and magnetic vibrations in order as it passes through it.[2] Other crystals, like quartz, also show the ability to order electric vibrations.

'The Power Stone is the ultimate crystal capable of ordering, amplifying and concentrating electrical vibrations of a specific nature beyond all conceivable limits. I have stated that the electrical vibrations needed for the Power Stone were of a specific wave-length. Now, mental energy consists, basically, of millions upon millions of infinitesimal electrical discharges occurring every second in our brains, and of the precise wave-length required to

---

2. What we now call the polarisation of light.

activate the Power Stone. Since most people have no control over their mental activities, the Stone is as useful to them as a fiddle to a cow. But for a trained master of the occult, who not only can project his cerebral impulses outside his brain, but direct them where he will, this crystal becomes a true Stone of Power. And it is mine.'

While Moriarty had been indulging in his long boastful lecture, I had arrived at the inescapable conclusion that we were all doomed if we did not do something, and jolly quick too. But what could we do? I glanced over at Mr Holmes to see if he had anything up his sleeve. But it was clear that there was nothing he could do without Moriarty noticing, for the Professor's full attention was directed at his arch-enemy. Indeed it was apparent that Moriarty's self-congratulatory and swanking speech was intended wholly for Mr Holmes's benefit. The rest of us — even I — were, intellectually, mere worms in Moriarty's eyes. It was a humiliating realisation, but it stirred the veriest beginning of an idea in my head.

Once again it would be up to me, Hurree Chunder Mookerjee (M.A.), to teach our arrogant Professor Moriarty (Ph.D.), a little lesson in Christian humility and common courtesy.

Mr Holmes was standing directly in front of Moriarty about twenty feet away from him. Behind Holmes were the two Lamas, both of whom, I am proud to say, were standing bravely erect not showing a whit the great fear they must have felt. I was to their right, a couple of yards away, a distance that I managed to slowly and considerably increase by the subtle performance of a series of almost imperceptible casual shuffles. When I judged that I could not proceed any further without attracting Moriarty's unwelcome attention, but that I was sufficiently beyond his immediate frontal vision, I drew in my breath and 'let slip the dogs of war'.

I was holding the dark lantern in my left hand. Deftly transferring it to my right, I flung it at the Professor. As the reader may have guessed, I was attempting to duplicate my previous incendiary success at the Chinese legation. Alas, it was not to be. Once again I missed Moriarty. The lamp struck the column and, bouncing off, clattered uselessly on the stone dias. No great gout of flame, not even a bally spark, came out of that damn thing. I had forgotten how robustly these modern safety lanterns were constructed. Moriarty — confound the man — did not duck, or even flinch at my attack, but laughed aloud in his sinister way.

'Ah ... how kind of you to remind me of our unfinished business. I had almost forgotten. Now ...'

'Look out, Hurree!' cried Holmes. But it was too late. Much, too late.

A brief current of light flashed from Moriarty's eyes to the Stone of Power. Suddenly a ball of fire shot forth from the Stone. It struck me full in the chest and threw me violently backwards. I seemed to lose consciousness for a moment, then I felt the pain, which was intense. It coursed through me like liquid fire. Then there was Mr Holmes crouching over my supine form, a look of intense sorrow and anguish on his face.

'Hurree, my friend. Can you hear me?'

I smelt the scorched flesh of my torn chest, and knew that it was all over; that I was now embarking on my final voyage on the khafila of life.

'I am dead, Mr Holmes,' I said simply. But it was not going to be as simple as that, for I heard Moriarty's strident objections to my speedy demise.

'No, no, my fat friend. Not so fast. You will burn for a long time before you perish altogether. Coals of fire. Eh! Coals of fire. Ha. Ha. Ha.'

Even in my final moments I was to be denied any peace or solace. Moriarty's maniacal laughter rent the air, and echoing off every point on the great dome of ice, filled the place with its horrid, exaggerated mimicry.

'Who shall it be now?' Moriarty cackled hideously. 'No. Not you Holmes. You will see this thing through to the end. It is necessary that you observe the suffering you have caused your friends by your impertinent meddling in my affairs. But where shall we start? Let us think. Shall we now see the Grand Lama onto his journey to the heavenly fields, as they so charmingly put it in this country?'

'Mr Holmes!' cried the Lama Yonten in despair. 'You must save His Holiness.'

'Old Fool!' laughed Moriarty. 'What can you expect this Englishman to do against my power — and the power of the Stone?'

'Listen to me!' the Lama Yonten shouted desperately to Sherlock Holmes. 'You are not really English. You are one of us. You have the power too.'

'What do you mean, monkey?' cried Moriarty, but the Lama Yonten's whole attention was focused on Sherlock Holmes, whom he was frantically shaking by the lapel of his Ladakhi robe. For the first and only time I saw Mr Holmes looking dazed. His mouth hung open and his eyes were glazed over. But the Lama Yonten desperately persisted in his attempt to persuade Sherlock Holmes of his rather lunatic conviction.

'Mr Holmes Mr Holmes. Listen to me. You are not Sherlock Holmes! You are the renowned Gangsar *trulku*, former abbot of the White Garuda Monastery, one of the greatest adepts of the occult sciences. The Dark One slew you eighteen years ago, but just before your life-force left your body we were able to transfer it — by the yoga of *Pho-wa*[3] — to another body far away.'

---

3. *Pho-wa* (Tib.) is one of the most jealously guarded secret yogic practises of Tibet. It is the yoga of transferring the principle of consciousness from one incarnation to the next without suffering any break in the continuity of consciousness.

'I cannot remember ... cannot remember ...' Mr Holmes mumbled and staggered back a few steps as if intoxicated.

'You cannot remember because you were unconscious and on the point of death when the *Pho-wa* operation was performed and the Aperture of Bhrama[4] opened to release the sacred bird. That is why we could not direct the principle of consciousness after its release and had to trust in the power of the Three Jewels to guide it to a habitable body.[5] It was the best we could do at the time.'

It may have been my proximity to death or the great pain I was suffering as I lay prostrate on that cold cavern floor that allowed me to hear this strange tale without feeling any real surprise or incredulity. In fact, in a semi-conscious, dreamy way, I found myself even beginning to agree with it. Mr Holmes a former lama? Why ever not? He was celibate, of noble mien and great wisdom. In accordance with the Mahayanic precepts of

---

4. The consciousness principle (or life-force) leaves the body through the 'Aperture of Bhrama' (Skt. *Bhrama-randhra*) situated on the crown of the head at the sagittal suture where the two parietal bones articulate, opened by means of the yogic practise of the *Pho-wa*. The bird flying out of it is the consciousness-principle going out; for it is through this aperture that the life-force quits the body, either permanently at death, or temporarily during the practice of *Pho-wa*. The process is a part of *Kundalini Yoga*.

5. Judging by the Lama Yonten's words, it would seem that in this case the process was not one of reincarnation with continuing consciousness, but a radical transfer of the consciousness principle into *the body of another existing person*. It would therefore seem that the yoga of *Trong-jug* and not the yoga of *Pho-wa* was performed in this case. The Babu is probably not to blame for this error in the narrative. It is most likely that the Lama Yonten made a mistake in his choice of terms, a perfectly understandable error considering the desperation of the situation.

altruism and compassion he had devoted his life to aiding the weak, the poor and the helpless against the powers of evil. He fasted regularly to clear the vital channels and bring about clarity of insight; and he had powers of concentration that would make many a practising yogi look like a rank novice. Never was an incarnate lama truer, or more deserving of his monastic robe and cap of office, than my dear friend.

Fresh spasms of burning pain racked my body, and for some moments I lost consciousness. When I recovered I was greeted with the offensive sound of Moriarty's chuckling.

'So, Gangsar, my pious, do-good classmate. You survived after all. Strange are the ways of karma, are they not? My two greatest enemies are actually the same person. Which is very convenient, when you think about it. One does not necessarily have to go to the blood-thirsty extent of the Emperor Caligula, when he wished that all Rome had just one neck, to appreciate the need for economy of action in these things. But we must see to the Grand Lama first. You will have to wait for your turn Holmes, or Gangsar, whatever you may wish to be called.'

'Holmes will do for the present,' said my friend in a clear strong voice, standing tall and erect, his arms akimbo, 'and you will not harm the boy.'

Though at death's door, I nearly cheered at this revival of Sherlock Holmes's strength. Indeed, his sharp eyes flashed like gemstones and all the outstanding aspects of his physiognomy: his fierce hawk-like nose, his determined chin, and his noble brow, seemed even more prominent and revealing of the greatness of the man. It was as if he had undergone transfiguration.

'Hah! Do I detect a note of defiance? Foolish. Foolish,' jeered Moriarty, shaking his long forefinger as if admonishing a child. 'Do you think that just because you have recovered your memory and some of your old occult powers, you can stand up to me? Have you forgotten the Great Stone of Power? Not even the combined strength of the College of the Occult Sciences, and all the Grand Masters, living and dead, could withstand its immense power. So how do you think you can stop me? It is beyond your capability to resist even an iota of its energy. Try!'

A ripple of movement flowed out of his eyes and, striking the stone, emerged as a kind of invisible wave of destructive energy that shot out towards Holmes and the two Lamas. Sherlock Holmes raised his hands and — as if he had been doing it all his life (which, in a manner of speaking, he probably had) — moved his fingers in a strange manner to form tantric gestures (Skt. *mudra*). Immediately, a barely visible barrier, a kind of curtain of shimmering energy, seemed to form before them. The force wave smashed into the psychic shield with the noise of a thunderclap. Holmes and the two Lamas were thrown to the ground; but they gradually rose to their feet, and it was apparent that, though shaken, they were happily unharmed.

'Good, Holmes, good,' crowed Moriarty, 'but not quite good enough, if you will forgive me the remark. You have obviously not applied yourself with sufficient diligence to the teachings of our old Master. The little finger should have unfolded like the petals of the *Utpala*[6] flower after the first rain, not hung hesitantly like a eunuch's *lingam.* So shall we try again?'

Again and again Moriarty attacked with the awesome power of the Stone, and again and again Sherlock Holmes threw up his psychic shield to protect the lamas and himself from annihilation. But it was tragically obvious that Moriarty was toying with Holmes and was — as he himself had earlier declared — using only a fraction of his power. Standing tall and erect, shining with vitality, he casually directed the murderous waves of energy at a rapidly weakening Sherlock Holmes.

---

6. Sanskrit for the Blue Lotus (*Nymphaea caerulea*).

Tears filled my eyes at the realisation that my noble friend was doomed, and with him the Grand Lama and the Lama Yonten; and then, of course, Thibet, that fascinating country to whose study I had devoted these many years of my life. Was it all to end in this manner? With myself lying useless and dying on the floor of this cold cavern, while Moriarty strutted about, brave as a cock on his own dung-hill, crowing his cock-a-doodle-doo of victory. It was hateful — intolerable. But what could I do? I could not even move. Or could I?'

Gritting my teeth I tried. I discovered that my entire body was useless and had no feelings nor functions, except for the right arm, which had retained some of its vitality — at least for the moment. Clawing the icy floor with my right hand I managed to slowly and painfully drag myself forward.

Moriarty had his back to me and was slowly advancing on Mr Holmes and the two Lamas, who were being flung further backwards in disarray after every shattering blow of the Power Stone. Oh, for my revolver! A weapon — anything. I looked about the cavern floor but could see nothing. Only my trusty old umbrella lay on the ice a little away from me, where it must have fallen after I had been struck by the fire-ball. Moriarty now paused for a moment in his advance to make some more sneering, facetious remarks, that he obviously regarded as hilariously funny.

'Have you now had enough finger exercises, Holmes? I should really hope so, for I intend to make our next lesson a more difficult one. Now what shall it be? Ah! I have it. You'll love this one Holmes. In fact it'll warm the cockles of your heart. Ha. Ha. Ha.' As the cavern dome echoed once again with his laughter, a jet of multi-coloured fire shot forth from the Stone. 'Hell-fire, Holmes! Hell-fire! Ha. Ha.'

Only just in time Sherlock Holmes managed to make some occult gestures and raised his psychic shield before the flames struck — and engulfed it. For a moment I thought with despair that they had been consumed by the blaze. But then, through the raging flames, I was able to see that Mr Holmes and the lamas were safely ensconced within a dome of energy, and safe — at least for the present — while all round them raged this magical conflagration.

Gritting my teeth I managed to drag myself to where my umbrella lay — and secured it. What I was going to do with it I did not know, but I grimly dragged myself towards Moriarty. On reflection, I can really provide no explanation how my shattered, near lifeless body managed not to just give up and expire altogether, much less move forward in this fashion. It may have been the overriding hatred I felt for this evil, sneering blackguard, or even the great love and concern I felt for my companions, that provided me with the necessary inspiration and reserve of strength to go on.

Now, as I neared my nemesis, the fire increased in malevolent vigour and began to take on a demoniacal life of its own. Strange hellish creatures: imps, monsters, demons and witches flitted and danced about the flames, sniggering, cackling and screaming at my friends within their perilously vulnerable haven.

I struggled forward until I was just behind Moriarty. But then I realised that I had, all along, just been deceiving myself. There was no earthly possibility that I could raise myself to my feet and knock the villain smartly behind the head with my umbrella, as I had vaguely planned to do. It was a miracle in itself that I had managed to just drag myself up to this point using only my one fit arm. Tears of impotent rage and frustration coursed down my cheeks and dropped on the icy floor. Through my misted eyes I now saw my friends in their final death-struggle.

The flames had greatly increased in energy. Sherlock Holmes, exhausted and beaten, was now down on both knees, his left hand resting on the ground, supporting his spent body. But that unconquerable, valiant soul still managed to hold his right hand high, the fingers still forming the *mudra* of protection (Skt. *raks mudra*).

The hellish creatures were beside themselves with rage and anticipation of victory. Three grimacing imps jumped violently up and down on the energy dome. A black satanic creature with flaming eyes attacked its surface with a fiery trident, trying to prise it open like a tin of bully beef. A coven of witches tore at the sides with their sharp claws, screaming and cackling in gleeful expectation — as the dome visibly weakened under their combined attack. There were many other such foul creatures in this ferocious assault, but it was not possible to see everything clearly in the hellish confusion and raging flames.

The dark figure of Moriarty seemed to grow taller, more sinister and satanic as he prepared to deliver his death blow. 'Well, Holmes,' he shouted gleefully above the roar of the flames and the screaming of his filthy minions. 'I trust that age hath not withered nor custom staled my infinite variety. This is just a foretaste of where I am going to consign you and your friends — forever.'

He stepped back a pace to prepare his stroke — and stepped right on my extended hand. I nearly yelled with the pain, but fortunately managed to swallow the hurt and remain still. Then a strange feeling overcame me, and I beheld the finger of God in this little incident.

'Goodbye, Holmes, everybody. Forever!'

Moriarty stepped forward. I clenched the end of my umbrella firmly and, whipping it forward, hooked the curved handle around his right ankle. Then, summoning the last remaining reserve of strength in my body, I pulled. For a moment Moriarty staggered backwards but then the full force of my pull caused his legs to flip back in the air and his torso to tumble forward. His arms instinctively extended forwards to break his fall — and he inadvertently released his hold on the Stone of Power.

The Great Stone of Power, propelled by the impetus of Moriarty's fall, sailed slowly through the air, glittering like the reflection of a full moon on the broken surface of a surging river

— straight past the demonic creatures and the conflagration, through the collapsing wall of the psychic dome — and plump into Sherlock Holmes's hands.

As Moriarty scrambled up from the floor, he visibly began to diminish and distort, till soon he was the old, ugly, crooked, bent, scarred, and lame bounder that we had known before. He looked about him confusedly but when he saw Mr Holmes coolly holding the Power Stone, his eyes opened wide with alarm. The alarm was justified, for the infernal fire and the hellish creatures around Holmes now turned their attention to Moriarty and suddenly surged towards him.

'No! No!' he wailed in terror, but they smashed headlong into him. For a brief moment Moriarty burned — and in seconds was only bones. These disintegrated, leaving a puff of smoke and fire which sped away with the other flames and creatures into the distance, and disappeared.

'NOOOOOOooooooooooooooo ...' the echoes of Moriarty's last desperate wail finally receded, and there was silence, and, at last, peace.

Sherlock Holmes walked slowly over to the monolith and replaced the stone. Then he quickly came over to where I lay on the floor, now at peace with myself, and reconciled to stepping onto another stage on the Wheel of Life. Kneeling beside me he inspected my wound anxiously. The Lama Yonten and the Grand Lama crouched beside him, their eyes filled with solicitude.

'I trust that my services have proved satisfactory, Sir?' I managed to whisper, my lips now experiencing the icy chill that had gripped the rest of my body.

'More, much more than satisfactory, my friend.' Mr Holmes's clear, hard eyes were dimmed, and his firm lips were shaking. 'Do not give up hope yet. There is a chance ...'

'No, Mr Holmes,' I interrupted. 'There is no time. I only ask you to give a full report of my service to Colonel Creighton. Also, if it would not be too much trouble, could you please scatter my ashes over the river Ganges. I am a scientific man but … but one cannot be too sure about everything. Now farewell, good Sirs.'

'There must be something we can do,' said Holmes in a despairing voice that wrung my heart.

'Perhaps there is …' said the Lama Yonten hesitantly, '… beyond the portals of the *mandala*. But how …'

'Of course,' cried Holmes, snapping his fingers. 'I remember the tale. We can but try. Come, Your Holiness. Only you can save our friend now.'

He led the Grand Lama by the hand to the stone platform. The lad seated himself, in full lotus position, before the Stone of Power, and closed his eyes in meditation. Sherlock Holmes crouched beside him and whispered into his ear. Whatever Mr Holmes was attempting, I knew that it would be too late, for I was fast slipping into unconsciousness. My vision began to blur until everything took on a far-away, dream-like quality; so much so that it is with much hesitation, and indeed against all my training as a scientific observer and recorder, that I now set down on paper what I beheld — or imagined I beheld — subsequently. I lay no claims of truth on the matter. Perhaps it was a hallucination. Let the reader take it as he will.

My fading vision was somehow compelled towards the Great Stone of Power, whose luminosity now strangely seemed to be the only thing of substance or reality around me. The light of the Stone gradually changed, becoming darker, but no less luminous. This wonderful phenomenon increased, until I realised that I was peering into some kind of dark, radiant opening. The black hole gradually increased in size until it filled the entire cavern — and then beyond it. Lying on my back and looking up I seemed to behold an endless and wonderful night sky, unlimited by any horizons, or the usual restrictions dictated by the limitations of the human eye.

This immense space was not static, but churned, nay, seethed with energy and movement, like gigantic whirlpools and waterspouts in a storm-tossed sea. The centre of this oceanic space seemed to tear open, giving birth to another vortex that gradually filled the previous space. Seven times it happened in all, till seven endless vortices, one within the other, stretched out millions upon millions of miles to whatever eternity lay in this universe of God's creation.

Then from the centre of the ultimate vortex emerged a small point of light, that, moving forward, gradually grew in size, till it was possible to appoint a definite shape to it. It seemed like a distant mountain, floating by itself — like Mount Kinchenjoonga seen from Darjeeling, that often floats serenely above a sea of monsoon clouds; or like Mr Jonathan Swift's 'Flying Island of Laputa'. The edges of this mountain-like shape glowed with a ring of fire, while its surface glittered with multi-coloured points of light.

As it came lower I could see that the shape was actually a kind of city — a celestial city, with soaring towers and marvellous palaces piled, *en échelon,* on each other like a Thibetan monastery — indeed like the Potala — but infinitely larger and higher. Millions of points of light flashed from every part of this city, while the many spires and curved pagoda roofs gleamed like molten gold. The city rested on a colossal circular platform many, many miles in diameter surrounded by rings of multicoloured fire that seemed to provide it with its vital source of levitational and motive power.

Of course. A *Mandala*!

A roar like that of a thousand giant Thibetan trumpets reverberated through the air as it slowly descended, burning so brightly with flashing, moving lights that my senses failed me for sometime. Then I felt myself rising towards the lights, which, strangely enough, did not discomfort me in spite of their awesome brilliance and energy. Then the brilliance changed to a comfortable glow like that of a well-lit room, and I imagined figures moving around me. I may have dreamt it for the figures, though vaguely human, were enormous — at least ten feet tall and clad in strange suits of iridescent armour, and grim helmets crested with nodding plumes of fire. Of course, the statues in the cavern! That's why I was dreaming all this. One of the figures walked silently over to my side and bent down. His face was that of a warrior, noble and stern, but he smiled kindly at me and put his hand on my eyes. I slept.

I dreamed I was lying on a high altar surrounded by faceless, white robed priests, who cut my body open with shining knives of light, and poured liquid fire inside me. But I felt no pain and I slept again.

23

His Last Bow

I opened my eyes to see larks flying high above in a clear blue summer's sky.

'Ah, Hurree. You are awake,' Sherlock Holmes's reassuring voice came from close beside me. He was sitting near where I lay on the grassy slope of a sun-drenched hillside, smoking his pipe contentedly. I was confused, but strangely did not care very much. I just felt wonderful to be alive. I touched my chest. There was no wound there — not the least trace. Had it all been but a dream? As I pressed my right hand on my chest I felt a twinge of pain in the *hand* — where a foot had trodden on it.

'Moriarty!'

'He has passed on to another existence, Hurree. Do you not remember how you tripped him up when he was preparing to deliver his *coup de grâce?* If they had such a thing as a public museum in this country, that's where your umbrella ought to be.'

Hearing our voices, the Grand Lama, the Lama Yonten, Tsering and Kintup now came up the hill from a small campsite just below. The Grand Lama came and draped a white silk scarf around my neck to thank me for saving his life. The Lama Yonten, looking none the worse for his ordeal, took my hand warmly and shook it again and again. Tsering and Kintup were very happy to see me up and alive, though ever after they stood in great awe of me, most certainly from hearing an exaggerated account of my feats in the cavern from an excited Lama Yonten, who had blown the story totally out of proportion in the recounting. All my efforts to set the record straight proved futile, even detrimental, since the two fellows attributed my protests to what they considered my natural modesty, and added it to their list of my virtues.

We were camped on a hillside some miles away from the glacier, which was visible to the north. The entrance to the temple was once again firmly buried under the ice, awaiting the advent of the next Grand Lama. One side of our campsite was taken up by our prisoners — thirty-odd Chinese soldiers huddled miserably together. The Grand Lama's guards, under the inspired leadership of our valiant Tsering, had not only succeeded in blunting the attack of the Chinese soldiers at the ice bridge, but subsequently, taking the initiative, had led a charge and routed them completely.

The next day we started on our journey back to Lhassa. On our way I questioned Sherlock Holmes about the extraordinary events in the cavern, and attempted to elicit some kind of rational explanation for them. He did not reply immediately but rode silently beside me. After lighting his pipe and drawing on it a few times, he turned to me.

'I value your friendship too highly, Hurree, to ever want you to think that I am not being frank with you. I am under a grave oath never to reveal certain secrets to anyone who is not of *us* — even though he may be a trusted friend and a great benefactor. I have discussed the matter with the Lama Yonten and he agrees that it is perhaps permissible to provide you a general explanation, without divulging specific information, that could be construed as a transgression of the vows of secrecy.'

Even on horseback, Mr Holmes managed to assume the slightly didactic air that he always did when discoursing on a subject.

'The Buddha once said that there were as many worlds and universes in the sphere of existence as there were grains of sand on the shores of the Ganges. Buddhist theologians believe that the "Wheel of the Most Excellent Law" has been turned in many of these worlds by various Buddhas of the three ages, and even by Shakyamuni himself. Many of these worlds are far in advance of ours, one in particular, ruling over a thousand other worlds in its system, is so tremendously ahead of our own insignificant primitive planet in matters of science and spirituality, that it would be impossible to explain its marvels to a modern man, as it would be impossible to explain the working of a steam engine to a savage Andaman Islander. To us, the beings of this world would seem god-like, not only for the unimaginable powers that they possess, but also for their miraculous longevity. But ultimately they are mortal. For as the Buddha has said, "all that is born must die — even the gods in Indra's heaven."

'It is believed that many aeons ago, in their quest for universal truth, these beings discovered "The Law," and since then, have ever sought to protect the Noble Doctrine wherever it may be threatened. They have always watched over our world, and, through a small community of fellow seekers in the remoteness of the Thibetan highlands, they have maintained a bond with humankind.

'You know of the prophecy of the Lamas, that when man succumbs absolutely to greed and ignorance, causing ruin and desolation everywhere on the land, in the sea, and in the very air; and when the forces of darkness with their engines of death and destruction have finally enslaved everyone, then the Lords of Shambala will send their mighty fleets across the universe, and in a great battle, defeat evil and bring about a new age of wisdom and peace.'

'Do you believe in the story, Sir?'

'It is not necessary to subscribe to such a belief to see where man's blind worship of money and power must eventually lead him. When the green and fertile land is destroyed to build dark satanic mills wherein underfed children and consumptive women are made to slave; when artless primitives armed with bows and spears are converted to our ideas of commerce and civilisation through the hot barrels of gatling guns; and when even that sport is now too poor and all the nations of Europe are fast becoming armed camps, waiting to fall on each other — then what can a discerning person really do, save tremble for the future of humanity.

'No, I do not think it would be simple-hearted to give serious consideration to this ancient prophecy, and also to take some solace from its hopeful conclusion. If, Hurree, the night is clear and star-lit, you might even look up at a far away immovable speck of light in the North, from whence may come our salvation.'

The coronation of the Grand Lama, or to be more precise his 'Assumption of Spiritual and Temporal Power', took place exactly a month after our arrival in the city. Moriarty's death had definitely drawn the fangs from Chinese plans in Thibet. Moreover the evidence of the captured Chinese soldiers proved to be too embarrassing even for the Emperor,[1] who hastily recalled the Amban O-erh-'tai to Pekin, and had him summarily beheaded as a stern warning to those who dared to cause misunderstanding

1. The ultimate political authority in China at the time was really in the hands of the empress dowager, Cixi, the ruthless, power-hungry, cunning, and treacherous aunt of the figure-head emperor, Guangxu, who languished in palace seclusion — on her orders.

betwixt a righteous Emperor of China and his revered chaplain the Grand Lama of Thibet. Without the Amban's support the Regent's power-base crumbled and he was subsequently arrested, tried before the Tsongdu, the National Assembly, and imprisoned for life.

Lhassa city, indeed the entire country, celebrated this joyous event. In the Great Audience Hall of the Potala Palace, before a vast assemblage of ministers, officials of various ranks, incarnate Lamas, abbots of the great monastic universities, and embassies from Nepaul, Sikkhim, Ladakh, Bhootan, China, Turkestan, Mongolia, and some small Indian states, the young Grand Lama was seated on the Lion Throne and presented with the Seven Articles of Royalty and the Eight Auspicious Emblems that confirmed him as Ngawang Lobsang Thupten Gyatso, the All Knowing Presence, in accordance with the precepts of the Buddha, the Ocean of Wisdom, Immutable, Holder of the Thunderbolt, the Glorious Thirteenth in the Glorious Line of Victory and Power, Spiritual and Temporal Ruler of all Thibet.

After this ceremony, to which Mr Holmes and I had been granted special seats, Mr Holmes and I, in another less elaborate but equally dignified ceremony, were presented with special awards for our services. A complete set of monastic robes was bestowed upon Sherlock Holmes, along with a cap of office granting him the rank of *Huthoktu,* the third highest rank after the Grand Lama's in the lamaist hierarchy. The young Grand Lama himself handed me a rare, fifteenth-century bronze statue of Atisha, the great Buddhist teacher from Bengal. I will remember forever, with reverence and affection, the words that accompanied this great gift.

'For a second time in our history,' said the young ruler, 'Thibet has need to thank a man from the sacred land of Vangala.'

The Grand Lama was no longer the sickly boy we had first met, but a strong and wise leader of his people. It was clear that whatever further obstacles and dangers would emerge during his reign, he would somehow overcome them.[2]

After the coronation festivities, Mr Holmes departed for the Valley of the Full Moon (Dawa Rong) in Southern Thibet, where his small monastery, the White Garuda Dharma Castle, was situated. A large retinue of monks and servitors accompanied him. There, in another ceremony, he was re-installed as the incarnate Lama and abbot of the monastery. He also underwent, for a number of months, a series of meditations, pujas, and initiation ceremonies (Tib. *wang-kur*) with his teachers.

Being granted a *laissez passer* throughout Thibet, Kintup and I, with Gaffuru and Jamspel, travelled to the great inland sea of Chang Nam-tso, the highest body of salt water in the world, to study its very unusual tides, and to survey the area around. (See my article, 'Record of Tidal Activities of a Thibetan Sea', Vol.xxv No.1 Jan/Feb, *Journal of the Geographical Society of Bengal*). We also travelled to many other lakes and conducted a number of geographical and ethnological studies, which it is not necessary to enumerate here. Finally, on receipt of the third of Colonel Creighton's harsh missives demanding my recall, I reluctantly decided that it was no longer feasible, on whatever account, to

---

2. Hurree was very prescient here. The thirteenth Dalai Lama not only survived a number of subsequent plots, but even after an exile to Mongolia and another to India, eventually succeeded in throwing out all Chinese influence and power in Tibet. He declared the independence of his nation on the eighth day of the first month of the Water-Ox year (1913). Besides making important reforms in the government and the church, he created a modern army that further defeated Chinese forces on the eastern frontier of Tibet, and gradually recovered lost territories of the old Tibetan Empire. For a full account of his life see *Portrait of the Dalai Lama,* London, 1946, by his friend Sir Charles Bell.

prolong my stay and studies in the Forbidden Land. Bidding a melancholy adieu to the Grand Lama, the Lama Yonten and Tsering, I departed from Lhassa on the 10th of November, 1892.

I travelled south, following the course of the Bramhaputra river, to the beautiful Valley of the Full Moon, to Mr Holmes's monastery, situated on a picturesque hillside covered with aromatic juniper trees. I stayed with him for a week learning much about ... let us just say, many things. He had decided to stay a year more in Thibet to complete his studies. But after that he would return to England[3] to finish his task of destroying Moriarty's criminal empire and removing his baleful influence once and for all from the cities of Europe. Only on the conclusion of this task would he finally return to Thibet.

'I have my orders,' said Holmes, 'and I must obey.' He did not elaborate about who had given those orders, and I did not ask.

The last sight of my dear friend will remain forever vivid in my mind. Attired in wine-red monastic robes, tall and imposing, he stood before a copse of dwarf pines by the monastery gate, accompanied by his disciples, who bowed low when I mounted my pony and rode away. Mr Holmes raised his right hand to bid me farewell and to give me his blessings. I never saw him again.

It has always been a dispiriting thing for me to leave the solitude and purity of the mountains and return to the real world, though this time my unique discoveries ensured that the world would greet me with medals, awards, appointments and all the other trappings of its respect and honour. Yet even in my new life of

---

3. Sherlock Holmes returned to England in the late spring of 1894. Soon after his arrival in London he succeeded in finally catching the elusive Colonel Moran in an ingenious trap, at the same time solving the strange murder of the Hon. Ronald Adair, which had left the fashionable world of London utterly dismayed (see *The Empty House*).

prosperity and prominence I have never forgotten the wise words of Sherlock Holmes — surely engraved in my heart as if on granite — reminding me of the sorrows and follies of this world, and man's inhumanity to man.

Just yesterday evening, I sent away my private carriage and driver, and walked home from the Great Eastern Hotel after the annual dinner of the Royal Asiatic Society of Bengal, where I had been invited to speak on Himalayan exploration to a group of sleek, well-fed gentlemen and their bored overdressed wives. Outside the hotel, hordes of starving children scrambled for leftover food from the hotel's garbage bins. I distributed what money I had on me amongst them. Then I turned away and walked through the dark back-streets.

It was a clear and moonless night. Once again I found myself looking up north, in the direction of the far Himalayas, at a sky blazing with stars ... *sic itur a mons ad astra* ... to paraphrase Virgil ...

But enough. I weary the reader with my unrelenting *cacoethes scribindi.* Let the tale now end.

Epilogue

The Thirteenth Dalai Lama, the Grand Lama of Hurree's story, died on the thirteenth day of the tenth month of the Water-Bird year (17 December 1933). A year before his death he proclaimed to his subjects his last political testament and warning.

'It may happen,' he prophesied, 'that here, in Tibet, religion and government will be attacked from without and within. Unless we can guard our country, it will happen that the Dalai and Panchen Lamas, the Father and the Son, and all the revered holders of the Faith, will disappear and become nameless. Monks and their monasteries will be destroyed. The rule of law will be weakened. The land and property of government officials will be seized. They themselves will be forced to serve their enemies or wander the country like beggars. All beings will be sunk in great hardship and overpowering fear; and the nights and days will drag on slowly in suffering.'

But the Great Thirteenth's warnings were forgotten by a blinkered clergy and a weak aristocracy, who allowed his monumental works and reforms to decline and fall into disuse;

so much so that the Chinese Communist Army marched into Tibet in October 1950 encountering only disorganised resistance. Then, the long endless nights began. After crushing all resistance the Chinese launched systematic campaigns to destroy the Tibetan people and their way of life. This movement reached its crescendo during the Cultural Revolution, but continues to this day, in varying degrees of violence and severity. Right now, in a deliberate policy to eradicate whatever vestige of Tibetan identity that survived previous genocidal campaigns, Beijing is flooding Tibet with Chinese immigrants; so much so that Tibetans are fast becoming a minority in their own country. In Lhasa Tibetans are an insignificant anomaly in a sea of Chinese. Even the Chinese police and military personnel, in and around the city, outnumber the Tibetan population. They are there to control and repress.

By latest estimates over six thousand monasteries, temples and historical monuments have been destroyed, along with incalculably vast quantities of priceless artistic and religious objects — and countless books and manuscripts of Tibet's unique and ancient learning. Over a million Tibetans have been killed by execution, torture and starvation, while hundreds of thousands of others have been forced to slave in a remote and desolate gulag in North-eastern Tibet, easily the largest of its kind in the world.

The refugees who escaped this nightmare tried to re-create in exile a part of their former lives. Monasteries, schools and institutions of music, theatre, medicine, painting, metal-work, and other arts and crafts began to grow in and around Dharamsala, the Tibetan capital-in-exile, and other places in India and countries around the world where Tibetan refugees found new homes.

It was in Dharamsala, where I worked for the Education Department of the government-in-exile, that I heard, one day, of some monks from the monastery of the White Garuda (in the Valley of the Full Moon) who had escaped to India. They had even managed to set up a small community of their own in a broken-down British bungalow, just outside Dharamsala town. An hour's hard walk up the rocky mountain path brought me to the dilapidated bungalow. A few old monks were reading their scriptures, sitting cross-legged on a scraggly patch of lawn before the house. I enquired of one of them if I could talk to the person in charge.

Very soon a large but cheerful monk, who looked startlingly like the French comedian, Fernandel, came out of the house and enquired politely as to my business. I offered him the sack of fruits and vegetables that I had brought along as a gift, which was, I was happy to note, welcome to them. I was offered a rather rickety chair in their prayer-room, now empty as most of the younger monks had gone to collect firewood from the forest nearby. There was a small butter lamp burning in a make-shift altar on the mantelpiece over the old English fireplace. A calendar reproduction of the Dalai Lama's portrait in a cheap gilded frame, was the centre-piece of this altar. Beside it stood two gimcrack plastic vases stuffed with bright scarlet rhododendron blooms that covered the mountainsides at this time of the year.

I made the customary small-talk with the stout monk, who was seated across me on a packing crate. Tea was served, made, inevitably, with CARE milk powder that tasted overpoweringly of nameless chemical preservatives. After taking a couple of mandatory sips from my cup, I got down to business.

I asked him if any of the monks remembered having a white-man, an English sahib, as the incarnate Lama of their monastery. I was really not expecting anyone to remember much, especially as it was now over ninety years since Holmes's presence in the monastery in Tibet, and also as only very few of the older monks had managed to survive the exodus from their burning monastery to this bungalow in northern India. So it was a pleasant surprise when the big fellow replied in the affirmative.

Yes, he remembered being told of the English sahib who had been their abbot. One or two of the older monks would remember this story too, though the younger ones, the novices, would not know. I questioned him a bit more, especially about the date of Sherlock Holmes's arrival at the monastery and the duration of his first stay there. The monk's answers rang true each time.

'Sir,' said he kindly, 'if you are so curious about our *trulku,* I can show you something that may interest you.' He summoned a monk and sent him off to fetch something. The fellow soon returned from an interior room, bringing with him a rectangular package wrapped in old silk, which he handed over to the big monk.

My host carefully undid the silk cover to reveal a rather decrepit tin dispatch box, the sight of which caused my heart to skip a beat. He opened the case. Within it, among a few objects of religious nature, was a chipped magnifying glass, and a battered old cherry-wood pipe.

For sometime I was unable to utter a word, and when I did I am ashamed to say that in my excitement I unwittingly made a very ill-mannered and ill-considered request. 'Could you sell me these two articles?' I said, pointing to the lens and the pipe.

'I'm afraid that it would not be possible,' replied the big fellow, smiling, thankfully not offended at my gaucherie. 'You see, these things are of great importance to our monastery. They also have some sentimental value to me.'

'What do you mean, Sir?' I asked puzzled.

'Well, these are the very articles I selected as a child when they came to look for me.'

'What!' I exclaimed, 'You mean ...'

'Yes,' he replied a mischievous twinkle in his eyes. 'You need not look so surprised.'

'But that's impossible!'

'Is it really, Sir? Consider the fact carefully,' he said in a rather didactic manner, 'then apply this old maxim of mine: "that when you have excluded the impossible, whatever remains, however impossible, must be the truth." '

As I sat across from him in that dark room, lit only by a single butter lamp, he commenced to laugh softly in a peculiar noiseless fashion.

J.N.
Nalanda Cottage
Dharamsala
5 June 1989

Acknowledgements

All journeys end in the settling of accounts: paying off porters, muleteers or camel-drivers, and rewarding the staff, especially the unfailing khansamah and, of course, the sirdar, the invaluable guide and caravan organiser. It is also the moment when one must seek adequate words of gratitude and recompense for the contributions of loyal companions, and least of all for the numerous acts of kindness and consideration one has received on the way.

First and foremost, I must acknowledge my overwhelming debt to the two greatest popular writers of Victorian England, Arthur Conan Doyle and Rudyard Kipling, from whose great bodies of work this small pastiche of mine has drawn life and sustenance — in much the same way as did a species of fauna mentioned in the story.

The sixty adventures of Sherlock Holmes recorded by John H. Watson are known to the followers of the 'Master' as the 'Sacred Writings'. This canon of Sherlockiana, which finds parallel in the 'Kangyur' of Tibetan Buddhism, was the all-important source of inspiration and reference; not just for facts, but for style and even the atmosphere of my work.

The general public is pretty much unaware of the tremendous bibliography of Holmesian criticism, which is referred to generally as the 'secondary writing', and which finds an equivalence in the Lamaist 'Tengyur', or commentaries. Many such secondary sources have been consulted for this project, chief among them are Vincent Starrett's classic, *The Private Life of Sherlock Holmes*, and of course, William S. Baring-Gould, *Sherlock Holmes of Baker Street*, and also his stupendous two-volume annotated collection of the complete Sherlock Holmes stories. I should also mention two earlier attempts to reconstruct Holmes's Tibetan period, namely Richard Wincor's *Sherlock Holmes in Tibet*, and Hapi's *The Adamantine Sherlock Holmes*.

The first germ of an idea for the *Mandala of Sherlock Holmes* was planted in my head by the late John Ball ('the Oxford Flyer'), the famous author (*In the Heat of the Night*, etc.), president of the Los Angeles Scion Society (of Sherlock Holmes) and a Master Copper-Beech-Smith of the sons of the Copper Beeches, of Philadelphia, who on a cold winter night at Dharamsala in 1970 examined me carefully on my knowledge of the 'Sacred Writings', at the conclusion of which he formally welcomed me to the ranks of the Baker Street Irregulars. (John Ball, 'The Path of the Master', *The Baker Street Journal*, March 1971, Vol. 21 No. 1, New York.)

Kim, Rudyard Kipling's great novel of British India, which Nirad Choudhari considers the finest story about British India, provided a large chunk of the geographical background of the story, the 'Great Game' milieu, and some of its characters — the most indispensable being our Bengali Boswell to the Master. Kipling's short stories, especially these collections: *The Phantom Rickshaw and Other Eerie Tales, Plain Tales from the Hills*, and *Under the Deodars* provided other details. I must, without fail, acknowledge the writings of Sarat Chandra Das, the great Bengali scholar/spy who is the real life inspiration for Kipling's Hurree Chunder Mookerjee. Chief among Das' works that animates this story is his *Journey to Lhasa and Central Tibet.* I must also mention Sven Hedin's *Trans Himalaya* which provided material for the preparation of Holmes's kafila to Lhasa.

For background on India and the Raj: Sood's *Guide to Simla and its Environs*, Charles Allen's *Plain Tales from the Raj*, and also his *Raj, A Scrapbook of British India*, Geoffrey Moorhouse's *India Britannica*, also Evelyn Battye's *Costumes and Characters of the British Raj*, for whom I am indebted to the description of the Bombay traffic police. For esoterica: Kazi Dawa Samdup and Evans Wentz for their writings concerning 'Phowa and Trongjug', Andrew Tomas's *Shambala: Oasis of Light*, and Carl Jung for the relationship of UFOs and Mandalas in the tenth volume of his collected works, *Civilisation in Transition*. Other scholars and writers whose works have either informed or inspired are acknowledged in the footnotes and quotations. Thanks to Gyamtso for the two maps and Pierre Stilli, Lindsey and especially Christopher Beauchet for their contributions to the first cover illustration. My thanks also to Esther for inputting the entire text on computer.

I am indebted to Shell and Roger Larsen for their warm and unstinted hospitality when I started writing the book and Tamsin for support. I am much indebted to friends Tashi Tsering and Lhasang Tsering for corrections, suggestions and relentless nagging to get 'Mandala' published; and also to Patrick French for sound advice and generous endorsement. I must thank my former editor Aradhana Bisht for helpful observations on Hurree's character. I am particularly grateful to Ian Smith, Anthony Sheil, Elenora Tevis, Susan Schulman, Jenny Manriquez, former American ambassador to India Frank Wisner, Tenzin Sonam, Ritu Sarin, Professor Sondhi and Mrs Madhuri Santanam Sondhi for their encouragement and help to get this book published. To Amala, Regzin, and most of all Tenzing and Namkha for love and unfailing support.

Glossary

A short glossary of Hindustani, Anglo-Indian, Sanskrit, Tibetan and Chinese words and phrases

Amban : the imperial Manchu commissioner in Lhasa (Manchu)

Angrezi : English (Hindustani)

anna : one sixteenth of a rupee

Argon : offspring of mixed marriages between Yarkandis and Ladakhis or natives of Spiti (Turkic)

arre! : expression of surprise (Hindustani)

Arya-Varta : Noble Land, India (Sanskrit)

babu : educated native in official employment (Hindustani)

badakshani chargers : cavalry mounts from Badakshan in Afghan Turkestan

bahadur : heroic, brave (Mongol, Hindustani) a Mogul, and later British Raj title.

baksheesh : alms, a *pour boire* (Hindustani)

bakwas : nonsense (Hindustani)

baapre-baap! : by my father! (Hindustani)
baraat : wedding procession (Hindustani)
bearer : waiter, house servitor (Anglo-Indian)
Benaras : holy city of Hinduism, on the banks of the Ganges.
betel nut : the areca nut. From the Malayalam 'vettila' (Anglo-Indian)
bewakoof : fool (Hindustani)
bhangi : sweeper (Hindustani)
bhisti : water-carrier (Hindustani)
bhotia : (bhutia) Tibetan, or ethnic Tibetan inhabitants of the Indian Himalayas (Hindustani)
bidi : a small native cheroot (Hindustani)
Bikaner : a former princely state and city in Rajasthan
bilaur : crystal (Hindustani)
bistra : bedding roll (Hindustani)
Bodhisattva : in Mahayana Buddhism, a person who is close to attaining nirvana but delays doing so because of compassion for human suffering (Sanskrit)
Brahmo Somaj : 'The Divine Society', founded by Raja Ram Mohan Roy, the great Indian reformer and doyen of the Bengal Renaissance.
budmaash : a no good, a villain (Hindustani)
bukoo : a Tibetan style gown (Hindustani)
bundobust : the faculty for organisation (Hindustani)
bundook : a rifle (Hindustani)
burra : big, important (Hindustani)
burra mem : important lady (Hindustani)

Cabuli : from Kabul in Afghanistan (Hindustani)
Chatter Munzil : palaces at Lucknow erected for the wives of a Muslim ruler
chale jao : go away (Hindustani)
chalo! : go, move on! (Hindustani)
chang : a light milky ale made from fermented barley (Tibetan)

chaprasi	: office servant, messenger, after chapras — brass buckle worn on belt (Hindustani)
chilingpa	: a foreigner, European (Tibetan)
Chini	: hill village on the Tibetan border in Kinnaur, now Kalpa
Chintamani	: the wish-fulfilling jewel of Buddhist mythology (Sanskrit)
chokra	: urchin, street boy (Hindustani)
chota-hazri	: early morning tea (Anglo-Indian)
churail	: ghost, spirit of a woman who has died in childbirth (Hindustani)
C.I.E.	: Commander of the India Empire, British title
collector	: chief administrator of district, originally collector of revenue (Anglo-Indian)
dacoit	: bandit, from the Indian dakoo (Anglo-Indian)
da dao	: large bladed executioner's sword (Chinese)
dak bungalow	: government staging house (Anglo-Indian)
daal	: lentils (Hindustani)
damcha	: water fowls (Tibetan)
dayig	: official missive, literally 'arrow missive' (Tibetan)
dawat	: ceremonial feast (Hindustani)
dekho	: look (Hindustani)
dekchis	: cooking pots (Hindustani)
deodar	: sub-species of cedar, native to the west Himalayas
dharma	: in Buddhism, universal truth or law, especially as proclaimed by the Buddha (Sanskrit)
dhoti	: loose loincloth worn by caste Hindus (Hindustani)
dorjee	: originally the thunderbolt weapon of Indra. Later incorporated into Buddhist symbology as the 'vajra' (Sanskrit), the Adamantine Sceptre (Tibetan)

double dorjee : crossed 'Adamantine Sceptres', Buddhist symbol of immutability (Tibetan)
drilbu : bell (Tibetan)
ducks : suit made of heavy plain weave cotton fabric of that name (Anglo-Indian)

Eblis : Islamic equivalent of Satan (Arabic)
ecca ghari : small two wheeled pony cart (Hindustani)
Eight Auspicious Emblems : the Parasol, the Pair of Golden fishes, the Conch shell (with a rightward spiral), the Knot that Has No End, the Banner of Supreme Excellence, the Wheel of the Law, the Vase of Great Wealth and the Lotus.

gadha : donkey (Hindustani)
Garuda : the phoenix or the roc, the all-powerful bird of Hindu and Buddhist mythologies (Sanskrit)
ghau : charm-box (Tibetan)

Great Game : Anglo-Russian rivalry and counter espionage on the northern frontiers of India

hai-mai : 'woe is me', wail of despair (Hindustani)
hakim : physician (Hindustani)
havildar : sergeant (Hindustani)
hawa-dilli : 'heart-lifter', an amulet (Hindustani)
hill station : station above 5000 feet to which state and central government transferred in the hot weather (Anglo-Indian)
hookah : the oriental water-pipe (Hindustani)
howdah : the canopied seat on the back of elephants (Hindustani)
huthoktu : high ranking lama (Mongol)

idhar aao : come here (Hindustani)
inter : intermediate, one of the many classes on

		Indian trains in the past. Between third and second class (Anglo-Indian)
izzat	:	honour (Hindustani)
jadoo	:	magic (Hindustani)
jaldi	:	quick (Hindustani)
jamun	:	an Indian and Southeast Asian tree, *Syzygium cumini* (family Myrtaceae); bearing an edible purplish-red berry fruit (Hindustani)
jehannum	:	Gehenna, Hell (Hindustani)
jhampanees	:	rickshaw-puller in Simla (Pahari)
jhula	:	crude suspension bridge (Hindustani)
ji	:	a suffix denoting respect to the person being addressed (Hindustani)
jingals	:	heavy match-lock muskets mounted on stands and worked by two men (Anglo-Indian)
kabari	:	shop for second-hand goods (Hindustani)
kacha	:	temporary, make-shift, fragile (Hindustani)
Kali	:	bloodthirsty female Hindu deity, much worshipped in Bengal
Kalka	:	a small town on the foot of the Himalayas, on the road from Ambala to Simla
kankar	:	limestone (Hindustani)
karma	:	Buddhist-Hindu belief, that every action brings upon oneself inevitable results, good or bad, either in this life or in a reincarnation (Sanskrit)
Kashag	:	Tibetan cabinet of ministers
Kashgar	:	large city in east Turkestan
Kathiawar	:	a peninsula on the northwest coast of India
Kayeth	:	a bazaar letter-writer; or of that caste (Hindustani)
Kesar of Oros	:	Czar of Russia (Turkic)
khabardar	:	an expression of admonition, 'take warning' (Hindustani)
khafila	:	caravan (Arabic)

khanda : a kind of sword (Afghan?)
khatag : white cotton or silk scarves extensively used by Tibetans as a token of greeting or offering of respect (Tibetan)
khura : hard Ladakhi biscuit
kismet : fate, luck (Hindustani)
Kotgarh : Christian missionary settlement northeast of Simla.
Kuan-yin : the female form of the Bodhisattva of Compassion, peculiar to Chinese and Japanese Buddhism (Jap. Kannon)
kuch nahin : nothing (Hindustani)
kunjri : the caste of vegetable sellers (Hindustani)
kusho : sir, or venerable sir (Tibetan)
kuttar : dagger (Afghan?)
kya : what? (Hindustani)
kay hai : what is it? (Hindustani)

la : a mountain pass (Tibetan)
lakh : hundred thousand (Hindustani)
lathi : bamboo staff (Hindustani)
Leh : capital of Ladakh and formerly great trading centre between Tibet, Kashmir and Central Asia.
lha : god, deity (Tibetan)
lha gyalo : Victory to the Gods! (Tibetan)
lingam : phallic symbol (Sanskrit)
Lingkor : the Tibetan via sacra circling Lhasa city.
Lopchag : annual tribute mission from the king of Ladakh to the Dalai Lama (Tibetan)
Lunkah : a strong cheeroot much favoured in Madras

mahasiddha : highly realised spiritual person (Sanskrit)
mahout : elephant driver (Hindustani)
mandala : intricate cosmic diagram (Sanskrit)
mani lag-khor : hand-held prayer wheel (Tibetan)
mantra : spell, invocation (Sanskrit)

mela	:	a fair (Hindustani)
momo	:	steam-cooked meat dumplings (Tibetan)
mudra	:	mystic gestures (Sanskrit)
Murree	:	hill station in northwest India, famous for its beer
mursala	:	king's letter, state document sent formally (Persian)
mussak	:	skin container for carrying water (Hindustani)
namaste	:	expression of greeting (Hindustani)
Narkhanda	:	small town northeast of Simla.
nickal jao	:	get out (Hindustani)
nizamut	:	criminal case (Hindustani)
norbu rimpoche	:	see Chintamani (Tibetan)
nowkri	:	service, employment (Hindustani)
Om Mani Padme Hum	:	Buddhist invocation (mantra), often translated as 'Hail the Jewel in the Lotus' (Sanskrit)
Oswal Jain	:	a particular subdivision of the Jain religious community, well-known for the commercial acumen of its members.
paan	:	a mild narcotic wad of betel leaf, chopped betel nut, spices and lime, habitually chewed by many Indians. It stains the teeth and lips red (Hindustani)
paan-bidi wallahs	:	vendors of cigarettes and paan (Hindustani)
pahari	:	hill man
P&O	:	The Peninsular and Oriental Steam Navigation Company, the largest and most popular shipping company for the English travelling to India and the East.
parao	:	wayside resting place (Hindustani)
Peshawar	:	at the entrance of the Khyber Pass, capital of North West Frontier Province.
phowa	:	yogic practise of transferring the consciousness

		principle from one incarnation to the next without suffering any break in the continuity of consciousness (Tibetan)
phurba	:	ritual three-edged dagger, mistakenly called 'ghost dagger' (Tibetan)
pie	:	the pie was the smallest fraction of the old rupee. There were 16 annas in the rupee, 4 pice in the anna and 3 pies in the pice (Hindustani)
poodle-faker	:	womaniser, especially in hill stations, hence 'poodle-faking' (Anglo-Indian)
poshteen	:	long sheep-skin coat from Afghanistan
pukka	:	a much used catch-all word with meaning ranging from sturdy, solid, well-built, to sincere or genuine (Hindustani)
pundit	:	learned man, teacher (Hindustani)
punkah	:	fan (Hindustani)
Puranas	:	eighteen sacred texts written between 200 B.C. and A.D. 800 containing epics, myth, popular lore, etc., embodying the principles of popular Hindu religion and ethics. Purana in Sanskrit means old or 'of old'.
puttoo	:	hand-woven woollen stuff (Hindustani)
PWD	:	Public Works Department
Rai Bahadur	:	an important title conferred by the Viceroy (Hindustani)
raks mudra	:	the mudra of protection (Sanskrit)
Ramasi	:	the language of the thugs
Rampur	:	town on the Sutlej river, northeast of Simla, capital of the independent hill state of Bushair
Rukho	:	stop (Hindustani)
saat bhai	:	Hindu secret society
sadhu	:	religious mendicant (Hindustani)
sais	:	groom (Hindustani)

sakht burra afsar : very important officer (Hindustani)

salaam : salutation, thus, 'Give my salaams to ...', also salaam wasti — to pay respects (Hindustani)

sambhar : large Indian deer

samsara : in Buddhism the process of coming into existence as a differentiated mortal creature. In Hinduism the endless series of births, deaths and rebirths to which all beings are subject (Sanskrit)

sanga : a crude bridge of wooden planks (Pahari)

sati : Hindu custom of widow burning condemned by Ram Mohan Roy and made illegal by the British (Hindustani)

seer : Indian measure of weight equivalent to two pounds (Hindustani)

serai : caravan halting station, also place for accommodation of travellers (Hindustani)

Seven Articles of Royalty : the Precious Queen, the Precious Minister, the Precious General, the Precious Wish-Fulfilling Gem, the Precious Wheel, the Precious Elephant and the Precious Horse.

sha! : kill! (Chinese)

shabash : well done, bravo (Hindustani)

shaitan : the Devil (Hindustani)

shamiana : marquee, awning, tent (Hindustani)

shikar : hunt (Hindustani)

sirdar : chief, leader, also organiser of a caravan or expedition (Hindustani)

sitar : multiple stringed Indian lute (Hindustani)

Sivaliks : a range of foothills in the Western Himalayas

Skanda Puranas : one of the eighteen sacred texts of the Puranas

Spiti : on the border of Tibet. In the valley of a tributary of the Sutlej

sanyasi : hermit, religious man (Hindustani)

TA : travelling allowance (Anglo-Indian)

talwar	: sword (Hindustani)
tantric	: esoteric Buddhism (Sanskrit)
tasam	: caravan: halting stations (Tibetan)
tat	: hill ponies (Hindustani)
taar	: telegram, literally 'wire' (Hindustani)
thana	: police station, jail (Hindustani)
thangka	: Tibetan painted scroll
Three Jewels	: the Buddhist Trinity: the Buddha, the Dharma and the Sangha
thugs	: an organisation of criminal assassins (Hindustani)
ticca ghari	: hired four-wheeled carriage
tiffin	: luncheon (Anglo-Indian)
tommies	: non-ranking British soldiers, after 'Tommy Atkins'
topee	: sun helmet, but literally hat in Hindustani (Anglo-Indian)
Trichinopoly	: a fine quality cigar made in Worur, a village near Thiruchirapalli in South India (Anglo-Indian)
trongjug	: the yoga of transferring the consciousness principle of a person into the body of another living person (Tibetan)
trulku	: incarnation of a lama (Tibetan)
tsampa	: roasted barley meal (Tibetan)
Tsongdu	: Tibetan parliament or national assembly
Tungan	: Chinese Muslim of Kansu
Tuticorin	: seaport on the extreme south-east of Madras, trading with Ceylon
uchen	: printed Tibetan script
umay	: cursive Tibetan script
Umballa	: older spelling of Ambala, capital of a district in eastern Punjab
Upanishads	: in Hinduism, any of a class of speculative treatises, usually in dialogue form and